More praise for the novels

"One of the finest, most erotic love stories I've ever read."
—Shelby Reed, coauthor of *Love a Younger Man*

"Sweet yet erotic . . . will linger in your heart long after the story is over."
—*Sensual Romance Reviews*

"The perfect blend of suspense and romance." —*The Road to Romance*

"A beautifully told story of true love, magic and strength . . . a wondrous tale . . . a must-read."
—*Romance Junkies*

"Darkly rich erotica at its finest."
—*TwoLips Reviews*

"A passionate, poignant tale . . . The sex was emotional and charged with meaning . . . yet another must-read story from the ever-talented Joey Hill."
—*Just Erotic Romance Reviews*

"This is not only a keeper, but one you will want to run out and tell your friends about."
—*Fallen Angel Reviews*

"All the right touches of emotion, sex and a wonderful plot that you would usually find in a much longer tale." —*Romance Reviews Today*

"Dark and richly romantic . . . a feast for your libido and your most lascivious fantasies."
—*Romantic Times*

A
Vampire's Claim

Joey W. Hill

HEAT
New York

THE BERKLEY PUBLISHING GROUP
Published by the Penguin Group
Penguin Group (USA) Inc.
375 Hudson Street, New York, New York 10014, USA

Penguin Group (Canada), 90 Eglinton Avenue East, Suite 700, Toronto, Ontario M4P 2Y3, Canada
(a division of Pearson Penguin Canada Inc.)
Penguin Books Ltd., 80 Strand, London WC2R 0RL, England
Penguin Group Ireland, 25 St. Stephen's Green, Dublin 2, Ireland (a division of Penguin Books Ltd.)
Penguin Group (Australia), 250 Camberwell Road, Camberwell, Victoria 3124, Australia
(a division of Pearson Australia Group Pty. Ltd.)
Penguin Books India Pvt. Ltd., 11 Community Centre, Panchsheel Park, New Delhi—110 017, India
Penguin Group (NZ), 67 Apollo Drive, Rosedale, North Shore 0632, New Zealand
(a division of Pearson New Zealand Ltd.)
Penguin Books (South Africa) (Pty.) Ltd., 24 Sturdee Avenue, Rosebank, Johannesburg 2196,
South Africa

Penguin Books Ltd., Registered Offices: 80 Strand, London WC2R 0RL, England

This is an original publication of The Berkley Publishing Group.

Copyright © 2009 by Joey W. Hill.
Excerpt from *Beloved Vampire* copyright © 2009 by Joey W. Hill.
Cover illustration by Don Sipley.
Cover design by George Long.
Text design by Tiffany Estreicher.

First edition: March 2009

Library of Congress Cataloging-in-Publication Data

Hill, Joey W.
    A vampire's claim / Joey W. Hill.—1st ed.
        p.   cm.
    ISBN 978-0-425-22608-7
    1. Vampires—Fiction. I. Title.
    PS3608.I4343V365   2009
    813'.6—dc22
                                                            2008039329

PRINTED IN THE UNITED STATES OF AMERICA

10 9 8 7 6 5 4 3 2 1

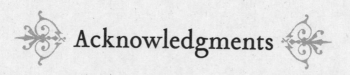 Acknowledgments

My thanks to the Berkley editing team of Wendy McCurdy, Allison Brandau and a wealth of other names and faces I do not have the opportunity to meet, but who work so hard on my behalf. Thank you for making my stories shine. It's been an amazing year!

I also have three wonderful critique partners, who shepherd my books through the painstaking author editing process and make them better stories as a result, every time. Thank you so much, Sheri Fogarty, Ann Jacobs and Denise Rossetti.

And for this book in particular, I need to extend an extra special thank-you to Denise. This lovely Australian lady and exceptional author kept her Yank friend out of too much trouble on the Australian setting and language for this book, all while juggling her own deadlines and travel plans.

As always, any errors or inaccuracies that remain are entirely mine.

1

Western Australia, 1953

*D*ON'T *go there tonight. Nothin' but trouble.*

As Dev passed the aboriginal elder, he heard the warning, muttered in the language the old man knew he understood. A wise man would listen to such a warning. But he wanted a beer. A bloody galah he might be, but hell, he'd been in the Outback more than sixty days. Even uncooled, the beer would bring welcome bitter wetness to his throat. A smooth bottle in his hand, the clink of the top falling away on the bar surface. His craving for it made a knight seeking the Holy Grail no more than a bloke who liked collecting fancy cups.

He needed the comfort of human conversation. At least for a night. After that, it would start to grate on his nerves, rouse old memories. He was like a seesaw, needing to descend into the embrace of humanity, but in short order he had to push off from that and let the other, darker part of him sink back into the vast emptiness of the harsh lands he called home. People were too full, and that fullness hurt the longer he stayed around it.

So, after his beer and some idle talk, he'd pay his tithe for the company and the wetting of his throat and head back out.

Unless there was a woman.

He snorted at himself. Not only were unmarried women few and far between out here, no decent woman put a foot inside a bar. An indecent one would be snapped up in a heartbeat by any bloke willing to shell out his last quid for her.

It didn't matter. As bad as lingering in human company could be, a woman's body was a drug that carried with it a hell of a hangover when he had to face himself in a mirror the next day. Unfortunately, he couldn't ignore the burning need festering in his balls. His mind had been dragging him into all sorts of unlikely fantasies for the past couple weeks. He'd risked fatally dehydrating himself, those nights he'd given in to the poor substitute of his hand. He might have to give it away, take the Ghan down to Adelaide and endure the mobs of people and noise, where women for hire were more plentiful.

Maybe it would be better that way. More impersonal and anonymous. Maybe he wouldn't imagine Tina looking down at him with shame and sorrow in her eyes, from the heights of a heaven he was never going to see.

Walling that thought off, he focused on an Adelaide whore. He'd want a soft and passably pretty sheila, one who'd smell clean. Who'd let him take her as rough as she could tolerate and still hang around to stroke his hair, curl in front of him so he could fit himself to her curves. Even have the pleasure of listening to her sleep, if he wore her out. Which, if he did her proper, would be the case.

Uncomfortably aware that his imaginings were far from the impersonal fucking he'd claimed to be seeking, he tuned back in to his immediate surroundings. The usual scattering of vehicles, mostly utes, were parked in front of Joe and Elle's place, a pub in the usual style. Two stories, the upper level for the hotel, the lower for the bar. A veranda that wrapped around the top level was for those who often preferred it to the stuffy rooms, if they had netting to guard against the bugs. A couple blokes sat out on it now, behind the lacy wrought iron railing, trying to catch the breeze.

Aside from the utes, there was a pair of expensive-looking Rovers, one being worked over by an agitated, grease-stained driver and another man. City folk by their appearance, but they wore appropriate clothes for the bush and appeared to be carrying the right supplies needed when traveling out here. That was a relief. Less chance the whole bloody town would have to mobilize to rescue them from some foolishness. Lord knows, the bush could surprise even the most experienced man. It could chew up tourists and spit them out like a pack of dingoes on a helpless sheep.

He took his swag into the bar with him as usual, because sometimes a light-fingered fella got to thinking you didn't need your pack if you left it sitting unattended. However, as he stepped into the bar, he forgot he was even carrying it. Hell, if asked, he doubted he could have told anyone his name.

While no respectable woman went into a bar, he wasn't about to cast any stones at the one standing at the antiquated jukebox Joe prized. Except for her, it was the only shiny thing in the dusty place.

Her back was to him, so her face might look like an aggravated camel's. But she had blond hair, tied in a tail that curled and waved across the narrow slope of her back like peaceful surf, touched by the gold of sundown. The track of it drew his gaze to the nip of her waist and down. Her arse alone would be worth overlooking a homely face, for the flare of her hips was well outlined in a pair of trim brown jodhpurs.

"Well, look what the cat's dragged in. Going to barter those eggs for a beer, Dev?"

In order to focus on Elle, Dev had to pull his attention away. He might have taken more time about it, but something in Elle's voice got his radar going.

Eleanor Waters was the exception to the decent-woman-in-a-bar rule, first because she was the licensee, with her husband, Joe. Second, she was as tough and no-nonsense as old Joe. She always said she'd seen it all, such that she kept a shotgun below the bar in case any of it came back twice. But she acted like something was bothering her tonight. The strangers, he guessed, from the scowls Elle sent their way. He wondered why. Though strangers didn't pass through all that frequently, it was rare that they caused trouble.

A glance about the occupied tables showed the woman was there with three men, in addition to the two out by the vehicle. From the way they'd checked him out when he stepped across the threshold, it was clear they were hired muscle. It was also clear she was the one who'd hired them, from their body language and glances toward her.

As he deposited his pack against the bar, taking off the slings that held his rifle on his back and the nest of billies at his hip, the blond woman turned at last.

Blue eyes. Jesus, so blue it was like diving the Reef. Skin so fair it brought to mind the fairy tales. But then there was that soft mouth, lush in ways that drove away all thoughts of children's stories and went into the realm of darker, more provocative tales. The lipstick she wore was deep red, wet. Normally, he would have scoffed at a woman wearing makeup out here, but wherever she wanted to wear it was fine with him. She wore a delicate opal amulet the size of his thumbnail. While it was a beautiful stone, he was far more distracted by how it glistened in the cleft of her breasts, above the slightly strained button of her white blouse.

He'd stripped off his shirt to carry the three emu eggs Elle had noticed right off, so the stranger's vivid blue gaze traveled with deliberate appreciation over his bare, sweat-stained shoulders and the expanse of his chest, passing over the scars, then lingering on each muscle in his abdomen as if she were tracing them with her tongue. When her glance went lower, just as slow and easy, her mink lashes fanned the cheeks of pale cream. She obviously didn't mind him knowing she was looking.

"*Dev.*" Elle's voice was a bit sharper.

Jesus. "Yeah, Elle. How ya going?" Clearing his throat, he put the bundle on the bar and took off his hat.

"Fair enough." Elle's solid bulk was a less unsettling sight to him as she slid him a beer. She had her brown and gray hair pinned up to keep it off her neck in the late-afternoon heat. "The Yanks elected that Eisenhower fella president. And the Queen's supposed to visit us soon."

Trying not to look toward the jukebox as the bar owner untied the shirt to give the eggs a critical look, Dev made a noncommittal noise. "Guess that'll be a right treat for some. You know the eggs are for Joe. I've got the money for the beer."

She smiled. "No, I was just teasing you. I know you've got the money. But I'll shout you the first one anyway. I asked you to bring them, after all. Had a few bad moments thinking of you lying out there with your head kicked in by an angry mother bird. Then I remembered how hard your head is." A warning flashed in her eyes as she said it, her gaze sliding to the jukebox and back. "Joe'll be so surprised for his birthday. He hasn't had a cake made of emu eggs since his nanna was alive. You can have the third, though. Only need two."

When the woman reached over, ostensibly to wipe the bar, she lowered her voice and muttered, "Unless a bird did kick you in the head, you'd best pay attention, you daft bastard. She ain't sweatin'."

Dev shifted his gaze. It was a sweltering sundown after a hot day, for sure. Elle had the fans going to help with it as well as the flies, but no help for it; a man was going to sweat. Not only the three musclemen his fair sheila had with her, but the group of blokes back at the pool table, some leaning against the wall with their drinks or tapping their smokes in the ashtray on the mantel of the fireplace that was never used. They all bore the signature sweat stains at the usual places. Chest, back, armpits.

In contrast, the woman's ivory cotton shirt looked as if it had just been pressed and pulled out of the wardrobe. White, always a favorite color for the flies, seemed to have no appeal to them while on her back. They weren't anywhere near her, whereas those who chose glasses instead of bottles had to keep a hand over them in between swallows to make sure the pests didn't go for a swim.

As the jukebox started to play the wistful ballad she'd chosen, she turned back to it. When she started to sway, those trim brown daks she wore moved with her curves perfectly. His gonads engaged again like bullets being racked into the firing chamber of a shotgun.

He wouldn't say she was oblivious to the attention she was attracting, but she didn't seem one of those shallow girls who needed it to thrive, her beauty her only sense of worth. Rather, he was reminded of a female predator who used wiles to attract her prey, just close enough . . .

His body and mind were screaming at him to go into that trap. Resolutely he turned back to Elle and his beer.

His forearm was braced on the bar, and so he was startled when a slim-fingered hand reached over it to cup one of the three eggs Elle had now placed in a bowl. Elle jumped, her eyes widening. While Dev managed not to react, he hadn't even heard the woman's slim, booted feet move across the wooden floor.

Her nails were a feminine length with clear polish, the elegant tips drawing attention to the grace of her hands. Despite the large size of the emu egg, the way she stroked the curves, he couldn't help but think of how those tips would feel moving over his balls in a similar way. God, he could smell her. All woman, fresh scents of soap and powders and the mysterious things women did to make themselves impossible to resist. And those miles of blond hair, waiting for deeper study, teasing his vision at the corner of his eye.

Forcing himself not to look, Dev nodded his thanks to Elle and lifted his beer to his lips, closing his eyes to savor it as he tilted back. Perhaps it was because he was so aware of her proximity that he anticipated the woman, but he caught her hand a moment before she would have touched his exposed throat. Opening his eyes, he kept his hand firmly closed on her wrist. Intrigued, he noticed her men didn't react, continuing their card game.

"Don't think we've been properly introduced, love," he said without rancor.

"I'm a woman who likes to touch fine-looking things," she responded. Her voice had a Brit and Aussie blending with an unexpected sultry cadence, probably because the sound of it had the smoothness of lava, pouring heat straight into his pants.

She might have said something else, but he missed the next series of words entirely. Like Elle, he wasn't knocked off his pins by much anymore. But now, confronted with her close up, he was knocked full on his arse.

Her face looked as fragile and protected as a prizewinning orchid. The blond hair was truly spun gold, like that found in the mines long ago, when the dust glittered on the walls like an enchanted castle.

Easy, mate. She's no whore, though by God she's acting willing enough to take you on. What in hell was a woman like this doing out here? The softness of the skin under his fingertips said she sure as hell didn't live in the Outback. He noticed how she'd come in on his left side, which avoided the straining long patches of late-afternoon sunlight coming in through the open door and windows.

Nothin' but trouble there tonight.

He'd gone and put his foot in it, hadn't he?

Shifting his glance to a watchful Elle, he said, "Elle, love. Can you lend me a clean bar rag?"

Elle slid one over. Picking it up, Dev released the blonde to clean off the sweat and grime he'd left on her skin. She had a narrow wrist, a gemstone on one finger in proportion to the one on her neck.

"Some nice baubles to be wearing way out here," he observed, trying not to focus on how easy it would be to make his functional scrubbing a teasing stroke over her pulse, a hint of what he could offer to other parts of her. As she lifted her hand to accommodate him, he could feel that pulse beating like a bird's heart. There was a delicate web of lines on her palm. Her lifeline was long, he noted.

"No sense in owning something if you're not going to play with it. Show it off." She turned her hand, interlacing a couple of her fingers with his own despite the cloth, and held them there at eye level, keeping his gaze focused on her face. He was a few inches taller than she was. "I'll tell you my name if you give me the extra egg."

Considering that, he gave her a half shrug. "Well, I haven't asked you for that, have I now? As pretty a name as I'm sure it is, it's not much currency for what could provide me a good meal or two. Barter again, love."

She studied him, her mouth curving up. "A dance."

"A slow dance." Dropping the rag on the bar and letting her go, albeit reluctantly, he took another bracing swallow of the beer and wiped his mouth with the back of his hand. As he did, he let his gaze move down and then back up, with as much brazen appreciation as she'd indulged herself. He thought he saw that hint of a smile reach her eyes at his boldness, but something else, too. Something darker.

"The kind of dance that tells a man what a woman's got to offer under her clothes," he added.

Elle muttered something under her breath. Dev was sure it was something like "stupid bugger," but because he was cracking on to the pretty stranger way too hard or because he was going hip deep into trouble and trudging along happily, he didn't know. Well, as for the first, the blonde had started it, hadn't she?

"Done," the woman said. "If you give me your name."

He took one green-black egg from the bowl and pushed it a turn toward her. "Devlin. You can call me Dev."

"Lady Daniela," she responded. The way she met his eyes as she said it made something reach in, wring his heart out like the rag. Pain came with it, of course, and the reminder of why he didn't linger long around civilization, let alone with a woman. "How do I know it's not rotten?" she asked. "The egg."

"You got a straw from your broom, Elle?"

Though the older woman gave him a narrow look, she plucked a good one, knowing what he was about. Dev took the other two eggs out and brought the three together end to end, nodding to his fascinated audience. "Now put the straw on the top of your middle one while I hold these to it." He shifted his body to block the air flow of the nearest fan.

When she did, he continued, "Now, if the straw spins, the egg's good for eating. If it's sluggish or dead in the water, well, I've given you a bad egg."

Lady Daniela watched, obviously intrigued, as the straw quivered and then began to move. Rapidly.

"Check the others," Elle groused. "I don't want you giving away a good egg and leaving me a bad 'un for Joe's cake."

He'd never bring Elle a bad egg and she knew that, but Dev let it pass. He tested all three to both women's satisfaction before returning the two to the bowl and putting the other in the cup of his hat.

When Lady Daniela reached out to touch her new possession, her fingers drifted to the hat itself, tracing the sweat-stained band inside, her gaze rising to his forehead, lingering over the strands of his hair.

"It seems I owe you a dance, then," she said. "Provided this bit of nonsense is true."

"It's true enough. What's a flaming Pom doing out here, love? One with a bloody title?" Now that he had her commitment to a dance, he saw no reason to rush what might end up being *only* a dance. Though when he took another swallow of his beer, he found the way she studied the motion, riveting on his mouth as if she'd like to lick the foam off, a serious strain on his control. But in England he'd once seen a very pretty snow owl who, despite the inviting look of her soft feathers, still had a beak as sharp as a spear and the eyes of a predator. Watching, gauging.

Sliding onto the stool next to him, she leaned back, the white shirt she wore tightening over her pleasingly shaped breasts, drawing his attention back to the crevice where the amulet hung. The brown trousers creased up at the top of her thighs, making him want to reach out and trace those tiny gatherings of fabric. Follow their diagonal slant across her inseam, push her thighs open so he could rub between them, feel her heat reach out to him through cotton. He would have paid good money for another look at her backside. Why in the hell did he care about her background? Why'd he even ask?

"I'm returning to my family's station to take it over." She studied her egg, a thoughtful look crossing her face. When she didn't say anything further, he cleared his throat.

"Sounds like you don't really want the job."

"It needs to be done." Her gaze shifted back to him. "You strike me as the type of man who knows his way around the business of a station."

"This a job interview, love?" He signaled Elle for another beer. He was setting too fast a pace, but if Lady D was going to dig around his past, he'd need to toss back a few more before he could accommodate her.

"You also don't strike me as a man looking for work. I'd be interested in your opinion, though." When the beer came into his hand, before he could pop off the top, she laid her own over it, preventing the motion. Her fingers curved in a bit, her nails pressing into the side of his hand.

"The current management is strongly opposed to me coming in and taking over," she went on. "Do I try diplomacy right from the off, or do I invite them to dinner and stake them out on an anthill, letting their screams be an example to the others?" She cocked her head. "Hypothetically, of course."

"Depends on whether you're planning on serving red or white wine with the dinner." When he directed a pointed look at his beer, she withdrew her hand, though with a smile. Ignoring the lingering tingle in his skin from her touch, he removed the top and brought it to his lips for a bracing swallow. He'd often wondered why men needed drink to give them courage around women. She was a blatant answer to that question. Her hand had settled on his thigh, was tracing it with a touch that was damn proprietary. He'd tell her to move it. After he finished the beer.

"The staking out seems a trifle heavy-handed. Might make them fall in line, but they won't respect you. They'll be afraid of you, and that's one step away from contempt. The moment you stumble—and you always stumble—they'll tear the flesh from your bones. Hypothetically, of course."

Hooking his arm on the back of his bar stool, he flicked a glance toward her hand. She'd turned it over, was stroking him with her knuckles way up high, too high. His cock was about to buck like a brumby in his pants. He cleared his throat. "But say you walk in, pull a gun and shoot two of them. Quick, no emotion, do the job. That says you're a right bad girl, but you're there with an objective. You're not making it personal. Then you bring in the fancy talk. Explain to those left standing why it'll profit them to look at things your way. Show them you're not afraid to seize 'em by the balls, but you'd rather make everyone rich and better off. Hypothetically," he added again.

Her brows rose, her hand stilling. "And where did you learn all that?"

"Oxford. School of Business. Some of it. The rest of it is living out here. There's some that respond to reason, some that respond to force. The wise leader is one that figures out how much of each to use depending on the situation. And also the one who listens to wise counsel"—he grinned, saluting her with the beer—"and doesn't get sidetracked by the opinions of lazy bludgers."

In his current position, he was half turned toward her, knees splayed and one boot hooked on the bottom rung of the stool. Such that when she turned more toward him now, her knees were between his, making their posture far more intimate. He could almost feel the warmth of her body emanating toward the strained seam of his trousers.

He wet his throat again. Beer had never tasted so good, nor could he remember ever feeling so quickly parched. "So you own one of those huge stations that take up half the grazing area of Western Australia?"

"It's just a bit of brick and tile and land." She shrugged. "You said I owe you a dance. You going to make good on the claim?"

"When I've a mind to." Which was right now, if he was being entirely truthful. Because if she kept her hand on his leg, he was going to slam her down on the bar and fuck her right there, until Elle had to shoot him like a bull gone mad with the heat.

Setting down the beer, he rose, shrugged his shirt back on but left it open. Then he put both hands to her waist to lift her off the stool. She'd made her interest clear, and he was fast losing the mood to play games. When she bumped against him as she stood, he didn't mind the contact, but slid an arm low around her hips to move with her to the open floor near the jukebox.

As they reached it, he took a quick glance to make sure his swag and rifle were still in his sight.

"Afraid I'm maneuvering you over here to have my men take your treasures?" she observed.

"There's only one thing going to be taken tonight, love." He couldn't help the underlying demand to the tone, or how it deepened as her blue eyes sparked in reaction. "You want to keep it safe, you'd best take yourself off soon."

She turned on the ball of her foot, moving back toward the bar. Dev didn't think, just caught hold of her arm, stopping her so they were shoulder to shoulder, him facing one way, her the other, but such that when she tilted her face up to his, there were only inches between them.

He wasn't one of those dickheads who wouldn't take no for an answer. He'd been without for quite a while, but he'd cut off his own balls before forcing a woman, no matter how loose she was. But it was as if her proximity had touched something even deeper than his eager body, and he was having a hard time remembering what was proper behavior. He didn't want to chase her off, despite his challenge, but it was only with considerable effort he was able to keep his grip firm, not bruising.

When she looked at his hand and then back up at his face, he saw something in hers that made his need even worse. Desire, goaded by his unplanned and possessive act.

"I'll be right back," she said softly. "I promise."

He let her go with reluctance. She did return a blink later with the rag from the bar, despite Elle's unfriendly look. Lady Daniela lifted it, that mysterious smile playing on her lips like the shadows playing among the lush mystery of a rainforest, concealing all manner of hazards among its beauty.

"You warned me if I was going to cuddle up to a bushman, I might get dirty. Thought I'd take care of some of the grime." Laying the cloth on his chest, she began to rub slow circles. Damn if she didn't tease a nipple with her clever fingers buried in the rag as she passed over it. His hand flexed convulsively at his side. "Plus I thought this cool cloth might feel good to you."

It did, primarily because she was the one wielding it. He couldn't imagine feeling the same way if Elle was swiping it over him like she would a dirty table. Of course, he'd never seen Elle wipe down a table the way this one did, following every contour of him intimately.

"God, you are something else. I bet the girls want to eat you alive." She lingered over the smooth flatness of his pectorals, the ridges of his sectioned abdomen, the curve of biceps. Dev knew he was in fighting shape because of the life he led, but having her appreciate it so openly, in such a tactile way, made him want to exercise some of that strength now. Put her under him, spread those slim legs and plow her like a wheat field.

"Don't have call to see many," he managed roughly. "I've had some roos give me an affectionate glance now and again."

She chuckled, and the sound was like a kitten purring, inviting his touch. As she made free with her fondling, he put his arm back around her waist, intent and easy as a python, flexing the muscles she was admiring to bring her closer to him. As she obliged, moving in another step, he rested his free hand on her shoulder, his thumb and forefinger cradling the base of her delicate neck. She didn't stop him, keeping on with her cleaning as if she were polishing him for her fancy walnut mantel, though he couldn't imagine how he'd fit with all the expensive and breakable things she'd likely keep there.

Her gaze wandered over the ridged circular scars on his chest again. Then she touched him there, the slow examination almost more than he could take and remain still. When she tossed the rag on a nearby table at last, before she could ask the inevitable question, he took her damp hand firmly in his fingers. "Let's dance."

True to his barter, he closed the last gap between them. Her eyes widened at the firm pressure of his hips against her pelvis. "Oh, my," she murmured. "Is that all you?"

Lord, he was twisted enough to enjoy the paradox of her, a fine lady behaving like a wanton. It was like walking into a minefield, terrifying and exhilarating at once, making his balls draw up as though to prove he was still alive. "I suppose that's what we're going to find out, hmm?"

Her hand drifted down his back, as welcome as only the caress of a woman's hand could be, no metaphor needed to enhance the simple truth of that. She curled her fingers into the loose fabric of his open shirt. "Not in a mood for courtship, are you?" she teased. "Wooing me with charm?"

"That's not what this is about. I'm not sure what your angle is, love, but I'm interested in following. That's what I can give you."

The next song gave him a hitch to his step. It was an old spiritual that spoke of a miner at the end of his life's journey, hoping that when he fell to his knees alone in the desolate rock desert, he'd fall into the cradle of God's hands. She had some odd tastes, this Lady D. But he pushed away his disturbing emotional response to the song and resolutely moved them into an easy, three-step rhythm. She followed with no trouble, moving with his body in a way that suggested to him a far less religious activity, though perhaps no less spiritual than the emotions evoked by the song.

"What is it you think that I want, exactly?" She made a soft noise of pleasure when his hand pressed on her lower back. With his blood stirring, he made sure their next turn changed the position of their legs so his was interposed between hers, rubbing a passing stroke over the sensitive pubic bone guarding her clit, sending an unmistakable answer to her question. Her lips parted, giving him a glimpse of tantalizing wetness.

"I do appreciate a confident man," she whispered, the words a teasing caress.

"I've been out bush over two months," he said with sudden desperation. He couldn't shake his innate sense of fairness, much as he wished he could. The song was too haunting. "This is no game to me, lady. I'm looking for a hard ride, the harder the better. If that's not what you're after, you'd best back off now and no hard feelings."

"The proper term is 'my lady.'" She never flickered an eyelash as she made the correction. "You've been with a woman before."

Puzzled, he inclined his head. "I think I made that obvious, love."

"That's not what I meant."

Halting midstep, he dropped his hands to the curve of her hips. A warning. "Don't," he said. "That's not a place you've been invited."

Something passed through her eyes again. A shadow . . . He couldn't tell if it was irritation with his reaction, which was too bloody bad, or something deeper, something he would like even less. Before he could put his finger on it, she moved her free hand to his chest, laying it over the ritual scars on his upper body again. There were two, each one curving up over the pectoral in a winged arc and circling the nipple, the outer rings dotted with bumps, scars made by putting clay in the fresh wounds. Her fingers passed over them like

Braille, which he knew in a way it was. "I won't step through a door where I'm not invited, but this is related, isn't it? There's magic to it. Significant . . . grief."

"Yeah," he said shortly, unsettled by the understanding in her tone. Thank God, the song was over. She nodded, then cupped the back of his head, fingers tangling in his hair. She'd willingly moved back onto safer ground. Respecting him. Showing compassion, not pity.

"I'm filthy." He gave a strained chuckle. "Likely to get all manner of things under your nails."

"I'll risk it." She leaned against him, so her body pressed into his as he turned them, now swaying without much in the way of steps while the jukebox crooned another, more popular but less poignant song. It was a tune he expected was played with full, wailing gusto in the clubs of the big city she was used to. But she seemed to like the quaintness of the tinny sound.

As for him, the music made no difference. The slow dancing he wanted to do with her wouldn't be obeying any tempo except the thundering of his heart against the wall of his chest, the pulse of need building in his cock and testicles. Did she have some strange ability to make a man, already in sore need of a woman, suddenly consumed by a maddening hunger for one? For her specifically?

"Tell me some of the amazing things a bushman can do. Like all city folk, I've heard the stories." She flashed him a mischievous look. "But I don't know if they're only stories now. It's been a long time since I've been home."

"Same as Knights of the Round Table or American cowboys. Romantic fantasy, for the most part."

She tilted her head. "Romantic fantasy is usually born from some piece of reality, even if it's only one man. A hero among the ruffians can transform the whole lot of them into legends."

"Wishful thinking can do the same. Some say Ned Kelly was a thug. Some say he was a hero. Only he knows the reality. I wouldn't get carried away by any of it."

She managed to slide an inch closer, such that he had the pleasurable and disquieting sensation that they'd become like two interlocking puzzle pieces. Every part fit together easily, no pushing needed. Though he wouldn't mind doing some pushing. Some thrusting, ramming, pounding. The need was becoming a raw ache in his gut, a hammering pain in his temples.

"Seeing as I'm holding a real man in my arms now, and I've had some quite fierce wishful thinking in my life, I can tell you that one would never be mistaken for the other." Reaching up, she laid her hand alongside his face. "Easy," she murmured. "We'll get there. At my pace, bushman. You understand?"

"I can't handle much more in the way of games, my lady."

"I never play games. It's all about what I want, and when I'll demand it. Now . . ." She put some more space between them again, let go to take a turn under his arm, and then came back to him, a piece of footwork that couldn't help but make him smile. "What type of thing can a *real* bushman do that will impress me? Quick, the first thing you can think of."

"I can guess your exact weight. We do that at the fairs. If I guess right, you have to buy me a drink." He gave her a wink, trying to regain some sense of the upper hand. In response, her thigh pressed to the inside of his so she grazed his aching balls. Her hip slid across his groin and her lips parted. The bloody tease.

"If your guess isn't ten pounds *less* than my actual weight, you'll owe *me* a drink." Her eyes glinted in that elusive way, a danger back in the air he couldn't identify. And didn't give a damn about anyway.

"I don't lie. But I can tell you, your body couldn't be more perfect." When he leaned in close to her ear, his nose against her hair, she stilled on the outside, while everything inside him just locked up. His nostrils flared, taking in the scent of soft female flesh. He wanted to taste her, put his lips under the ear, bury his nose deeper into spun gold silk. He made himself rein it in. Settled instead for caressing with his breath the shell of an ear so delicate it looked like something found broken on the beach sands. He hadn't been to the ocean in a long time. Surfing at Cottesloe . . . He shoved that thought out of his mind and whispered the number to her.

When her head turned, he stayed where he was, so her nose brushed his jaw and he could see the moistness of her lips up close.

"That's my exact weight. So according to my terms, you owe me a drink." Her fingers skimmed the line of his jaw, several days' worth of stubble, down to the vulnerable Adam's apple, his jugular. "Again, when I demand it."

"I never agreed to the bet."

By all the cruel gods, she felt good. Good enough to suffer that crushing despondency he'd feel in the morning if he took her to bed. It was looking like a closer-than-distant possibility, and he already knew he wasn't smart enough to walk away.

Her breasts were firm and soft at once, and she didn't seem to mind his hand was low enough on her trim waist to graze the top of one fine arse cheek. As he said, he wasn't a dickhead. He didn't grope, but Jesus, he wanted to fill his hands with her. Maybe he'd be better off with a whore. His wants tonight were tumbling off the edge to savage, and while she sparred a fine game, he wasn't stupid enough to think she was ready to take a rutting beast to her bed.

"I noticed you carry a whip." She nodded to it, coiled on his pack, the handle slid through a loop. "Are you a fair hand with it?"

He tried to pull his thoughts back in order. "Passable."

She chuckled. "You said you always tell the truth."

"Well, there're degrees, love. There're men tons better than I am."

"Then I have no one but myself to blame if I don't believe you." She leaned back in his arms then, way back. Dropping her head and shoulders in an elegant and impressive dip, she trusted him to hold her by the waist as she did it. The strands of her tied-back hair brushed the floor before she straightened, displaying a grace and dexterity that caught every man's attention with its obvious implication. When she'd come all the way back up, he made sure she was so securely held in his arms there wasn't air between them. *She's mine tonight, mates.* He could feel their attention and envy pressing in on them like wolves, and wanted to make it clear who was alpha this evening. No matter the men she'd brought, she was sending out a strong message with her behavior that could turn this lot into beasts in truth if she wasn't careful. That was likely why Elle was so stirred up over her.

She'd chosen him, though. Over all of them. The thought roused something just as primal in him, only it would make him far more dangerous than the other blokes.

Her breasts were pressed to his chest, her hips against his arousal, her mouth so close. He put his lips there, brushing the fullness of hers as she spoke. "Tell me, Dev. Can you strike me without marking my skin, so that it feels as good as your breath on my flesh, like right now?"

It took him a minute to remember her question about the whip. The smile had left her lips, and her blue eyes were focused, intent.

"I'll do whatever it takes to be sunk to the balls inside you, to have you under me." He wasn't going to dress it up for her. Oh, hell, it wasn't that. He was a coward. She was making him feel a hundred different ways he couldn't afford to feel, and he was resorting to crudeness. Part of him cursed himself, for he was going to lose her with the defensive tactic. Another part hoped it worked, so she wouldn't tear his guts out.

When a shiver rippled through her body, his arms tightened around her.

"I'm at the boardinghouse down the way," she said. "Once the sun sets, I'm going to take you there. I'll show you what scraps of fancy I've got on under my clothes. We'll see then if you can curl that whip around me without the slightest pain. You show me you have that kind of control, no matter how worked up I've made you—and we're nowhere close to how worked up I intend to make you—and you can dish out whatever pain you want. I'll take every bit of it. But you *will* owe me that drink."

"God, you've no sense of fair play, do you, love?"

"Play assumes a game, Dev."

He'd lost his mind. "Whip's mainly for cracking. Strikes are usually trick stuff."

"But you can do both." She wasn't leaving him any room for escape.

"Maybe I should leave it at the one dance," he said. She really didn't understand the extent of what he wanted tonight. He wasn't sure himself anymore.

"Elle, do you have a back room?" Lady Daniela spoke as if she'd known Elle all her life. As if she were a family servant. Dev almost winced at the imperious sound of it.

The woman gave her a gimlet eye, jerked her head at a door on the back wall.

"Good, then." Lady Daniela turned to lead the way. Gathering his wits back about him, Dev shot Elle an ironic look. But he followed the Lady Danny, as he'd dubbed her in his mind. While her eagerness to get him alone for whatever reason was flattering, he was prepared for her reaction when she turned the knob and pushed her way through with confident determination.

Or so he thought.

She stepped right into the light of a sun a breath away from setting, because the door led not to a back room, but to the yard behind the building.

He'd been right on her heels and so pulled the door firmly closed, eager to have her to himself, only to find she'd spun on her heel and thrown herself into him with a gasp of genuine alarm. Reacting instinctively, Dev swung her behind him, back against the door to protect her with the shadow of his body. He was uncertain what the threat was, but he suspected his city lady had startled a snake on the back steps.

"Inside." As she made the demand, she shoved at the door so the jamb splintered. It had a history of being stubborn, but apparently it had rotted through at last, though the shards of wood that fell off looked sound enough. He pushed it open for her with his palm on the panel above her head and she quickly lunged back into the bar. It was then he smelled burned flesh.

The three men were on their feet as she made a direct line for Elle, moving so swiftly Devlin couldn't catch up in time. Elle was going for her shotgun, but before she could bring it out, Lady Daniela had caught the woman's collar and hauled her halfway over the bar one-handed, as if Elle's stocky body weighed as much as a doll.

"You human bitch," she snapped. "I paid in advance for your drinks. Not to mention the filthy rooms at that boardinghouse leased by your cousin."

"Love." Devlin eased up beside her, quickly taking in the light burns on her exposed forearms. He hoped he wouldn't have to get physical to intervene. Only an idiot got between two women in a blue. "Elle was getting back at you for putting on airs. Let her go now. She didn't know you had a sun allergy."

"I'll be happy to give all your money back if you take you and your mob elsewhere." Elle spat it out. Dev had seen Elle take an indifferent attitude toward foreigners before, but this was active dislike, tinged with the stink of fear. *What the bloody hell is going on here?* "I'd even lend you transport, but it won't have those nice dark windows. It'd be a shame if the engine died right before dawn."

He realized he wasn't disrupting a possibly entertaining brawl of hair pulling and female slaps. His own hackle-raising intuition, as well as the tense reaction of her men, told him that Lady D's level of violence could be anything but entertaining. Another piece of the puzzle, one he was sure keyed in to both the aborigine's and Elle's not-so-subtle hint that he was playing with fire. And it was likely he was going to get sensitive bits of himself scorched.

"Elle, leave off." As he reached out, Devlin judged Lady Danny's temperament much as he'd gauge a croc's appetite before he knelt by a creek to refill his water supply. When he put a hand carefully on her wrist, she flicked him a glance. "My lady, let her go. Look, the sun's said its final farewell for the day. You know how it is here. Sunset and then boom, it's night. And just to be sure . . ."

Determining that it was reasonably safe to step away a moment, and glad Joe wasn't around to mix things up further, he turned, scanned the bar and found what he sought. Going to that corner, shouldering past the few men watching, he procured the paper parasol that Elle had as one of the decorations for the place. "I'll bring it back," he promised, before Elle's scowl got any darker. He gave it a twirl, drawing the lady Danny's attention.

"A parasol to shade you, my lady. It's even got this pretty picture of a Japanese lady on the outside, sitting beneath a bamboo tree." He cocked a brow and won a quirk of Danny's lips, though her eyes were still shooting sparks. Lord help him if her temper didn't make her even more breathtaking.

"Dev, not for a million quid would I go anywhere with her and this lot. She's not right. She—"

"Neither am I, Elle." It was a gentle reminder, but he gave her a hard glance that said he wouldn't be dissuaded. "And I don't need a million quid, do I?"

Lady Daniela abruptly let Elle go, giving her a scathing look. "I paid for the room, and I'll be staying. But that's the last time you annoy me." Her gaze flickered over Devlin in a way that made his skin tingle and his cock jump to new life, brainless appendage that it was.

"He's mine for tonight. And he appears more than willing. Don't interfere again."

2

H<small>E'D</small> never thought of himself as belonging to anyone, but as for the rest . . . well, there was no arguing with the simple truth.

Devlin stepped out into the night, offering his companion a hand down the rickety back steps this time. He'd brought the parasol, but as soon as he verified the sun was truly gone, he left it inside the door. He'd recovered his belongings, so they sat comfortably on his back again, a weighted reminder of reality he needed right now.

"The sun just said its final farewell? A bit poetic for a bushman."

"Oxford, remember? See, it's right pretty out here. Though we might get eaten by mozzies."

A pair of kookaburras perched in a stately gum tree over the small billabong. The birds' raucous, laughing cry always made Dev think they were expressing their amusement at human folly. Appropriate for this moment.

"The bugs won't bother either of us, as long as you're standing near me." As she surveyed the water hole, he got the impression she was drawing in the night air, settling down. Perhaps trying to regain her composure.

"So why did you want to bring me into a back room, love?"

"To start what I intend to finish in my rooms. I can be impatient, on occasion. The perils of youth, I've been told." An ironic quirk of her lips again, suggesting her good humor was returning.

Now it was his turn to steady himself. The effect of her bold words was dizzying, as more blood rushed downward than his brain could spare.

"Looks like this is a favorite gathering space." She nodded toward several rough-hewn benches and chairs.

"Yeah, there's a nice wind off the water, when the creek bed's not dry." He knew it because he actually preferred this area. Usually he ended up back here, where he could breathe better. He'd nurse a beer, get up a card game, stumble off to his swag on the veranda only when he was well buzzed and too sleepy to dream. Wouldn't be that way tonight, though. He couldn't imagine her preferring anything other than a soft, clean bed, a courtesy he was sure she was used to having from a lover.

She'd traveled a few steps away, releasing his hand, and now she turned. "I shouldn't have lost my temper like that," she said. "Sometimes I let it get away from me."

"You don't owe me the apology, love," he said mildly. "Talk to Elle."

Lady Daniela snorted. "I don't owe that one an apology. She knew what she was doing, right enough. I just mean control is important."

"More important than anything else?"

"Pretty much." She threaded her manicured fingers through some loose tendrils of blond hair, but her gaze was riveted on him again. "Though there are always things that tempt me to think otherwise. Do you know your Australian history?"

He grunted. "As much as any lad with more interesting things to do."

"Liar. Oxford scholar. 'All I see I claim.' " Her gaze coursed from his toes, moving slowly . . . so slowly. "That's what the first settlers said. No wonder they felt that way, looking at terrain that could give them so much. If they understood its mysteries."

"Let's go to your room." He straightened, his voice thick. Stepped toward her. "You can claim everything you want from me, love."

The pupils of her eyes had dilated in the near darkness, grown larger so he was actually having some difficulty seeing the blue. "Rooms. I have the whole upper floor," she said. "The windows are open, and there's a door to the veranda. You won't feel trapped."

"Why does one woman need a whole floor of rooms?" He decided not to comment on how she'd picked up on the fact he didn't like to feel closed in.

"My needs are not small. And tonight I intend for a bushman to demonstrate his prowess with a whip." That smile again, feral enough he wondered if it was a smile at all, or more likely the expression of another species whose language he didn't yet know.

∼

The small boardinghouse was nothing fancy, of course, a frame building set up on pilings for air flow. Basically, it served as an alternative to the hotel, which housed mainly single stockmen. But it was clean and they'd tried to create a parlor for guests to play cards or keep one another company. There was even a brace of not-too-dingy lace curtains at the doors leading out to the veranda. He watched, bemused, as she slid the meager furniture of sofa and chair against the wall to clear floor space before he could join her to assist. For all she looked so refined and willowy, she was a strong thing.

"Take out your whip," she said. And without further ado, she began to pace back from him, until she was near the opposite wall. Then she started to slip the buttons of her white shirt.

That froze him in place, watching the cleavage evolve into the high white curves of her breasts, like a bird's wings. And she didn't wear some practical brassiere bought out of a catalog, like most women he'd known. Her bosom was held in a lacy, transparent garment that not only made it look ready to spill out at any moment, but showed him the soft smudge of mauve nipples. Saliva gathered in the back of his throat as she shrugged out of the shirt. When she loosened her hair, it drifted over the molded cups and swung back over the upper arms, her rounded shoulders.

"Come here and take off my boots."

He moved, even though the commanding tone bothered him

some, as if she fully expected to be obeyed. *Don't make an issue out of it, mate.* Wryly, he suspected that quelling directive had been barked straight from his cock to his floundering brain.

"Lady Daniela." He wet dry lips. "So you never explained that. Am I with nobility, then?"

"Aristocracy. Nobility is a virtue. I have few of those."

He let his gaze drift appreciatively. "I'd argue that, my lady."

When he reached her, she was leaned up against the wall, folding her hands almost demurely beneath the cushion of her backside. Even though the pose lifted those breasts, drew his hungry attention to them, she lifted a leg, braced her heel on his thigh, stopping his forward progress. "My boots, Dev. If you'd like to see the rest."

Picking up her ankle, he slid to the heel to take hold. While she hadn't said to do it, he also took off the thin sock beneath, his hands whispering along bare skin now, the slope of her calf and delicate structure of her ankle, the arch of her foot. Her lips parted, her breath raising those lovely breasts on a trembling sigh. She liked his touch, then. That was good. Because he intended to touch her a lot, for as long as she'd put up with him.

She shifted, placed the other foot high on his thigh again, earning a hungry lunge from his cock contained only by the tough fabric of his moleskins.

Once he slid that boot and sock off, she straightened and opened the clasp on her jodhpurs. One teasing wriggle and they slid down her flesh like a waterfall, no resistance from her silky skin. As if she were one of those Roman goddesses, it was like she was meant to stand like this, in an elegant, nearly naked pose. He was all for it.

More lace, more transparent fabric that hiked high on her legs and the delectable arse. He'd bet it was round and soft-looking as a pillow. He was a sucker for a fine arse. He liked all the parts, but that one . . . He couldn't get enough of ogling, squeezing, smacking . . . even buggering. Tina'd always laughed and said she had to keep her back to a wall—

He pulled back, startled by the thought. Lady Daniela glanced up at him. "Something bite you?" That seemed to amuse her for some reason, but there was a serious question in her gaze.

Nothing but memories. But as he well knew, memories did more than bite. They tore, ripped, mutilated . . . refused to leave you alone— or dead. He wouldn't care which they did, as long as they'd stop their tormenting.

As if she knew that, she crossed the room, putting that distance between them again. He'd never seen a woman walk like that. Not the exaggerated saunter of a whore, or the self-conscious movements of a modest woman deprived of her clothes. It was the way he imagined a goddess to walk, fully aware of her sexual power, willing to be generous with it if the man was worthy. He wasn't, but at this point he was willing to beg, as soon as he could find his tongue. She was giving him a hell of an eyeful, driving coherence away.

High, firm tits, arse shifting along just right, smooth, pale legs. She was a vat of cream, for sure, and he was the hungry tom who wanted to lick it all up.

"So here's your chance, bushman." She posed there, a hand on her hip, cocked provocatively, and tossed her hair back. "Touch me with that whip from the farthest reach possible, without leaving so much as a mark, and I'll give you everything you want. If you hurt me . . . I'll get what I want." She smiled, unexpectedly. "Of course, it's all the same really, isn't it?"

It broke some of the tension, making him chuckle. But as he measured off the pacing he needed, he felt a moment's uneasiness. There was a reason the stockman's braided kangaroo hide whip was called his third arm. He had as much control over it as his own limb. But the one appendage Dev didn't seem to have any control over, his cock, could seriously disrupt that control, and a stockman's whip could carve a brand in a steer's hide.

So focus, damn it. You don't want to hurt her.

Or did he? Fleetingly, he wondered if he might cheat a little . . . just to see what she'd demand of him. The look in her eyes was the way a lioness centered herself before chasing down that helpless buck. He did and didn't want to do it her way. Some part of him wanted to go to her, bury himself in wet heat, feel the desperate clutch of her hands as he drove her to climax. Because after he exploded inside her, for a short time he could drift in the fantasy of a reality he'd had for too short a time. A reality he'd never have permanently again, because his heart wouldn't survive its loss twice.

Stop it. Control wasn't only important in the use of the whip. It was what was most important of all. As long as you had it, it implied you had choice. Startled, he realized he'd echoed her words by the billabong. Control was what was important, above all.

He uncoiled the whip with one deft move of his wrist. "You sure you might not enjoy feeling a touch of pain, my lady?"

"That's beside the point." She curled her lip, showing him a flash of her canines, which seemed particularly sharp. "The bet is no pain, or I get to take everything I want."

He could curl the whip around her body for hours, twirl her in a dance, touch the end of it to any pink, fragile part, tease a nipple or the hint of her pretty pussy beneath the gauzy fabric. Or cut a brand into her flank as intricate as he might wish. His cock hardened inexplicably at that thought.

As she posed there, beautiful, statuesque, something far beyond his reach, her blue eyes never left his face. Then she destroyed him by raising her arms above her head so her breasts rose, the skin stretched over her rib cage, making it more defined, vulnerable. She stayed that way, as if her hands were bound from the ceiling, and his blood fired.

The whip sang out, the pop striking right where he intended. A spot high on her perfect right breast, the first place he'd put his lips to soothe the skin. He put enough recoil into the strike that the effect was a bee sting, raising a blush on the skin. No cut, but it definitely hurt. Proving that he could do it without pain, and had made the conscious choice not to do so.

Sometimes he thought his roughness with women, the need to hurt them a little, came from the fact that none of those women was the one he missed so much. But there was a different component to this. Bloody oath, she didn't even flinch. But he sensed something change in the air as he brought the whip back to him, coiled it up in an efficient movement. If he had to give it a name, he'd say it was a wave of feral satisfaction, emanating from her like blazing heat.

Holding the whip in a clenched fist, he saw her gaze travel to where his cock was straining against his trousers, then back over every tense muscle in his body. As her attention went up his bare chest, it reminded him of her touch through the bar rag, the way she'd seemed to savor every inch of him.

"I assume you're a man of your word?" she asked.

"I am." He found his mouth was dry.

"Take off your shirt." When he complied, she began to move toward him. As her hips moved like the pendulum of an elegant clock, her breasts quivered in the cradle of that bra. He was sure the underwire beneath the lace was far more unforgiving and cruel than his hands would be. Or maybe not.

She stopped before him, gazed up into his eyes. Dev was unable to move, the proximity of her body to the raging need of his own overwhelming, paralyzing him. "When we're alone, you may call me Danny," she said. "All right?"

"Yes, my lady." He wasn't sure why he couldn't comply with it just yet. Maybe he needed her remoteness. Maybe he was afraid that what was inside him would swallow her whole if she left no barriers between them.

"There's something in your eyes, bushman," she continued softly, looking up into them. "I want to keep this moment quite real between us. You said you'd let me have anything I want."

"There's not much to take, love." And he was afraid what little there was, he might give her. He'd immersed himself in women before to keep the darkness at bay, but despite the fact that this woman looked a handful of years younger than him, it was as if she understood the deep intricacies of the world, how they were heartbreaking beyond bearing. She wasn't soothing him or telling him to shut it out. Instead she was throwing him a line, making him accept the port she was offering from his storm.

Her hand slid over his on the whip, started to uncoil it again. When he reached for her with his free hand, she caught his wrist, guided it behind him, then the other, the whip still in his grip. Before he could object or try to overpower her, she'd lifted on her toes and brought her mouth to his, pressing those straight-from-heaven tits against his chest. The bra was so thin he could feel the pressure of her hardened nipples.

Opening to her, he gave her his tongue, teased her with it, demanded with his lips what his body had to have. He was vaguely aware of her tangling his hands in the whip, and now he'd no objection to her game. Until he felt the kangaroo leather cinch on his wrists, one shot past painful, and found she'd securely bound his wrists behind him.

She backed away from him then, holding the tail of the whip through his legs. When he started to move forward, she lifted it between them, putting an uncomfortable pressure against his testicles. Her blue eyes had sobered, but he found it somewhat reassuring they still reflected the raging desire he was feeling himself.

"Did you know that when a convict was brought here, sometimes he didn't even know the length of his sentence?" Her voice had become that sultry murmur again, despite the grim topic. "Perhaps the judges forgot to tell him, or didn't think him worth the effort. I think that would be the worst part of his lot. Truly helpless to his fate, forced to trust his master to tell him when his release would come."

He told himself all he needed to do was twist to yank the whip from her. Instead, he remained still, watchful. "You didn't jump when I marked you. As though you expected it."

"I did. You don't do what you're told, because you want to defy the consequences. Prove you can handle them." She came back to him then, one step, two . . . three. Reaching out, she caressed his jaw, then tipped his chin back, slowly, her nails digging in a little. She liked using her claws. A further tip, straining his neck some, a deeper gouge of those sharp edges. "Plus, I trusted you. Can you trust me?"

Her breath was on his flesh, near the artery pulsing in his throat. For some reason Dev heard his blood pounding through it, his ears, his chest, as if rushing water were closing in on him.

"I doubt it."

A soft chuckle, then the pressure of the whip against his testicles loosened, brushed against his buttocks as she dropped the tail and reclaimed it in the back, guiding a length of it across his tense buttocks and fondling him with greedy fingertips. When she took a handful of muscular meat and squeezed it against the braided leather in her palm, he growled and stepped forward, bumping her. Her other hand found his cock and balls, ready to explode out of his trousers.

"My God, Dev."

"Let it out to play, love, and you won't be sorry." His urgency had the edge of desperation. Even if he'd been a man dying of thirst in the desert, he would have taken a lick at her pussy over water at this moment.

"Is this how you do it, Dev? You assuage the need and then go back into the bush, until it becomes unbearable again? No working mates, not even a dog to keep you company. Maybe Elle's right to worry about you."

Before he could respond to that, she was continuing on, her fingers teasing, stroking. "There's only one reason God gives a man a gift like this. I think you should stay with me awhile, see if burying yourself between my thighs often enough will slow those demons chasing you."

His arm muscles strained against the restraint as he pushed her back a couple more steps, a challenge, an attempt to get her to shut up. She moved with him as easily as if they were dancing again. Cripes, what kind of knot had she tied? He was testing it, but he couldn't tell. In truth, his brain was so fogged it could have been a simple shoelace tie.

"Why only between your legs, my lady?" He rasped it against her temple, groaned as she squeezed him, letting him feel her nails again. "You strike me as the type that appreciates a good arse fucking. And then there's your smart mouth."

"Be careful, bushman." Her throaty voice, the taunting laughter in it, vibrated against his skin. "Or I'll wash yours out."

"Well, there's plenty of fluid soaking your knickers now, isn't there?"

As she tipped her head back, he saw she'd closed her eyes. They'd almost reached the wall. Bending his knees, Dev put his hips hard between her legs, taking her off her feet and slamming her back into it with the pressure and strength of his upper torso and legs. Her eyes flew back open. Grinding himself against her mons, the swollen clit he knew would be vulnerable to such an attack, he earned a gasp as she caught hold of his back and neck.

He stopped at that point, though, so hard he was on a dagger's edge, unable to move unless he wanted to come in his pants. But more than that, there was a violent pain in him, and he was afraid he was going to put her through the wall to deal with it.

"Shhh .... shh now." She wasn't fighting him, struggling to throw him off in anger as he likely deserved. Instead her touch, the blue of her eyes, drew him in, eased him like a soft sea air.

She lowered her hand to open his trousers, and then closed over him, cool, firm pressure against pounding, insistent heat. She was trembling, and it was only that which recalled him, though he was certain it wasn't fear. While he pressed his forehead to the wall to the left of her fair skull, he kept her off her feet between him and the wall, determined not to let her get away, trying to rein it in, trying to protect her. All long fine limbs, fragile face . . .

"What made you what you are, Dev?"

Though it was phrased as a question, in that seductive whisper she had, it resounded in his mind with the ring of command. When he shook his head, his gut knotting, her fingertips grazed his nape, played in the strands of his hair.

"Many things make us who we are," she continued, a relentless angel. Not the kind that you put on your mantle as Christmas decorations. The kind that fought Satan to the gates of hell. "Changes us, from year to year. But one main event shapes us, defines us. Tell me yours, Devlin."

"I didn't invite you there, love. I told you that."

"You want past this gate"—she rubbed herself against him—"you pay the fee."

"I didn't take you for a whore, love."

Her nails stabbed into skin, sending a shudder jolting through his spine. "You won't play with me, Dev. Your soul knew what I was, the moment you walked into the pub tonight. Tell me. How did you lose her?"

He closed his eyes. He wanted to tell her to go to hell, but he'd only be there waiting for her. He'd been there so long he should have forgotten the time before, when he wasn't scorched in its agony, but part of the agony of hell was the inability to forget.

It was just a handful of sentences. In a book or film, they'd be thrown in to make an otherwise wretched bastard a sympathetic character. As a scholar, he'd done everything to those sentences in his mind. Diagrammed them, broken them down. As if he could scramble the tense or arrangement so it wouldn't be true, would change the story after it was written, a quick redlining and destruction of those ill-advised pages.

In real life, speaking those sentences gave people something to talk about in their own blissfully mediocre lives . . . *Heard about what happened to that bloke's family, the one running a station outside Blackall? What a terrible thing . . .*

So he'd never said them, though they ran through his head like a ticker tape on the stock market all day long, with no closing bell. He'd studied business as well as literature, because a good business mind helped run a station. But in the end, he'd become this, a wanderer, belonging nowhere. Haunted by the ghost of the rare woman who'd loved the Outback as much as he had.

He couldn't say the words. They represented the chasm in his soul that was always there, burning . . .

His family had ties with the aborigines, dating back to when his ancestor escaped from Moreton Bay in the nineteenth century and lived with the black fellas long enough to marry into one of the clans, become part of a tribe. Some of that blood ran in his veins. Though it wasn't much, not enough to show and cause him any problem in the white-run world, those ties still existed. He knew they could offer succor, paths to walk to heal his pain. Then there were the bars, with the temptation of gleaming bottles. Or he could lose himself in the dark corners of the world where opiates could be found.

Instead he'd chosen the Outback, for he couldn't cope with anything that didn't offer him honesty. And the bush told him, every day, that the world was cruel and beautiful both.

He'd left the green and fertile fields, the wild mountains of coastal Queensland, gone deep into Western Australia. What he sought in those lonely, wild areas was inside the woman before him now. Beneath the creamy skin and blue eyes, there was that same call . . . something savage and violent, even deadly. Something like the Outback, requiring his full attention so there wasn't time to dwell in the desolation of his soul. And if he plunged into her deeply enough, perhaps he would find permanent oblivion.

"They came to the station while I was gone. Raped and beat my wife to death. Killed my son when he tried to do my job. Tried to protect her."

Her arms closed around him, holding him, but not to give pity, which he could not have borne. She lifted his chin, made him look at her.

"Give me your soul, Dev," she murmured. "Sometimes it's much easier to let someone else carry the weight of it for a while."

Her lips curled back then, so he could see the sharp canines elongate, become tiny, needlelike points. There was a weight on him, something that made it not matter that he was seeing something he'd never seen before, except in horror films. She was right. He had known the danger of her the moment he'd walked in tonight. And the feelings that rose in him now were acquiescence, the fierce desire to accept, to give her whatever it was she wanted. They raged through him, full of his lust and pain. It was nothing she was compelling or forcing from him. In the fight-or-flight scale of reaction to fear or great emotion, he'd always been a fighter. His lack of choice at this moment had to do with what his own soul was demanding, not hers. He had to have her. Take her. He'd accept whatever price she demanded. No matter what she was.

Her hand slid behind him, and the whip dropped to the floor with a heavy thud. "Do as you like, bushman. I promise you can't break me."

Obeying mindless, primal need, he tore the swatch of panties from her, found her wet opening with his broad head and shoved her down on it, a sword determined to fit into a small scabbard, even if he tore her open the way she was tearing him.

She sank her fangs into his throat, filling her mouth with his blood. Her cry at his penetration allowed some of it to escape and trickle down to his collarbone, leaving a drop on her breast right over the red mark he'd made with the whip. His blood slid down and stained the edge of the bra. Yanking it off her with the noise of ripping fabric, he filled his hands with her curves.

Blood. Pain. Release. Flesh and pleasure. Woman. He seized her buttocks then, gripping as he thrust against her against the wall, beating a tempo. She was so tight and perfect, all the way to her womb. She didn't tell him to stop, didn't make him back off, as he would if he'd had a mind to be the considerate lover he knew he could be. But at the moment he had no control.

It didn't seem to matter. Her body rippled with desire against his as she undulated with lithe grace, keeping right up with him in ferocious urgency. Her hair caressed his face, the curve of his shoulder as she nourished herself at his throat. He felt her strength again in the unshakable grip of her arms, the resilience of her bones as he shoved her against the shabby wall. She didn't seem to notice or care.

He maneuvered his hand in between them, lubricated his fingers in the slick fluids dripping around her opening, stretched impossibly by his cock. Teasing her clit until he won a gasp, he moved around to slide those fingers into her tight arse before she could deny him. He wouldn't see her after tonight, but by the Devil, she was going to remember him for days afterward.

She bucked up against him. While she didn't loose her clamp on his throat, he heard her whimper, felt her pussy muscles contract on him, her clit harden, ready to go. He loved a sheila who liked having her arse played with, almost as much as he enjoyed the wet heat between her legs. He wanted to fuck her, lick her clean, get her creaming again and start all over, until she was hoarse from screaming and unable to walk.

Until he was hoarse and unable to walk.

She was having a hard time keeping her mouth on him now. More blood was trickling down his chest and she was flexing her body into a crescent, lapping up the stream like an eager kitten, reaching his nipple, her nails raking over his shoulders, drawing blood there as well. Bending his head, he put his lips over the red mark he'd left on her plump right breast, as he'd first desired, and that stilled him for a moment, so he could almost stand outside his mind and feel the rushing urgency of their bodies. Their temples brushed, and he thought they might look like two strained curves of a heart, quivering with near explosion.

"Come for me, love," he demanded roughly. "Let me hear you."

She stiffened, resisting, but he withdrew and then slammed back in, letting her feel the length of him stroking against the outer lips, finding the dense spot within her and rubbing against it on the way back to her womb. That was the good thing about being cursed with an organ the length of a horse's cock. He could make that feeling last a good . . . long . . . time. He withdrew, slid back in again. Moved his mouth to a nipple, scoring her with his teeth, sucking on her relentlessly.

"Give over," he snarled against her flesh.

His wrists were burning where she'd bound him and he'd fought the restraints. Her skin was abraded by his whip. Small sacrifices of flesh to one another. They were both caught up in this, on sacred ground indeed. He'd never look at the dingy second level of this boardinghouse the same way again.

Swinging her abruptly from the wall, he crossed the short distance from the parlor to the small bedroom. He wanted to take her on her back. He needed to feel her legs high on his spine, her body open to his, pressed beneath him. It gave him the angle he needed, a friction against her clit she couldn't resist any longer, though he sensed her scrabbling attempt, just as he sensed her aversion to the position he chose, as if she was used to or preferred to be on top. But when their eyes locked once more, it didn't matter. Two puzzle pieces were two puzzle pieces, no matter what way you turned them. And when all was said and done, it didn't change the fact they were still a puzzle.

He was a lost soul. She was a vampire. Everything was bloody perfect.

Her screams resounded through the building as he began to come with her, both of them finding their temporary release. He from the wasteland of his memories. She . . . Well, Dev didn't claim to know any woman's mind, let alone that of a supernatural one, but from the bite of her fingernails, the beautiful artwork of her pleasure-suffused face, he thought he'd served her well despite it all.

As his blood and seed were drained from him, as the orgasm ripped through him like bushfire, only one fleeting question remained to worry his mind. And that made only a negligible dent in his already battered shields as he drifted into a hazy aftermath.

What happened to a man after he handed a vampire his soul?

3

FROM the start, he'd warned her. He might not control himself. Might use her too hard, take her too rough. A halfhearted attempt to protect her from *him*.

What a fucking joke.

How much time had passed? Sometime during the early morning hours, she whispered something about how he'd persuaded her to take an extra day here. *I'll punish you for that, bushman.*

That threat, delivered in a soft breath of air against his ear, had left him wrung out and drained. Again and again. She had the stamina of a male beast in rutting season, and she didn't take no for an answer. She didn't even ask the question. He found himself servicing her mindlessly, again and again, however she demanded it. And when he flagged, her mouth, hands and body would drive his cock to obey her once more.

Since Tina, he'd probably spent less than forty-five minutes alone with a woman. Most he pushed away after about twenty minutes. He wasn't a bastard. He left them satisfied, but he had nothing to offer but a good fuck and picking up the beer tab before he took off. Like most men, he wasn't into the cuddling aftermath, but unlike them, it wasn't because he feared intimacy. It was because he remembered what true intimacy was like. The mockery of it flogged self-loathing to life. If he was in range of alcohol, he'd be forced to get off his face to bury it again. Otherwise it drove him mad enough to do violence.

She didn't care about that, the dogs he was afraid to loose. She herself had broken the chain holding them back. She reveled in his savagery, his attempts to fight her for control. She took him on like a she-wolf. At one point, he remembered staring at her through the darkness, for by that time Elle had cut the generator, leaving them only the option of candlelight. He'd seen a hint of his blood smeared on Lady D's full bottom lip, the stain of it gleaming on a fang.

While he remembered nothing about the passage of time after that first coupling, everything else had the sharp edge and accuracy of a carved spear. She'd reversed their positions, shoving him to his back on the bed. His eyes had widened when she produced iron manacles from her belongings. Like those clapped on the wrists and ankles of his convict ancestor. He'd seen a pair under glass at a museum, and had imagined them, hard and unforgiving on a man's legs or arms, limiting his choices.

With movements faster than he could follow, even if his chest hadn't been working like a bellows, his dizzy brain still reeling, she had him bound again. There was the disturbing click on each wrist and ankle, four separate suspensions of time. She used her belt to bind the leg chain to the foot rail, his belt to make fast the wrist manacles above his head. Frissons of shock jittered through him, a strange, unsettling venom that compelled him to fight. However, the way her blue eyes intensified beneath the fringe of gold lashes as she studied the flex of his muscles, the bowing of his body, a thin line of perspiration along his neck, made him grow still again, shallow breath held.

She'd recovered his whip and held it in her hands, the braided length passing through her fingers, while she stood at the foot of the bed.

Despite the fact she'd just milked him, his flagging cock wanted to strain like a dying man, ready to pull itself over sharp rocks toward her.

"What . . ." He licked dry lips. "Love, what—"

"You may speak as you like," she said. "Except to question anything I do to you. That's up to me, and none of your business to decide. I'm a fair hand with a whip myself, Dev."

And he felt it, enough to make him jump. The tail popped so close above his nipple the faint sting came from the snap of the air. Despite himself, his cock slid from his thigh back up toward his belly, an animal reawakening.

"You do have some of the way of it, then," she observed. "Though I'll bet that's a bit of a surprise to you. Has no woman ever mastered you? Taught you to respond to her slightest touch upon your mouth, guiding your head? Made you give her everything, letting her ride you past the endurance of your great heart? Like a stallion trained to go on until you'd let it explode in your chest rather than fail her."

Christ, she was a sight. Talking like that, naked as a savage, her long blond hair loose and flowing along her arms and shoulders like a mane.

"That what you're fixing to do, love?" he managed hoarsely. "Ride me to the end?"

Her gaze flickered at his deliberate disobedience. This time the pop hit his abdomen with a singing pain that arched him off the bed, sent fire coursing through him and brought a curse to his lips.

"No," she said softly. "I want to make certain you'll go that far, if I demand it."

That powerful first time must have addled his wits, because he never had his feet back under him again. She brought him back to life with her sultry taunts and the painful caress of the whip, the brush of her body, her hair across his chest, and then she rode him to another climax.

Living in the Outback so long, his body had adapted so he didn't waste water easily. He wasn't one to sweat profusely, but nothing could dehydrate a man quicker than fucking. She didn't give him water, or any type of relief for a while. She changed the manacles, spread his body wider on the bed, making his shoulders and hips ache.

The next time, she commanded his erection to life by running the whip under his arse and gripping it in both hands to hold him to her as she teased his girth with her small mouth. Slid his cock through the cleft of her breasts, using her own fluids to lubricate the valley. But what sent him back to groaning stiffness was when she turned, made him watch his cock pump up and down the channel between her cheeks as she straddled him backward. The flex of those lovely buttocks, gripping him, moving up and down, feeling her flesh clench his organ, made him leak out and slick the passage further, increasing the torment.

When he thought he could stand no more of that without the tearing agony of a forced orgasm, she backed over him, filling his vision with the heart-shaped backside as she leaned forward to go down on him and stroked him beyond speech with the hot, sucking pressure of her lips, the grip of her fingers, moist breath on his broad head. Her pussy was over his face, but strain as he might, she kept it out of reach, though the fluids collected over her aroused cunt lips before his glazed eyes. He opened his mouth to take in the slow drops that eventually fell, sweet as hot molasses, on his tongue, his lips.

At one point, he demanded she rub it in his face, that she ride his cock. She did neither until he begged, pleaded.

After the third time, or maybe it was the fourth, she'd had water brought, and food. But she hadn't let go of the upper hand then, either. Putting the water in her mouth, she cradled his jaw in one hand, her other loosely on his neck, so the pressure of her palm was against his ragged pulse. Coaxing his mouth open, she let the fluid trickle in and hydrated him that way, one painstaking mouthful at a time. By the time the slow, sensual process was over, he was high and proud again. He was going to be fucked to death.

Death by fucking he could take. It might even be welcome, though it would mean he was surely going to hell. He hadn't lived a good enough life to earn heaven, and only a god with a macabre sense of humor would give him every man's wish for his last act on the earth before plunging him into the fires that would scorch the memory.

True to her word, he wasn't allowed any questions about what she was doing or why. Every attempt was met with a punishing strike of that lash, as opposed to a teasing lick from it, and she was liberal with both, for he was hardheaded, when all was said and done.

Occasionally, the restraint, the pain of it, brought forth a surge of emotion so strong he had no control anymore. He raged at her, thrashed against the manacles until they scraped the skin off his wrists, enraging him further, pulled at the unrelenting iron headboard. He called her foul names, demanded she release him, the demon-bitch from hell.

Her answer was more devastating than simple pain. She let him run out, then shifted her legs beneath his head and shoulders, slackening the hold of the manacles enough so she could cradle his upper body in her lap, stroke his head. Wouldn't let him snap at her, holding his head fast and gently applying pressure to his windpipe until his vision blacked and he settled down out of self-preservation. Still, he thought she was taking a risk with her more tender appendages when she brought her nipple into the proximity of his lips. But at that point, gasping for air, his mind whirling, he was nonplused when she pulled her hair to one side and then poured more precious water down the curve of her breast, exercising such steady control that it was a slow, precise trickle down that luscious hill. The way it arrived at the nipple, skirting around it across the mauve areola, with his mouth so close, made it the simplest thing in the world to close his lips over it and begin to suckle, take in the fluids he now desperately needed. The feel of that taut nub against his tongue, the need to flick against it even as he drank, tasting her with the life-giving water, was something he couldn't deny himself.

It took some time, but as she crooned softly to him, one after another, each taut muscle that had been struggling like a wild creature for release began to relax. He kept suckling, his breath and heartbeat steadying. She kept up her purring, replenishing him from her breast.

Christ, it was the oddest combination of sensations. One minute, a killing rage if she didn't let him go. His instinct could turn him into a beast when cornered, as she'd just seen. But there was apparently an even deeper, more primitive instinct she'd uncovered that put him in this strange trance, a stupor of zealous devotion and fascination with her at once. His mind was in some fucking bizarre limbo, no longer wanting to question or want. She was the beginning and end of it all.

Then, holy God, she started all over again.

~

By the last time, many hours later, it had become painful. It was as if she'd flogged his cock the way she'd striped other parts of him with his own whip. His balls ached, burned. There was nothing left, there wouldn't be. Still she urged him on, demanded, and as she'd threatened, he was working everything he had for her. His whole world was about the fierce victory of putting a flush on her silken skin, hearing a catch of breath in her throat, raising the level of arousal in her eyes, to see if he could get it higher than last time. He couldn't explain it, why it was so easy to abandon everything to her, even hope. There was no responsibility for him in this, just in serving her.

She understood the power of it, the sheer abyss of oblivion that he'd not found in his long years in the emptiness of the Red Center. He'd found it here, in a small, stuffy room, physically overpowered and unraveled by a slender blond vampire.

He didn't have to explain it. She knew.

"Don't think I . . . can, love," he gritted that last time, even as he pumped his hips up from the bed as best he could. Christ, everything hurt, and yet the slippery purse of her cunt clutched him, demanding, keeping him hard.

"You can. You will." She put a finger in her mouth, two, then three, and then, as sly and sinuous as a carpet shark, she slid that hand down between his thighs, caressed the joining point between balls and cock, causing a shudder to run through him. She carried the movement right in between his sweaty arse cheeks, already lubed up from sweat.

"Don't . . . no. Ah, God." He bucked up from her touch and impaled her mercilessly, playing deep, going where no one ever had. She leaned forward, bringing close the wet red lips, pale skin, and cruel intensity of soft blue eyes that should have been on a child's doll.

"Don't ever say no to me, Devlin." Her fingers adjusted, found what she sought, that gland, and her lips curved, celebrating her sinful victory as he convulsed, tongue tied up by that unusual but unbearably good stimulation. She knew her business there. With a wrenching that he thought might be from his guts twisting around her fingers, he began to come again. Dry this time, for he had no semen left to offer, leaving him painfully hard when he was done.

Tossing back her head set her breasts quivering. Exhausted as he was, he couldn't not look at the spread of milk-and-cream thighs, the slope of her abdomen, glistening from his sweat. Before this round, she'd given him water again, the same way, and the tracks of his mouth were on her damp breast. The nipple he'd latched on to with the furor of a newborn at her guidance was still hard and a darker red than the other.

He did his best, kept his hips working, dragging in and out in rhythm with her, determined to give her the full amount of pleasure. Her eyes were closed, soft whimpers coming from her throat. He wanted to hear her scream and so redoubled his efforts, ignoring the spasms in his back muscles, the gray settling into his vision, the fact he had no more oxygen left. He was going to do her right and proper. Ride her to the end, as she'd said. If his heart did explode in his chest, if that made him daft, he didn't give a damn. There was only this. No more thought.

She cried out as he rammed up hard, giving her the full measure of him. "Don't get shy on me now, love," he managed, making sure she knew he had fight left in him. "Take all of me in that eager cunt of yours. Take me deep, if you dare. Most girls . . . won't . . . can't. If . . . I bent you over the table and put myself up your arse, you'd think I'd split you in two. Make you cry pretty tears, even as you'd gush all over my balls."

She met his gaze then, the spark there telling him he was a complete dill for challenging her again. Her body shifted, enveloped even more of him, took him deep, all the way, so he felt the cervix give way, right into the uterus. Most women found it too uncomfortable, but he saw the pain of it ripple through her gaze and then become something else that hardened her clit and the walls of her womb around him.

"Ride me to the end, love," he snarled. "You'll never need another mount."

Her nails dug hard into his chest, gouging the countless welts she'd already made with the whip. A couple times she'd sliced hard enough to shred skin, then lapped at the blood with her tongue.

The release of pain, the demand of pleasure. He'd used them separately to absorb that constant burning in his gut, the memories that battered him. He'd never known the power of using them together. She'd brought him that. If endlessly serving her was a punishment in Purgatory, he'd take it.

Summoning all his strength, he bounced her on his loins, a bucking that slapped her flesh against his, brought her clit down against his taut body. "Spread wide for me, love," he muttered. "Let me hear how much you like it, my fucking you."

She shrieked like an animal as she went over, her nails sliding down, pulling skin with them, her inner muscles convulsing in a way that took him with her. Lord, she had a grip, and she fit him so perfect, so bloody tight and slippery at once. She pistoned her hips, matching him blow for blow, her lips stretched back to show those fangs, a guttural sound of release coming from her absurdly fragile-looking throat.

He couldn't get enough breath, couldn't draw in enough air, his limbs quaking so the manacles that had cut cruelly into his flesh rattled harshly against the iron headboard. When at last she slid from him, the limp length of his cock lay like a heavy trout along his thigh. It stirred weakly, the last throes of a dying soldier, as her body pressed on the inside of his leg and her breath touched it, a dainty tongue sweeping over the ultrasensitive flesh.

"I've taken so much," she whispered. "Left you almost nothing." Her nose nudged his cock aside, and her teeth grazed his thigh, the fang pressing with enough pressure that he was aware of the erratic beat of the vital artery behind the flesh. "But you've drained me as well. Can you feed me, bushman? I'm hungry for your blood again."

His eyes were closing, his grasp on consciousness slipping. Though he felt like a desiccated lizard, he didn't begrudge her whatever was left. But he could tell his response was important, even if her intent was to finish him off. "You told me . . . not to tell you no again." It curved his lips, but the rueful comment twisted something sad and exhausted within him. "Do as my lady desires. It's all yours, Danny."

His last conscious thought was that the sensation this time was different, as if the puncture of her fangs jolted him with electric current. His leg jumped, but her gentle, powerful hands held it fast. "My parting gift, Dev," he thought he heard her murmur. "So I can check in on you now and again." Her hair brushed his balls, his cock, a fond caress as his lady's mouth drew sustenance again from his body, a body willing to give her everything.

Was that a magic she had? Or had the desolation of his soul responded to her as if hell had finally beckoned, ready for him at last?

He'd given up thinking a few hours ago and he sure as hell wasn't up to any weighty thoughts now, particularly when it really didn't mean a bloody thing. He drifted away, not caring if he ever woke again. Dust and oblivion. That was heaven for a man like him. The only heaven he'd wanted for five years. But the bloke who'd impaled Jesus on a spear had been doomed to walk the earth for all eternity. Why should his punishment be less?

Blasphemous, Tina would have said, giving him a light smack. But consciousness left him before the ache of tears could come.

~

He surfaced with no sense of what day it might be, but it was nighttime again. Maybe about nine or ten o'clock. She'd drawn the windows and curtains during their daylight time together, but now they were open, the screens keeping out the flies as the wind moved the lace curtains. As he woke, for a wistful moment he'd hoped that breeze was the light touch of her hand.

Struggling to his elbows, he surveyed his body. He was naked except for one leg snarled in the sheet. Cripes, he felt like he'd fallen into spinifex grass and been dragged for miles. Had he said light touch? He'd been trampled by cattle with kinder feet.

But the cruel and the sweet together was what had made it addictive. The way her eyes had softened when she nursed him at her breast. Or the couple of times she'd curled up next to him, laying her head on his shoulder. Though the extra weight had added to the strain on the joint, the way she'd wrenched his arms up so high and held them there, wrapped around the top railing of the headboard. He remembered once—and only once—she'd offered to loosen the bonds. As he'd stared into her eyes, his throat had thickened, saying the incredible words which made no sense.

"No, love. If it gives you pleasure . . . leave me as you wish."

From the flare of desire and what he forced himself to acknowledge as possession in her eyes, it had been the right answer. The stroke of her hands had alternated between playful wisps along his flesh and sudden pains as she'd drag her nails through the welts she'd reopen, making him jump. On other expanses of skin, she'd simply traced circles on him, spoken in quiet tones, murmuring noises like he might use to soothe stock animals.

He could see all those marks now, cuts, welts and bruises. Feel the ache of pulled muscles. However, where he'd expected to see a bloody, sweaty shambles of bedclothes, he found he was on clean linens. The places where she'd broken skin had been dressed with a mint-smelling salve that cooled his flesh and the inside of his nostrils as he inhaled it, easing him somehow. Then his gaze found the pitcher of water beside the bed.

By the time he slowed down, he'd drunk more than half. He, a swagman who knew the value of water, who would never think of guzzling it like he was bellied up to a bar in Perth. There was also a covered plate, heaped with a feast of cold lamb and roo meat, plus a hunk of bread wrapped in a separate cloth. He wolfed it all down, sitting there naked like some kind of famished animal, which he guessed he was.

Despite the hard use of his body, he had to acknowledge that inside was a different matter. His spirit felt almost . . . easy. Knots hardened by the salt water of unshed emotion were now loosened a bit, letting him breathe. He normally felt a bit easier for having lain with a woman, despite the painful yearning aftermath, but this was a grade or two above that. Bless the fine-arsed darling. The blood-sucking fiend.

He winced over the smile. She'd bitten his mouth as well as his tongue, left cuts on both. Though he knew she was gone, he still looked for evidence of her in the room, other than the things she'd left for his care. Then he noticed that underneath the plate he'd pulled from the side table over to his lap was a folded square of paper.

She didn't know everything, that one. He might have missed it if he hadn't felt a need to eat in the bed, lie back against the pillow to steady himself as he put meat and water in his gullet. Then again, he expected she'd treated other blokes to this, so maybe she did know what she was about. It made him frown, though getting jealous over it made no sense. He'd been her dinner, and she'd been kind enough to show him a roaring time in payment. He thought about the paid women he'd hard-used and ruefully acknowledged the scales of justice had a way of righting things.

Christ, how civilized did that sound, when there'd been nothing civilized about this at all? He focused on the note.

I can use a station manager. If you're interested, I'll be at Thieves' Station.

The paper had a rough sketch of the location, though of course he knew of it. If Elle had known Lady D's destination, that also explained her attitude toward the strangers. The place didn't have the best reputation, though Dev had never been in the vicinity to find out if the rumors about it were true, or bush lore to scare and entertain the kiddies.

Danny had signed the note with a press of her lips he was fairly certain were inked with his blood, a sharp smear suggesting the hint of a tooth. Beneath, she'd written, *If not, no worries. It was aces, bushman.*

Simple, like a mate might write it. Nothing to hold him or make him feel any guilt. Fair dinkum she was. But strewth, the room felt empty without her. She'd beaten bloody hell out of him, nearly killed him with sex and pain, administered in ways he hadn't dreamed were possible, and he was missing her. What a bloody twisted bugger he was. *It was aces.* In a pig's arse. That didn't capture the half of it.

He always felt this way at first, he reminded himself. A sheila always came with a cost, bringing a mob of memories of another woman's scent, her skin. Her laughter. But there was a particular bleakness, an extra weight, because bloody oath, it was *her*, Lady Daniela, he missed this time.

He hoped Tina couldn't see him now. They'd been two groping kids when they married. Had learned the way of it all together, not afraid or ashamed to try anything, all innocent to it. While she wasn't a wowser by any means, she'd been a good girl.

'Course, he wasn't worth a zack to her anymore, so it didn't matter. Squeezing his eyes shut, trying to dispel the lingering memory of blue eyes that seemed to understand so much, he threw off the sheet with a curse and forced his body to do what it had always done. Survive, and keep moving until the devil caught up with him, or he turned and cornered the bastard himself.

It was time to pack up and return to the bush. While he didn't doubt Danny's offer was genuine, he couldn't afford her. He might survive the kind of job he'd performed for her these past . . . Christ, how long had he been in this room? But when she was done with him, he wouldn't care for that cast-off feeling one bit. Or hanging about to see the next hapless but also lucky bastard she took beneath her. Best to leave things as they were.

He began the painstaking process of making his arse move, along with a few other loudly protesting parts. He expected he now had a far better understanding of the Yank term "rode hard and put away wet."

4

"WELL, you look about as I expected," Elle said, sliding him a beer when he put his pack down next to the bar. Though she'd been closing down for the night, about to cut the lights, she'd been merciful enough to give him the parting drink, though he expected part of it was curiosity. Her shrewd eyes covered the open throat of his shirt, where the scars from the lady's nails were as prominent as a tiger's.

"Leave it, Elle," he said shortly. "Joe get back last night?"

"Night before last." At his startled look, she cocked a brow. "You've been under quite a while. Your lady friend left at sundown."

Dev covered his surprise by picking up the beer, taking another deep swallow. Christ, he couldn't seem to get enough fluid. Guess that was what happened when you let a sheila drain your cock *and* your blood. "You don't seem sorry for her to go, though she dropped more than a few quid."

"We get by without their type."

"World takes all kinds of people."

"She ain't people," Elle said sharply. "She's part of the Thieves' Station mob, as you should know if you did anything other than . . ." She bit that off, though it visibly cost her. Since she was old enough to be his mum, Dev knew the usual topics a respectable woman avoided discussing with a man weren't going to be off-limits to Elle for long. "And trouble's already following her," she added. "Best all around that she left."

"What do you mean?" Dev made a careful shift against the bar to avoid contact with the sore spot high on his thigh. The place she'd bitten him that last time. He recalled the unusual tingle of feeling that came with it.

"Kim over at Carson's Creek Hotel, hundred miles from here, radioed for a bloke who was interested in what route your lady friend might have taken. Seemed anxious to catch up to her. Lucky her driver asked me about the roads, so I had an idea of what to tell him."

Dev put down the bottle. "Why do you think that means trouble is following her?"

Elle shrugged. "'Cause Kim called back an hour later, asking me what it was about. He said that bloke and his mob had just left his place, looking like a hunting party. I told him it involved Thieves' Station, so it wasn't our worry."

As he stared at her, Elle gave him an irritable look. "Nothing good comes out of Thieves' Station, Dev. You've heard the blacks mutter about it. Go walkabout out there and you're never seen again. The men who work at Thieves' keep to themselves, don't say nothing to no one when they come through. Don't even use outside help at shearing time, none that comes from around here, at least."

"Last I heard, they raise merinos. Smaller flock. The rest are stories to scare the little ones, Elle. Bull dust." Rising, he laid down his money for the beer.

"You going to say that after what you rooted with last night?" Her gaze scorched him, though a flush stained her cheeks at her own crudity. "Thought you'd be wrung out enough now you'd be thinking with something above your belt, but sounds like the kangaroos are still loose in your top paddock."

"I know what she is," he said evenly. "It doesn't mean there's a bloody haunted station out there."

Elle's arm shot out to snag his collar, startling him as she yanked the fabric aside to reveal the puncture wound at his throat, the long rivulets down his chest.

"You aren't an idiot, Dev, even when you act like one. I know you're a grown man, and you see to yourself your own way. But you listen to me now. Something like her will take everything you have. And you don't have much left to you. That's just the truth of it."

As he held her gaze, Dev forced himself to look past the flash of his own anger to see the concern there, the care. Because of that, he kept his voice steady when he said, "Let go of my shirt, Elle. If you know her route, see if you can raise the places with radios along the way, verify if she's been by or leave a warning for her. She dealt fair with you. She deserves a fair go at this. If you refuse," he added, "I'll hop over there and do it myself."

Muttering, she released him and went to the radio behind the bar. As Dev listened to her rattle off the call signs, making contact with the small handful of stations and hotels like hers along the three possible routes, he marked them in his mind. Two verified that they'd seen the Rovers come through at different times through the early part of the night, but up between the Wattle Grove and Smith Town hotels she'd apparently gone off road, which was about right for where her station was located on the rough map she'd left him. She must have a damn good guide, or a damn fool one, traveling off road in the dead of night, though at least there was a bright moon. Of course, he knew that area pretty well himself.

She could make it to Thieves' in one night from here, unless she ran into trouble. Since trouble was something experienced bush travelers always counted on, he assumed those special tinted windows had been in case they had to travel during daylight hours. Though from her aversion to being anywhere near those patches of late-afternoon sunlight, he couldn't imagine it would be comfortable for her.

But that wasn't what was making him uneasy. His gut and the hair on the back of his neck told him that something was off. Draining his final beer, he shouldered his swag as Elle turned to him. "I'm borrowing one of your motorbikes and taking a couple spare tires and some petrol. I'll bring it back on my next go round, but I'm going to catch up to her."

"What if I lift this shotgun, and call Joe to hog-tie you?"

He gave her a wry look. "Every man makes his own fate, Elle.

Here." He produced a gold nugget he'd found from some idle fossicking, pushed it across the bar to her. "That should cover the bike, if you never hear from either of us again."

"Oh, rack off with you, then." Her earbashing didn't cover her worry, so he leaned over, kissed her cheek, though she scowled at him.

"You're a love, Elle. She'll be apples, you'll see."

"She's back of Bourke by now. You'll never catch her."

As he looked toward the window, the truth of her statement goaded the uneasy feeling he had. At sunrise, the fierceness of the day would bake a lizard. To the fair skin of a blond vampire with an aversion to daylight, it would be lethal.

Danny might have been able to allay some of Dev's concerns. Knowing the hazards of traveling the bush at any time of day, she'd hired two of the reputed best guides for traveling off road, warning them ahead of time she'd be traveling at night. She'd also included her specially coated canvas coverings, which could be draped and pinned over the Rovers like a wide tent, in case they ran into trouble and had to camp out during daylight. Of course, she hoped for a smooth passage, for even under those coverings and behind tinted windows, sun glaring off the desert sand and temperatures capable of rising well over a hundred would make her feel as if she were cooking. No, it wouldn't be a pleasant day. She'd handle it if she had to, though.

The guides, Mal and Pete, didn't know her kind, but Harry, Roy and John, her personal security detail from Brisbane, were all long-term employees. While she typically would use her night vision to warn them of trouble spots, she found the guides were anticipating well, and after a time she relaxed. She really didn't want to pass the time conversing with the two in the front seat as she might have done. Much of the trip she'd remained aloof, studying the passing terrain.

Being able to see in pitch darkness had its advantages. She could make out the groupings of gums and wattle. Low patches of mulga bushes, the various grasses. Occasional movement from groups of kangaroos or emus. Some rabbits and dingoes came close to their track, foraging in the cooler night air, but the guides could see them only if they passed ahead, where the headlights caught the brief shine of their eyes. There'd been some rain recently, so she knew there might still be some newer green leaves on the shrubs or patches of wildflowers that sprang up quickly after the blessing of water.

No more than a couple centuries ago, a handful of outcast Europeans had been forced to put down roots here. But a small group of those had seen something different when they looked at this country. Wide, open spaces. Freedom of determination. No bloody Poms telling you what to do. There was something old, wild and primitive in Australia, like a goddess of an ancient religion, amused and yet indifferent to the antics of the younger continents. A goddess who embraced those few who understood Her independence, Her dark and light spaces, Her harsh and unforgiving wisdom.

Ironically, that special group of white settlers who'd bonded with this land, the Outback in particular, had that in common with the even smaller smattering of vampires out here. While more dangerous conditions for vampires couldn't be devised, even by dedicated vampire hunters, there were at least fifty in the Northern Territory and Western Australia. The only vampire she knew that lived in harsher sunlit conditions was one in the Sahara, and Lord Mason had reputedly lived there for centuries.

Of course, that was where the connection between the humans and vampires here ended. While Danny had no tolerance for the woman's insolence, she couldn't dispute Elle's reaction. Thieves' Station had been no friend to its neighbors, white, black or vampire. She hoped to change that.

Unfortunately, she was on her own for that. As she'd learned only too well on her recent trip to Berlin, the Vampire Council had as little concern for what happened here as the rest of the world. Out of sight, out of mind. Why care what atrocities the Northwest Region Master, Lord Charles Ruskin, was committing with humans, as well as with his own kind?

She'd deal with it. But first she had to deal with Ian. Damn it, she wished she'd brought the intriguing swagman with her. Her mind drifted back to the pleasant, feral memories of the past day. God, he'd been unexpected. She hadn't had one so tempting in more than a century. That hard body, firm, clever lips and magnificent cock were certainly memorable all on their own. But she kept coming back to the sea green eyes, so sad and fierce at once. A lost warrior. One who'd failed to protect his family, and so had sentenced himself to solitude.

All those unresolved emotions had become luscious, dark needs, which betrayed him through his body's cravings. The resilience of the human animal. The primal beast never stopped wanting to live, even when its intellect tried to convince it life wasn't worth living.

But she wasn't alone, she reminded herself. Those three men, her employees, each carried two of her marks. The first mark was a simple geographic locater. The second allowed her to be in their heads, speak to them or see their thoughts, though they, of course, did not have reciprocal access to her mind. While to humans who served a vampire it might seem an intimate bonding, for a vampire, it was merely typical and a wise security measure to have second-marked household staff. It wasn't the same level as the intimacy of shared emotions, passion—things she supposed a vampire *could* share, *if* she chose to do so—with a third-marked, full servant.

The thought made her shift in her seat. She'd shared such intimacy with Dev, without any marks at all. Not all of it had been voluntary. A wicked smile touched her lips, but with it she felt a twinge of something else. She missed him. *Strange.*

Most vampires took their first fully marked servant by the time they reached a hundred. She was nearing her second century and had never taken one at all. During the period when convicts were still being brought to Australia, her mother had acquired some for labor, like a lot of landowners, and Danny had made use of dependable ones in her youth for second-mark purposes. That had always seemed sufficient to her, even as she matured.

Perhaps she'd take one eventually, but for now, such long-term commitments didn't suit her. They brought irritation. Tedium. It wasn't worth the bother. But she hadn't been able to resist marking Dev once, so she could reach out and find him if she chose. Make sure he still shared the world with her and hadn't succumbed to the discouraging fragility of human mortality.

She bit back a sigh. She'd done the right thing, leaving the choice up to him, even though she'd been tempted to roll him up in his swag while he was unconscious and bring him along. They'd made less progress than she'd hoped. Traveling off-road in the Outback took time, even in broad daylight. One had to maneuver among the wiry and twisted tall eucalyptus, saltbushes and grasses like spinifex that could foul the grille, and watch for ruts and deep gullies. Mind the bands of sheep and cattle. Desolate open spaces could hold peril. The stability of creek beds had to be established before crossing, determine if it was possible to work from boulder to boulder on the few that still held water. So far they'd done a bang-up job. Her two guides' blood was worth bottling. An Oz colloquialism about courage she found quite amusing, all in all.

Dev likely knew the dangers of this type of route quite well, including how to handle them. *Ah, hell, Danny. Stop it.* He was a human. A meal. But there was no reason she couldn't divert her mind from a simmering anxiety about the approaching dawn by thinking about every inch of his pure male body in slow, lingering detail. The sculpted muscles and rugged hands, the sun-browned flesh that gave his face such appealing lines. He'd had strands of copper in his unruly red mane. The red suggested an Irish or Scot in his background, but his accent was pure Oz, that brusque Cockney mixed with the laughter of the Irish. The tragic warrior bard, traveling alone, mourning his love. She saw her fingers, passing through the russet strands of his hair, and she curled them on her knee as she remembered. The way he'd gone so still, watching her, his body restrained, but quivering with a power great enough to snap a man's neck, she was sure.

She hadn't needed to ask what had become of those men who'd taken his family from him. She'd been around long enough to know the haunted look of a good man who'd stained his soul with murder. It gave him a dangerous edge, because the man who'd done murder once would always be more capable of doing it the second time. And he'd already done it more than once.

"Lady D?" Harry, one of her men, leaned in to her window. They'd stopped to investigate a fallen gum during her musings, and she'd been only absently following their progress. "Getting close to dawn. It's going to take us a bit to move that tree off the road. Sand's too deep to go around it. You want us to rig that canvas over your Rover until we get moving again?"

"That'll work fine." She nodded. "You boys holding up well? Do you need to have tea?"

He flashed a grin at her. "No worries. We'll hold. We're taking shifts on the driving, and we'll all rest better when we have you safely at home."

Home. She hadn't thought of Thieves' Station that way for a long time, but she guessed that was what it was going to be now.

"All right. Go ahead and—"

The only warning was an odd whistling, the way the wind sounded when it was being cut by a projectile moving fast enough to slice it. Harry pitched forward. His arms, which had been dangling with casual ease on the sill of her window a moment before, now dropped limply into it with the rest of his upper body, showing the hilt of the knife lodged in his back, severing the spinal cord.

Lunging over him, Danny yanked the blade free and shoved out the opposite door, hitting the ground and rolling beneath the vehicle as a man shouted. The Land Rover up ahead exploded. With her vision, she had the horrifying ability to see the projectile hit the side, a canister that punched into the engine compartment a blink before it detonated the excess petrol. Mal and Pete disappeared in the flame that shot through the interior. The impact lifted the Rover into the air, tossed it up and over, against the troublesome gum tree, breaking it in the middle and catching it on fire as well. Fortunately the Rover had been parked far enough ahead to avoid igniting her cover.

It wasn't much comfort. Three men, taken out in the first strike. She should have been more vigilant, watching for more than ruts in the road. It had been a niggling worry in the back of her mind since she'd received the letter from the solicitor. But that nagging feeling hadn't been worth a zack, since she obviously hadn't anticipated Ian trying something like this. She was a fool.

She cried out despite herself as her remaining two men, John and Roy, went down under a peppering of gunfire, this time coming from the driver's side. They collapsed some ten feet away from her, Roy's eyes full of an apology she didn't deserve as the life died out of them. His rifle had fallen close to his nerveless fingers.

The fire swept down a eucalyptus, fueled by the flammable oil, and had already hopped over to another cluster of bushes. Bloody hell. She pushed away the pain, let fury take her. Fighting the automatic panic caused by so much fire closing in around her, she marshaled her thoughts. Gunfire from the driver's side. The canister shot immolating the Rover had come from the passenger side. As she quickly shifted around to the rear of her vehicle, an Essex pulled up behind, skidding to a halt.

Her fingers clutched the knife. Hand-to-hand guerrilla tactics were not her best skill, but she was far stronger and faster than a human and so far she'd sensed no vampire presence. *Letting your minions do your dirty work, Ian? You bloody bastard.*

God, why had she come out here? The first frisson of fear, that sense of being a doomed, trapped animal, gripped her, and she pushed it away again, more viciously. *Think.* Did they know she was under here?

"Here, kitty, kitty . . ." Two sets of feet stopped on the left side, another on the right. "Why don't you come out from under there, and we'll make sure you don't get a bad sunburn? Only a few minutes to sunrise, you know. Somebody wants to see you."

With a snarl, she dropped the knife, rolled, caught both ankles of that one set of boots and yanked. It knocked the man off his feet, and she hauled him beneath, hand over hand, jeans to belt to shirt front, and had his throat beneath her palm before his scream of terror could split the air. She tore out his larynx and shoved, sending him twisting and spinning out the other side, ramming the legs of the man there, sending him stumbling back with a surprised oath. Seizing the knife again, she began to scramble forth and screamed as a flood of flame met her. She rolled back up toward the front wheels, knowing it was futile. *Christ, not burning.*

"Bloody hell, Rogers! You want to blow it up with us standing right here? Shoot the bitch. It won't kill her, but—"

"Cripes, look at Tim. I'll show her." A succession of gunfire. *Thunk, thunk.* Though she flinched, anticipating the engine block igniting, she realized quickly they weren't shooting for her. Air whistled out of the tires. The vessel lurched, the punctured tires rapidly deflating. Gasping, she shoved against the undercarriage as it pressed toward the earth, sinking lower into the sand. Jesus, this was heavy. She hated the feeling of being closed in. Could she toss it toward one of them, use the distraction?

The sunrise was coming. She could feel it, the heat rising in her skin. If she rolled the vehicle and fire destroyed it, she had no cover, no protection from the sun's rays, because the coated canvases had been in the other vehicle. Another stupid decision. She'd been in the city too long.

"He wanted her alive."

"He said if we couldn't make her come, to kill her. You hear that, love? You've left us no choice, unless you're willing to let us stick this tranquilizer into your bum."

"Try it," she hissed, baring her fangs. "You'll look like your mate."

"Have it your way, then," he responded shortly, but she had the brief satisfaction of hearing a faint quaver in the unnamed man's voice. "Step back and juice up the flamethrower, Rogers. Reconsider, darling. We've got a nice canvas in the ute, so the sun doesn't fry you like an egg. Otherwise, we fry you here."

"Go to hell."

As her arm muscles strained, she realized her quick plan wouldn't work. She'd never actually lifted anything this heavy, and while she could hold it off her for a while, tossing it like a soccer ball was out of the question. She heard the roar of the flamethrower, saw the flash of light as it was triggered. The men had split, one to each side, backpedaling, apparently prepared to detonate the vehicle with the combination of flamethrower and gunfire. While she didn't need to breathe, she was gasping, and she recognized it as fear catching up with her racing mind. Her skin was already crawling, anticipating the suffocating inescapable burn of the fire or the sun, the predawn light starting to show in the scrap of sky she could see.

No. She wouldn't die this way. She wouldn't surrender, but they sure as hell wouldn't outlive her. Twisting her body, she shot out from beneath the Land Rover, darting under the spout of fire. Ignoring the crackle of flames that could easily spark in her hair, she channeled her terror into a predator's rage. She swerved, leaped behind Rogers. His neck cracked beneath her hands, but then, with a deafening roar, she was tossed as the vehicle exploded. Twenty feet she sailed, thudding down in a patch of sharp barbed grass that stabbed through her clothes. Bloody perfect. At least it served as somewhat of a buffer to the fall, though her bones did not easily break.

Scrambling, she turned and saw the other man thought too damn fast on his feet. He'd seized up the abandoned flamethrower and now redirected it toward her, a wild arc that caught the brush as she dropped to the ground beneath the wave of it. It surrounded her, licking greedily toward her legs as the man advanced, yelling.

He'd panicked, though. Misdirection of his weapon and the flame of the second Rover had caught the tires of his vehicle. It would be going up in a matter of minutes. As she crouched, she had the satisfaction of seeing the fear as he met her gaze. *Yeah, you worthless bastard. You're dead, no matter what happens. This far out, no supplies, on foot, you'll cook as good as me. You'd beg me to kill you.*

Then he stopped, the flamethrower stuttering to a halt, dropping out of limp fingers. Fear became confusion and then vacancy as he fell to his knees, a knife protruding between his shoulder blades, the same fate as Harry. Dev charged around the petrol bonfire that was her remaining Land Rover, snatched his blade out of the man's back and came toward her. Danny didn't give herself time to think, just focused on a clear spot and leaped out of the flame. Fire grabbed at her calves, licking up toward her hips. As she landed, she stumbled, her usual vampire balance abandoning her such that she almost dove into the flames of the Rover.

Dev caught her, rolling her to the ground to douse the small licks of flame before he hauled them both outside the range of the rapidly spreading fire. Her startled cry was muffled when he twisted her beneath him, sheltering her with his back as her attacker's vehicle went up in another wave of blasting heat and noise.

"Christ, just what we need." He was up and pulling her forward again, even as he swore and muttered. "Come on, I have a bike over here."

"Dev, sunrise. Everything to protect me—"

"Is gone. I know. Come on." He got her to the motorbike, about a hundred yards away. Yanking his swag out, he removed the pack of belongings it held and then tossed the swag across the ground, unrolling it in a deft, practiced move. "Lie down on this."

"It won't be enough—"

"It's what we have. It's thick. Come on," he snapped.

Behind him there was a dramatic backdrop of flames. Men's bodies littered the ground. Not only the bastards who'd attacked her, but two innocent guides and three men she'd known for several years. Men who'd let her into their minds, who'd protected her when her strengths could not. Who'd tried to do that, even to this end. And now here was another man, risking himself for her. Pressing her lips together, knowing now was not the time for regrets, she lay down.

Without another word, Dev rolled her in the swag, tucking the ends around her, working the ties with fast fingers, handling her as impersonally as a bundle of stones. The heat of the flames was being encompassed by the building light in the sky, which she could feel to the marrow of her bones. The sun was about to crest, turn the world around her into a hell on earth.

"You don't need to breathe, right?" She nodded, a quick jerk. Before he brought down the full hood he'd fashioned, he nodded toward a cluster of rock formations in the distance, a series of pillars and hillocks. "It's going to take me about an hour to get us there, long as we don't have any problems. If we're lucky, we'll find a cave or at least an overhang with a shadow. I assume that would get you through until night."

She didn't have to agree or disagree. There weren't any other options. Still, at his light shake, she managed another nod. "And this cloth? Will it protect you enough to get you there?"

It was all they had. He didn't have to say that, either. "I'll be a bit uncomfortable, but I'll manage."

Perhaps it was because they both knew the Aussie gift for understatement, or maybe there was a shameful quaver in her voice. Regardless, Dev studied her with serious green eyes, a momentary assessment, and she saw the man whose bush craft was the only thing between her and a very painful death. "All right, then. You hang in there, you hear me? I didn't drive my arse off through the night and miss out on a piece of Joe's birthday cake so you can die on me." Then he cinched down the hood, shutting out light, most of the air and any sense of direction. She was giving herself completely into his hands.

He lifted and set her on the bike sidesaddle. Another precious few moments passed as he used some type of cords to secure her to both him and the bike. Finally, as he kicked the bike back to life, his hand squeezed her leg. "She'll be right, love. I'll take care of you, I promise."

She couldn't hold on to him, clutch at another living thing, her arms pressed against her body as if she were in a coffin. But she was tied to him so that her body leaned into his. She held on to that, the sense of his heartbeat through his back, against her shoulder, her hip pressed against his buttock.

She should have told him to stake her. That was far preferable to being slowly burned alive.

$\sim$

He didn't want to think about it, but it kept intruding. The wet blood on his knife. Explosions. Leaving fire and mayhem at his back. He'd been there before, reveled in it like a savage, even as he'd been tempted countless times to let the flames consume him.

After Tina and Rob, he'd taken himself off to war, finding a place for the rage he told himself God would overlook. There was plenty of death to go around on the Kokoda Track, as he and his mates did their best to keep the Nips from making Australia part of the bloody Japanese empire.

Then, after the war, back to the Outback. There were no accusations here. Just emptiness, blessed silence. Well, with some exceptions, like the past few minutes.

He didn't have time for ruddy flashbacks. Her life depended on him. He pushed the bike, but he couldn't go too fast. There were too many things out here that could pop a tire, flip them. The light was rising, which improved visibility, but when the first red and gold ray of the sun painted the horizon, he heard her breath draw in as if it were a needle that pierced the canvas of his swag. He had to shut it out. He had to get them there safely, and if he rushed it, wrecked them, she was as good as dead.

God, it'd been a sight, though. The two explosions had sent percussions through the air he'd felt a mile away. He'd arrived in time to see her fly out from beneath the Rover before it exploded. She'd caught that one bastard up and broken him like a rotted branch. When she'd spun, that golden-blond hair glittering in the fire, her fangs bared, she was vicious, magnificent, deadly. And frightened, which made her all the more lethal.

He knew what Elle would say. But he couldn't turn his back on Danny. She hadn't spared him during their remarkable time together, had used him hard, just as she'd said she would. He'd craved every minute of it. He'd also heard the catch of her breath in her throat, seen the softening of her gaze when she touched his face with light fingers, passed them over his lips. Once she'd smiled, a tender girl's smile, when he'd kissed her mouth unprompted. He remembered the arching of her body, offering herself to him as pleasure swept over them both.

Hell, he didn't know anything about vampires. But life was apparently precious to vampire and man alike, and that said, there were things they both needed, wanted. Feared. Quite simply, he couldn't bear for her to be afraid.

Whether vampires needed to breathe or not, he heard her breathing now. She was rasping. He felt the convulsive kneading of her hands against herself, a vibration of her body. Heard quiet noises of distress. Worse, he smelled that acrid, charcoal smell that he knew all too well was burning flesh.

It was good that she was tied to him, because he opened it up then. Taking hillocks in leaps and rough, jolting bounces, putting his booted foot down to steady them when the wheel scalloped in the thicker sand, vegetation ripping at his trousers. The hard landings wrenched pitiful choked cries from her he could tell she was trying to bite back. He thought of her blond hair spread over his skin as she suckled and nipped her way down his body, the tickle of it along his abdomen, his arms. Once, when she'd leaned over him, a handful of silken strands had fallen into his palm like a gift. He'd curled his fingers into it, holding her until she tilted her head, gave him a considering look, waiting him out until he released her. He'd liked that look, which seemed to collect heartbeats between them, hold them in the intent moment, an unexpected, quiet intimacy.

"Getting closer," he muttered. If only he'd heaved his sorry arse out of bed sooner, moved faster. Ah, hell, that kind of thinking didn't do any good. The bike stuttered, and his heart stuttered with it. *No. Don't you do it. We only have a couple miles to go.*

But it had done its best, and he'd pushed too hard. He was damn lucky the tires were still inflated. It ground to a halt, the rattle telling him he'd likely jarred some important part loose, or the age and condition of the bike had made it a lost cause to begin with. Another time he could have stopped, tinkered with it, figured out the problem and likely had it running again. He'd have to come back for that.

Jerking the ties loose from himself, he slid off the bike, steadying her.

"Wha—what is it?"

Her muffled voice was thin, tight. In terrible pain.

"Bike's bung. Going to have to hike it. It's only a couple miles. Fireman's carry, love. Hang on there."

"No." She batted at the canvas, but a child playing inside a thin parachute would have demonstrated more strength. "Sharpen a branch and take me out now. Better than burning. I can't . . . Dev, it hurts too much. I can't do any more."

"Too ruddy bad. Stop your whinging." He made himself say the cruel words, saw her stiffen briefly. *Yeah, she had pride.* It helped. "You can, because I say you can. It's just pain, love. You can make it through pain. Pain goes away. Death doesn't."

There was a choking sound, a strange, alarming gurgling, but he thought she might have cursed him. When he hauled her onto his shoulder, she cried out, an involuntary sound of anguish. In this position, the charcoal burning stink was worse. Strewth, he wondered if vampires could pass out from too much pain. So far, it didn't seem so. He'd have to come back for the swag contents. Speed was the most important thing. He set out at a jog, fast as he could pace himself toward the shelter of those distant rocks.

Please God, let there be a cave. Or at the very least, an alcove formed by centuries of runoff. Anything that would do a better job than the too-thin fabric of his swag.

5

B<small>Y</small> the time he made it to the first pillar his legs were trembling and his shoulder muscles had passed from excruciating to aching numbness. When he made it around the base so the twenty-foot-high rock swallowed the morning sun behind him, he could have sighed in relief, if only he knew the condition of the woman he was carrying. At one point, every pounding stride had brought a whimper from her, a wounded animal unable to bite down on its pain anymore. But he'd experienced second- and even third-degree burns before, so how she wasn't screaming, he didn't know. Until he shifted her at one point and saw blood staining the canvas where he guessed her mouth might be. She'd likely pierced her own tongue with her fangs. God, she was a dinkum thing. Tough as they came. Other places in the fabric were damp, where viscous fluid had soaked through.

As much for the hope of his own comfort as hers, he murmured, "We're out of the sun, love. I'll find you that shelter. Hang in there a bit longer."

The response was inarticulate, but it was there. He left it at that and made his way along to the next hillock. Next to the pillar of rock, the two had looked like the engine of a train. While he'd targeted this section because it appeared the one most likely to have a cave or fissure, Rob had liked trains. As he studied the rock face, he found what he sought and blessed that brave young spirit for guiding him. Easing her onto a flat ledge, he scrambled up fifteen feet to explore the cave opening. No current animal inhabitants, and he saw evidence from drawings on the walls that it had been used as an aborigine camp. Which suggested there was water somewhere not too far. Best of all, the cave was deep enough that when the sun crested and came down on the other side of the rock this afternoon, the occupant could stay out of its direct light.

According to the aboriginal Dreamtime beliefs, the land had been created for them by ancestral heroes and heroines. When those creators disappeared, they believed they weren't gone, but had remained in secret places in the natural features in the land. He tended to have an easier time with the idea of those types of guides than an omnipotent God who was supposed to prevent bad things from happening, so he didn't have a problem offering quiet thanks for the shelter as he returned to retrieve Danny. He might have his grudges, but the clan had taught him well enough not to piss off the ancient spirits of the land needlessly.

Brute strength more than finesse got her hauled up the steep cuts he used as steps in the rock. Which would teach him a lesson. Having wild sex with a paranormal creature for hours left a bloke poorly set up to race across a couple hundred miles of terrain to rescue her.

When he entered the cave mouth, he carried her to the back. The temperature drop was considerable, a blessing. It registered in the tense torso draped on his shoulder as a sick spasm of relief.

"Okay, here we are, love." He put her where it looked like the rock was flat and smooth. Of course, once he unwrapped her, he could make a more comfortable bedroll out of the swag, even though he remembered that even the touch of air hurt burned skin. How could he bring relief to a badly burned vampire? He could retrieve his pack, find her some water. That might help, but it was precious little.

As the thoughts chased one another through his mind, he forced himself to go slow, be patient when he released the cords and pulled back the flap of the hood he'd made for her face.

She had bitten through her tongue and her bottom lip to keep from screaming, as he expected. Both were swollen, explaining why her responses had been so garbled, beyond the muffling effect of the covering. At first, he felt a sweep of relief, for while her face and throat were lobster red, it was no worse than a very bad sunburn. Then he remembered she'd turned her face into his back, holding it there most of the time. The viscous spots were on her back and side, the parts of her she couldn't press against him. Though she said nothing, her eyes were open, finding him. Tears had marked her face, apparently until she ran out of fluid to give to them. Her breathing still sounded labored, indicating pain, as well as the obstruction of her swollen tongue and lips.

Swallowing, he ran his knuckles alongside her face. "I'm sorry I didn't get here sooner," he said. "This is going to hurt."

"Just do it," she said in her thickened speech.

The best thing for the spots that had adhered to her skin was to pull the clothes off without hesitation, he knew. But he prepared as much as he could, unbuttoning her shirt, opening her trousers and removing her boots, which fortunately had protected her feet better than the clothes and his swag had been able to do. He turned her onto her stomach as tenderly as he could, then steeled himself.

Regardless, when the first hoarse scream tore from her throat, it almost ripped his heart out. Forcing himself to keep his movements smooth, swift but unhurried, he manipulated her body as needed, removing all her clothes except her knickers.

Holy Christ. He was glad she couldn't see his face when he first viewed the charred expanse from the tender nape, down the slope of the lower back, to the beautiful arse and long legs. It was like looking at overcooked barbecue, an analogy he dearly wished hadn't occurred to him, for he doubted he'd ever enjoy a good barbecue again.

"Bad?" she croaked. Her head was tilted away from him, as if she was staring at those red and white clay paintings on the cave wall.

"Yeah, love. Tell me what I need to do."

With the side of her face pressed to the stone, she placed a trembling hand on the hard surface as well. "Take the rest off, so it's done."

Unfastening the bra, he slid it off her arms, left the cups cradling her breasts and worked her knickers off her hips, clenching his jaw against another anguished mewl. Then it was done, and she was naked. She flattened herself against the rock like a lizard. "Cool . . ." she mumbled. "Just . . . leave me be. Need the cool. Rest." At first he thought she was talking about herself, but then her eyes opened, the blue focused on him. "Dev, rest. Now that I'm out of . . . sun. I'll heal. Just . . . need . . . time. You rest. There'll be more . . . later."

She was advising he take a nap while she lay there, one part of her broiled and the other part shivering? There was a gleam on her forehead, like sickly perspiration. Water would help, he knew. Would help them both.

"I'll get us some water first," he said. "I need to go get my pack, but I'll be back soon. I won't be far."

Her head jerked once, acknowledging. Dev folded her clothes, set them to the side, an absurd use of time, but he felt it might help, her seeing that he'd done something so practical and normal, so unpanicked. And truth, it steadied his own nerves. When he left the cave, he jogged out to get his pack, but had to walk back to conserve his energy in the heat. Circling the base of the rock formation where he'd left her, he used his probe to find the soak, a shallow water source in the sand. He filled a medium billy, and then worked his way up the rocks again. She was in the same position. No change in her skin, but she did seem easier, more alert as she looked up at him when he came to her side.

"Can you lift your head for some water?"

She shook her head. "Not yet," she slurred. "Don't touch."

"No. I know it hurts." Sitting down cross-legged by her head with the billy and a mostly clean cloth, he soaked it, then twisted the end into a teat. "This is the way I used to water a dehydrated lamb." He did have to slide a hand under her jaw to guide her face, and though she winced, it seemed bearable to her. Bringing the twisted cloth to her lips, he let some of the water dribble into her mouth, watched her swallow. "Christ, you're a mess, love."

"I'll heal . . . fast. Just . . . little time."

As he dipped the cloth several times, he studied the swelling of her tongue, the punctures. "You could have screamed, you know," he said gruffly. "It was only me and a few birds about. Maybe a dingo or two. None of us would have minded."

Danny's cracked mouth almost moved in a smile. "I'll be . . . fine. Bushman rescued me."

He tightened his jaw. "You think they'll come looking for that lot?"

He watched her consider it. The way thoughts moved behind her eyes told him she hadn't lost her mental acuity, a considerable relief. Her lips moved at last. "Not for a while. He wouldn't waste more men. He'll assume"—she swallowed, forced the words to come out as clearly as she could manage—"successful. Remembers me younger, less sure."

"So you know who sent them."

She nodded, closed her eyes. "Later. More. Rest, Dev. Will need . . . your blood. You need rest." Then her eyes reopened and she gave him a considering look. "If you . . . okay with that?"

"The lady only has to ask," he said at last. He sensed it was significant, her asking him, though he wouldn't have hesitated to give her what she needed, no matter what.

"Good. Lie down. Shut . . . up."

With a forced half smile, he stretched out beside her on the rock, though not before he arranged the swag into more of a mattress, so she'd have something to shift upon if she chose to do so. He noticed then that her hair, which he'd swept off to the side, had trickled back along the slope of the rock to touch her shoulder, making the skin beneath twitch in an irritated way, reminding him of a horse with flies. Turning onto an elbow, he lifted the strands away from her flesh, gently scooping them forward to gather and braid them. Tying it off with a short cord from his pack, he wound it into a knot on the back of her skull, tucking it in. But he stroked his knuckles over it, wishing he could do the same to her temple, soothe her some. The pain was making her tremble, and he couldn't touch or warm her.

But she was here, she was safe. Whatever she needed, he'd figure it out. A more complicated problem was what needed to be done about the dead men lying out around the burned-out Rovers. They were almost on the edge of Thieves' Station property, though still about sixty miles from the actual homestead. The nearest place from here, if he remembered correctly, was about fifty more miles.

Fortunately, the Rovers had detonated in a relatively bare patch, and the wind had been down, so the fire had died out before it could become one of the devastating wildfires that could take out thousands of acres and attract too damn much attention. While the residual smoke might be seen by another station or settlement, her land was one of the rare sections that had a scattering of mountain ranges and rock formations amid the desert sections, so it might not prompt a radio call. However, if a mail plane or the Flying Doctor service passed overhead . . .

Cripes, eight dead men and here he was, trying to think of ways to conceal them. Maybe Elle was right. The kangaroos weren't just loose in his top paddock. They'd soared over the fence and had gone walkabout.

"Danny," he murmured quietly. "About the men."

"Know." Her eyes opened and they stared at each other. "We'll send someone . . . clean up. After we get to station. Don't like to think . . . dingoes. But might be for the best. The heat. No families."

Though she didn't say it, he suspected that was a personnel requirement for her. His gut tightened. "How long do you think it'll be before you're ready to travel, love?"

"Bored with . . . babysitting. Already?"

Despite the words, he didn't see much in her eyes except exhaustion, and that weariness wasn't merely physical. She was fencing with him out of habit, not real spirit. Putting his hand next to hers on the rock, he overlapped her smallest finger with his.

"You're a braw lassie, as my Scots granddad might have said, but I'm not seeing you as the bat-in-a-cave type of vampire."

"No?" She arched a brow, a gesture reassuringly similar to the confidence she'd shown in his arms at the pub.

"Nope. You're more the lady-of-the-manor type, ready to spear the help with your fangs over a chipped china dish."

Her eyes closed, her tongue coming out to lick her lips, which seemed to help with their movement. "Shows what you know. I'm . . .

pleasant boss . . . compared to other . . . vampires." Her mouth thinned. "Except still . . . get killed . . . working for me."

He slid his hand completely over hers this time, though lightly, and her eyes opened again. "I'm sorry."

"Me, too. Good men . . . who deserved better."

He knew when to keep silent and so he did, watching her as she appeared to drift off into a doze, tempered with the occasional jerk or painful shudder. Her lack of concern over authorities finding the bodies struck him as curious. But then, Thieves' Station had been surrounded with dark rumors for some time. It suggested the land-owners had a contingency plan for that—deep pockets or another manner of compelling law enforcement to overlook such things or downplay them, so they were treated as exaggerated local gossip, as he'd implied to Elle.

The current management is strongly opposed to me . . .

All these things should set off alarm bells, and they did. But when had the world—or his life—ever made any bloody sense, after all?

"Giant kangaroo."

He saw her gaze was back on the wall. Twisting, he looked past the Rainbow Serpent done in white and red earth by a more recent aboriginal group, to a much older scratching that had used gold and blue as well. Lord, nothing wrong with her eyes. He had to leave her side to go make it out. It showed a group of stick figure men hunting a kangaroo that towered over them.

"Could be." He ran his fingers over it. "Looks pretty old. They say kangaroos grew past ten feet, thousands of years ago. Wombats were the size of that crispy Rover of yours."

"Don't believe it." She studied the wall, obviously seeking things to distract her from the pain racking through her in short convulsions that had his own skin flinching in sympathy. "Things don't survive . . . thousands years . . . by getting weaker . . . smaller."

"Depends, love." He looked at the wasteland of her body, the beautiful face. Remembered how she'd commanded everyone's attention just by existing, the second she'd stepped into Elle's. "Sometimes seeming like less of a threat is the best survival technique of all. I suspect you were attacked because somebody decided you're far more than a pretty face."

~

"Dev. *Dev.*"

He'd gone to sleep with his rifle and knife close to hand, so he had the latter tight in his grip when he came up out of a murky dream, responding to the urgency in her voice.

"Yeah." He rubbed his eyes, turned to her. During the past six hours, after periodic awakenings where he'd told her stories about the bush and a variety of other nonsense to help her drift back into a doze, the open meat of her back had begun to scar over. But she was still shaking. Putting his hand on her forehead, he found she was burning up, literally so hot he had to remove his hand. "What's happening, love?"

"Sun poisoning . . . the vampire version of it." She closed her eyes, apparently to manage a hard spasm that rocked her against the stone. It passed as if she'd been rolled by a wave and was bracing herself for the next one. "I need a little blood now, for strength to fight it. From your arm. Don't . . . let me take too much."

Her tongue was also healing, for her voice, though low and hoarse, was much clearer, and her lips looked less bee-stung. Nodding, he straightened up and leaned over her, taking his wrist toward her mouth.

"No." She recoiled, her hands curling into claws. "Cut . . . drip it in my mouth. *Don't* let me have your arm."

Frowning, he did as bade, making a shallow cut on his forearm and then positioning it over her mouth. It wasn't as easy as letting her put her lips on him. The blood kept rolling down his elbow, but most dripped onto her tongue or splashed her lips, where she could lick it off.

After she'd had about half a cup, she nodded and turned her face back toward the rock. A couple of last drops hit her cheek, making her flinch. "I don't like you seeing me this way," she said. "My mouth open, like some gaping fish."

He hadn't thought about it that way at all. He was humbled by it, how she turned her face up to him, golden lashes fanning her cheeks as she parted her lips, her delicate tongue twitching, waiting for the sustenance from him.

"Don't be daft, love," he said. Holding pressure on his wound to help it clot, he put his other finger to her cheek, collected the blood on it. Her gaze turned back to him. She might have been about to warn him again, but he put the bloodstained fingers to the corner of her mouth, teased her with it. Watching him in a curiously immobile manner, as if she were trapped in a suit of armor—and perhaps that wasn't inaccurate, hampered as she was by so many healing burns—she parted her lips. He stroked the bottom one, her fang so close it scraped his knuckle, causing a flicker in her eyes.

"This will get bad," she whispered. "Worse before it gets better. You ever treat anyone in a fever delirium, Dev?"

"Once. My boy, Rob, he caught something. Tina and I took care of him. Thought we were going to lose him for a bit there."

"Tina. Your wife?"

He nodded, a short motion, and her expression softened. "A nice name. I bet she was pretty, delicate. But strong of heart. Loved you."

"Better than I deserved," he said gruffly. "Love, don't—"

She shook her head. "'S okay. The fever, it will be like that. But I'm going to be a hell of a lot stronger than your boy. You're going to look like a slab of blood-soaked beef, and I'm going to be a starving shark. You need to leave. Go somewhere else for a while. A half day maybe."

"Ah." When he sat back on his heels in that comfortable manner bushies and blackfellas had, as if they could squat for days, Danny found it unexpectedly calming. "What if I give you some blood, about every hour or so?"

"You'll get weak." She shook her head.

"But you'll heal faster, get you back to yourself."

"You need to go," Danny said stubbornly. Even though an idiotic part of her wanted him to stay. She didn't want to be alone during this.

He studied her. "You're not the best liar, love."

"I don't need to lie. I'm not the noble type, remember?"

"Maybe not entirely. But your chances will be better if you have a blood source."

"You won't leave." She realized it from the set of his jaw.

"No."

Danny bit back a sigh. "If you change your mind, I won't think the worse of you."

"Well, on something like that, it's not your opinion that counts, love."

She didn't need to second-mark him to guess what was going on behind those sea green eyes. She let her own narrow. "You've nothing to prove. I'm not your family. I'm a vampire that took you to my bed. Treated you like my slave."

"And I let you. I wanted you to, Devil help me." He bent down to her, ignoring her hiss of warning, bringing the rich smell of his life and heartbeat close. "Maybe I want you around to do it again."

"Back up," she said unsteadily. "Dev, I mean it."

Her fangs were lengthening, and when his gaze flickered, she knew he'd seen the red tinge coming into her irises. A man who'd obviously confronted predators before, he did a slow and easy rock back onto his heels, nothing quick or startled. God, he could get her worked up even when she was like this. And he shouldn't have been any prize right now.

Crusted with sand and ash, a few scrapes and burns from getting too close to the Rovers, he smelled of smoke and sweat. But she couldn't dispel the effect of his provocative comment, the way he refused to flinch, no matter what danger she threatened. As if it had a rope on it, her mind tugged her gaze to the slope of his fine chest beneath the open neck of the shirt, the muscled line of his arm, the way his forearm rested on his thigh, his hand loosely dangling. And since she'd gone that far, she might as well indulge in an appreciative look at his groin, the curve of testicles and that amazingly large cock, emphasized by the spread of his thighs.

She was in roiling pain, unable to even hold herself up on her trembling arms. But that wouldn't be the case for long. Even now, the stirring in her lower belly was ratcheting up her bloodlust. She shoved it away, while she still had the sanity to do so, and chose anger instead. Because if he was doing what she thought . . .

"I am not going to be your bloody death wish," she snapped. "Do you understand that? I will stake myself first."

Anger flashed in his gaze. "It's not like that."

"Isn't it? Rack off. Now." She firmed her lips. "I don't need you around for this."

A muscle twitched in his jaw. However, instead of saying anything more, he picked up the cloth he'd kept in the billy of water, wrung it out. As he wiped the cool dampness of it across her brow, he spoke low. "You're sweating." Then, even more quietly, "I won't leave you like this, Danny. And you damn well can't make me."

The gentle stroking, at odds with his words, made her eyes close. "Bloody hell, Dev. I want the pleasure of you in my bed again, too. If you let me kill you, that's not going to happen."

"Well, when you put it that way. I'll leave you to care for yourself, then. Even a man with a death wish will live another few hours if he thinks he might have one more naughty out of it."

She smiled, her eyes still closed. "Worthless larrikin. All right, have it your way. Give me a little every hour, about as much as you just did. If I latch on to you at any point, you do whatever you have to do to knock me off you. The butt of your rifle might be best. Shoot me if you have to. It won't kill me."

"I'm not going to hurt you when you're already in pain."

She opened her eyes then, forced herself up onto her elbows, hissed at him when he reached forward to help, arresting the motion. Despite her pain, she made sure the command she injected into her voice was that of the woman who'd bound him to a bed, teased and tormented him for hours, who'd drawn pleasure from goading him to climax with the lash of his own whip. "Dev, there are only three things that can kill a vampire. Prolonged exposure to sunlight, cutting off my head, or a stake directly through the heart, which is much harder to do than most books and films tell it. Everything else will fix itself. In several days, any trace that I've been burned will be completely gone. But when a burn is this bad, there's delirium first.

I'll be mad for blood, little better than a rabid animal. No rope in your pack will hold me." She paused, considering. "Though it would slow me down. Ever done a hog-tie on a person? Wrists to ankles to throat?"

"What?"

She made an impatient gesture. "If I try to get free, I'll choke myself. It can weaken me, make me pass out. Though since I don't need oxygen to live, lack of air won't kill me."

"I'll just bind your wrists," he said uncomfortably.

"Dev." She forced herself to patience, though part of her wanted to scream. Perhaps this was why so many vampires liked having full, third-mark servants. No need to explain everything. Merely open that part of your mind and they'd understand. "The healing will continue, even under the rope. As I said, the question isn't *will* I heal, but how fast. You're right; regular blood throughout will help with that, but if you're determined to stay, then you do it my way, damn it."

Despite the ripple of raw pain that came with it, she turned to her side, staying up on one arm. The braid he'd tucked into a knot had loosened and now fell forward to brush against the curve of one breast, the pink tip of a nipple. As she saw his eyes follow it, she remembered how fascinated he'd been at the boardinghouse, when her hair was loose and reached the cleft of her buttocks. She remembered how his shoulders had tensed, the muscles in his arms rippling against his bonds, conveying his need to touch her. Bloody hell. Just the heady memory, combined with the pain, made her sway. Ignoring her warning once again, the stubborn idiot had his hands on her, steadying her. Saliva gathered in her mouth, wanting to tear into him.

"You're not like any woman I've ever known," he said.

"Of course not. I'm not human." She turned her head to look up into his face. "Don't confuse me with her, Dev. That's not safe for you. Plus, it would make me quite angry."

He held her there, his large hands on her shoulders, feeling every quiver and twitch. He didn't know what a lethal concoction was simmering beneath his touch, her pain and bloodlust, as well as plain physical lust. "Tie me the way I said, Dev," she said shortly. "All right?"

He nodded at last, went to his pack and came back with a coil of rope. As she eased herself back down to her side, she found herself holding her breath, watching him measure it out, the rope sliding between his fingers. The way he studied her body as he did it. When he dropped to one knee by her, she reminded him with a voice now thickened by things other than pain. "Wrists to ankles to throat."

He turned her back onto her stomach, and she laid her cheek down on the rock, a quiver running through her as he guided her hands to the small of her back, making the soft breast flesh and tender nipples rasp against the rock. Steeling herself to that, she folded her arms in a box position. "Wrap them," she said. "From wrists to elbows. It will be stronger that way."

As he did it, she was conscious of his heartbeat, his increased breath and the conflict it likely caused within him. "Don't beat yourself up about it, bushman," she murmured. "It's in you, pleasure from dominance. It's one reason it was such a pleasure to master you. You understand the way of it enough to get aroused on either side of the coin."

"But you're a bleeding mess right now. I feel like a bastard, getting hard . . ."

"I'm wet for you, Dev." His words clogged in his throat, and she would have smiled, if she wasn't in such pain and trying to bite down on any show of it to keep him on track. "Vampires mix sex and pain so regularly, I'd have to be dead to be immune to your arousal. As I said, don't confuse me with a human." Clearing her throat, she felt the prick of her fang. "Now the ankles. Hurry." She was sweating again, a sickly shudder running down through her back. His heartbeat was getting louder, only it was the volume of her senses increasing it, a tempting drumbeat in her ears.

He was efficient and smooth, telling her he hadn't lied about his experience as a stockman. He knew his way about a rope and worked quickly. But still, by the time he adjusted the cord around her throat, she was growling low in her chest, her jaw clenched against need, the sharp stab of lengthened fangs. She'd rebuked him twice for not making it tight enough. When he'd finally obeyed, cinching the line between wrists and ankles, and then taking up the slack between ankles to throat so she was well arched, her breasts rising off the ground, the moan that slipped out was caught between ecstasy and agony.

He straddled her, one knee on one side, his other leg stretched out so her cheek was against his boot, her body under the triangle formed by his as he finished the knot at the base of her skull. His fingers followed the line of the rope directly under her jaw, her chin, caressing her sensitive throat. Then he shifted her to her less burned side on the swag he'd folded to create a bed for her.

There was an attractive flush at the base of his neck, and it seemed he was reluctant to slide his hands off her, one resting on her hip, the curve of her flank. His eyes kept returning to the way the rope collared her neck, the arched display of her body. He was fighting his reaction to her with a delicious guilt that was almost palpable.

But even as he fought with his lust, he apparently noticed other things. Like the way she was sweating. For now he brought the cool cloth back, ran it under her chin, into the pockets of her collarbone, the sternum above the beginning swells of her breasts. The soft friction rippled all the way to the hardened points, making them jut at him in a way that only a dead man could ignore. She wondered if he was thinking of how he'd suckled water off them. She knew she was, and the memory wasn't exactly cooling.

"Touch them," she whispered, though she knew she was being foolish. If the bloodlust grew too strong . . . But she needed him to touch her, now, when she could still hold the reins on herself, though the grip was getting tenuous. "Torture me the way I tortured you."

"It's still torture to me, love," he said, his voice sexy in its rough need. "Because I can't do much about it, no matter how hard I get over it."

"If you were a vampire, you'd take pleasure in my pain, grasp me by the waist, dig your fingers into my burns as you shoved your cock into me."

His gaze flickered up to hers, and the green in his eyes had become brilliant, filled with lust. Lifting the cloth to her face with great deliberation, he wiped it along the line of cheek, her chin and faintly quivering lips. Then he used her own logic on her. "I'm not a vampire. Strewth, you're hotter than fire, but you're pale. You need more blood."

"Wait a little longer," she said. "It hasn't been an hour. Give me too much, and it'll come back up. Makes a mess."

"Right." He pressed his lips together, kept touching her flesh with the cloth. Light, easy, cool, and it was driving her crazy, as if he were deliberately teasing her. Because some touches felt simple, easy. Others exacerbated the burns because even the gentlest of contact hurt.

"Vampires like restraining their servants," she said, her gaze clinging to his sensual lips, remembering them on her breast, between her legs. God, she was hot, needy, while the burned skin beneath the tight hold of the rope was enough to make her want to writhe and scream. "I've suspended a man from the ceiling, his wrists and ankles manacled. Positioned his face over a female servant's spread legs. She was staked to the ground, so neither of them could move except as I desired. The wheel kept lifting and lowering his cock into her mouth, even while he was straining to bury his face in her pussy."

"Christ." He shook his head. "You vampires are strange creatures."

Dropping the cloth, he cradled her right breast in gentle fingers, an unexpectedly soothing, relaxing touch, a knead of sensation as he weighed it in his palm. It was sexual, creating a liquid yearning, but more than that, it was a reassurance, a demand that wasn't demanding. As he passed slow fingers over the nipple, they both watched it change to a taut point before he ran his knuckles down the curve, to her flat belly, the indentation of navel. Then further, his fingers passing over her mons, feathering her clit and the lips, her thighs. He'd wrapped a length of rope around them as well, so they couldn't part beneath his touch, only tremble in reaction.

"You're right," he said, low. "You'll come good, no time. And maybe you'll let me keep you tied up a bit, see where this might go. Until then, stop being such a bloody tease. I'm not going to bugger you like this, no matter how you bait me with it." He brought a smoldering gaze up to hers. "I'm here with you, to the end of it. All right?"

"Can't change the nature of man or vampire, bushman." Danny

tried to hold her voice steady. "You're a pretty interesting man, though."

He shrugged, gave her an odd smile that twisted something within her. "No different than any other. Just the fool you're stuck with to get you through this."

He might be a fool, but she found his presence comforting, amid the roaring pain from her nape to her heels, exacerbated by the tight chafe of the rope. And though she'd said her libido could be kindled no matter her physical state, it was still unexpected, how he'd roused it this strongly amid the discomfort.

If she had the choice of anyone in the world, she would choose this man to watch over her. The startling thought was followed by another, equally disturbing.

From her limited understanding of such relationships, that was the way a vampire felt about her fully marked servant.

FIRE. Sun poisoning was like fire rushing through a vampire's blood, scalding her from inside even as the burns healed rapidly on the outside. The only thing for it was replacing the blood, bringing in new infusions of it, pushing the poison out through the pores. She'd told him the first part before coherence deserted her. She'd forgotten to tell him there'd be weak tracks of blackened blood oozing out all over her healing skin.

He had his hands full, all right. No more than an hour after he tied her, she was thrashing against the restraints, snapping at the stone like a rabid dog. He wished he dared get close enough to wipe away the blood, keep bathing her in cool water, but it was clear he had to limit his risk to what would help her the most. Each hour, he maneuvered over her, held the taut line running from throat to wrists to bent legs against the stone floor with the weight of his boots. As everything tightened, her wild gaze would swivel up to him, watching hungrily as he cut his wrist and let it drip over her mouth again. The blue was gone. Her irises were as red as a sundown, all the way out to the corners, the black pupils huge.

At one point she was too far gone to drink. She wouldn't stop her flailing, the whipping of her head, the choking against the rope. Knowing he was being an idiot, still he wrestled her down, twisted her upper body to her back so he could hold a forearm against her throat and bring his cut arm close above her mouth. Christ, she'd been right. She could throw him off with her bucking, even bound as she was. She managed it twice, sending him rolling, before he maneuvered her close enough to the wall so he could put weight and leverage into it, pushing against the cave wall with his heels, his knees digging into the stone beneath them until he forced that first drop to go onto her tongue. That caught her attention, turned her from her delirium to the base desire for food. Still she growled, snarled, raged, even as she convulsively swallowed, watching the slow drip of his blood welling from the cut. Once he was done, he jumped back fast, because he found she could roll herself pretty fast if she wanted, and discomfort didn't slow her down.

Once he wasn't cautious enough. She reared up like a striking snake and clamped on his arm like a vise, even as she started to choke from the stranglehold of the rope. He'd had half a mind to let her do it that way, for she settled right down, like a baby on a tit, until he quickly realized how fast she could pull the blood out of him. Yanking back did no good, nor shoving or shouting at her. Her eyes turned even deeper red, the flaming colors of hell.

Self-preservation kicked in. While he had to close his eyes when he did it, he managed to reach his rifle and brought the butt smartly down against her collarbone. She'd screamed, making his gut wrench as she fell back, wriggling away like a legless crab to hole up against the side of the cave, glaring at him. He scrambled to the opposite wall, holding the rifle in clutched hands, getting his breath while she cursed at him in unintelligible animal noises, blood smeared across her mouth.

Please God, let her return to herself soon. The scars were healing with amazing speed, and as sundown approached, her strength was increasing. Conversely, she'd been right about the weakness. Every hour, he gave her a half cup of blood, until he was feeling dizzy with it. Breaking out his rations, he plowed through them, giving himself energy, watching her out of the corner of his eyes. Jesus. She was like one of those bloody motion pictures, the monster trussed but staring with red, soulless eyes at the hapless soon-to-be victim it would eat when it broke loose, as it always did.

She'd called it hog-tying, right enough. A couple times she'd struggled until the rope dug into the veins in her neck, made them run purple and oxygen-deprived, her breath rattling in her throat. He'd had to fight hard as hell not to go to her. Only the fact she was trying to get free so she could tear his throat out kept him out of her way, watching her roll and gag. Once she'd seemed to pass out, only to revive fifteen minutes later and do it to herself again.

He slid down the side of the cave wall now and decided to stare back, holding that inhuman gaze, watching her lovely chest rise and fall in quick pants. Their wrestling matches over the blood had resulted in her upper body being smeared with it so she had the look of a crazed Pict, or someone who'd escaped from one of those films he'd been thinking about.

I'm not scared of you. I've faced far worse things, love. He held on to that fierce determination, even as he knew those ropes wouldn't hold her forever. The hog-tying had, in fact, kept her from trying too hard, but once or twice he'd feared she might snap them anyway. Would he kill her to save his own skin, if he had to do so? Should he prepare a stake, just in case? She'd tell him to do it, for sure.

She'd never know how close she'd come to seducing him into buggering her, even with her wounds. He didn't know if that was a nod to her powers of temptation, right up there with Lilith, or how much of a bloody monster resided inside him. That said, any other bloke seeing her right now wouldn't touch her for all the gold that had ever been dug out of the earth. After the skin beneath knitted, the burned flesh sloughed off in an unattractive fashion, a serpent depositing its latest sheath. Her hair was unbraided again, hanging lank around her feral face. Her fangs were still almost as long as his smallest finger, making her look half woman, half beast. The guttural, constant growl coming from the back of her throat only added to it. She'd dug her fingers into her own arms, half-circle marks that bled, again and again.

Yeah, she didn't look like anything he'd let anywhere near him, let alone into his bed. So maybe when this was all over, he'd be shoulder-ing his swag, giving her a short nod and putting her behind him, a campfire story to share with himself on occasion, or with the aborigi-nal kinsmen who sometimes walked with him. But he'd said he'd stick by her. *If you change your mind, I won't hold it against you . . .*

She'd killed people before yesterday, he was sure of that. There'd been grief in her eyes at the loss of her men, but no shock at the deaths.

He'd become proficient at continuing to walk in one direction when he couldn't decide if a turn was the best course of action. But this was pushing it. Why was he still here? Was it because he couldn't help noticing the old sheath left gleaming skin in its wake? In her case, that skin was pale and smooth, a deadly invitation to touch.

His insane tangle of thoughts froze at the yip, a howl. Jesus, night had fallen, bringing a new problem. The dingoes had smelled the blood. Retrieving the pistol from his pack, he checked the ammo for it as well as the rifle. He needed to build a fire, but his gut told him not to betray their location. He'd moved the bike under a screen of brush, but if a plane sighted the burned Rovers, someone would be sent to check it out, and if that man was a good tracker, they'd be easy to find. It would be a little problematic to explain why he had a naked woman covered with blood trussed up in a cave. Of course, once they wrestled him to the ground and untied her, she'd eat ev-eryone, so no worries.

His lips twisted at the thought as he positioned himself at the cave mouth, at the bend where he could still see her, and yet also see the approach the dingoes would most likely use from the ground. If he shot a couple of them, maybe they'd get involved enough with the fallen fellas to leave them alone. Predators were drawn by warm, fresh blood, after all. He steeled himself not to think about that. About the red, still eyes that had followed him across the cave and were fas-tened on him still.

~

Three more feedings. Two dead dingoes. He leaned his head against the cave wall at his sentry position, the moon fuzzy around the edges. Like one of those funny flowers . . . dandelions. The kind that you blew so they flew away in the wind, drifting to plant in new places. Create more fuzzy little balls. Funny. Nice to be a fuzzy little ball, something simple, short-lived and yet continuing on, forever and ever.

He stumbled to his feet. Another feeding. "Bugger," he muttered as he tripped, fell to one knee about five steps in. Using the rifle to get himself back up, he found her in the gloom of the cave. An hour or two ago, she'd stopped making the hair-raising growls and hisses. The pale wisps of skin appearing among the burns had now become a reassuring wide cream expanse, where he could see the delicate bumps of her spine. However, fuddled as he was, he came to a dead halt when he realized her arms were in front of her. The snapped rope lay like a sprawled snake between him and her, one end disappearing under her hair, up over her shoulder. His grip on the rifle increased. As he hobbled around her cautiously, he considered his options. She hadn't come at him while he was at the entrance, so maybe . . .

When her gaze rose as he moved around her feet, relief flooded his chest. Her eyes were blue, only a tinge of red left. "Danny?"

She gave him a tired smile, and the fist squeezing his gut eased further. Her close scrutiny was intelligent, aware, not feral hunger. Lowering himself to one knee next to her, he used the rifle to prop himself. "Do you need—"

"No. You've done enough. More than enough." As she started to lift herself up on her arms, he reached out with clumsy fingers, and drew the loosened rope away.

Danny watched him, saw the shadows go through his gaze at the bruising around her throat. It moved her, even as she knew it was absurd. If her burns had vanished in less than a day, the bruising would be gone in barely a blink. He was so pale. Given the amount of time that had passed, she assumed he'd given her far too much of his blood. If he'd lost that much all at once, he would have gone into shock. As it was, even over time, it was far too much.

With three marks, it would have affected him far less, and she could have replenished him with her own blood after she recuperated.

While she saw signs that he'd been smart enough to dig into his provisions, she also smelled the blood of the wild dogs and knew he'd been fighting a battle on two fronts.

She could also smell herself. Stale saliva and metallic dried blood. Discarded spaghetti in a garbage can likely looked more appealing than her hair at the moment. Even so, he reached out and touched her face without hesitation, brushing his knuckles along her cheek, under that limp fall of hair. She had to quell the overwhelming urge to give him the second mark then and there, because she wanted to know what was going through his mind.

"Good on ya, love. Nice to have you back."

Swallowing, she put her hand over his on her face, the large, capable fingers. He was cold—the blood loss, she knew—but beneath that was something that warmed her in a way she couldn't explain.

"Why are you still here?"

"I said I'd stay," he said simply.

"So you did." She managed another smile. "You gave too much. You're weak."

He shrugged. "I expect you'd like to get cleaned up."

That was an understatement. All vampires were vain, but when reduced to this, fussing with her hair or wiping some blood off her chin wasn't going to cut it. Nothing would suffice but a full bath.

"Is that possible?"

"How strong are you?"

When she gave him an ironic look, he chuckled. "I mean, there's a small billabong, a little under a mile away. It's about midnight. We have time before daylight to get there and back with an easy walk. There's also a moon tonight, so we'll have enough light to likely stay out of much trouble. And the dingoes—" He cut himself off, gave her a shrewd glance. "'Course, you don't have to worry about that, do you?"

"Now that I'm back up and about, the dingoes shouldn't cause any problems. Most scavengers and predators won't come near me unless I'm wounded," she reminded him. Her lips curved. "Though reptiles can be a bit thickheaded about it, kind of like bushmen. I don't think the problem is if I can make it. Can *you* manage it?"

"I'll do." His mouth tugged up as well. "And you're strong enough to carry me if you need to."

~

Though she stayed close enough so that he could lean on her as much as his pride would allow, Dev did manage. He was quiet, scouting his surroundings in a way that appeared casual, but she suspected was a detailed surveillance. Apparently he'd been doing it long enough that it was as second nature to him as breathing. She felt the twist of guilt again. If she'd been equally vigilant, would her men still be alive?

The moon bathed the land, the expanses of sand among the vegetation and trees gleaming like the shimmer of a tranquil ocean. Great, vast, unaffected. Yet intensely sentient, listening and alert.

When she first scented the water, her pace quickened, though she tried not to push him, knowing he'd feel it necessary to keep pace with her. She felt like a dog who'd enjoy a good full-body roll in scratchy sand. She'd used a little of the water in the pot back at the cave to take the worst off before she donned her clothes, but she couldn't wait to be fully immersed.

At the same time, she keenly missed the maidservant she'd kept in Brisbane to help her with things like back scrubbings. As pleasurable as it would be to coax Dev into that duty, she didn't think he could afford to have any more fluids drained out of him at the moment.

She felt gloriously alive. *If you gave him the second mark right now, it would help restore him a bit. Though not as much as the third mark . . .*

However, it wasn't only her knowledge of his physical condition holding her back, but that quiet that had settled between them since the cave. He squatted by the billabong now, in profile from her, filling his large billy so that when she was ready for soap, she could use the cloth-wrapped cake he'd brought along. At a distance from the watering hole, of course, so she wouldn't contaminate the water for other creatures. If he was her servant in truth, he'd haul the rinse water, pour it over her, maybe pass his hand over her flesh, make sure all the crevices were free of slick soap . . .

Stop it, Danny. That gentle caress on her face in the cave, the moment of relieved levity, that was the brief bond of two people who'd shared a rather intense experience. One that was now over. He'd come out here on a hunch, thinking she was in trouble. Now that she wasn't, maybe he was feeling trapped, his sense of nobility chaining him to her side until she reached her destination. And he'd had to kill for her.

Bugger it. Moving off to a nearby tree, she bent to unlace her boots, pull them off, hopping a bit, then shimmied out of her trousers. As she shrugged out of the shirt, she did a quick pirouette to flash him a smile. "Come in if you dare, bushman. I'll protect you from the beasties."

"Hold up a moment."

She paused. As he moved toward her, the moon glanced off the planes of his face, the sensual mouth. In darkness, the green of his eyes had some of the gold and gray of hazel. Though she liked watching him move, the sinuous play of muscles at abdomen and waist beneath his shirt, she tried to keep her expression indifferent.

Patiently, he gathered her clothes and put them together in one spot, stuffing the socks in the boots in a way that reminded her horrible things could crawl in while she was gone. A spider or lizard might not be able to hurt her, but she didn't relish the idea of one scuttling over her toes as she poked them back in. She made a mental note to shake out the boot, even with the protective sock in it.

"You can't cross this ground with those soft, pretty feet." Despite the weakness she sensed was still hampering him, he nevertheless guided her arm around his broad shoulders, bent and lifted her, moving forward toward the billabong. She was beginning to wonder if he was made of iron, or if he was too stubborn to know he should be falling down, not hauling her about.

Green rushes moved at the edges of the pond, whispering like spirits about their peculiar nighttime visitors.

Even as she caught her breath at his arm around her smooth back, the other crooked beneath her legs, she chided herself. She wasn't a green, fresh girl. Hell, she'd practically raped him less than a day or two ago, taken him places he'd never been before.

But he wasn't afraid of her. Not in the least. Though it was a vague, bestial memory, she remembered latching on to his arm. Even then, she'd seen the will to survive in his eyes, but no fear. Nor did he appear to have a fascination with danger. He was just . . . he was like this billabong. A couple weeks ago, it had likely been a dry bed. But the rain came, and now it was this, a quiet pool in the moonlight, wildflowers and grass springing up on the banks, creating a thing of beauty. No big fuss about it, though it was a miracle. It simply was. Like him. And like him, it would disappear again in the normal cycle of things.

When he let her legs down, her feet touched the cool mud of the bank. She kept hold of his shirt. She easily could have reached up and kissed him then, wanted to, but more than that, she wanted to see what he wanted. So she stood there, staring up at his face in the moonlight. Then she changed her mind, couldn't wait. "Dev," she murmured. "Kiss me."

Cocking his head, he studied her features, then his hand came up again, this time to slide beneath her hair, cup her jaw, pass a thumb over her cheek, the corner of her mouth. "You make things in me hurt, love. Hurt so bad I think I'd rather take a gut shot. But here I am, anyway."

"A true masochist," she whispered. "Vampires have a sadistic streak, you know. Maybe you're attracted to the pain I can give you. And not only to your body."

"Yeah, maybe." He'd bent closer now, though, and her lips parted, her heart accelerating. *God, kiss me.* Danny could have closed the gap, but maybe she wanted the torture as well, because waiting for him to make that decision was a delicious longing that bordered on an ache in her vitals.

"But then again," he murmured, a breath away, his eyes dominating her vision, "if I could freeze this moment, I'd stare at you naked in the moonlight, your mouth waiting for my kiss, your body swaying toward me. I'd be willing to stand in front of something like that forever, without ever going one step forward or back."

"Well, time does go on," she managed. "Dev, are you trying to make me beg?"

"You've put me on my knees often enough, love. Truth, I haven't been off them since the first time I saw you." The green in his eyes had become stormier, increasing the need within her even more as his voice dropped to an active stroke along her nerves. "The man who enters Aphrodite's temple has to take a bit of time to contemplate her, you know. Worship the very miracle of her existence, before he dares to touch her. She's uppity that way."

The scholar. "God, you're a strange one," she whispered. "Damn it, *kiss me*, Devlin."

With that appealing tug at his lips, he bent his head and pressed them upon hers. He curved his arms all the way around, one high on her back, the other low on her hips, bringing her full against him, hard, lean male, the muscular planes of his body, the cool metal of his belt buckle, the impression of the knife he wore on his hip. Smelling of sweat and blood. Emitting a relieved sigh into his mouth, she whimpered in soft approval as he buried his fingers in her hair to deepen the kiss. His tongue was wet heat, stroking along hers, making her press closer, feeling his stiffening reaction to her naked body against his clothed one. She wanted him now, wanted him inside her, filling her, a basic hunger, no matter how weakened his body was. One part of him was obviously able to handle it.

Vampire sensuality was always filled with delicious power games, teasing, a buildup of need until the culmination was explosive, on the edge of violence. She loved it, but perhaps because the past twelve hours had been brimming with violence and power, and she'd brushed so close to the end, bringing him to that edge with her, she didn't care about any of that now. There was only this, an overwhelming need to have him.

"Dev, fuck me." Her voice was hoarse, almost as guttural as when she'd been mad with bloodlust. This seemed no less intense.

He glanced around, and before she could ask him what he was about, he'd lifted her onto his front, hitching her legs around his hips. Despite the shaking she could feel in his limbs, he staggered the few short steps to a mature gum leaning over the billabong, the cascade of rain from its branches likely one of the reasons a pool formed here.

She clung to his shoulders, pressing her face against his neck. She was filthy, she knew. She didn't care, because he didn't seem to care. She didn't have to be beautiful, polished or in control. He'd saved her life. Kept her alive, and not judged her for who or what she was. If she ever did contemplate having a fully marked servant, she wasn't likely to find a better one.

Jesus, was it like this for all vampires when they found their third mark? As impossibly romantic and illogical as the way humans claimed to fall in love? Damn it, she *would* be rational. She could give him the second mark now, only the second mark, and that would be best for them both. With the second mark, she could restore some of his strength, because bloody oath, he was going to try to fulfill her wishes, and if he fucked her, she'd likely kill him with the effort.

Best of all, she'd be part of his consciousness, and she could allow him into hers when she chose. He was already bound to her, in ways neither of them had expected. So it was a simple, additional step. He didn't even know he carried the first mark, anyway.

He brought her up against the sloping angle of the tree, and oh, holy hell, the bark was a blessing. Despite herself, she wriggled, and a relieved sigh escaped her lips. "This is why bears do it," she observed.

"I assume you mean scratching their backs on trees." His lined, tanned face was filled with that familiar touch of laughter, but determined desire as well. "Let me see if I can help. I'd thought I'd start by scrubbing your back, but . . ."

"Later." She felt the heat of him touch her thigh when he opened his trousers. Then he found her opening, already eager and wet for him. "Oh, God, now." She constricted her arms around him, brought him in, and cried out as he sheathed her fully, that turgid, enormous length. This time he didn't hesitate, just pushed all the way into her womb, in a way that was burning pain and pleasure at once, because it told her he'd missed her. He was matching her need. No foreplay or fondling. This was simple, needful fucking, two bodies who'd brushed too close to death, now with one goal in mind.

He pushed against her, thrusting in and dragging out, raking her up and down a handspan of the tree's length, intensifying the ecstasy and discomfort at once. When he drove her harder, she cried out, encouraging him, wanting him to pound her against the tree, wanting to feel the unyielding power of his body, knowing he didn't fear hers. She bruised with the forceful grip of her fingers. She remembered how he'd removed the rope from her neck, so gently, but lingered there on her collarbone with that intriguing look in his eye. She imagined him bound to her in a similar way. Her collar on his throat, the visible knowledge that he belonged to her, willingly. It had to be like that, for it to be the way it should be between a vampire and her servant.

He was flagging, as she knew he would. Despite a great heart and tremendous strength, Devlin was human. Too much blood loss and lack of sleep were taking their toll. He should have passed out by now. His hand gripped her waist hard, leaning them both into the tree for support, but she saw from the set of his jaw he'd keep going until he dropped.

The second mark would allow her access to that delicious mind, all the twists and turns of it. Take away some of his emptiness. If she asked, he wouldn't agree to it, not consciously, but she knew in her heart he needed it. Wanted it.

She reared up, curving her arms around his shoulders, bringing her in close to his throat as he pushed closer to the tree in response, sandwiching her between it and him, to work her in smaller, more intense thrusts that had her body vibrating, jerking with the movement, her clit rippling with every contact. He liked doing a woman rough, she'd felt it in him from the first. It was so powerful, his need, that she could imagine any woman being a little intimidated by it. Had his Tina been able to take his dark hungers, take him fully into her body without discomfort? Or had he coddled her, leashing all of it back because he loved her so? Had those dark needs even existed before he lost her, before he learned the price of his soul?

She gasped against the side of his throat, the pulsing life there as he changed his angle. When she sank her fangs into his throat, the wild rush of the blood, pumping hard during physical exertion, sprayed into her mouth so that she had to use her tongue to control the flow. Holding that pressure, savoring the taste of him on her tongue, she released the silver flow of the second marking into his bloodstream.

He caught one hand in her hair again, holding her head there, telling her he liked it, liked her feeding from him. He needed her to need him. Needed a woman to care for.

She closed her eyes, letting the swirl of thoughts flood her mind as his taste had flooded her mouth, the way his seed would soon be flooding her body. Savored all of that, past, present and future. He thought no mortal woman safe with him anymore, with the violence of the needs he had. The rage in his soul was so great it made her tremble. It was so carefully layered—not like the strata of the earth carved by wind and water, but like bricks. A brick wall, constructed by human hands. He stayed in the desert because he was afraid people might break that wall and he wouldn't be able to control the rage.

With the mark came the renewal of strength, surging through him so rapidly she felt it like glory. He slammed her against the tree hard enough to catch her breath in her throat. She began to work her hips on him, taking control, drawing him up with her, refusing to leave him behind, joining him to her climax the way she'd just taken another step to join him to her mind.

His hands were gripping her buttocks now, fingers seeking that tight opening, the scoundrel. She rocked up, taking more of him, drawing back from his throat now to clasp his shoulder and ride him like the magnificent mount he was. When her breasts quivered with the downward impact, it of course drew his eye, though his attention slid over her fangs, wet with his blood and the silver marking in the moonlight, she was sure.

"Come over . . . with me," she gasped out, and then they leaped together, his body spewing inside hers with liquid heat, while she threw her head back and cried out, working her cunt on him, the tree raw on her skin, his fingers bruising her, his cock fair splitting her in two, such that the pain was a euphoria all its own.

～

As they slowed at last, she was aware of the night creatures, the far-off call of a dingo, a few bird noises. And the twinge of guilt, though she tried to dispel it by sliding her fingers into his unruly red hair, licking along his neck to get the last of the unclotted blood. She'd done two marks before. It wasn't a big deal. Fine. So why hadn't she warned him? She'd warned others of her staff, what to expect, why she was doing it. It was always to increase staff efficiency, her security. Someone whose mind couldn't hide from hers could hardly orchestrate a betrayal with her enemies.

She'd never done the second mark merely because she had a powerful hunger to invade a mind, roll in the flow of its thoughts, see those images through his eyes. She'd certainly never done it as a stopgap measure to keep her from yielding to the temptation of the third mark.

"What . . ." He gripped her hard about the waist, letting her legs down, but then he lost his balance, stumbling back, forcing her to catch him. He pushed her away, however. "Don't move. Told you, you can't walk out here. What did you do? This is like that last bite. The first night. It felt different."

"I gave you the first mark then. It's only a locator. It lets me know where you are." *That you're alive.* She did it automatically, finishing the thought in his head, and his eyes widened. He straightened, but his focus was inside, even as he swayed on his feet. She could see them, his whirl of thoughts. There were vampires that could be inside a human mind without any detection at all, from the very first moment they second-marked a mortal, but she wasn't old or experienced enough to make that seamless transition. Since she was there now, the nagging sense of being watched inside his own head was impossible to mistake for anything else, even if it took a leap of credibility to comprehend it. However, considering the events of the past couple days, she suspected the leap wasn't much more than a stride for him.

"It's called the second mark," she said quietly. "It helped restore what you lost with the blood. But it also . . . it allows me into your mind. I can read your thoughts, speak to you in your head, over reasonable distances. I can feel what you feel, when you're afraid . . . or angry."

He stared at her. "I feel like I have mozzies in my brain. And like I'm seasick. Is that permanent?"

"No. It's a good analogy. It's a lot like acquiring sea legs. You get used to it."

"You didn't think you needed to ask me before you gave me nowhere to hide from you?"

"No," she said evenly, despite the twist in her lower abdomen. She felt the trickle of him down the inside of her thigh, and God help her if the feeling didn't make her shiver, her nipples tighten again. He saw it, his expression darkening as his attention rose to her face again.

"Christ, it doesn't even bother you."

"It's not the third mark, Dev," she pointed out irritably. "That's a much more permanent bond, and truthfully, that would have restored your strength even faster, because you could have taken in my blood."

"A good night's rest and a heavy breakfast would have restored my strength as well."

"It just . . ." She shrugged. "I wanted to be inside you. Wanted to hear your thoughts."

"Well, as long as it's about what *you* want . . ." He put both his hands to his head as he moved a few steps away, apparently trying to get his bearings. Danny moved toward him and yelped as something stabbed her foot.

"Jesus Christ. You are a bloody piece of work. I told you not to move." He turned abruptly, only staggering a bit, and scooped her up in his arms again, lurching an alarming moment so that she caught his shoulders as he righted himself. Automatically, she reached into his head, helping him steady, and he stiffened at the feel of it, going still a blink or two before he jerked into movement again.

"Here." He worked his way over to the billabong. "You wanted a swim to rinse off. You go ahead while I sit here and decide if I should find a pointed stick and harpoon you with it. Now I know what drove Ahab."

"What does that mean?" She gave him an indignant look.

"You figure it out. So this means you can automatically read my mind?"

"When I choose to. At the moment I'm not—"

"You should have been. Cheers, love." And he tossed her, the force of his anger and his own natural and now augmented strength launching her out a good fifteen feet so she landed in the deeper water with a resounding splash.

She took on a mouthful of water with her yelp, and sank, not having had time to mention that vampires weren't buoyant. Not that she thought that would have elicited any sympathy from him. Particularly since she'd already told him they didn't need to breathe. However, as she made it to her feet, she found the water was only about chest deep.

She had half a mind to come back onshore, lay him out on his back and show him exactly how tolerant a vampire was of human cheek. But in truth, to him it probably seemed she'd been too impatient to wait on his recuperation for a good fucking. That would actually be amusing, if it was true. Maybe she should have asked, but . . . oh, bugrit. Everything he'd done for her in the past two days, he *had* deserved better. She'd just been so sure at that pivotal moment that he needed to let her in, whether he thought it was best or not. She couldn't stand him being so weak from caring for her.

She wasn't certain she didn't still feel that way, but he was now carrying two of her marks, and hadn't even agreed to be in her employ, in any capacity. The problem was, she'd actually forgotten that for a few minutes. The way he acted toward her, the way he responded to her, and she to him . . . Damn it, what was she doing? She'd gone two hundred years without a full servant and suddenly she thought she couldn't do without one? And not a human with the proper qualifications. This man.

Humans were inferior to vampires, she reminded herself. They were intriguing, thought-provoking, and could create sentimental reactions in vampires, but a servant was a vampire's property in the eyes of other vampires, to handle and treat as he or she chose. To a human, that sounded like slavery. But to a vampire and servant, where the human came willingly, it was entirely different, below the surface of perception, a compelling bond that really couldn't be defined. So she'd heard. And that was the way she felt with him. Shit. Shit. *Shit.*

This was ludicrous. She rinsed her hair in the water, rubbed her flesh to get rid of the stiff feeling of dried blood and saliva. Rinsed her mouth. She pointedly ignored the shore, even though she could hear muttering from it. If she chose, she could find out exactly what was going through his head. She wasn't sure she wanted to do so, but . . .

Conniving, supercilious . . . Making decisions for me like Winston bloody Churchill . . . I should have let the dingoes have a go at her. Then, startling her, *You getting all this, love?*

Loud and clear. You needn't get all shirty about it.

"Shirty?" He stomped down to the water's edge, glared out at her. "I've got you fucking around in my head, and you act like I'm only narking."

"No need to shout," she said coolly. "I can *hear* you, after all. Inside and out."

His eyes narrowed, his jaw muscle flexing. Bloody hell if it didn't get her juices flowing. "Get your arse out of that water so I can blister it all over again."

That capped it. She moved forward fast, intending to come right up under his nose.

The croc caught her in the shoulder, a stunning blow as the beast attempted to knock her under, roll her to the bottom and drown her for dinner. The poor creature didn't realize she couldn't be drowned. With a snarl, Danny ducked under him, seized the weak front leg, slapped her palm beneath the broad snout and heaved.

Dev was already halfway into the water, knife drawn, when she sent the crocodile flying. In hindsight, he realized it had actually been a controlled move, to keep the beast close to the water where he wouldn't be harmed by the impact. She accomplished it magnificently, for the croc landed on his back with a loud, brutal smack that had Dev wincing from a recollection of a childhood belly flop. The stunned creature floated a second, then turned, sinking beneath the surface, the movement of the water suggesting he was headed for the far end of the billabong, as swiftly as a dazed croc could.

It was unusual to find one this far out from a steady water source, but he also knew there was no end to the things one saw in the

Outback. Like a female vampire materializing right before him, her preternatural eyes glowing in the moonlight.

She clamped down on the wrist holding the knife, her body so close to his the tips of her wet breasts brushed his shirtfront. A brief, distracting impression as she twisted his arm, forcing him to drop the blade and driving him to one knee in the shallow water. The blue eyes that stared down into his face were not those of the impassioned woman of a few moments ago, or even the feral madness of a vampire with sun sickness. It was the look she'd given Elle.

"You've made your point," she said icily. "You didn't appreciate me giving you the second mark. I am grateful for everything you've done to save my life, Dev, and I apologize if I offended you. But do *not* push me."

He stared at her. "If the apology means anything, then you take your hands off me."

Danny studied him, the granite expression, the tension under her grip. He might not be able to hurt her, but by God, it was clear if she pushed *him*, he would try. Fearless, as she'd thought. Stepping back after a moment, she spoke in a quieter tone. "I've not taken away your free will."

"But it's easier to do it now, isn't it? Compel me, like they say in the books."

"Dev, all vampires have some compulsion ability, even on unmarked humans. But I don't need to compel your free will. That's not why—"

"Well, that makes me feel loads better," he retorted, springing to his feet, though he didn't back off a step. "As long as you don't need to do it, I'm free to walk around and do as I please. Until you decide I'm not. Do you really think I'd just say, 'Oh, well, bugger. She can read my mind and take away my choices. Guess I'll go have a beer or two and she'll be apples'?"

Her mouth pressed into a line. "No, that's not what I'm trying to say. You're not my full servant, Dev."

"What's the bloody difference?" he snarled.

"I haven't asked you," she shouted.

"Why bother?" Irish temper had flared and his green eyes were like brilliant emeralds, flashing in his furious face. He yanked at the collar of his shirt, opening it several more buttons. "Sink your little fangs in once more and consider it done, since it's so fucking obvious that's what you want from me."

Danny blinked. She was experienced enough to mask her reaction to anything, but she couldn't find anything to say to that. Though she knew it was rather important that she think of something. A denial? Some type of retort that would turn this conversation in a different direction? Because the truth, that she was entirely out of her depth on this, was not an acceptable admission.

Dev turned away from her with a look of disgust, retrieved his knife and walked back to the tree where he'd fucked her senseless. Danny stood watching him, an uncharacteristic shiver going through her. She usually didn't feel the cold, but for some reason where his anger had stirred her, this abandonment left her feeling . . . wrong.

When she pushed past that into his mind, she found nothing. He wasn't thinking anything. Just . . . he was tired. Very tired. And sad. An overwhelming wave of loneliness hit her, so hard she almost staggered backward several steps. He wanted to go back to the way his life had been several days ago. Where solitude was his primary craving. Where he carefully managed his feelings so he didn't feel too much. She'd disrupted that. But instead of feeling gratified by the thought, she felt shame. Even more disturbing, her heart twisted, seeing those desolate thoughts in his mind.

She was a young vampire, but she knew the warnings about caring too much for humans. No one denied that fully marked servants, bonded to a vampire's very soul, were cherished in the unique and various ways that vampires expressed such affection. But while humans might be valued highly for their intelligence and resourcefulness, it was important not to lose perspective.

She also knew that, though many vampires might mark a human once or twice at will—or even on a whim, as she'd done it—only a fool made a human a full servant when it was not something the human desired. That was what Dev didn't understand. Of course, sometimes it seemed he understood more about their situation than she'd even admitted to herself.

She moved out of the water, intending to dare the possibility of damage to her feet to get to her clothing, and the boots he'd thoughtfully stuffed with her socks to keep creepy-crawlies out of them. She wasn't going to enjoy putting the same dirty clothes on, but at least her body was cleaner.

"You said you wanted me to scrub your back," he said.

She turned to where he was sitting in the shadow of the tree. He had his hands linked over his knees.

"I figured I'd asked enough of you for one day."

"I'll give you anything you ask, love. Anything." His voice was low, thick. "I only mind what you decide to take."

"I don't know how to say I'm sorry for it, Dev. If it helps, I didn't intend to hurt you with it." She turned to him, feeling oddly vulnerable without any clothes on, him sitting on the ground studying her.

"Can you explain why you did it, then?"

Good luck with that, when she couldn't explain it to herself. "I just . . . maybe I got a little carried away in the moment, is all. The . . . It's intimate, the ability to link with your mind. Speak with you with no one else hearing."

"Can I get into your mind the same way?"

She shook her head. "Only if I let you. I can let you hear thoughts I speak to you, but typically a vampire doesn't give a human full access. It's best all round. It could be disturbing, for one thing."

"And what is the difference? Between two marks and three."

Everything. But she stuck to the physical considerations. "The third mark triples a human's mortal lifespan. Enhances healing power, speed and strength, as well as the mental connection of the second mark. It also links Master and servant irrevocably. If the vampire dies, the servant dies."

"And if or when the servant dies?"

"The vampire lives," she said.

Though it was akin to having the heart ripped out of one's chest. So she'd been told by her father. *There's a sense of closeness, of binding, greater than you will ever feel with any other living being, maybe even God, while in your earthly form. Most human life forms spend their whole lives feeling lonely, Danny. But vampires have a way to feel completely connected to someone, no guessing or faith to it. Forever.*

"Mmm." Rising, he picked up the billy and the soap, bringing both to her. In the darkness, his silhouette was broad and tall, shadowing her. "Turn around, then, love. Let me do your back."

She nodded, uncertain what else to say. When the soapy cloth touched her back, began to rub, she could barely resist the urge to arch and purr. He moved her hair forward, over her shoulder, smoothing it down over one breast, taking advantage of that, but in a quiet, sensual way that merely sent a ripple of pleasurable response through her.

His mind had gone quiet again, focusing on simple things, like the shape of the moon, the gleam of it on her flesh. How he was going to get her to the next pub, get her a safe transport out to Thieves' Station.

"How do you do that?" she asked.

"What?"

"Your mind . . ." She realized she might be touching back on a sensitive subject, when his hand with the cloth paused, but she pressed on. Best to seize the bull by the horns. She couldn't pretend it hadn't happened. Hell, she couldn't even pretend she hadn't wanted it to happen. "It's . . . I can tell it bothers you, very much, what I did. But you've put it aside, or something. Your mind is . . . vacant. Smooth. Like a lake."

"Are you saying I'm empty-headed?"

She bit her lip against a smile, felt things loosen in her lower abdomen. His hand started rubbing again, working out dirt and blood, stroking responsive skin. "No. Still, calm. You've just chosen not to think about anything more than this moment. And practical things."

"Like my diabolical plan to leave you stranded out here?"

"No." She closed her eyes as he put down the cloth and began to massage her flesh with two soapy hands, nothing interfering with contact between their skin. His strong fingers eased the muscles at the same time he rubbed the flesh.

She imagined him doing this for his wife at the end of the day, after she'd been doing any number of the things a wife handled at a homestead. He'd have her sit in a chair while he did it, his gaze caught by the sable silk of her hair, the way it exposed her neck so that he leaned over and put his lips there. Her laughter was a breathless shiver. *Dev, you daft man. I'm much too dirty from cleaning. And pregnant as a cow, on top of it.*

He'd had the ability to arouse her with a touch, that bare caress of lips. She could see it in the face the woman . . . Tina . . . turned up to him, the love and desire shining in her eyes, her parted lips showing her willingness even as she chided him. And he'd taken advantage of it, too, lifting her out of the chair and turning her, bearing her back to the table and taking her right there. Rucking up her skirt, finding her wet and willing before easing into her, gentle, holding back, pleasing her and finding his own pleasure. He'd curtailed the raging desire in his gut to rut upon her, exercise the lust he felt for her in the most primal way. His hands had cupped her belly, and, even as he stroked inside her, he'd bent, put his lips over the child they'd made.

She'd made him feel as if he was the center of her world. And she, and their son, had been the center of his. It made sense. No one understood the agony of eternal loneliness until he'd had the exact opposite, lying like the simplest of gifts in his palm.

Danny opened her eyes, gazed into the night. Her imaginings, or his, had led her into his memories. Was there anything more attractive than a man who knew what it was to truly love a woman? Who remembered the joy and wonder of it, so it was stamped on him, forever felt by any woman graced by his touch, his smile, or his attentions? He didn't have to guess to know what was the right thing, the right feeling or touch. He'd been there. Perhaps some women would have been jealous of the memory, afraid of its hold on him, but because she could wrap herself in those memories, she saw how they enhanced him, how he was integrating them into this moment. While it made him pensive, it also guided him as he kneaded, rhythmic and slow, his fingers fanning out over her back, the thumbs dropping like the stem of a bird's wings as his touch rolled across her firm skin and muscle.

"Will you tell me how you do it, Dev? The stillness."

She saw the flash of resentment in his mind, the thought that she could just go fossicking for it if she chose. But rather than reacting to that, she waited him out.

"My ancestor lived with the black fellas in Queensland for about thirty years. My family has always been connected to that clan, even as we've all been moved around a bit. Some of my growing up was with them, in the Outback. One of the Elders of that tribe taught me things about being still. Inside and out." He nodded toward the land rolling out before them, mostly flat until it reached their rock formation in the distance. "You know, in brightest daylight, ten aborigines could be standing within a hundred feet of us here, and if they didn't want to be seen, they wouldn't be. Part of it is understanding the land, the ability to blend, but a large part of that is blending your mind with your surroundings, as well. Letting it go completely still, so that you can find a center. I can do it when something bothers me more than it should. Later, when I go back to it, it seems more manageable, somehow."

She nodded. Not only from the shifting images in his mind, but also from the inflections in his voice, she knew that ability had been a desperate need for him, particularly in the past decade. But she let that go for now as his hands slid down her rib cage, back up again, using the washcloth to drain more water on her skin, lubricate the avenue he followed across her body. His hands spread out farther, traveled to more distant points. It became a sinuous dance, her body moving with the motion of his hands. Back down again, around, his palms molding her buttocks, lifting them as one of his hands came around her front, flat on her stomach, anchoring her as he gripped the buttock, bent and pressed his lips to the curve, taking a nip that made her jump. "You've a beautiful arse, love."

She picked up the thought from his mind, tilted her head to look over her shoulder at him. "You're thinking that getting to put your cock there is even payment for me invading your mind?"

"Nope," he said, unruffled. The cloth slid down her flank, tracing the cleft between her buttocks, his fist squeezing so the water trickled into the sensitive area. The traitorous coiling in her lower belly left her worrying her bottom lip. "Not even close. But it's a start."

She intended to toss a disdainful look over her shoulder, but he dropped to one knee, his thumbs inserting themselves in that seam as if splitting open a succulent piece of fruit. Abruptly she swayed forward, drawing in a surprised breath as his lips and tongue began to collect the water he'd drained in that cleft, easing in so he was teasing her rim with the heat and moisture of his mouth.

Sensation shot through her. She twisted around, mindful of staying in one place, not wanting her tender feet to be pierced by the dangers on the darkened ground. As she gripped his shirt, she wasn't sure if it was to stop him or steady herself.

"That's enough," she managed, feeling heat in her face.

When he looked up at her, a drop of water was on his upper lip. He wiped the back of his hand across it. "No man's ever buggered your arse, has he?"

She raised her chin. "A crude way to put it."

"You can read my mind, love. No sense in prettying it up. You get it the way I'm thinking it, right?"

"Even if I can read your mind, manners are still important," she said primly. "And I'm not constantly inside your head. Mostly it's a functional connection. Harry, John and Roy were all second-marked, and I didn't . . . They were my employees."

"But at one time, you had them. You wouldn't keep any man around you that you haven't had beneath you. I'd bet my last quid on that." When he rose, he turned her so that her feet found the tops of his boots, a safe resting place, at least from the dangers of the ground. When she closed her fingers on his shoulders to hold on, he settled his hands down on her hips, anchoring her there.

She really needed to establish some space between them, some sense of his place with respect to a vampire mistress. Though he hadn't agreed to accept her as a mistress. This whole situation, the way it had happened so suddenly, hadn't left any room to lay the normal groundwork for what liberties he could and couldn't take. Of course, those quelling thoughts didn't make her pulse beat any less fast, or the vibrating response in her pussy ease, with a matching throb between her buttocks.

"I'd love to be the first." His eyes were intent, hard to resist. "The only. It would hurt, a lot. But I'd make you come through the pain, so hard you wouldn't know if you were screaming in pleasure or agony."

"I need my shoes," she said. "My clothes."

"I didn't finish washing you."

"Then you need to do so." She had to take control back, couldn't give him the impression of more power over her than he truly had. That would be dangerous for both of them. "After that, we should return to the cave. It's too close to dawn." She gave him an even glance. "Remember. Don't push me, Dev."

Grim amusement laced with male frustration flickered through his gaze. Though he might not have access to her mind, Danny reflected with wry despair that he seemed damned adept at reading it. The croc may not have been a hazard to her, but this rough bushman apparently was.

7

"So, do you have any thoughts on how I can get to Thieves' Station from here? Sixty miles is a far distance to walk, at least between sundown and sunrise."

"Maybe you should forget about that, let me get you inland again, love." When they'd returned to the cave, he'd prepared a meal for himself out of the tucker in his pack and was currently shoveling food in his mouth. He didn't look up as he spoke. "It makes no sense for a vampire to risk conditions out here. The city offers you a lot more options. And everything about you says you've lived most your life there anyhow."

It offended her, tweaked her pride. Until she saw into his mind. The daft man felt she needed to be *protected*. Of course, considering he had come to her rescue, she couldn't claim invincibility, but it was an unusual reaction for a human.

She set aside the comb he'd lent her, frustrated with the snarls in her hair anyway, and leveled a glance on him. "I'm going home to *my* station. And one setback doesn't mean I can't handle it."

He lifted his head, leveled a green stare on her. "Setback? That's what you call getting blown up and fried like an egg?"

"Vampires lead interesting lives, Dev," she said mildly. "We're nocturnal predators, like dozens of other creatures out there. While the sun presents a challenge, very little else about our environment does. We aren't affected by extremes in temperatures, bugs ... We have no predators of significance. Truthfully, our greatest enemies are others of our kind."

A shadow crossed her mind at the thought, at the reminder of why it was imperative that she return to the station. "But you're right. Many of our kind do prefer urban life. It does provide more ... social opportunities. The percentage of us who choose the Outback are probably similar to the percentage of humans who do the same."

"Probably less, I'm guessing," he grunted. "Seems a bit wobbly for someone like you, though, love."

"Noted," she said coolly. "You didn't answer my question. Is there anything useful you can offer about getting me to my station?"

"Depends on whether you need more men and weapons to deal with what you find when you get there." At her sharp glance, he shrugged. "Doesn't take much of a leap to guess the threat was dispatched from there. Want to fill me in?"

"Why?" She held his gaze. "I thought you were turning down my job offer."

"Whether I am or not, I plan on getting you there, safe and sound. The more I know, the more help I can be on that."

"We'll see. You've done plenty enough." At his steady look, she sighed, picked up the comb again and ran her fingers over it. "All right, then. To put it simply, we have a Vampire Council that runs everything, worldwide. Then we have Region Masters who cover groups of territories. Below them are territory overlords, who rule over the rest of the vampires in that area. I left my station about forty years ago, because my mother had taken up with a bit of a bastard called Ian. We didn't see eye to eye on him, and so in the end I left. My mother was the territory overlord, and Ian liked sharing that responsibility with her, though there are only about twenty vampires in our territory. There are not a lot of us in Australia, and as you guessed, even less in the Outback."

"So what makes your mother more important than the average vampire, that this gold digger would want to latch on to her?"

"Vampires are very hierarchical. Very conscious of lineage, particularly between made and born vampires."

"I thought they were all created through a vampire biting them. At least in the storybooks. Can't say I've had much personal experience with them, except in the past couple days, and just the one at that."

She watched him set aside his plate, pick up his tea. He'd made a small fire, since it was dark, and now he nodded to the water. She shook her head. "None for me. Not right now. Some vampires are born," she continued. "Usually from a vampire and human parenting. Born vampires have a higher rank than made ones. On extremely rare occasions, a child is born of two vampires. It's happened a handful of times at most. I'm one of them."

She thought about trying to pull the comb through her hair again. God, she missed having a maid. Plus, there was a strand of russet hair in it that she'd managed to twist around one finger and she wasn't done worrying it. "On top of that, my mother was the child of two vampires. It makes me the top of the heap, with respect to bloodline, but that doesn't mean I have a tremendous amount of power or influence, unless I've proven I can wield it. My mother didn't care about that, and neither did I."

As if he could read her thoughts himself, Dev spoke them aloud. "But there are always those who do care about it. The wrong sort."

"Yes. I'm a gentle sort of vampire." An ironic smile touched her mouth, reflected in his arched brow. "Believe me, there are those who are far more brutal, who care little for human life or rights, even the lives or rights of other vampires. They believe power makes the rules. The Vampire Council, through the influence of some vampires who fortunately do not feel that way, puts a cap on the number of humans a vampire can kill." As Dev's brow furrowed, she inclined her head. "For survival purposes, a vampire needs to kill one human a year, mortally drain them. We call it the annual kill, and it's necessary to keep our blood rejuvenated, our minds sharp."

"And what's the limit?"

"A dozen." She shook her head at his expression. "Believe me, Dev, it was a miracle the number was that low. Because the purpose of that and other Council laws is not the humane treatment of humans. It's to keep vampire bloodlust in check. Your friend Elle picked up what I was, but to the majority of the human world, we're the work of fiction and nightmares. We're sensible enough to know that's best. We may be more powerful, but there are a great many more of you.

"Unfortunately," she said, her tone becoming more leaden, "infractions occur. And the Vampire Council is little different from other national governments, when it comes to Australia."

"Nobody cares what happens here," Dev murmured.

"Not exactly on our mostly European Council's travel roster," she agreed. "So, about ten years before I left, a vampire named Lord Charles Ruskin became Region Master of the Northwest Region, which, like it sounds, straddles much of the northern and western territories of Australia." Her lip curled. "He's a brutish, nasty piece of work who was part of the English aristocracy during the seventeen hundreds. He still carries the same notions of imperialism and loyalty to the mother country."

Dev snorted. "Not much different from most here. Though there are those of us who've felt differently, ever since the Poms gave us up to the Japs as part of their war strategy."

She nodded. "Lord Charles resents the fact he's been stalled as Region Master here, but the Council is smart enough to recognize a vampire that doesn't need a more powerful position. They feel like he's contained here. He and Ian became fast friends, because Ian is also ambitious and of course, Lord Charles is the most powerful vampire in this Region. I suspect Ian feels, when Lord Charles finally gets his coveted post back in Europe, that he might recommend him to take over in his stead. Unlike Charles, Ian has no problem being the large fish in a small pond."

"So you think it's Ian who sent the attack against you? I don't understand. Isn't he the overlord? Why would you be a threat to him?"

"My mother was the overlord," she reiterated. "Ian was her consort. A few months ago, my mother died. She chose to meet the sun. And no, I don't want to talk about that," she added, shifting her glance back out into the night. "Vampire Council rules dictate that when a vampire dies, his or her property and position pass first to the oldest child, if there is one, reinforcing the importance of being a born vampire. In my absence, or the event of my death, it can then go to whoever is willing to fight for it, and that of course would be Ian, who likely has his backside comfortably entrenched there."

"And there are no repercussions for him trying to kill you?"

"Not exactly." She gave up on the comb and instead ran her fingers through the mop on her head, trying to dispel the unbidden image of the times her mother had helped her dress it. Playing with different styles, woven in ribbons she knew Dev would like . . .

Let me do that.

Surprised, she looked toward him. Heavens, he was a fast learner. Rather than saying it, he'd spoken in her mind, taking her mind from her disquieting thoughts.

While she could have made him come to her, he was sitting on a rock, so it made more sense for her to rise and settle between his knees with easy grace, though he gave her a hand to lower herself. As she leaned against his leg, curling her fingers around his knee, she gave a snort.

"You just couldn't help that image, could you?"

"Well, love, when a woman kneels down in front of a man, his mind's going to go to certain things, no help for it."

"Hmmm." She returned his comb to him. "Prove your usefulness, then, and I'll overlook it."

"Here I was thinking I'd already done that," he said.

"That was then, this is now." She shrugged, but smiled as he gave her hair a sharp tug before starting to work it with the comb. "Where was I?"

"No one's going to drag this Ian off for trying to cop you on the back roads."

"No, because it wasn't entirely motivated by a desire to see me dead. If it had ended up that way, he would have been fine with it. I don't mean that, but it's also about impressing me. Vampires form alliances based on strength and sexual attraction."

"Hold up." Tilting her head back, he gazed down at her, those green eyes remarkably close. "You're saying he's as happy to bugger you as to kill you?"

"When it comes to women, most men feel that way." Her lips curved. "You've already had both thoughts. And that's in the short time since I've been able to read your mind." Because she couldn't help herself, she put her fingers against those firm lips before forcing herself to remove her touch and resolutely gaze toward the fire again, waiting for him to start.

Instead, he slid his hand along her jaw, compelling her head to twist up toward him again, only to meet his mouth as he leaned forward, pressing against her back, a different heat from the fire before her. He took his time, keeping his fingers along her cheek, making light tracings on her skin along her nose, her jaw, close to where their lips were joined. She got lost in it, a swirl of taste and scent.

She'd thought it frustrating at first, having someone who could switch off his thoughts, but in a sense, it was restful, too. As if that stillness wrapped itself around her so she could let go, float in his mind, such that when he raised his head, she found herself in a similar place, where nothing seemed to matter but this very moment.

"I think it's a little bit different, him and me," he murmured.

She was fully pressed against his inner thigh now, her other hand gripping the opposite one, the posture of a woman immersed in the sensual attentions of a man. As her fog cleared, she gave him a bemused look. "Felt you had to prove something?"

Shrugging, he sat back and studiously repositioned her to start combing her hair. Tina's hair had caressed the top of her buttocks, like Danny's when she was naked. To him, it made a woman's arse appear even more soft and vulnerable, a fragile, tempting part of her, like the nape of the neck, the small of the back.

She suppressed a shiver. "God, Dev. You could at least try to guard your thoughts."

"You wanted in. No sense in me concealing anything now, is there?"

She gritted her teeth, bracing when he hit a snarl, but relaxed when he carefully parted it, worked it out with his fingers, not causing her a moment of discomfort. Even so, she added uncharitably,

"You're determined to make me sorry for doing it. I *did* apologize for it."

"So you did. Your chagrin was overwhelming," he said dryly. "But we're back to my original question. How many more men and weapons will you need to storm your castle, take it back?"

"None." She stared forward. "He's made his attempt. He's shown his hand, and he's done now. He'll wait to see how I respond. I have a plan in mind. It would be useful to have you stick around a bit, watch my back against whatever human vermin he's got hanging about."

He kept combing. She wouldn't beg or ask twice. Since he seemed to have a tendency to think things through before he spoke, she'd give him time to sort. And she wouldn't pry into that part of his head while he did so. She wasn't sure she wanted to hear his thoughts on the matter, anyway. Instead, her mind went back to the firefight, the way he'd handled himself, and wondered if he'd handle himself as well at the station, against greater numbers.

"You were in the war," she said.

Given his age, it would have been odd for him not to have fought, unless he'd had an exemption for running his station to meet the war's supply needs. But she'd also seen scars on him other than the self-inflicted ones. Possibly bullets, or shrapnel, scattered over his torso and limbs. One rather harrowing mark, high on his thigh.

"Don't want to talk about that." His short comment had the same warning note as hers about her mother. She respected that. However, as she anticipated, it dredged up thoughts that slipped under his shielding.

Had she said there was a stillness in him? As the tranquil cloud at the surface of his mind shifted, she dropped beneath it and found herself in a maelstrom, a swamping, choking sea of emotion, riddled with blood and screams, gunfire and bombs. Images of soldiers and battles that had been savage struggles for every yard of ground. Tedium was a horror all its own. Waiting and waiting, nerves snapped to the breaking point, looking for the enemy in the jungle shadows. Constant guerrilla fighting, muddy trails where the boots sank in to the ankles.

He'd done the most dangerous scout work, taken some of his opponents out with his bare hands and a rage in his soul to kill, kill,
kill. Every confrontation fueled by the last images he had of his son
and wife. So much blood, his wife naked and torn. That beautiful
sable hair he'd brushed had been used to choke the life from her,
probably as they'd raped and beaten her to death.

The stark image was so desolate. It was the fear of every living
thing, to end life helpless and terrorized, in horrible pain . . . He
hadn't been there. He was the husband, the father, the head of the
house. It had been his responsibility to protect them or die trying.
Instead he'd been the one to dig their graves, a punishment straight
from hell. Clean and arrange their bodies, see every mark of violence, every violation.

It was all connected, one memory flowing to another in rapid
succession, just a flash through his brain she saw all at once, like a
mud slide into her consciousness. But after their deaths and before
the war, there'd been one more prong to add to the barbed wire
cinched around his heart. The murder of the men who'd done it.

He'd tracked them, nearly been killed taking them down, three
to one. Jesus, he was barely more than a kid then, but apparently the
rage of angels had fueled him, guarded his back. The scar high on his
thigh had come from that fight, not the war. He hadn't killed them
slow, the way he'd dreamed of doing, but he'd cut their lifeless bodies apart with the hatchet he still carried in his pack.

When he was done, he'd been drenched. It had been night, and
dingoes had gathered, a circle of shining eyes in the darkness, called
by the blood. But as he walked off, passed through their ranks as if
they weren't there, they shied away from him. Though he'd been
covered in blood, their animal instinct knew he was the most dangerous predator in the bush that night.

Oh, God, Dev. Perhaps the architects of human justice would say
he had no right to go after his family's murderers, but seeing the image of the two people he'd loved so much, what had been done to
them, she knew no male of any moral substance would have done
differently.

As she moved out of those images, she realized that, while he resented her taking the choice from him, he didn't really care about her being in his mind. To him, what he kept behind the gate of that stillness was a barren field. The history lingered there, but he had no expectation that it would again hold treasures or secrets worth keeping.

"I'll get you to your station, stay around a bit," he said, breaking into her thoughts. Danny realized her fingers had tightened on his knee, and he'd put his hand down on it, apparently thinking she was goading him for an answer. "It'll be your choice on whether or not we share a bed, but once you start sharing it with another, I'll be off."

She looked up into his resolute face as he continued. "I know you'll say I have no claim on you, and maybe that's true, but I don't share a woman."

He was oblivious to the dynamics of vampires, but she held her tongue. She liked the idea of him being in her bed, very much. More than she wanted to let on. But she did owe him some honesty, and gave it now. "I won't force you to serve my will, but I can't let you defy it more than once, either. It's our way. You'll learn more when we get there, and then see if you can stand it. If you can't, you'll be free to go."

Her fellow vampires would call her a young fool, but while she demanded loyalty and a certain level of obedience from the humans she claimed, she had no desire to force them to serve her against their will. Though like all vampires, she was capable of it.

"Fair enough." His hands had worked out the tangles, and it was now a smooth, silken mane again, such that she closed her eyes as he kept combing it for her pleasure, and maybe his own. Deep, easy strokes that massaged her scalp, eased some of the tension in her shoulders.

"I never knew a man's hands could feel so good doing this. I may never go back to having a maid."

"Well, my lady, as long as you don't want me to wear one of those little white caps, I reckon I can help you brush your hair. Bathe you, rub you down with those soft lotions you girls like so much . . ." As he leaned in, his breath teased the side of her throat so she tilted her chin, giving him better access. "If that's what you're looking for from a station manager. Easier than managing sheep."

His arm slipped beneath hers, and his large, capable hand cupped her breast, bearing its weight, his fingers tracing the outer curve, leaving the nipple taut, begging for attention.

He was almost as insatiable as she was. Swallowing, she increased her grip on his leg, though she had enough of a mind to avoid bruising him. For now. "It's getting close to daylight."

"Maybe I'll give you a thing or two to dream about."

"You're a very confident man, Dev."

"Out here a man's either good at the things that matter, or he's dead."

"Oh." Her lips curved and then pressed into an aroused, straight line as his lips found her throat, brushed the large artery and scored it with his teeth so that her grip went beyond consideration into demand. Now he had both arms around her, his thumbs making a single, too brief pass over her nipples. In another moment she was going to shred his shirtfront and sling him to his back, mount him in a single movement and ride them both into near unconsciousness. She didn't want to rush it, and the fact she could, but fought her own desire to do so, only spiked it, as if the sun were burning inside her, immolating her vital organs.

"And what use is this particular skill . . . out here? Thought you said . . . only the roos gave you affectionate glances."

"An unsatisfied roo is a deadly creature, love."

She snorted on the unexpected laugh. "You dill."

But then the amusement died out of her as he turned her in his arms and she looked up in his face. Kneeling between his knees, with both of his hands now cupping her face, she was conscious of what a searingly sweet, romantic position it was. The expression in his eyes was tender and thoughtful, the poignant pain of his past and his desire for her in the present combining in a way that held her.

So many had cast a careless, distasteful eye over the landscape beyond this cave, seeing a few shrubs and craggy-armed trees, the blistering sun that could boil the unprepared traveler to death within a couple days. But she'd always looked at it and seen why it was said that God had created Australia as a unique gem, something that couldn't be found anywhere else. There was always far more than could be seen on one glance, or even a thousand. And so it was, looking into Dev's face.

She'd never been in love. It was such a startling thought, she almost pulled away from him, but she stopped herself, falling back onto a vampire's innate ability to mask deep emotion or reactions. She certainly wouldn't fall in love with a human. No sensible vampire would. Or was it that no sensible vampire would admit it?

Maybe she was an odd vampire. Or maybe she was normal. Vampires didn't talk about such things among themselves. Maybe that's why they had humans, to give themselves permission for vulnerability, since humans weren't a threat the way their own kind were.

Like how humans loved a pet, she thought, gaining confidence with the analogy. They believed they'd do anything for their beloved mutt, but if the human was trying to get out of a burning house, and the dog was trapped in a back room, the undeniable survival instinct would kick in, claim superior value. That human would cry bitter tears over her dog's loss, agonize over the creature's inevitable pain and fear in those final moments, but she'd save her own skin. No one else would castigate her for it, as they would if she left a human the same way.

Well, that was a pretty crook thought. Maybe others wouldn't castigate her, but what if her conscience knew the pet was a far nobler creature than the faithless master? God, she was out of her element here. Best to be straight up about the things she *did* know.

"I can't love you, Dev," she said, more harshly than she intended. "You can't hope for that." Her voice faltered, though, as his mouth hovered a few inches above her lips, which were already parted, not only with the words, but her eager need.

His green eyes never left hers, but his thumb swept her temple, a gentle reproof. "That's all right, love. I can't love you, either. You'll have what I can offer, though. I won't hold back on any of it, as long as I'm with you."

Her eyes closed, accepting that as the heat of his mouth closed over hers. Circling his neck with her arms, she rose on her knees as he slid down and met her, bearing her back to the cave floor, his weight pressing into every curve of her body with lean, sun-toughened skin and corded muscle. His mouth took over her tongue and lips, making her body strain up against him, her legs rising to clasp his hips. A sound between a growl and a plea clogged the back of her throat as his enormous cock pressed between her legs, a promise indeed of what he could give to her. Her core was already aching for that sweet split between pleasure and penetrating pain.

Indulging herself, she pushed his open shirt off his broad shoulders. She liked his aborigine tendency to wear clothes as a second thought only, at least his shirt. His heat burned beneath her fingertips, the dampness of his nape, the brush of his abdomen. A silken spear of hair arrowed down it, the mink pelt of an animal against her own hairless body. As if matching the direction of her own thoughts, his fingers, having opened her trousers and now playing inside them, smoothed over her mound, the crease of her thigh. "This isn't shaved, is it, love?"

His voice was husky, filled with lust in that rough, male way that made her tremble and be glad she was female, able to enjoy the benefits of it.

She shook her head. "Vampires only have hair above the throat."

"It makes your skin so smooth . . ." He got the trousers and knickers off her so he could continue tracing her with his fingers. A feathery touch slid along her inner thigh now, down toward her knee, then drifted back up. Shifting onto an elbow, he leaned over one of her thighs, pinning it there as he eased the other one outward. His eyes glowed with green fire once he'd settled his gaze fully on what he'd spread open before him. She watched, somewhat discomfited by his piercing regard, but unwilling to admit it and be anything but the sophisticate she was supposed to be before this uncultured bushman. She couldn't even imagine him as the bookish Oxford scholar right now. He looked far readier to ravish her body, take over her senses and then leap up and fight off an army than settle down with sonnets.

Bending, he pressed his lips to her inner thigh, so close his cheekbone brushed her vulva, making her hips twitch, jerk. He turned his head, slowly nuzzling her, inhaling right up against her flesh. Closing his mouth over the entire area, from clit to the perineum, he pushed her legs wider to accommodate him. His tongue made a long, thorough lick that managed to penetrate and sweep between the lips, finishing with a light swirl up over the clit.

Young vampires, those under fifty, never had carnal relations with a human without another vampire present. It was a protection for the human. Not only to keep from sucking him dry during hungry passion, but to avoid the possibility of cracking the spine with the force of desire. She had to remind herself of that now, forcefully, as her leg lifted to clamp around his back. Instead, he caught it, guiding it back down, a gentle pressure, but one that fired her inclination to possess, dominate, control. She had to close her hands into fists to quell that. When he took one, drawing it down to his mouth, raising his head enough to kiss the white knuckles, he spread the fingers out the way he'd spread her legs. She speared them through his hair, tangling in the red mane, finding the tendons at the back of his neck and gripping him there with bruising pressure despite her struggle with herself. Catching her wrist, he lifted his gaze to hers.

"Don't force me, love, and I promise you won't regret it. I'll make it that much better. Let me savor you."

She nodded, a quick jerk. Releasing him, she put her palms back at her sides, dug her fingers into the rock and gave herself over to his mouth.

Holy God, what a mouth. He knew the way to dance his tongue over a woman's clit, how to ease his fingers inside her, curving them forward in that lovely come-hither motion that sparked the sensitive place inside her. In no time, her hips were lifting to his mouth in an insistent rhythm, her head beginning to toss from side to side, making a tangled mess he'd have to work out for her again.

God, here she was, the least ambitious vampire in the world, intending to reclaim her station, put her mother's consort in his place, and then address the problem of a Region Master who'd overstepped Council rules. Even though she'd be far happier living in this cave for a while, enjoying the adventure of learning how he lived out here, letting him take care of her needs as they made love and explored the desert in the night . . .

Stop thinking. Just . . . feel. His hand slid up to her thighs, her hips, and then he was lifting his body over hers, his mouth glistening with her arousal.

Yes. Now.

This was the far more gratifying side to the second mark she could offer, the way the mind could express emotions far more vividly than vocal cords. His cock responded with an impressive flex, pressed against her. As she bathed herself in his flood of need, possession and hunger, she merged it with her own. *It can be a curse, Dev, but it can also be this.*

The dew-kissed petals of the rose are said to be red from the blood drawn by its thorns.

Warrior poet. As she pulled him down to her with insistent hands, he pushed into her, his gentleness a different devastation from the previous times. While she was all wet heat, God, was he huge. She let out a guttural cry as he worked his way in, laying a path of caresses along her throat with his mouth, then down to her sternum. When he cupped her breasts together and began to tease the nipples, suckling her, remembering how he'd drawn water from them, that image softened her muscles.

She arched with a moan and he expertly used the undulation to slide all the way in. Her body clenched down on him at once, welcoming him. He'd pushed his trousers to his ankles, as if knowing she had no patience to wait for him to remove his boots, and it stimulated her further, seeing the masculine boots, his heels pushing against the heavy rock he'd been sitting upon, using it to add force to his thrusts as she locked her legs over his bare buttocks. When her fingers dug into his shoulders, those self-inflicted scars of grief on his chest were a sweet friction as he moved against her, seeking, needing. Incredibly, his size increased, pushing into pain, making impending release ruthless, inevitable.

While her body prepared itself, her clit hardening, her vision narrowed to his rugged, handsome face. He wasn't pretty. It was like looking at Ayer's Rock, that incredible sandstone monument rising mysteriously out of the Western desert. Only ten percent of its actual face showed, so much of what it was still below the surface. But on that face, time had sculpted its map, its beauty in its mystery, unable to be captured by words. The meaning of the universe lay in it. She'd been in the city so long, she'd almost forgotten that the Outback offered that. Until she looked up in his face and saw it there.

"Come for me, bushman," she urged. She pierced him with her nails, drawing blood, reminding her of other hungers he could sate. As she clamped down on him with her wholly female muscles, she reared up, brought her mouth to his throat. At the same moment, as if anticipating her, he tilted his head, averting his chin. He offered to her, even as she had the need.

God, he would be a perfect full servant.

The astounding thought pushed her over the pinnacle, making her scream out her release even as she pierced him with her fangs. His blood and seed filled her at once, an ecstasy she couldn't deny herself.

Even as she knew she'd be left only wanting more.

8

W HEN she woke, it was midday. Uneasiness had roused her at the unexpected time. He was gone, along with his pack of loose belongings. She saw he'd left her some water in the billy to wash up, as well as the swag on which she'd fallen asleep at dawn, curled comfortably across his body. Her body was apparently still rejuvenating, because she hadn't felt him slide out from beneath her. He'd left her clothes in easy reach.

Because she was disoriented, for an instant she forgot about the second mark, instead immersed in a painful ripple of betrayal, which was followed closely by anger.

Idiot. Find him. She shook her head at herself. Reaching out with her senses, she did locate him, about five miles away, which wasn't exactly reassuring. She tried to sound calm, relaxed. *Dev? Haven't run off and left me, have you?*

A sense of a start, a grunt. *Christ, that takes some getting used to. Like having you pop up right behind me in the middle of a piss.*

That isn't what I interrupted, was it? She pressed her lips against a smile, suppressing her relief at his relaxed tone, then wondered why she was restraining herself when there was no one to see.

No, but would have served you right if you'd interrupted something worse. I found us some transportation. I couldn't fix the bike, but I used a couple of its parts to get this dinosaur running. Another grunt, a muttered curse. He was working hard at something. Through his mind, she picked up that he'd found an old ute, one that had apparently bogged in what was now a claypan. The owners hadn't yet returned to claim it. At first he thought it'd been the old bomb of a group of aborigines and they'd figured it was easier to move on without it, but it was odd, the amount of supplies left, including partially full petrol and water tanks wired into the bed. He was digging a giant hole in front of it.

The second mark could give her some impressions of physical condition, though not as deeply as the third mark. He'd very nearly worn himself out in the hundred-plus heat, so it seemed to her.

What are you doing? Are you drinking enough water?

His patronizing chuckle rankled her, though it didn't dispel her curiosity. *Don't worry about me, love. Though, strewth, if I had any sense, I'd be doing this after dark, instead of when the Devil's out trying to cook my brain. But I've got a demanding boss who has places to be.*

"Doesn't do me much good if you have a stroke. Why are you digging that big hole?"

Tire anchor. Winch didn't work on its own. Sand was too soft. You have to bury the spare tire about five feet down, then attach the winch line. That should pull it out where the ground anchor couldn't, if I can jack up the back wheels enough to get enough rough stuff beneath them. She heard another inventive curse. *Don't know why the owners didn't try it themselves, because they had all this in the cab. Then again, we're on the edges of your territory, love.*

She could tell he regretted letting her have that thought, but her senses sharpened. *You're seeing something.*

Yeah. Looks like a pack of animals attacked, but the human kind. I see footprints. Small ones. Kids. The driver may have had kids. There was a tightness to his voice. *No remains. Just a bad feeling to it.*

Uneasiness rippled through her. *How much longer will you be there?*

When I get it free or decide to hell with it.

"Dev, get back here before night falls." She said it aloud, the emphasis intentional. She sensed him stilling, cueing in to her reaction.

You know something?

No, she responded. Technically an honest statement. *Just a bad feeling, like you said. I'd rather have you close.*

No worries, love. I'll hurry.

From his tone, he thought she was worried for herself. He thought like a man, protective of a woman. She rather liked that about him, and in this instance, she was fine with him making that assumption. Because she was also certain he was male enough to ignore her if he realized her concern was for *him*.

~

Dev did make it back right before sunset, which was good, because she intended to go after him, take a strip of his hide for worrying her. Hearing the welcome rumble of the engine, she cautiously approached the cave mouth, shielding herself from the sun's lingering rays while watching the dust trail behind the old bush bomb. It had seen better days, but he'd fixed it. God, the man was able to unbog a vehicle by himself through patience, sheer muscle and will, and hotwire it to boot . . .

Despite the fact she'd had a few hours to lecture herself on not getting too carried away with the idea of him being her full servant, so far he'd proven himself more than capable of it out here. He knew the Outback, as well as how to manage and operate a station, apparently having vacillated between homestead owner, stockman and swagman enough during his lifetime to learn the skills of all three. Another benefit of the second mark was the ability to plumb a man's capabilities with a quick search, though in truth, she'd been able to pick it up from what she knew of him so far. He'd never make more of his skills than they were. In fact, much like his skill with the whip, he'd more likely underplay them.

He was also a war veteran who'd killed a man in her defense. There hadn't been even a flicker of hesitation in his eyes when he planted his dagger between her attacker's shoulder blades.

A silly man who spoke poetry and had hot flashes of temper sprinkled with distracting moments of vulnerability. A decent man who could be counted upon, a rarity in any world, in any society she'd experienced.

Pushing that away, she focused on the present. He'd left the vehicle where it could be seen directly from the cave, and disappeared under the lip of rock.

While today wasn't even the hottest she knew it could get out here, a temperature over a hundred was going to have an effect on the human body. Therefore, when he made it to the cave mouth, she was already moving to meet him. He stumbled when he hit a bump of rock across the threshold. Though she was ten feet away, it was nothing for a vampire to cross in a blink and catch him, hold him up. "About time you dragged your sorry carcass back here," she said.

"Well, you know I had to stop and shout a round at the local pub," he managed, though he let her ease him down to the cool rock.

"And didn't even bring me a cold one, you piker," she returned in true bushman style, winning a tired grin.

"You find a place round here that can afford to keep their beer cold, love, I'll gladly hike out another five miles for it."

"Shh," she said firmly. "Enough." Using the soaked rag, she pressed it to his neck first, then began working her way across his bare chest.

"I'm fine, love, really. But that feels good. Don't stop. Just completely knackered."

Worried, she worked the cloth over his chest, the raised scars, then down his belly, sweeping his ribs, up under his armpits. His eyes were already falling shut, but when she took it up to his brow again, his mouth tilted in a sleepy smile as he turned and kissed her wrist.

Vampires possessed highly sensitive erogenous zones in the same areas where they ironically were most likely to bite their prey. Even in his current state, he had the ability to arouse her. Fortunately, he'd dozed off. But his hand had moved, curling over her arm near the elbow, his head pressed into her hand holding the cloth, lips resting against her wrist.

"Good man," she murmured, finding herself reluctant to move yet. Glancing up, she saw she was in a position to watch the sunset without being burned by it. As it was off to the left, she couldn't see the orb itself, only the panorama of colors it flung against the sky. Red and gold, violet and pink. Opening up her mind to the sleeping Dev, she gave him the beauty of it to soothe his exhaustion into deeper sleep.

When she'd been younger, long before her father had been killed, she hadn't been sure whether she liked living in the Outback. There seemed to be so much space, and the sunlight was fierce, and frightening. Then one day, her mother took her into a room where they could be out of the sun's direct light, like this, but she could still see the full tapestry of a sunset. There'd been nothing in its way, for it was the side of the house that didn't face the mountains. Just the clear, flat expanse of the bush, the occasional tree or hump of scrub. And the sky and the colors were so immense . . . so . . .

It makes you feel like nothing, which at times can be the most comforting feeling in the world.

He'd opened his eyes. She'd let her thoughts as well as her vision fill his head, so now she closed the connection, softly, as she might a favored book, and looked down at him. "I told my mother our land had reached out and marked me, as surely as we bind others to us with our blood."

"Is that how you do it? The third time? The servant drinks from you?"

The air stilled between them as she saw his gaze move over her throat, considering. It was as heavy and momentous as the artistry spread beyond the cave entrance. His fingers were stroking her arm, absent movements that rippled all the way to her toes.

Then his stomach gurgled at her. The dangerous moment passed, the question left unanswered, for both of them. Danny laid a hand on his abdomen. "Why don't I put together something from the tucker you're carrying? I'm not a bad cook."

That surprised him, she could tell. "Why would a vampire cook?"

Rising, she went to the pack, began to rummage. "You can savor food without eating it. You focus on the smell, appearance . . .

texture. You can enjoy just the taste, letting it rest on your tongue, swirl it in your mouth like wine. It's a very satisfying experience." Giving him a sidelong glance, she added, "I love to watch a man cook for me. The way his hands move over the food, creating something tempting to all the senses, not merely weight for his gullet. It's very . . . stimulating."

He snorted, pulling himself into a sitting position, bending his knees and linking dirty hands over them. "Well, I got a ton of metal out of the muck for you, love. I'm a bit jagged out. I'll amaze you with my culinary talents another day. Don't want to overwhelm you all at once, after all. But I might be able to handle the stimulating part."

She tossed him a reproving look. "You keep letting your cock do your thinking, it's going to kill you. You stay there and rest."

He smiled again. "You're a tease, love. Don't think I don't know it." Then he sobered. "Once I eat, we should get on our way. We can make it to your place by sunrise if we don't run into any other problems."

"Like the vehicle dying?"

He shook his head. "It's old, but it's a Studie. It's got some heart, though it'll likely rattle our teeth loose over this terrain."

Though she wished she had enough experience driving off road to offer to take the wheel, give him more of a rest, she nodded. Instead she put her effort into reviving their small fire, now that night had descended, using the kindling he'd thoughtfully collected. With his intrigued direction, she used his odd assortment of stores, including tubers, bark and flowers he'd picked up on today's travails, to make a passable meal with his dried meat.

When at last she brought him the plate, Danny had a strong desire to feed him with her own fingers, but suspected that might lead her into selfish temptation to do more than that. He was so tantalizing, she couldn't help herself. Curbing the impulse, she handed him the plate, taking a seat on the nearby rock. "What happened to your station?" she asked instead. "The one you had before the war."

She wasn't sure if it was a painful topic, so his shrug was a relief as he began to work on the food slowly, building fuel again. "When I joined the militia headed for New Guinea in '42, I gave the place to a mate of mine. Tom. Him and his family."

"I suppose you got a good price for it. Pretty land up in Queensland."

"You've been prying, love. But not deep enough. I didn't sell it. I gave it to him." At her startled look, he shrugged again. "He needed it, I didn't. Tom does right by it. He knows the business. Plus . . ."

Dev put down the tuber that had cooked up with a sweet yam smell, wiped his fingers on his trouser leg. "Well, he watches over them for me, Tina and Rob. I told him Tina's favorite wildflowers, so he could bring them to her stone when the wet grows them. After I signed up for the regular army, he wrote and told me he put a swing out near there for his kids. So Rob would have friends. Tina would have liked that. My word, she loved to watch that kid. Sometimes I'd come up on her, just watching him grow. She'd forget what she was doing entirely. Once I even had to scold her, because she forgot to cover up the grain bin. Got distracted playing with him, and the chickens got all in it. He was such a strong little chap, a fierce fella."

He stared at the plate. "Sounds crook, but I'm glad she died with him. She wouldn't have survived losing him like that."

"I don't think you survived it," she observed softly. At his look, she added, "That man is gone, isn't he? You're never going back."

"Well, my favorite chair has the shape of Tom's bum now, instead of mine. No point." He extended the plate to her. "Thanks for the meal, love. If you get our camp cleaned up, I'll give that old ute one last check and load us up."

～

As they trundled along in the darkness, Dev keeping his gaze focused on the terrain they were covering, Danny gave him more details of what lay ahead.

"Ian won't deny he was behind the attack," she explained. "If anything, he'll cheerfully admit to it, ask if I was impressed. All the while plotting how he'll have me staked by the end of the evening, either literally or in a far more carnal manner." At his startled look, she waved a hand. "He'll provide us dinner first."

"Oh, well, since you put it that way, no worries. And what should I be doing?"

"Keeping your eyes and ears open. He'll have a human staff, and most of his stockmen likely do double duty as his thugs." Putting out a hand to make him bring the ute to a stop, she drew his full attention. "If his intent is to stake me, rather than work out our differences another way, and he manages it, you are released from any other responsibility to me. Vengeance, while a sentimental and appreciated notion, is entirely foolish and unnecessary in this case. For one thing, there's no need for you to get involved in our bloody politics. As much as you know about me, I could be as bad as any of the lot. So don't sacrifice yourself."

When he would have spoken, she held up that hand. "For another, you won't have any chance, fighting against a vampire and his mob. In vampire fights, humans are nothing. And that's not the good kind of 'nothing,' like sunsets. More like the way aborigines used to be viewed by settlers."

"Hmmm." He gave that noncommittal grunt that was changing Danny's opinion of his ancestry. She suspected he had some Scot mixed with aboriginal and Irish blood, for that grunt held a wealth of meaning, none of it satisfying her as an agreement. "You old enough to remember that, love?"

"Yes." The blacks had been hunted like vermin, a nuisance. Some of the settlers, those who hadn't wanted to waste ammunition, had offered damper to traveling groups of aborigines as an apparent kindness. A gift infused with poison, like baiting traps for rats. Yes, being "nothing" in this country also had its downside. She knew that firsthand, because she was about to be back among the sort who took great advantage of it.

~

She said little else on the drive through the darkness, though she didn't hesitate to use her exceptional senses to warn him of unexpected animal crossings, the signs of deep sand or other things he'd see, but only a precious few seconds later. He suspected she'd make a hell of a tracker, what with her superior eyesight and speed. Of course, vampires being predators, he likely wouldn't want to know how she employed the skills.

She hadn't yet told him how old she was, but he found her short answer to his question fascinating, because it was obvious she could speak to things directly that were unfortunate historical facts to him, or things his grandparents had told him,

However, it was unlike her to be so silent. He didn't think her increasing pensiveness was due to somber reflection on the tragedies of the past. She wasn't a female chatterbox, but he was used to her dry wit, catty observations and the occasional question. As he glanced over, he noted her stillness was becoming predatory again, the way her head turned, the glitter of her gaze in the semidarkness like a waiting croc. It had him inventorying the weaponry he had, and figuring how much could be worn to dinner without offending their bloodsucking host.

"We're about fifteen minutes from the house now," she said, pointing to a stand of eucalyptus, a post marker. "Do you remember all I told you?"

"Yeah. When we get out of the car, I give this Ian a smart thump in the teeth."

"Dev."

He waved a hand. "I cover humans, you handle vampires."

"Follow my lead," she added. The darkness had turned the blue of her eyes black. "While you're not my servant, you're in my employ and marked twice. They'll expect you to defer to me as such. If you don't, it will undermine my authority. That's a perception we don't want them to have."

He inclined his head. "Understood. I can tug my forelock and 'marm' with the best of them."

"If only it were that easy," she muttered. At his askance look, she shook her head. "Just follow my lead," she repeated.

A couple miles from the property, Dev stopped the vehicle for the last time. He holstered his pistol, put his rifle within reach so he could feed it down his back sling when he got out. His full complement of knives was already firmly strapped at his ankle, thigh, waist and back as well. Danny said little, watching him adjust the weaponry, then asked his assistance to check her own unique arsenal.

Before they'd started off, she'd used their water and cloth to scrub her face, and he'd helped comb her hair and French braid it. She'd worn a wrinkled but clean T-shirt from his pack, tucked into her belted daks. Those were filthy, but her bearing pulled them off as merely a trifling inconvenience. He inclined his head. "You'll do. You look fine."

"Not that we have one handy, but my inability to look in a mirror is unbearably irritating."

Despite himself, he grinned. "Well, next to me, love, you look as if you could go to tea with the Queen."

"You're supposed to look scruffy and dangerous," she informed him.

"Scruffy is hardly intimidating."

"It is, if it implies an overbearing stench."

He gave her a narrow glance, but put the vehicle in gear. A few minutes later, they pulled through the pole fence surrounding her childhood home, which backed up to the dark shadow of low hills. It was a good setting for a sheep station in a country that ran more to cattle. Dev stopped a moment, letting the engine idle. It was a nice-sized home, a two-story wood frame with a wraparound porch, secure weatherboard and corrugated iron roof. There was a handful of outbuildings that he identified as a couple bunkhouses for unmarried stockmen, a cottage or two for a foreman or married blokes. A stable, sheep-shearing shed and storage for equipment. It also had a diesel engine, likely for powering the generator for the house and well pump as needed. A windmill.

However, it was the house that reclaimed his attention. Though it was silhouetted in darkness, it appeared that the rear half of the home was embedded into the hills that folded back into the low mountain range behind it.

"That's where the bedrooms are," Danny explained at his intrigued look. "A study and alternative parlor. It works wonderfully for vampires."

As they drew closer, the skeletal remains of what used to be watered perennials lined a front walkway, made up of crushed shards of termite mounds. Unkempt, tougher scrub would close in on them in no time. Dev noted Danny's eyes touching upon those dried-out plants. He didn't need access into her thoughts to recognize lingering evidence of her mother's presence in what was obviously now an all-male domain.

There were men standing on the porch, as well as in front of the bunkhouse. In the open doorway of the barn, two more men stood, watching their approach. One had a cut on his eye. The other looked as if he'd recently been burned.

"Two of my attackers apparently made it away before we got them," she noted. "I'm surprised they're still alive, if they came back without proof that they'd done their job. God, I wish there'd been somewhere for us to stop to clean up."

He found it remarkable that was her primary concern. He'd noted three other men who'd come out of the stockmen's quarters, giving them the same unfriendly once-over, as those two from the barn started to make their way to the porch. He also suspected there were reinforcements hidden elsewhere in the buildings. Five Rovers in excellent condition were pulled up front, suggesting Ian had additional visitors.

"How many vampires did you say are in your territory?" he asked.

She shrugged. "Probably about twenty. In all of Australia, there are less than two hundred, and like the humans, most live in the cities on the coast. There's only about five thousand in the whole world. That we know of," she added.

A pack of dogs had come out of the shadows and were milling, yipping. Danny, unconcerned, started to get out of the vehicle, when Dev put a hand on her arm. "Why don't I get the door for you?"

She blinked. "Guess I need a reminder about appearing all uppity, don't I?"

He offered her a smile, because in that brief moment, the mask of calm slipped, and he saw some of her nerves. "I'm here, love. Least if we get torn to pieces, we'll have each other for company."

"A comfort," she said dryly, and gave him a steady look. "Dev, whatever else happens tonight, whatever I have to say or do, however I make you feel, I want to say thank you. You've been a true friend these past few days, and I've met precious little of them in my life, vampire or human."

He nodded, meeting her eyes in a perfect understanding, for at least that moment. Then he opened his door. Whatever was going to happen tonight, she apparently expected him to be so horrified by the end of it that he'd need what he suspected was a high compliment. For her kind.

When he offered her a hand out of the ute, she took it. He made sure his grip was strong, steady. He had a fleeting sense she wanted to hold on, but she released him at the proper moment, stepping away from him.

Stay about two or three paces behind me, Dev. It's not a protection issue.

The front door opened, and a man stepped on the porch. Even without the slight stiffening of Danny's shoulders, Dev would have known it was Ian. He hadn't really been giving it much thought, but now he realized one thing about the lore of vampires was true. They were all beautiful. Dev's tastes didn't run toward men at all, but he had to acknowledge the man would earn the stares of either sex. His hair was sleek as a show horse's mane, and lying on broad shoulders. A trim coat with open-necked shirt beneath, along with polished riding breeches tucked into boots, gave him that careless lord-of-the-manor look, which Dev suspected was intentional. The eyes he fixed on Danny's were green, like Dev's, but Ian's were as brilliant as the verdant farmland outside Victoria. No blemishes or scars, no lines of age. He looked like a young man of twenty-five, though from Danny, Dev knew he was looking at a vampire more than four hundred years old.

But despite that, there was something off about him, flash as a rat with a gold tooth. Danny flicked her gaze at the two stockmen from the barn who'd joined the men on the porch. Picking up her cue without even a thought to back it up, Dev hooked a hand on his belt, his smallest finger resting with import along the pistol. He kept his eyes moving among all of them, and of course they were studying him as intently, gauging his mettle. He recognized the coil in his belly as anticipation. A fight had long ago lost the ability to make him nervous, and odds didn't worry him that much. However, it had been a while since it meant more than the opportunity for violence. Now he was mindful of his responsibility to protect and serve the lovely blonde ahead of him. While he logically knew she wasn't threatened by these thugs, the natural compulsion to keep himself between her and the line of fire was strong, despite her command that he stay back.

Steady, Dev. A soft whisper in his head. "Your men need further instruction on how to take out a vampire, Ian," Danny said coldly. "You inconvenienced me greatly on this trip home."

Ian shrugged. "If I inconvenienced you, then perhaps I also managed to impress you a little bit. Can't blame a man for trying."

Danny studied him, her face impassive. "Your grieving period is short. Not that I'm surprised."

Smiling like a benevolent angel, Ian moved to the bottom step. His well-manicured hand curled around the post, the other lying on his thigh, drawing attention to the well-muscled column held in the snug stretch of fabric, the curve of groin. With one booted foot on a lower step, it was an attractive pose, an obvious display of what he might have to offer her.

In contrast, she hadn't had a full bath in a couple days. Wore a man's shirt—Dev's shirt—tucked into her dusty trousers. Yet dirt couldn't mar the fineness of her features, the direct courage of her gaze. The way she held her shoulders back. Pure class she was, up one side and down the other. No matter what she said about the pretensions of nobility when it came to vampires, Dev thought it was obvious she was aristocracy, the man before her little better than a gigolo, hoping to scheme or ingratiate himself to achieve what she would acquire by right.

Ian kept himself on that bottom step, towering over her, which would force her to continue to look up or come to him. Which, whether he realized it or not, made him appear that much pettier.

"If you remember," he said at last, "I offered you a place at my side, while she lived. I was willing to cast her aside for you. It was you who walked away."

Danny's expression remained unreadable, cool. "I don't try to take another woman's possession. Nor do I care for her leavings."

His lips tightened, a flash of anger. But Danny turned, unconcerned, toward Dev. "Bring our few things inside. My bedroom is on the second floor, last room on the right. Instruct the servants to draw me a bath, and notify me when it's ready. I'll be in the parlor." Turning back after a brief eye contact, she added, "I would enjoy taking tea, Ian. Is there any to be had in this nest of testosterone?"

"I can certainly provide you tea, my lady," he said. While the anger was gone, there was a new note to his voice. Challenge. "But my servant, Chiyoko, has that room—"

"She will remove herself from it. Now." Danny did not move, but her frigid tone caused an uneasy shifting on the porch. "It was my mother's room. As mistress of this house, it's now mine. I question what you have become if you are allowing a human to claim a vampire's status."

"You needn't stoop to petty insults, Danny." Ian's expression was masklike, the genial smile strained enough that Dev was reminded of a dog on the verge of snarling. "She only stayed there to be available to my needs in the suite next door. We didn't expect you so soon. I have already told Chiyoko to vacate the room."

"I wish it thoroughly cleaned during dinner, Dev," Danny said. "Please see the housekeeping staff about that as well."

"My lady," Dev murmured.

"You are determined to make this unpleasant, aren't you?" Ian eyed her. "And while I'm entertaining guests. Your timing couldn't be worse."

"What guests am *I* entertaining, Ian? What other vermin do you have sullying my carpet?"

His lips stretched in an unpleasant smile, his eyes glinting in anticipation. "Our Region Master, Lord Charles. I believe you've met him? He's joined us for the weekend for some fox hunting, his favorite pastime."

"While Lord Charles and I do not see eye to eye, I am certainly honored that he has chosen to visit my home." She visibly relaxed, cocked her head. "Perhaps your standing in the world has improved since I saw you last. Is it deserved, or have you learned to play your underhanded games that much better?"

"Perhaps you will find out at dinner." Ian managed to cover the flash of surprise passably well, though Dev caught it. In a less belligerent tone, the vampire added, "You will honor us with your company, I hope? I would suffer even a venomous tongue for the pleasure of looking at you."

"A nice touch of charm. You've always had that. Very well." She shrugged. "I will join you for dinner. If you come down here and welcome me properly, rather than standing up there like a gorilla in a tree, about to beat his chest."

Ian's lip lifted in a sneer, and then he was directly before Danny. It was a movement so rapid, Dev hadn't seen him leave the step. Whereas Danny hadn't so much as twitched. When Ian stood before her, only several inches between them, she tilted her head back to study his perfect face, eyes roving over his high brow, the straight nose and firm lips. His challenging look became more speculative as she took her time about it. His hand closed over hers at her side, lifted it toward his mouth. Since they stood so close, his knuckles brushed her sternum, the curve of her breast, before he brought the fingers to his lips, lingering over them, even giving her a little nip with a fang, though he didn't break the skin.

She raised a brow, pressing her lips together, moistening them. "I'm no longer a child, Ian," she murmured. "Forty years have taught me many things."

Dev pushed down the simmer of irritation. She'd said that vampires played games with one another. She had to figure out how to outmaneuver him, get him to leave her property. To do that, she might have to cozy up to him some. It didn't mean Dev had to like it. In fact, he was quite certain he was revolted by it. The Region Master's visit seemed to be unexpected, and though her reaction appeared neutral, he suspected the chess pieces were scrambling in her busy little brain.

He missed that cave.

"I look forward to learning what those things are. Your mother found me a willing pupil. Perhaps in time you will consider me the same." His jaw hardened. "But I'm not a fool, Danny. Don't take me for one."

"I don't take you at all, Ian. Not yet." She extricated her hand in a smooth slither. "Since this is my home now, I suspect you need to prove to *me* it's worth my while to keep you around. Or kill me. Though I'd prefer you wait on that until after I've had a nice bath."

Moving around him, she nodded to Dev, then proceeded up the stairs without so much as a dismissive glance at the other men, making it clear she didn't consider any of them a threat of consequence. "I hope you haven't disposed of my mother's clothes. I'd like to select something suitable to wear for dinner."

Dev noted not a one of them, even Ian, could keep his eyes off the curve of her perfect backside, the pendulum sway as she gracefully ascended, letting her slim fingers slide along the wood railing. When she reached the front screen door, she gave the man closest to it a significant glance. He jumped to open it, tipping his hat. It was one of the men who'd tried to kill her. An ironic smile twisting her lips, she swept inside.

Though Ian had enjoyed the view, cold calculation took over when he turned to face Dev. While he'd love to plug him full of holes right here, Danny had said decapitation, burning or staking were better methods.

He was sure he could find a match somewhere.

"You are Lady Daniela's servant?"

"No," Dev replied. "She hired me." He steeled himself to immobility as Ian drew closer, far closer than most men would stand to another male. His nostrils flared as he inhaled.

"That may be. But she has marked you. In multiple ways." The words were spoken in a feral, suggestive manner that had Dev's hackles rising. "Interesting. There were times I thought her cunt was a block of solid ice. Apparently you know the rare art of ice fishing."

When Dev locked eyes with the vampire, the men on the porch shifted, muttered, a warning. Ian's gaze frosted. "I've no chance of holding my own against you," Dev said. "But each time you insult her, one of your men dies. Good stockmen are hard to find."

Ian's lips lifted in a fang-baring sneer. "You've got Buckley's of outdrawing—"

The fire of the pistol was loud in the echoing dome of the night, a sound that would carry for miles, make the heads of night creatures jerk up, looking for danger.

He managed two quick shots, but almost as the second one left the chamber, Ian shoved him back five feet, slamming him against the old ute with bone-crushing force. His arm compressed Dev's throat, cutting off breath. Only the sound of two heavy thumps on the porch saved the windpipe. The vampire's head whipped around, in time to see two men drop to the porch boards, the pair who'd been part of the aborted attempt on Danny's life.

"You said one, human."

"Well, they botched their job," Dev rasped. "So I figure you'd consider them the same value as one." Plus, he knew he was saving Danny time and effort later.

Ian's lips curved in an unexpected, cold smile. "You've no fear in you. That's unusual. What if I sank my fangs into you, tasted the blood-of-the-moment Lady Danny seems to fancy?"

Dev got one finger on his knife but that was all. He was thrown face forward into the dirt, the vampire's boot on the back of his neck, the other pressed hard on the small of his back. "All I have to do is lean, and your cracked back will turn you into a helpless crab. I could order every man here to bugger you while you lie like this. You'd die long after you wished you were dead, and at dawn I'd have you tossed outside the gate for the dingoes to finish off." He stepped back and spat, the saliva striking near Dev's face. "Don't you *ever* look me in the eye again."

"Ian." Danny's voice came from inside the screen, and though Ian's tone had been cold, hers was arctic. "I've not given you leave to take up a grievance with my employee. You have a problem, you address it with me."

Ian muttered an oath, but left Dev with a short kick that effortlessly flipped him over onto his back.

Red rage clouding his vision, Dev had his hand back on the knife, ready to stick it into the arrogant bastard's hamstring while he was distracted.

Easy, Dev. The thought was a sharp command, sharp enough to stop him. *This is the way the game is played. Believe me, at this point, it's all fun and games.*

His fat aunt. He didn't hear any indication in her thoughts that *she* considered this fun and games. However, he cleared his anger enough to note the other hands were pressing close, bodies ready for violence. Neither one of them had a friend here. Except each other.

He looked up toward her, met her eyes. *I'll race you back to that cave. Last one there has to wet the billy.*

Her delicate nostrils flared and she glanced toward the fallen men. "I want to taste the blood of those who tried to kill me. Tell the kitchen staff to draw me some of it. Dev, supervise that personally. I like to know my blood is clean." Her gaze came back to him. "Bring it up to my room. I think I'd rather take my tea up there, with my bath, Ian. Before I can be polite company, I need to wash off this filth."

With that, she turned and disappeared in the recesses of the house.

9

ONCE he'd gone to a fair where they had a tent show with a rotating stage. Each scene in the rotation was different, as if the audience sat outside the Wheel of Time, watching its progress. He had that same kind of rotating stage in his mind.

One scene was sunlight and quiet, the winds moving grasses on the earth, the sheep calling out placidly. Then the sound of surf hitting the shore as he shouldered a board, nothing on his mind but showing his boy the way to ride the waves. Next scene, finding his wife and that same boy in the eerie stillness of a house that had seen unspeakable violence, all the elements of a peaceful life shattered in the form of dishes on the floor, the excrement of men left behind as a taunt. A territorial marking saying they'd claimed all that was of value here. Then there was war, the sound of bombs and gunfire almost reassuring against the eternal silence of that house, which had relocated and buried its foundations deeply into his mind.

A hundred different scenes like those, rotating around one another, connecting, touching, bumping, overlapping. Reality versus the surreal, until he'd realized one could be a mask for another. Sometimes he thought it was always a mask, and a man was no different from the mouse circling the snake lying still in the grass. Innocuous as the log it impersonated, it was ignored while that mouse climbed over it, playing, foraging. Spinning mouselike dreams, until the snake turned and struck, and the mouse realized he'd always been food . . .

So given all that, maybe he was uniquely prepared for a vampire dinner. Taking a leisurely meal in the open maw of a poised tai pan was okay, as long as a bloke ignored the venom and hungry saliva dropping off its fangs onto the shoulders of his elegant dinner jacket. Oh, yeah. He'd have a ripper of a time.

After Ian had followed her into the house, Dev had obeyed her unlikely instructions, even though he'd dearly wanted to stay at her back to keep that bastard away from her. But she was counting on him to keep his wits and not go all wobbly on her.

So he'd found the kitchen, and the kitchen staff. Two men and three women. He didn't know their relationship to Danny's mother or Ian, but he brusquely relayed Danny's commands about a bath and the blood. From their wary reaction, he could tell they realized the balance of power might be shifting, and it was important not to come down on the wrong side of it. Most were obsequious to the point of being irritating, with the exception of one young woman with a pretty, fresh face who simply studied him as he explained what was needed. She volunteered to take care of the bath and quickly disappeared from sight.

Another maidservant, attractive enough with neat brown hair coiled on her neck and a voluptuous form beneath her dark uniform dress and starched apron, retrieved a container from the shelf and left for the porch from the kitchen exit. Mindful of Danny's advice about monitoring what she was going to be putting in her mouth, Dev followed the woman. When she knelt by the first body, she calmly grasped his hair and lifted his head, studying the bullet wound.

"You need to cut him and drain it into the container. I'll hold it."

It was certainly not the most terrible thing he'd ever done or seen, but it was unsettling, her matter-of-factness about squeezing a dead man like an orange for his fluid. It made him feel a twinge of shame for the act, a long-dormant need to say a prayer.

Instead he nodded, drew his knife and squatted next to her. A cooling dead man gave her a meager flow, but she pulled the container away after only a small sampling. Since she was far more accustomed to preparing tea for vampires, he wouldn't argue. As she rose, Dev rose with her. Some of the stockmen were still about, and he met the gaze of the nearest man, holding the dark look with one equally intimidating. But he could feel it as much as they all could. A sense of anticipation had descended on everything human on the station. Nobody was going to fuck around with anyone else until the vampires decided how things were going to be. That made things a little easier on him, at least, though he didn't envy Danny. It was good that his sheila appeared to have nerves of steel. She was going to need them.

When he returned to the kitchen with the woman, she put the blood into a teacup and poured Earl Grey over it. She prepared a tray with sugar, cream and a couple biscuits. Handing it to him with a short curtsy, she returned without another word to her duties, preparing dinner. He found the biscuits odd, but then he remembered what she'd said about vampires enjoying food without consumption. Well, the biscuits did look good. Maybe Danny would balance them on his nose and, if he performed the trick well enough, let him have them. He was getting hungry himself.

He shouldered his swag, the sum of their belongings, and headed for the stairs to the second level. As he did, he glanced in at the rooms he passed. The décor was the dark furniture and overly formal look of an English estate, down to an ostentatious painting of hunting hounds over one of the fireplaces. The dogs stood against a lush hillside that looked nothing like this part of Australia, or any part of the country he knew. These had to be Ian's choices, for Danny had implied her mother had a bond to the land that she herself possessed. Thank God.

When he reached her room, he knocked.

Come in.

It reassured him, the voice in his head, which probably proved he'd turned the corner. As he stepped in, he found he was right about who'd chosen the interior for the rest of the house. The first thing he saw when he stepped in was a series of Outback watercolors, small, quaint landscapes. The room had rustic furniture, a large quilt on the bed. Because this was the part of the house buried in the hill, it was blessedly cool, and a group of candles gave it a light that made him think again of the solitude of their cave, with more creature comforts.

When he set down the tray and turned, she was emerging from the washroom. He could see the bathtub behind her, water ready. She'd stripped out of the T-shirt she'd borrowed from him. Wearing brassiere, trousers and bare feet, she came to him, took the cup and downed the contents in several swallows, a look of ferocious satisfaction crossing her face before she tossed the delicate porcelain aside, letting it shatter on the floor. Seizing the back of his head, she drew him down to taste the blood on her lips, the taste of her beneath it. Struggling to catch up, he gripped her hips, as much for anchor as to return the pleasure, and she growled, moving into him. Her breasts pushed against his chest, her flat abdomen sliding along his cock as her leg insinuated between his.

If he touches you again, I'll kill him, I swear it.

The sheer raw possession in her thought took him by surprise. He sure as hell didn't like Ian touching her, or thinking about how many blokes Danny might have chosen to touch. But this twisted something unexpected in him, all the way down to his balls. It was beyond jealousy. She viewed him as belonging to *her*, and had taken great offense at Ian manhandling him, not just with the suggestion of violence, but sexual violence.

"He's not my type, love, no worries," he managed against her mouth, trying to lighten things. Though his voice was hoarse, and the look she flicked up at him didn't even register as human.

"I need this now. To do the rest." Before he could guess what she meant, she made it rather obvious, shoving him to his back on the bed even as she was tearing her trousers off her legs, along with her knickers, leaving her gloriously naked.

"Open them. Now." She gave a short nod to his strides, staring at what was already straining beneath, as if she could command it to arousal with one demanding look, and she probably could. The air around here was rife with the idea that vampires could control and direct anything they damn well pleased. While he couldn't very well argue that, not after Ian had knocked him into the dirt and held him there with as much effort as it would have taken to hold down an infant, Dev's hackles rose.

"You going to make me if I don't, like your friend down there?"

He fought her, but it made little difference. She was too damn fast. She didn't take them off. He cursed her as she shredded one of the two pairs of pants he owned, tore the seams of the boxers beneath and ripped open his shirt, leaving it in strips on his broad shoulders. She didn't touch the knife harnesses he wore beneath his clothes. A message that they were useless against her. She left all that on, but took everything else. As she straddled him, she held him down with one hand pressed hard against his throat. She was dripping and hot already, so he couldn't help but groan as she sank down on him and began to ride. Even as his mind was spinning, his body was ready for her, hard and thick, making those cunt muscles of hers strain to take him, where she outmatched him physically everywhere else.

"You did this, Dev." There was anger in her voice, warring with lust. "You stood up to him, you foolish, *stupid* man. You killed those two men because they tried to hurt me. You didn't care about the consequences."

No teasing seduction. She rode him, ruthlessly using the lust of one body for another, something that couldn't be denied. He didn't know if this was punishment or desperation, but he gripped her hips, hung on as she bent, lithe and flexible, and sank her fangs into his throat, drinking deep, letting him feel the unnerving rush of blood from that major artery flow into her mouth. She swallowed against him, close enough the quiver of her breasts brushed his chest as she kept moving rhythmically, demanding his surrender.

She was still drinking when he came, crying out hoarsely, his hands digging into her arse as she made a noise of approval against his skin. Her body shuddered, an intense but short climax of her own that seemed to paralyze her for a moment, her forehead pressed hard against his jaw. Then, still impatient, she was sealing the wound with strokes and pressure of her tongue, her fingers burying into his hair, squeezing past the point of pain, her mouth still on the side of his neck.

But when she slowly rose, her lovely abdominal muscles contracting as she straightened without the use of her arms, he saw she wasn't done with him yet.

She stepped away from the bed, their mingled fluids trickling down her thighs, the dark pink of her flushed and swollen sex visible to him. "Clean me, Dev." She said it softly, but it was still a command. "With your mouth."

To do it, he had to leave the bed, go down on his knees before her. Technically, it wasn't difficult, because he didn't think his legs were quite ready to hold him and it made sense to give her that cosseting as a continuation of the passion between them. However, when he slid out of the bed, she moved back two steps, waited for him, brilliant eyes resting on his face. A taunt, making it clear she expected him to walk those two steps on his knees.

To hell with that, was his first thought. Then he looked at her. Her hair poured across her pale shoulders, her breasts high and proud. But beneath that, a tempest, so many things obviously swirling in her mind as she stood before him.

She was a garden behind a stone wall, protected by a dragon in a moat. When she let him into that garden, when he was deep inside her—God help him, he might be insane—he'd discovered rare and fragile blooms. He saw them in her eyes, in the tremble of her body, her response that couldn't be feigned. And it wasn't just a response to his body or what he was doing to hers. She was responding to *him.*

She was the dragon, the wall *and* the garden. So though her challenge brought forth an instinctive rebellion in him, he thought the dragon *expected* to be fought, maybe even relished it. But somehow, ultimately, it was surrender that would bring him over the wall, into that garden, her innermost self. Would bring both of them into it. Taming the dragon, at least temporarily. When he was in that garden, he never wanted to leave.

It was a strange mélange of thoughts, but he was at a loss to explain most of his reactions to her. He didn't know why even this demand made his cock give an unexpected contraction, another small expulsion of semen that caused a gasp, a little bit of a forward pitch. Her hand was on his shoulder then, steadying him. She guided him as she put one foot on the bed, widening her stance.

"Every drop, Dev. Let me feel that clever tongue."

Placing his mouth against her cunt, he closed his eyes, immersed in the scent of her. When he placed hands on her hips, her own landed on top of them, closing over his wrists, a light manacle. He began to lick, circling his tongue over the damp, still-aroused clit, goaded by the guttural sound that emitted from her lips. He kept going, kept his focus on actually cleaning her, which he understood was what she wanted. He was performing a task for her.

In return, she rewarded him. Or tormented him further. With her, the line between pleasure and torture was slim.

Opening a window in her mind, she showed him other times, when she'd bedded men to add spice to the blood she took from them. Afterward, she sent them away and let her maid do the cleaning honors with a soft washcloth. The maid she'd used in Brisbane had been young, her fair skin flushed a pretty pink as Danny taught her best how to pleasure her Mistress, to bring her to climax again. Then one night Danny had laid the young woman down on the bed and removed the knickers beneath the short black skirt. Fingering her moist, virginal lips, she had the girl writhing until Danny removed her own knowledgeable hand and made the girl finish herself, enjoying the maid's discovery of her own sensuality.

He gave her labia a light nip. *Could have done without the first part, love, about you and those other blokes. But the rest . . .*

Holy God. The visual of her and the maid had his drained cock struggling to rise again. The brainless appendage didn't realize it would take a miracle for a normal man to get it up after such a fucking, and Dev was a heavyweight.

But when you're standing behind my chair tonight, you'll think of it. If you don't, I'll send other thoughts your way. I want them to see that erect cock straining and know that it belongs to me. I want them to envy me until it borders on the edge of hatred.

The venom in her mind was alarming. He paused briefly. *Love?*

Her fingers dug into his scalp again, though her voice gentled. "All the way down the leg to my ankle, Dev. You missed a drop."

He followed the track, suckling with his mouth, and then he realized the appearance of it, as he went lower, lower, his hips necessarily sliding back toward his heels and then having to lift his arse in the air as he bent all the way to the ground, to the foot she had braced on the carpet. Her tiny foot, the precise arch, the fragile bones of the ankle.

Don't think, Dev. Just do it. Leave your mind out of it and decide what you want to do.

He found her arch with his mouth and dwelled there, feeling her fingers trail down the bridge of his back, the bullet scars and other signposts of his life. She adjusted her stance so the foot shifted under his mouth. Then she lifted her foot off the bed to prop it on the small of his back, right above the curve of his buttocks. It was where Ian had placed his boot, only this was her delicate foot, her toes gripping his skin, teasing the cleft, her cunt positioned over his head, so that he could have turned on his back and stared up at it, the petals of slick flesh. But for now he paid homage to her foot, teasing it with his tongue, his teeth, the suckling of his lips. Then he heard a soft moan. Remarkably, a drop of moisture fell on his back, anointing him where his hair had slid forward, baring skin at his nape. Lifting his head then, he worked back up the leg, holding on to it to steady her. She shifted the other leg back to the bed so he could work back to her cunt, then across and down to tease that foot as well.

Oh, God, Dev, you are too good at this. A tug of his hair, and she moved away, her foot easing out from beneath his mouth as he sat on his heels again. She moved back another step, studying him. "I intended to teach you a lesson."

"Consider it taught, my lady."

She closed her eyes, and he had the fleeting, amused thought she was counting to ten, something his mother had done . . . well, countless times. Then her eyes opened and his amusement shriveled up like a man's testicles before an icy wind. "You're in a den of lions here, Dev. If you challenge Lord Charles the way you challenged Ian, he won't hesitate to rip your throat out."

"If you wanted a submissive puppy who wets himself if someone scolds him, you brought the wrong escort to this party." He stayed on his heels as he retorted, because it didn't matter if he was laid out flat on the floor. He wouldn't be anyone's doormat.

Her shoulders lifted in a sigh. "Yes, I did. I'm sorry for that. I've brought you into hell, Dev." She shook her head, turned away. "You can go now. I'll tell them I dispatched you on station business, but you can simply go . . . wherever it was you were intending to go before we met."

He blinked. "Is that a command, my lady?"

Danny stopped, spun around and leveled a glare on him. "Don't be thickheaded. You don't belong here, Dev. Which means you'll die here, and I've no desire to see that happen. You've played your part in this little drama."

"You didn't answer the question." He watched the irritation flicker through her gaze, a muscle flex in her slim jaw.

"And if it is?"

He rose then, aware she might be stronger and faster than he was, but he'd always be taller. Her eyes narrowed at his matter-of-fact mental taunt as he moved closer.

As far as hell goes, I've been there, a long time now.

Putting his hands on her shoulders then, he slid them up under her hair, and forward, to her jaw. She'd gone tense as a snake about to strike. While he expected her to do just that, he simply bent, brushed his lips over her mouth. *I'll try not to let the arrogant bastard—either one of them—get under my skin. A man's will can't be taken, and my will, for the time being, is to be here with you.*

What about when I no longer give you the choice? When I refuse to let you go, no matter what your will is?

Letting his hands glide back under her hair, he caressed her nape, twining the strands, his thumb teasing the artery in her throat as her gaze went opaque. *It might be a moot point. Maybe there's already nothing I'll deny you.*

For a moment, there was such raw emotion in her face, he knew he'd stepped right into that fragrant garden, past moat, dragon, drawbridge and bailey. Everything about her was within his grasp, only it was so elusive he didn't dare move at all. It raised an odd, hungry yearning in him, as if he'd walk on hands and knees through scorching sand to touch her foot with his lips again.

Then it was gone, the dragon returned. Clearing her throat, she stepped back and away. "Time for me to get dressed. If you insist on coming along, I need you to dress for dinner as well. Fortunately, you're of a size with one of Ian's staff. They're supposed to bring you a change of clothes. You can wear your gun and knives over them." She caressed the strap of the scabbard for his hunting knife, her fingers trailing over his bare groin. "I like this look, very much."

Turning and moving toward the tub, she tossed over her shoulder, "So you never said. How do you like my station?"

"Oh, it's beaut. A real warm and welcoming feel to it. Particularly the part where they offered to break my spine and bugger me."

She chuckled, bending over to test the water, her blond hair falling forward over her shoulders. It was a lovely view, and he forced himself to focus before she laughed or snapped at him. "If a human holds a vampire's gaze for too long, it's considered a deliberate sign of disrespect."

"Hmm." He grunted, decided to park his bum on the edge of the bed until his legs stopped having that unmanly tremor that accompanied a hard climax. "Well, good. I did something right then."

When she straightened and turned, he saw more of the Danny in the desert, though there was still enough of the ruthless vampire to make him wary. She came back to him, stood between his splayed knees and settled a firm grip on his shoulder, making him raise his attention from the lovely breasts so close to his chin. "You've got a head like a rock, bushman, so let me say it once more. *Let me deal with the vampires.* Everything Ian said he could do to you, he *can* do, if I don't protect you from him. With Lord Charles here, I'm outnumbered. We have to depend as much on diplomacy as strength. I don't doubt your skills. They're formidable, but without the element of surprise, you've got no chance at all. Even when relying on the unexpected, your margin for error is nonexistent. You miss, you're done. And no one relishes pain and torment the way a vampire does. It's a drug all its own."

As her gaze coursed over him, he knew the feral look was intentional, but it still caused a cold shiver to run up his spine. Even as it perversely made his balls ache with desire, because it came from her. Noticing it, her voice dropped an octave, bringing a dangerous purr. "I think you've started to realize that for yourself. None of us are immune to it, though some of us keep it on a closer rein than others."

"You're the gentle vampire," he recalled.

When she met his gaze, surprised, her mouth eased back into a smile. "Scoundrel," she murmured. She moved back toward the tub, speaking over her shoulder again. "There's a room across the hall with a bath and shaving gear for you, as well as the clothes. It will be your room while you're here. So you can be available to *my* needs." With an ironic look, she stopped at the doorway, her hair caressing her hips, not a stitch of clothes on her lean, perfect body. It made him think of a water nymph.

"What will Ian have to say about that?"

"This is not his home." Her expression hardened. "He'll challenge that eventually, particularly with Lord Charles here, but for tonight he'll let it go, if for no other reason than we all need to behave for dinner. The two of them are such bloody Brits." With a roll of her eyes and a toss of her head, she closed the washroom door, apparently done with him for the moment.

Surrounded by Poms *and* vampires. Bloody hell.

10

I T was peculiar to have danger weighing so heavily over a room set up for a formal dinner. Expensive china, all the forks and spoons in the proper place with napkins folded in an artistic display. A brass candelabra twined with wildflowers, a surprising touch. A subtle welcome?

Danny had suggested he familiarize himself with the house and immediate grounds until he was summoned for dinner, and he'd started in the dining area. A turntable was playing classical music. Mozart, Dev thought. A maverick in his own time, one who had a wildness that suggested a bit of the vampire. Christ, before it was over, he would be seeing monsters everywhere.

Ruskin, as Danny had implied, was solidly seventeenth-century British. Dev caught a brief glimpse of him when the Region Master joined Danny and Ian, already in the library, for before-dinner cocktails. He was tall and kept his hair trimmed short, emphasizing the pale ice of his blue eyes, the chiseled jaw. Everything in his studied manner reminded anyone blessed with his presence that he'd been titled aristocracy as a mortal. From the disdainful veneer that layered all of his comments that wafted outside the library, it was apparent he found it insulting to serve as a Region Master here. Though he allowed that the hunting was exceptional for its lack of restrictions.

Dev's inquiries of the household staff revealed he'd once been a duke close to the monarchy, if his remarks about it were to be believed. Until he was turned, a made vampire, and of course had to fake his death, since it became difficult to explain the lack of aging. Like many British outcasts, he'd ended up in Australia.

He could have made overlord in Europe by now, but he's not willing to kiss arses that low on the totem pole to position himself accordingly to get back into England. He wants them to hand it to him like a damned royal scepter.

Better to reign in hell, hmm?

Something like that.

It was remarkable, how she had no trouble participating in animated conversation with Ian and Charles at the same time she was tuning in to Dev's thoughts. He was doing his own tracking as well. She sounded as if she were at tea in her own garden, all gracious beauty and seductive appeal. Apparently, their physical exercise before dinner had helped. He was glad for it, though he was going to have bruises the size of fists.

I'll kiss every one of them.

Promises, promises.

He'd also discovered the station wasn't completely a nest of testosterone, besides the maids. The staff had indicated Ian's and Charles's full servants were both female, though he'd not yet seen either.

For reasons that should be rather obvious to you, vampires choose full servants that mesh with their sexual preferences. While Ian and Ruskin can be adventurous, their primary preference is women.

Well, that's less than comforting, love. I'd much rather worry about my throat being ripped out than being buggered.

Stepping out onto the porch, he saw an old swagman stacking wood next to it. Every staff member he'd encountered was as wary as a beaten dog. However, when the man looked up at him, Dev was surprised to see a straight glance. The old man nodded. "It's good to have the lady D home again," he said in a voice made of gravel. His eyes were squinted and watery, a sign of permanent sun blight. "She finally got herself a human servant. Good. I'm Jim."

"Dev. But I'm not her servant," he replied. The man gave him a narrow look; then his shoulders rose in a shrug.

"Dim-witted girl. Shoulda known."

"Hold up." Dev arrested him in midshuffle, heading back to the shadows. "You've known her awhile, then. And Lady Daniela has never taken a full servant?"

"Not that anyone's heard about." Jim scratched at some blistered skin on his nose. "I came onto this place when I was barely twenty, stayed to work for her mother and then her. Knew she'd be back, so I stayed. *For her.*" His tone made it clear he didn't give a spit about any of Ian's lot. Dev bit back a smile and wondered how the old bloke had lived to his current age, but then realized he was making it clear where his loyalties lay, the first staff member with the guts to do it. He sharpened his attention.

"Her mother used to get after her about it, said it was dangerous not to have one," the old man continued. "But that girl, she was always a free spirit. Kind of like a bloke about marriage, way she acted about it. Keeps herself shielded on all sides, that one."

"Well, you keep yourself protected on all sides, can't be buggered by no one, can you?"

Jim gave him a tobacco-stained and mostly toothless smile. "Except yourself, mate. That's the rat bastard you really have to look out for."

Before Dev could respond, he hiked off, one bum leg making it more of a hop. Ian's man materialized at his elbow, fast enough that Dev spun in defense, knife half drawn. The man halted, eased back. "Truce, mate. Ain't no call for any mischief until they finish their dinner. I wanted to know what old Jim had to say to you."

"He's planning to stake the lot of them and take over the place at midnight. He'll give us the go signal by cackling like a kookaburra."

"Think you're a smart bloke? You haven't been among 'em long, have you?" The man grinned, showing yellow teeth, but his eyes were shrewd and dark, not entirely unpleasant. While Dev didn't take his hand away from it, he slid the knife back in place, putting a hip on the rail.

"Not in a place like this. Only out there." He nodded into the darkness, toward the desert and hills. "They're serious about their dinner, then?"

"Oh, yeah. Aren't we all? Name's Bill." Bill glanced toward the windows where the maids were lighting the candles at the dinner table. "If they don't kill one another or someone else as the predinner sport, they have a pretty reasonable meal and tea and cakes afterward. Then they have their games at the end. Though those don't involve killing." He flashed a grin, gave Dev a quick once-over in his formal clothing. "If you're going to be in there, you'll find out what I mean soon enough. Hell, mate, you may even get to be part of it. Don't know if that means you're a lucky or sorry bastard."

"Hey, Bill. Rattle your dags, mate. Don't want to handle this on my own."

The voice came from the square of light of the open barn. Bill gave Dev a nod and headed in that direction. Dev heard the shrill whinny of a horse, and Bill's pace increased, as if he had cause for alarm. But he called out something brusquely and entered the barn without any apparent concern, so Dev relaxed.

We're ready for dinner, Dev. Come meet me at my chair and see me seated.

Dev took another look around in the dark. For some reason, facing blood-crazed dingoes and her raving, violent delirium seemed more appealing after Bill's unsettling comments.

Ah, fond memories. Come to me, bushman. This is just dinner.

When he came into the dining area, the vampires were entering from the opposite hallway, Danny preceding them, courtesy to a lady. He didn't realize he'd stopped dead in his tracks until his lady's soft voice spoke in his mind.

Dev? You look like a gaping trout. Only she didn't seem entirely displeased, considering she was the cause of it.

He hadn't seen her when she came down from her bath, before she went into the library. She and her mother had shared the same build, because the dress she wore fit her perfectly. The silk gold taffeta skirt fell to midcalf. Strapless with a neckline that had a scalloped plunge between her breasts, there was a tiny row of decorative buttons down the front that had a sparkle to them. She'd piled her hair on her head except for one artful lock that fell to her shoulder and lay in a curl above her right breast, rounded and high from the hold of the wiring of the dress's bodice. She also wore another opal centerpiece at her throat and matching teardrops. The white dress gloves she'd donned fit her fingers and arms tightly, erotic in the way they molded her flesh but hid it, the candlelight reflecting a light sheen all the way to her upper arms.

In the service, he'd occasionally had the opportunity to view one of the scratchy films for entertainment they got through the supply lines. She was Grace Kelly, that timeless perfection, coupled with a danger that lovely lady had never projected.

She'd reached her chair now and laid a hand on his arm. Smelling like some kind of exotic perfume, she'd touched her mouth with a wet lipstick that urged him to suck on her lips, bruise them to even riper fullness. And that couldn't help but make him think of the ways he could cause the lips between her legs to swell with arousal. With a sudden hunger that was uncanny, he imagined hearing that rich taffeta rustle as he pushed it out of his way.

She'd wanted him embarrassingly erect. She'd managed it, and he hadn't even needed the memory she'd given him. However, as he should have expected, she wouldn't be satisfied until he was about to explode out of his britches.

Everything beneath is bare flesh. Just garters and stockings. When he dumbly pulled out her chair and she swept her skirt around her, he saw small heeled slippers. A tiny bow on the top of each, with a scattering of diamondlike beads dangling from them over the toe. *My feet are still thinking of you. Your mouth upon them, your body kneeling beneath me, that fine broad back of yours serving as a prop for my foot.*

Strewth, she was fair killing him. When she took her seat, he brought her up to the table. He noted then that Ian wasn't looking particularly pleased, probably because she'd taken the seat at the head of the table, and Ruskin had taken the other head. However, he settled and rang the bell for the first course.

The two female servants had been behind their Masters, and now Dev emulated them, taking a step back to the wall behind his lady's chair. With the vampires engaged in light discourse, it gave him the chance to give them the once-over, the way they were doing to him, with covert glances. He tried to ignore the fact that his interest went beyond simple information gathering. He wanted to know what a third-mark servant looked like, how they acted.

Did vampires choose their full servants for their beauty, or was that a side effect of getting that third mark, like a vampire's unearthly good looks? Because the two women were stunning. Ruskin's was an Asian Indian named Aapti, according to the staff. She had dark hair nearly to her knees and wore a sapphire and silver sari with matching jewels that made her appear as a princess, except for her submissive pose behind his chair, her long-lashed eyes down, hands folded. It took him a moment, still recovering from the shock of Danny, to notice the sari she wore was sheer, as was the halter piece beneath, so there was the suggestion of her sex and nipples beneath the flowing garments.

When he shifted his gaze to the other, he recalled Ian had called her Chiyoko, and registered for the first time that Ian's servant was Japanese. An unusual sight in Oz, when anti-Nip feeling still ran so high. He didn't have much problem with it, though, because he'd met enough Japanese villagers during his tour to know there was a difference between the enemy you fought and the people caught in between. Though in war, he acknowledged there was often no time to sort out the difference, for either side.

Again, silky black hair, and she wore a black cheongsam with gold and crimson dragons embroidered on it. The cheongsam was cut all the way up beyond the thigh to the waist, so that when she moved, it was possible to see the neat curve of naked arse, the dusky crease to her sex. The frog clasp neckline followed the shoulder, but the front bodice was open cut, her breasts completely bare to a man's gaze. A crisscross of ribbon over them held the shape of the dress and served to lift the small curves. It appeared there were some kind of clamps on her nipples, screwed in to hold them taut, with a delicate beaded chain running between them. Another series of chains ran up to her throat, and he realized then that the clamps attached to a collar she had fitted beneath the standing collar of the cheongsam.

Holy Christ. When he'd taken whores, they'd been the simple kind that might hang about a pub and give a man a good go, but basically average girls. Before that, he'd been a husband with a trusting, adventurous wife, but they'd been kids. Even as a soldier, there were dark places he hadn't gone during his tour of duty. He felt like a youngster again, agog at the underwear section of his mother's mail-order catalog.

They play their real games after dinner.

He pushed away his uneasiness about that, though he couldn't ignore the weight of the glances they were giving him. Or the looks he was getting from Ian and Lord Charles, though he made sure to keep his gaze on the back of Danny's chair, aware of their regard but not meeting it. It rankled, but he knew being a stubborn swagman wouldn't help Danny now. In fact, he was getting the distinct feeling it was a liability of some kind, not having a full servant. It affected her standing in this gathering, which made it more important that he try to observe the niceties. *Bloody hell.* He could drown in waters like these.

"Are you still fencing, Lady Daniela?" This from Ruskin, as he was brought his glass of wine. A glance at the sidebar told Dev it wasn't the cheap plonk he was used to. Still, without prompting, he moved there, chose an unopened bottle, and waved off the manservant who'd poured Ruskin and Ian's. Conscious of their regard, he nevertheless drew his smaller knife, cut a vein and let his own blood flavor the wine he poured in a glass and brought to her.

She chose to take it from his hand, her gaze rising to meet his as their fingers brushed. "Thank you, Dev."

I don't trust anyone in this den of thieves.

She gave a slight acknowledgment, a flit of her lashes. Then she turned her attention back to Ruskin's question. "Of course, Lord Charles. I prefer the saber. The footwork is more challenging."

"I remember being surprised when your mother told me that," Ian put in. "Most women are attracted to the foil, for it relies more on light finger work, not so much wrist strength. Constance preferred light fingers."

"In profession, my lord. Not in swordplay." Danny chuckled. "But she would appreciate your wit. She herself was actually most fond of the cavalry sword. She could be terrifying on horseback. I think the staff was afraid she'd try to practice beheading when she was in a temper."

"Perhaps we could have a match later tonight?" Ruskin suggested, tracing the rim of his cup as he studied her.

"Of course. I'll need to change. I wouldn't want my dress mussed for sport alone. This was my father's favorite." She glanced toward Ian. "Since it was toward the back of her wardrobe, I am assuming she rarely wore it for you."

He gave her a humorless smile. "She preferred the past to remain there. Her focus was on our future together."

"Perhaps that's why she chose to meet the sun," she rejoined sweetly.

"Children," Ruskin said mildly, though there was anticipation in his gaze that made Dev wonder what agenda the old bastard had himself. "Let's drive the tension between the two of you in a more pleasurable direction. Perhaps you could suggest an entertainment for us during the soup, Lady D?" His gaze rose to Devlin. "You have a fine-looking servant attending you. I'd like to see his capabilities."

"His capabilities are far beyond the scope of a dining room, Lord Charles. This man is my new station manager, here tonight merely for form, because he is my most highly ranked employee. Not my full servant. You know how I hate to be hovered over." She cocked her head. "But I would take great joy in watching your two servants pleasure one another. I expect it would not distress either of you as well."

"Lady Daniela thinks only of us. So generous. But I must challenge the truth of your statement. Not because I doubt you, but because of the man himself." Ruskin raised that cold gaze to Dev as he struggled to keep looking at the wall, Danny's nape. "He carries two marks, according to Ian. And his eyes follow you with such hunger, he's obviously under your spell. As are we all," he added with malicious gallantry. "What will he do for that hunger? Is he ravenous enough to go against his nature? Earlier you questioned Ian for elevating a human servant to the status of a vampire in this household.

I question the strength of a vampire who has a human in her employ she can't command to her will."

"I've stated my preferences, Lord Ruskin." Danny's voice turned cool, though her pose remained relaxed. "Are you denying me my preferred entertainment? While we are far from the formal dining rooms of England, I expected you, of all people, to know our rules of social etiquette. You invited me to call out the first entertainment. I have done so."

A silence around the table. Dev knew Danny's casual demeanor had to be a deception, but damn, she pulled it off well. He didn't like the satisfied light in Ian's eyes one bit, though. The bastard felt he'd one-upped her.

"Aapti." Lord Charles turned at last, nodded at his servant. "You and Chiyoko, move there." He gestured to the open area of the floor, the wood covered by a colorful Persian carpet. The scattering of pillows against the wall reminded Dev of the palaces in India. As the two women complied, a study of sensuous movement, Ruskin cocked a brow, spoke tonelessly. "Lady D, it is your show."

Danny nodded. "Kneel facing one another, but leave about three feet between you. Remove everything except your shoes and jewelry."

He would *not* give away his complete lack of experience in such things by spewing all over himself like a boy. Instead, he'd settle for swallowing his tongue. Dev watched, amazed as Aapti unwrapped the sari, let it float to the floor around her, and then removed the bodice beneath so she was standing before them only in the shoes, bracelets, rings and heavy brace of gold necklaces that stacked high around her throat, keeping her chin raised.

Chiyoko also unhooked the frogs and the side fastener to step out of the cheongsam, leaving on her high-heeled shoes. Now he could see the collar attached to the chains that ran to her nipples, and realized a chain also ran down the back of her collar, into the cleft between her buttocks. Then under and up, splitting her cunt lips and going straight up her shaved mound, hooking onto a tiny silver bar pierced through her navel. In the open space between her navel and the nipple clamps, an elaborate tattoo had been inked across her upper abdomen. The design was that of a delicate tree, its many leaves and branches etched out in fine black dye, with several Japanese characters aligned alongside it. The whole display was one of the most erotic things he'd ever seen, and he shifted, feeling a need for adjustment.

No need for self-consciousness here, bushman. No one in this room objects to seeing you handle your cock.

That's what concerns me a little bit.

Would you like me to do it?

As she tilted her head toward him, there was a touch of laughter in her mind-voice at his sudden flood of panic. But he noted the humor didn't reach her eyes. She leveled her gaze on the two women again.

"I did have in mind to use one of the household servants, my lord," she said. "Mary."

A maid who'd entered, carrying the soup course, came to a halt. She managed a brief curtsy, keeping her eyes averted from both Danny and the display on the other side of the room. "Marm."

"Mary, how long have you worked in this household?" Danny studied her, and Dev didn't think she was missing anything, from the woman's sudden pallor, to the tremor that ran through her fingers on the grip of the tray.

"About ten years, ma'am."

"Did you like my mother?"

The maid's gaze darted up, then over to Ian.

"Answer the question," he barked at her.

The tray wobbled, then steadied. "Y-yes, my lady. She was very . . . kind."

"Even when Ian, tiring of my mother's melancholy, chose you over her to warm his bed, to spend his seed in your cunt?"

Ian's gaze narrowed. "I didn't . . ."

"It's all right, Ian." Danny waved a dismissive hand. "I know it's difficult to deal with a vampire with the Ennui. Though perhaps it gave Mary some delusions of grandeur for a while, I'm sure you reminded her of her place." She turned her attention back to the hapless maid and spoke, almost gently. "Did my mother ever draw you into her lonely bed, trying to absorb a modicum of the heat that Ian left vibrating on your skin?"

The young woman's face flushed, confirming the truth.

"You are most provocative in your choice of dinner entertainments," Ruskin commented in a neutral tone.

"Ah, Lord Charles." Danny leveled an amused glance on him, gesturing to Mary to distribute what was on her tray. "You should go to Sydney sometime. See the glittering shows that can be put on there by the Region Master, Lady Elwyn. My favorite night was when she had a dappled Percheron brought into the very dining room, a mare with ribbons twined into her mane and tail. Those ribbons were woven around the servant she had strapped high on the mare's back, the straight line of her spine aligned with the creature's neck, held in place with a bearing rein. She was a very petite thing, this servant, a lovely Irish girl with flame red hair and fair skin."

Danny closed her eyes, remembering, her lips still curved. But as Mary put the last bowl at her setting, Danny reached out unerringly, clasped her wrist, held her there. The girl jumped, almost spilling the soup, then held still, her gaze flashing to Dev's face and then back to Danny's hand, holding her fast.

"He'd brushed the girl's hands and feet with a glittering silver and black paint," Danny continued. "Wherever she pressed the soles of her feet or clutched at the animal in arousal or distress, it left beautiful marks. Her backside was positioned onto a sizable saddle pommel, holding her anchored. Legs spread and bound around the mare's girth. Each vampire used a polished wooden set of stairs to mount the horse and put his pommel, so to speak, inside her, when it pleased him or her to do so. Periodically, her hands were redipped, and the horse walked about the room to display her, as well as to keep the poor creature from getting fractious. When they let the mare's head down from the bearing rein, the servant's body was stretched out further. She cried out in a lovely way, because, of course, the pommel was designed to shift with her, create a different discomfort and pleasure at once. It was delicious, the perfume of the girl's arousal mingling with our dinner in a most stimulating way."

"I've seen such provincial performances. Like carnival side-shows." Lord Charles shrugged. "Tanks of sea snakes, where a vampire may enter the water to feel their bodies twine around your limbs, slither across your bare skin. Quite affectionate creatures, but venomous. We had far better entertainments in the mother country."

"I find that hard to believe. I've been to England, and they are far less imaginative than the Australians." She gave him a conspiratorial wink, lessening the barb. "Go to Sydney, Lord Charles. You won't regret it. But for now, we shall make do, won't we?" Her gaze shifted to Mary, still helplessly manacled to her.

My lady, she's trembling. You're frightening her.

She will not be harmed, Dev. No more than she deserves. Do not worry for her.

On that less than comforting thought, Danny rose in a rustle of taffeta. "Go stand with Chiyoko and Aapti," she ordered. As Mary complied, Danny circled the other side of the table, moving behind Ian's chair. Letting a white-gloved hand trail along the chair back, she brushed his shoulder, giving him an amused look and Charles a speculative one as she made her way to the women. Mary waited between the two servants, her head bowed, lips pressed together. Dev wasn't sure, but he thought her perilously close to tears. He didn't like this, though he held his tongue, waiting to see what his capricious sheila had in mind. But it was an effort.

"Easy, dear maid. You shall only give us pleasure tonight." Danny stopped beside her. She was about three inches taller, but the stature difference had nothing to do with which of them had greater height. "The first task shall be easy. Kiss me, Mary. Do your best. Imagine I am who you love best here. I will discern who it is."

Mary swallowed as Lord Charles's and Ian's attention sharpened like the end of a spear, pointed toward the four women.

Dev was as riveted as either male vampire as Mary lifted her face and awkwardly pressed her lips to his lady's mouth, her hands fluttering nervously, alighting in tense fists just short of Danny's body, the maid obviously uncertain if touch would be welcome. Aapti and Chiyoko had taken a knee on either side of her, naked and patient, but their eyes were locked upon the display as well. Dev noted Chiyoko's nipples hardened further in the clamps, obviously stimulated by the merest twitch of the chains placed in her nether regions. Aapti, while equally attentive, was entirely still, waiting, which suggested she was the most experienced. In fact, her gaze slid briefly to Dev while the others were distracted, marking his reaction, obviously gathering information for her Master, before it went back to Danny.

Danny chuckled against the girl's mouth and in the next moment gripped the back of her head, tumbling off the white lace cap, tearing out the pins so her mouse brown hair tumbled down. Mary gasped, but Danny forced her harder against her lips, tunneling her fingers in the girl's hair, the other arm snaking around her waist and clamping onto a buttock, bunching up the fabric of the black uniform. Mary made a noise of part pleasure and fearful discomfort as Danny's hand gathered up the skirt, slowly revealing the generous bare bottom beneath. Dev's eyes narrowed. It was bruised and marked with red welts. Belt marks. Danny's fingers traced over them, the movement of her lips showing that she was plundering Mary's mouth fully, tongue tangling with hers, nipping at her so a trickle of blood ran from the corner.

He wasn't sure which way to look. His lady was surrounded by enemies, but he wasn't sure if she wasn't one of them at the moment. Then he noted that, as she kissed Mary in such a hard, brutish way, Mary's initial resistance was melting away. She was leaning into Danny's body, tentatively grasping at a fold of the taffeta skirt, making soft whimpering noises as Danny alternated between petting the marks and cruelly pinching them. He tried not to notice, but Mary had a fine, fat arse.

Finally, Danny pulled back. She held the girl away from her as she strained for a moment, too carried away from the passion to recall herself. When she did, she flushed and tried to gaze down.

"No need to be all prim and proper now," Danny observed mildly. "Though that's your appeal, isn't it? You're so innocent. You came here a virgin, didn't you?"

The maid nodded, a quick jerk of her head. Danny made a satisfied hum. "You have a good eye, Ian. Or my mother did. Was she a gift?"

"Yes. One I am very fond of. Your mother had an aptitude for finding them, the innocent ones who craved Mastery."

"She did at that." Danny glanced at him. "Well, let's see if we can erode some more of that innocence. Strip off your clothes, Mary, and get on your knees between them." She nodded to the two servants kneeling on the floor.

The maid haltingly untied the sash of her apron. Danny took it from her, and then watched as the maid struggled with the zipper in the back of the uniform, wriggling in a way that had Chiyoko wetting her lips and Ruskin taking another generous sip of his wine. The staff had smoothly taken over Mary's duties, removing the appetizer dishes from the previous course as Mary stripped down to the bare skin. Danny shoved her to her knees before she could kneel, so the girl landed heavily between the two servants. However, before she came to harm, they had her arms, only to wrench them back as Danny knotted the sash of the apron around them and crossed it up the back, tying it around Mary's neck in a neat bow. Like a more feminine version of a man's tie, so the maid had to hold her arms up at an uncomfortable angle to keep pressure off her throat.

"Now, these two very experienced ladies are going to do as they like with you. Suckle you, fuck you with fingers or anything else that comes to hand. If you come before you beg me to do so, this nice gentleman behind my chair will fuck you in the backside. Believe me, that will hurt like nothing you've ever felt. You'll cry pretty, pretty tears, and I'll kiss every one of them away before I take your sweet blood." She glanced at the two women on their knees before her. "I trust you'll take the choice out of her hands, ladies. I'd like to see those tears."

Elegant as a lady of the manor should be, she turned on a heeled slipper, this time passing behind Ruskin. He put out a hand as she reached him, and she allowed him to take it, press a kiss to her hand. "I believe I owe you an apology, Lady Daniela. You have a fine grasp of what we would best enjoy."

"Well, I will forgive you this once, Lord Charles." She extricated her hand before he could linger, but with a smile that ensured it wasn't an insult.

Dev.

He needed the prompt, though he had a difficult time focusing on the simple act of holding out her chair.

I don't like what is being done to this girl, love. It's pissing me off.

Steady, Dev. Trust that I know what I'm doing. She will come to no harm.

Chiyoko and Aapti had descended on the girl, despite her protests. Though he was disturbed by her cries, Dev couldn't ignore the dripping slickness of Mary's cunt. As Danny's mind directed his attention there, he recognized undeniable evidence of a delicious mortification, a nectar she obviously fed upon in this depraved household. Aapti spread the maid's legs and put her mouth to work on her, while Chiyoko straddled Mary's face and made her eat her pussy. She massaged the girl's breasts, pinching the nipples enough to earn yelps that vibrated pleasurably against her, if the way she tightened her knees on Mary's skull and ground her sex in her face were any indication.

Danny had opted to let her chair stay somewhat away from the table, so he was startled when her hand drifted back. He moved forward a step or two, took the hand.

Step to the side of my chair, Dev. Put my hand on your cock. I want to feel how hard it is.

The two men were, of course, more absorbed in the women, but they were not ignoring Danny's actions, either. Dev was in a room of hawks, whose sharp eyes missed nothing. He'd definitely never indulged in public displays like this. Maybe her command now was driven by spontaneous arousal on her part, goaded by the scene before them, but for some reason, nothing felt spontaneous. However, when he hesitated, Ruskin's gaze honed in on him. Anything that suggested less than complete loyalty could undermine her. He comprehended that. But she'd put him on the spot, hadn't she? She wasn't giving him any answers or direction, and though he was sure she could hear the questions, it seemed as if this quite significant choice was all his.

Keeping his eyes on the women, avoiding eye contact with the two men, for reasons that had nothing to do with pretended deference, he molded her palm over him, feeling the silken stretch of the erotically snug glove over her fingers, the bumps of her knuckles. He had to stifle his own groan. She teased his hard length, not at the easiest angle at the moment, having come to the erect state beneath the slacks and him still too much of a wowser to handle himself in mixed company. Mary made a plea, and Aapti gave her a hard, strong lick, worrying her clit, making her scream in short bursts. The Indian woman's silken hair pooled on the floor. Indulging herself, Chiyoko reached past the struggling maid to stroke her fingers through it, straighten it, but then took one of the small pillows and forced the edge of it into Mary's mouth.

"Bite down and be silent," she commanded, and Dev knew the order had come from Ian, from the faint displeasure on his face at the noise.

"Now, in deference to Lord Charles," Danny said, a quiet purr, keeping her eye on the women even as she let her knuckles glide across the straining fabric of Dev's pants, "I did witness a marvelous entertainment in Berlin. They blindfolded a man, his body bound on a St. Andrew's cross. It was unfinished wood, and they'd dragged him over it several times first, so splinters had embedded themselves in his back, his buttocks, thighs, the backs of his arms. It was rope crucifixion, but the cross was tilted to a forty-five-degree angle. The point was the edge of pain, not agony.

"They brought woman after woman to him, impaled them on his cock, and yet he didn't know who or what he was fucking. They kept teasing him to arousal, never letting him release. It went on all night. Every once in a while, his Mistress would bring him water and food. The tenderness with which she fed him, stroked him, whispered to him of her pleasure—for it was all *for* her pleasure—was so moving. Particularly the way he strained to kiss her, in a way he hadn't strained for the others. Emphasizing that, for all of them, he was performing. But with her, it was no performance. That was the true artistry of it, seeing the contrast between what was real, and illusion. What was art and what was mere entertainment."

"A romantic interpretation," Ian scoffed. "Typical for a female."

Lord Charles lifted a shoulder. "Perhaps. But I think the point

Lady Danny is making is a sound one. For younger vampires, it's about cock and cunt. But simply skimming the surface of physical pleasures can sap the mind. To really live, a vampire must seek deeper, explore all the facets of who we each are, what drives us. What the need for blood really means."

"And we each interpret that differently." Danny inclined her head to him, lifted her wine. Then she altered the direction of her gaze, considered Ian. He met her look with a studied one of his own, let his gaze drift down over her breasts. His intent focus moved to the way her hand stroked over Dev. When it resulted in a look of displeasure on Ian's face, her lips curved, half invitation, half challenge. It gripped Dev's gut unpleasantly, even as he couldn't stop the occasional slight jerk into the knowledgeable grip of her hand. With her free one, she dipped her finger in her wine, trailed it down her neck pulse and lower, to the ripe curves that held Ian's attention beneath her pendant. Distantly, Dev noted that Ruskin was keeping an interested eye on all of them.

Mary was making rapid, muffled bleats into the pillow. "Let's tone it down some, ladies," Danny commanded. "I want to draw this out, turn her into a mindless animal before she comes."

I need your mouth, Dev. I want it between my legs.

11

A T his startled glance, her blue eyes, smoldering dangerously, lifted to his. *Yes. Right here, right now. Serve me before them. Show them what you have that they do not. The ability to make me scream in pleasure, far louder than Mary.*

Her grip flexed, causing his cock to convulse and hampering his ability to think clearly. He knew she'd already coaxed moisture from the tip with her knowledgeable fingers, for he could feel the damp spot in his shorts. *I won't bugger that poor girl in front of them, whether she comes or not.*

Even though you can't help thinking of it, bending her over the table and making her take every inch of you? Her gaze flickered. *Like me, her capacity for pain is almost limitless, in human terms. You could cut her with your knife and she'd curl her blood-soaked fingers around your wrist, plead with you to cut her again.*

She was good, absolutely ruthless, but maybe because sharing thoughts like these made it impossible to completely block everything she felt, he caught something. He thought it might be pity. Or maybe that was just his futile hope.

I won't do it, my lady. Play your games with them, not with me. An idiotic thing to say, of course, as he stood before a group of strangers, letting her stroke him to the edge of spurting. He grimaced at her ironic brow.

Of course, I never said you had to bugger her before them. You imagined that. What if I sent her to your rooms after we retire tonight, order her to stay there until you've fucked her to your heart's content? That arse is perfect for you, soft, like holding on to the two sides of a welcoming pillow.

The only arse I want is yours. The only woman I want is you. That's why my cock is hard. Because you orchestrated this, because you're what's driving all of us half mad with lust, the female alpha of the pack, and you bloody well know it.

Though he had the heat of anger, the surprised flash through her eyes at the deeper emotion behind it had him fighting the urge to put his hand on hers, tell her to give over, bring an end to this circus and let him sate her lust in the privacy of her rooms. Serve her in the way he knew she preferred. Knew it to the bottom of his soul.

But it didn't change what she had to be in this company.

"Are you and your *nonservant* having a disagreement?"

Ian's mocking voice grated on Dev's nerves. He could piss off. Because Dev was about to make a damn fool of himself without his help. Summoning up a memory of Shakespearean theater and praying he didn't look a total idiot, he dropped to one knee by Danny's chair. Bowing his head, he let his hand fall, brush the toe of one slipper, let her feel the heat and strength of his palm as he closed his fingers around it. "My lady, how may I best serve you?"

When she'd talked about the Mistress feeding her blindfolded servant, her voice had thickened. In her rooms earlier, he'd realized there was a vulnerable core to a dominant woman that only the man who surrendered to her might get to visit, perhaps even dwell there forever, if he won the right to a permanently open door. As her fingers whispered over his ear, he felt the tremor, realized the truth of it again. But her voice, when she spoke, was almost indifferent, though laced with a glittering lust that would stimulate the other two men in the room. Whether to lust or fury, he was uncertain.

"You may pleasure me, Dev. Use your mouth. Show these two vampire lords what you can do for me."

A pressure on his shoulder then, pushing him down. Then her hands were gathering the taffeta, the gold fabric draping over his head, and he understood. He bowed even lower as she adjusted, one slender leg under his arm, the other guided over his shoulder as he moved forward in the darkness, toward the scent of her arousal brought to the edge of the chair. He found her garter by touch, the attachment to her stocking, and he slid his thumb under it, following the stretched line of it up to her hip, while his other hand discovered the crease between thigh and bare sex. Christ, she'd been telling the truth. The only things under here were the garters, stockings and her.

Modest before them, she was. An aristocrat. She'd let him eat her pussy, but in a way they could only see by suggestion, and by her reaction.

Can you make me come hard and long, bushman?

I suggest you hang on to the arms of that chair, my lady. And hope they're sturdy.

He didn't know someone could laugh in their mind, particularly not in a soft, seductive way that gave his cock another hard jolt. It had a different sound, softer even than that earlier purr for Ruskin and Ian. What was the act and what was real? He wanted to believe this was the reality, the rest the illusion she'd described. He couldn't do this believing otherwise, God knew.

He liked it like this, where all his focus was here, on her cunt, the rest disappearing in a dark void, his hearing muted by the dress and the clasp of her thighs around his head, increasing as he tasted her, teased the outer labia, tracing the line of it all the way around, overlooking the clit as he warmed her up elsewhere, flicking between the outer and inner sensitive lips. Breathing on her, delving into her drenching honey as her hips rose to his face. From the tautness of her body, he knew she had in fact gripped the arms harder.

Dimly, he could hear Mary's pleading noises, which fair begged for a climax, the clink of silverware as the staff came and retrieved the final course, probably to replace it with tea. He wondered if the server was having to step over his bent legs to retrieve one set of dishes and replace it with another. Bloody oath, what a world. But he didn't give a damn at the moment. All that mattered was this, the fact she'd now let go of one arm to grip his shoulder, finding him beneath the jacket to grip the thinner fabric of the pressed shirt. She yanked on him so hard he felt the seams tear, the spasm of her fingers a welcome caress.

Now at last he moved to her clit, working beneath the hood, biting gently, then moving his tongue over it in a leisurely coil, like a snake winding about on a rock in the sun, spreading a full measure of warmth over the expanse of sensitive nerve endings. She gasped, let out a harsh moan. The table protested as someone shifted. Perhaps Ian or Charles had turned his chair with uncharacteristic lack of grace, their attention now divided between the two stimuli. Even so, the hair lifting on the back of his neck told him more than physical lust was rising in the room. It wasn't much of a leap to realize it might be inadvisable, having a human service her needs when there were two alpha male vampires in the room. Well, she'd said she'd handle the vampires, and until they hauled him out back and tore him limb from limb, he'd trust in that.

"Chiyoko, Aapti, stop now." Danny spoke abruptly. "Mary, return to your duties. As you are, without any of your clothing. You will stay that way until sunrise. Let it be known that any man on the place who wishes to have you tonight may do so. As often and however he wishes, though I will hold them accountable if you are unable to perform your duties tomorrow evening."

Christ. Damn it, Danny—

She is fine, I promise. Obey me.

Her commanding tone was punctuated by subtle breathlessness, but he still had to marvel at her control, because her cunt was rippling against his mouth.

"Now, you two. Come enjoy my bushman. He deserves a reward . . ." She stopped, her hand molding over his forehead, only the thin taffeta between them. It broke the contact with his mouth, but her leg pressing into his back told him she wanted him to stay where he was. "For the treasure of his tongue," she finished, though the hard spasm that went through her thighs told him how close he'd come to sending her over. He struggled to obey the clamp of that thigh, the alpha in him pretty worked up as well.

Remember that blindfolded servant, my love. Focus on serving me instead of your own desires. It's important.

He did, but it was difficult to stay still when feminine but quite bold hands touched his back, his buttocks. Long, stroking touches, the hands of women who knew exactly what they were about. He'd thought of whores earlier, but this was far more than that. They were like the temple priestesses of ancient times, for whom coupling was an offering to their Goddess, women who possessed the skill and intensity that came with loving the act, considering it a sacred power of its own almost without equal.

Oxford scholar . . . your mind is as stimulating . . . as your mouth. Stop thinking, though . . . Just feel.

She'd eased the pressure of the leg, and so he laid brief, teasing kisses against her wet lips, trailing his tongue along the inside of her thigh as the servants touched him.

Then he stopped, tensing. Tugging off his jacket was fine, but now they were unbuckling the knife holster, the pistol.

The weapons have no use at this moment, Dev. And they won't leave my sight.

One of them had unlatched his belt, and her clever hands had unfastened his slacks. He did not know either woman enough to know whose hands were doing what, but they were equally confident. One set pulling the shirt and collar off his shoulders as another pair ran over his chest, then down, down, gripping him as they took his pants down, past his knees, sliding them off with his boots, leaving him uncomfortably bare-arsed, totally naked. But before he could worry too much about that, Jesus, they widened his stance, tugging on one knee until he obliged.

I'm feeling forgotten, Dev. She was teasing him now, bloody woman. *Concentrate on me, not on them.*

Forgotten? He plunged his tongue deep inside, suckling her lips ruthlessly so she arched and gasped. His hands were free, so he used three of his fingers, sinking them in, knowing his calluses would rub against the tender flesh, be a delicious friction.

He started as a soft female body pressed against the inside of his calves, one of the servants having obviously lain down between them and used the leverage of her hands on his spread thighs to put her head on the floor between his knees. At the brush of chain against his skin, he realized it was Chiyoko with her nipple clamps. Aapti's hand, then, was the one that gripped his cock and levered it down into the other woman's waiting mouth. They had to be twisting around him and Danny like sinuous cats. A moment later all speculation or coherent thought of any kind abandoned him, for both mouths were teasing his cock, making him realize Aapti had slithered through the rungs of Danny's chair to come at him from the front. Now Chiyoko gave the whole of his cock to Aapti as she began to suck his testicles into her mouth, stimulating the sensitive stretch of skin between balls and anus with clever skill. He let out a guttural, purely bestial sound against Danny's flesh, feeling his seed boil up in him.

Not before you make me come, Dev. Or I will *make you take Mary's tender backside tonight. I'm strong enough to shove her down onto a table and slam you down right on top of her, feed that enormous cock into her while Charles and Ian hold your arms.*

He heard a threat in her voice that made him believe it. She'd do it, not because this was one of her games, but because, though she'd commanded these women to arouse him, his first duty was to her. She would tolerate nothing else.

Trying to hold off the overwhelming pressure building in his balls, his lower abdomen, the muscles tightening all along his body, preparing for explosion, he mindlessly tickled, teased, flailed and licked her clit until she was bumping up against his face rhythmically. The grip of her hand on his shoulder became painful, almost bone crushing in its strength.

At this point he was like a wolf with the scent of blood in his nose. Aapti could deep-throat a man all the way to her lungs—that lucky piker Ruskin didn't deserve her—and was working his cock in and out of her mouth and throat, a slick, entirely pussylike passage. She'd likely have tears at the corners of her lips for a few days, for she had a blissfully small mouth. He noticed such things, having a cock the size he did. Danny had a fairly small, bow-shaped mouth, the kind he most liked to shove his cock into. That was what he'd like to do to his fair, beautiful sheila, have her service him like this, feel her take all of him . . .

She gasped, her body spasming again, and he wondered if she'd seen that image. He hoped so. "Come," he whispered against her flesh, making it quiver further. He wasn't loud enough for them to hear, but he wanted her to feel the words, as well as hear them in her head. "Come, my lady. Scream for me."

At that moment, the one suckling his testicles teased his anus with a finger, and he detonated. As Danny began to come, crying out her pleasure, he shot his load down the other girl's throat. His wild animal growl vibrated against his lady's flesh, driving her higher, if the punishing grip of her thighs around his head was any indication, the hard grinding of her wet pussy in his face that smothered him for a few dizzying moments.

As he eventually slowed, making unexpected grunts similar to the soft gasps of Danny's aftershocks, his body jerking and convulsing against the women's mouths and fingers, he collected enough brain cells together to wonder what the other two vampires were doing. If it had been him, he would have been yanking his servant away and fucking her senseless on the table.

He'd never been so saturated with sexual energy, surrounded by it, driven by it. If this was the way they usually conducted their dinner parties, he didn't wonder that the participants were mostly full servants, with the enhanced abilities Danny had mentioned. Sex like this could kill a mere mortal in short order.

While he was winded, his mother had raised a gentleman, though it had been a long time since he'd thought of himself that way, and certainly not in this context. He finished with tenderness, giving her a brief cleanup with his tongue, gentle kisses, rubbing his clean-shaven jaw against the softness of her inner thigh, pressing kisses there, too. Her hand was still relaxed, almost limp, as she stroked the curve of his skull through the light fabric, the line of his shoulder. He wondered about the picture she must make, a languidly sated woman, her legs spread and yet all but her calves covered, the shape of his body provocatively outlined beneath the skirt.

The women withdrew, their hands caressing as they moved back. Curiously, they clothed him again, sliding his shorts and pants back on, tucking him back in and zipping him up with care, which he appreciated. His blindness made the metallic music of their jewelry, and some breathy giggles, sound like small bells, all the more distracting. Then they were threading the belt, tucking the shirt, their hands teasing and provocative. They left off the collar and tie, which he didn't mind.

Stay where you are, Dev. On your knees, facing my chair.

With lithe grace, using the leverage of her heeled slipper against his back, she rose. Her skirt drifted off his head and shoulders, leaving him blinking in the candlelit room. His lust still high, he imagined how the fluids he'd been unable to reach with his tongue would now be trickling down her leg, marking her. Turning his head, he stayed where he was, but discovered Ian straightening, arranging his clothes. He'd obviously kept Mary in the room, for she was bent over the table to his left, her hands fisted in the tablecloth, tears on her face from how hard he'd worked her, her body shuddering as if in the aftermath of climax. Either she'd been ordered to be quiet about it by Ian, or Dev had just been too absorbed in himself to hear her.

Ian took his place again, tossing a leg over the chair arm, hooking his arm on the back, the picture of the careless, dissolute young nobleman in his own hall. "Now you can go, Mary," he said, tossing Danny a smirk. The maid didn't need to be told twice, pushing herself up from the table and gathering her clothes to leave the dining room.

"A moment, Mary." Danny's voice brought the woman to a halt at the door, though Mary kept her head down. "Please tell the staff we do not wish to be disturbed until I send Dev for them."

She nodded, bobbed another quick curtsy, with remarkable grace considering she wasn't wearing a stitch, and disappeared, closing the double doors behind her. Dev noted that Aapti and Chiyoko had taken a place against the wall behind the empty side of the table, remaining naked as well. Aapti had her arm around Chiyoko's waist and was fondling the woman's small breasts as the Asian girl leaned in to her, her hand reaching back to find Aapti's hip, caressing. Their movements were languid, unhurried, the intent obviously to provide ongoing visual entertainment for the vampires, not to bring each other to climax again, though it was clear they would keep each other well stimulated. Dev knew he would have had a hard time tearing his eyes away as well, except that Danny's instruction to the maid had drawn the attention of the two vampires.

"More games, Lady D?" Lord Charles raised a brow.

Danny gave him a smile that Dev suspected would have tempted any man down the road to perdition. "I find this has just whetted my appetite. But if you don't mind, first, more wine. No, I'll get it myself. I can tell Ian likes the way I walk." She sauntered in a relaxed, sated fashion over to the side bar. Since it was behind Ian's chair, she leaned forward until she was eye to eye with him, and the deep plunge between her breasts couldn't help but command his eye. "You imagined it was me when you were fucking her, didn't you?"

Lord Charles's chuckle caused a scowl to cross Ian's face. When Danny reached out a hand, trailed a fingertip along Ian's jaw, Dev tensed as Ian seized her wrist, holding her there, the tension between their arms suggesting he'd tried to unbalance her, haul her forward.

She neither moved nor flinched, simply stretched out her fingers and continued to stroke up to his cheekbone. Then across his lips in a deliberate way until they parted, touched her with his tongue, showing the needle edge of one fang. "And who were you thinking about, my lady," he said huskily, "when that mongrel was eating your cunt?"

"Why, him, of course. Look at him, Ian. Why would I want to imagine Dev as anything but the perfect human specimen he is?" Arching a brow, she glanced over at Dev.

Ian gave Dev a narrow look that suggested he'd be happy to see him crucified with railroad spikes. Dev mentally thanked whoever was responsible for getting the women to put his pants back on, for now that his focus was changed, he had no wish to be bare-arsed before the other vampires. In the corner of his eye, he discerned that Ruskin was also watching him, and there was no friendliness there, either.

While he dearly would have liked to give both bastards a *bugger-*

off look that couldn't be misinterpreted, he wasn't as hardheaded as Danny feared. He knew it was best not to do something to piss someone off until he was sure what the hell was going on. She'd intended to provoke them by letting him pleasure her; that was easy enough to understand. But he wasn't sure if she sought to stoke their anger, lust or something beyond his comprehension.

With a snort, Ian released her. The red imprint of his fingers showed on her white skin. Dev indulged in a graphic visual of breaking each one of them.

"You're baiting us," Ian said. "You like to tease, Lady Danny."

"Perhaps." She straightened with that same smile in place. "But as I said, Ian, I am not the same woman who left here over forty years ago. What I want to know is if you are the same man. Can you satisfy me enough to make it worth my while to keep you around? More wine, Lord Charles?"

Moving behind Ian's chair, she let her hand trail along his arm, up to his neck, even teased the queue of his hair, drawing Lord Charles's eye as she gave him a bold stare that caused his brow to crease, a smile to curve his lips as he shook his head, noting his glass was still half full.

"That depends, my lady," Ian said. "But I suspect I can more than adequately supply what you need."

"Then you won't mind a small test of that?" She gave him a look that had an unmistakable sexual challenge in it as he shrugged, spread his hands.

"I'm at your disposal, my lady."

Picking up a strawberry from the side bar, she inhaled the aroma, then bit halfway into it, apparently letting it tease her taste buds, before she leaned over the top of the chair. When she brought it to his mouth, Ian covered the fruit and her lips with his own, one hand rising to twine in that single lock of hair. She drew back as he bit down, taking half of the strawberry from her lips. Since she remained leaning over him, he withdrew the fruit from his mouth and used it to mark a faint crimson cross on the high pillow of one pale breast. Her lips parted, showing a hint of fang, her eyes flashing with obvious lust. Lord Charles chuckled appreciatively.

"I think Lady Danny has learned a great deal on her travels. She no longer seems the angry child you told me about. I'd hold on to that invitation."

"I might at that." Tilting his head back, Ian stared up at Danny as she settled along the top of the chair, letting her hand tease his cheek. He turned, nipped her, and the tooth raked her palm, pearls of blood welling from the track.

"The responsibilities of an overlord are much for one person," she commented, letting Ian play as she glanced over at Lord Charles. "Particularly for me. I wish to honor my mother. If Ian served her well as a partner, I see no reason not to continue with that, for the time being." She picked up another strawberry from the side bar.

"Will you seal that bargain with a kiss, my lady?" Ian's eyes were bright on her face. "And let me take you to my bed tonight?"

"Perhaps I will take you to mine. And it is not a bargain. It is a trial period," she amended, with a cooler smile. "I am not so easy as all that. Close your eyes, Ian, and let's see if you can see the difference between a plump strawberry breast, and the taste of strawberry on my lips. I'm feeling generous."

Dev's brow had creased throughout the exchange, and now his blood heat rose in violent reaction as she leaned down toward the male vampire once again. He knew she could hear him in her mind, wanted to fire something suitably scathing at her, but held it, his jaw clenched. Less than a couple hours ago, she'd taken him into her body. Maybe she thought what he said about tolerating other men only applied to human males she took to his bed. He wasn't sure how a vampire thought about such things, really. Bloody hell.

Her blue gaze softened, just a touch, painfully reminding him of how she'd given him a similar look. When her thumb dropped to cradle Ian's jaw, the intimate gesture made bad go to worse. He knew it was a game, that she loathed Ian, but how could she perfect the exact same look, unless both were an act to get each of them to do as she wished? She'd said politics had to be played. Well, to hell with that, and her. He preferred the straightforward survival needs of the bush. If she kissed Ian, he was going to murder someone. That was the end of it.

A vampire could move faster than a human eye could track. Dev already knew that. But it still caught him off guard when Lord Charles surged up from his chair, violently enough it turned over and hit the wall.

A blink later, Ian's head toppled off his shoulders, bouncing off the chair arm and hitting the floor.

12

IT made a hard thump, reminding Dev how much the head actually weighed, a nasty tidbit he'd learned during the war.

Severed arteries sprayed blood, spattering the walls, Lady Danny and her lovely gold dress, even the elegant china tea settings.

A choked scream from Chiyoko sent Dev lunging around the table, helping Aapti to catch her as she fell to the floor, the Asian girl convulsing. Dev ripped off the collar to give her the ability to breathe, but Aapti's expression, the knowledge there, brought Danny's words back to him brutally.

A third-marked servant dies when the vampire dies . . .

Aapti covered her fellow servant with the arch of her body, her hand in her hair, her soft voice murmuring to her. At her calmness, Dev wondered how many sights such as these the Indian servant had seen. Except for a subdued quivering, she had no outward display of shock. A moment before Ian's decapitation, she'd had her mouth brushing over Chiyoko's, sharing their pleasure in each other, even if it was for the primary benefit of their Masters.

While he knelt by the Asian girl, feeling the heat leaving her hands, Dev saw the bloodstained wire clasped in Danny's hands. He recalled the artful and provocative way she'd trailed her fingers across the tops of her breasts, as accomplished as Salome, the way she'd teased her cleavage as she'd cradled Ian's jaw. The approach of her lips holding the strawberry, the sense of her breath on his face, would have made Ian's eyes half close even if they weren't closed already, preparing for the coming bliss, the spike to his lust.

It was all she'd needed. It was easy enough to reverse engineer now. She'd pulled the wire, cleverly threaded into the underwiring of her bodice, looped it around his throat and yanked, no more than a blink with vampire speed and the element of surprise.

Without the element of surprise, you've got no chance at all . . . Her gaze met his, then shifted to Lord Charles. He was still on his feet, though now he appeared to be waiting on her, rather than preparing for attack. "Under Council law," she said, "I am overlord of this territory. His attack upon me in the desert, where he intended to take my life, entitled me to retribution."

"Council law supports that." He inclined his head. "But you also know that my permission is needed to take a vampire's life in my territory. There will be a cost."

Her expression didn't flicker. "You are Region Master, Lord Charles. I certainly have no wish for discord between us. Since I owe you a fencing match tonight, perhaps we will discuss it before or after that. Will you allow me to handle this household matter first?"

At his nod, she shifted her gaze to Dev. She might have been a living corpse such as Stoker imagined, as little life as he saw in her eyes. "Dev, please ask the staff to gather out front. All of them."

She stood to the left of a headless vampire's body, slumped over the side of the beautifully carved Queen Anne chair, his servant dead at Dev's feet. He found he couldn't respond until she prompted him again gently. *Dev, can you handle it? Or do you just want to go?*

From the Region Master's scrutiny, Dev knew he was expecting him to jump through the hoops properly for her. Despite that, once again she was giving him the chance to get the hell out of here and not look back.

Maybe anyone else would have leaped at that chance. He could think of a lot of other places he'd rather be right now, for certain. However, during the grueling New Guinea campaign, he'd learned to split his mind into two parts. He'd process all sorts of data—enemy movement, the location of his mates, whether his weapon was ready to fire, the placement of his feet and body for the action he would face. He was hyperalert to every whisper of wind, crackle of grass, the scrape of a boot on a rock. And yet he was entirely numb to clambering over fallen bodies, the rage that made him scream like a madman as he fired, not caring about life or death.

Some part of him knew, when it got quiet again, there'd be something worse than death to face, the two parts of his brain coming back together whether he wanted them to or not. So he'd learned that what was important in the face of the unthinkable was not to make any big decisions right then. Only the little ones, the ones that moved you moment to moment.

Yeah. I can handle it.

She nodded. "Please inform Mary I expect her to take the next available transportation off the station. She is discharged. I don't want her here."

He looked down. "My lady, what would you like—"

"Please select a few of the men to carry the two bodies outside, where the assembled staff can see them."

"My lady." Lord Ruskin held out his arm. "What say we retire to the study a few moments, share another glass of wine while your man gathers the staff and follows your direction?" His gaze traveled over her. "I am assuming you do not care to change until they've seen you, to underscore the point."

"As ever, you understand a great deal." Danny inclined her head. "Perhaps my grievances about you with the Council were rash, youthful. Sometimes stronger measures are needed to handle matters."

With another glance at Dev, she exited with Ruskin, her mind silent, though he didn't know what she could say that would make him feel better about this. Or if she even felt it was necessary to try.

Chiyoko had fallen gracefully, and her legs were folded together, one foot slightly turned over the other, like a babe in the womb. Aapti layered her hands on her chest, closed her eyes. While he wasn't sure why he did it, Dev figured out the nipple clamps, removed them, as well as all the chains, to leave her in only her flawless skin. Aapti didn't look at him, but he saw her lips press together, and a tear trickle down her cheek.

Rising, mind numb, Dev headed for the kitchen to do his lady's bidding.

~

There were about eighteen people who belonged to Danny's station. Household staff, and those who maintained the building and merino sheep. In gathering together the latter, Dev quickly pieced together that Ian had allowed the flock to dwindle to such a low number it barely qualified as a hobby, keeping the men dangerously idle except for violent pursuits like Danny's ambush. Dev suspected she'd have to dismiss most of them and start from scratch.

Lord Charles's men stood off to one side, below where Charles stood on the porch, leaning against the railing. Those in the courtyard had their eyes fastened on their new Mistress, who'd stepped out in the blood-spattered taffeta dress. The torchlight made the fabric shimmer, fire glittering in her golden hair. There was a slash of blood across her cheek. Dev noted old Jim off to the side, and the old stockman looked . . . relieved. Remarkably unsurprised by this turn of events. Strewth, Dev apparently had a lot to learn about vampires. The question was, did he want to know any more?

"Ian is dead because of his attempt to kill me." Danny addressed them all bluntly, glancing toward Ruskin. "I have reclaimed my mother's station. You stay, work for me, you'll get a good wage. If you aren't a good worker, I'll sack you. You can hike the twenty or so miles to intercept a truck train to take you out of here." The frost of her eyes increased, made brilliant by the torchlight, as if a demon within surged to the forefront, capturing their attention. Dev noted no one coughed or shifted. There was no muttering. They were riveted upon her.

"Betray me, and I will stake you out on the fence, give you enough water to keep you suffering and alive for days, and let the sun, bugs and the limitation of your frail human body kill you. Do *not* make the mistake of thinking I will not employ violence when necessary, simply because I am not as violent as Ian." She looked toward old Jim. "Put Ian's body out past the fence to burn when the sun rises. Have the maids prepare his servant's body for burial. Put her outside our family plot, but give her a decent marker." Her attention moved back to the assembly. "I will give her that. I've no idea of her character, but her judgment in relationships was poor. Bear that lesson in mind."

Her gaze then shifted to the maid staff. "After I change, Lord Ruskin and I will have a fencing match in the courtyard. Please have brandy brought there. Oh"—she stopped in midturn—"Devlin is the new station manager until I say otherwise. You will bring any questions to him. That is all. Go back to your duties or your sleep."

～

He saw their speculative looks. What they didn't know was he had as many questions as they did. She hadn't given him much of a job description up to now. It wasn't the first job he'd had to learn by the seat of his pants, and a description seemed a bit laughable in any case. They hadn't talked wages, either. Another absurd topic, really. But after he assisted old Jim and the rest of the staff in cleaning up the aftermath of her coup, he decided she owed all of them a raise.

He'd gone from the graveside of his son and wife straight into the army. It wasn't until that was over that he'd known he wasn't returning to his station, ever again. Instead, he'd gone on walkabout. He came in and out of towns, worked here or there as he wanted or needed to. Being a swagman had become a state of mind, a drifting to find something of meaning. A purpose, an arrow of sorts? He certainly felt he'd been shot by one.

He'd thought it over and couldn't do this. He couldn't live in a world like this. That was the end of it. He'd stick with her through tonight, though. When these immediate tasks were handled as best as could be managed, he'd find her to let her know. That was the type of message she deserved to have delivered in person.

Plus, she'd been silent as a stump in his mind since she left the porch. He was learning her voice came from a certain direction in his mind, for lack of a better description, and right now there was a solid wall in that spot. He wasn't even sure if he "thought" his intentions at her, she'd hear them.

So when at last he went looking for her, he found she hadn't come back down yet. Probably still getting ready for her fencing match. How in the hell could she manage an idle sport after that? He shook his head, closed it off. Not his issue, really.

But as he reached the top of the stairs, prepared to move down the main second floor hallway, he stopped. Her scent, that light perfume she'd worn for dinner . . . it was here, as if she'd recently gone this way. Turning down a narrower, left-hand corridor, and obeying that instinctive sense of her, he put his hand on the doorknob of a room he hadn't explored and turned it.

It was a smaller bedroom, though it had a washroom like the master rooms. He moved around the bed, studying the simple, elegant arrangement of a guest room, similar to where Danny had put him.

The mirror in the washroom confirmed this area was intended for human habitants. He almost turned away, since he didn't see her in the reflection that showed the rest of the bathroom, then he stopped. While he'd already learned some lore about vampires wasn't true, and some of it was unimaginable, it was possible that certain things, like the inability to cast a reflection, could be fact. He leaned into the room.

Since he'd met her, she'd overwhelmed him sexually and emotionally. He'd seen her fight like a tiger for her life against superior numbers and firepower, overcome third-degree burns, and tonight, single-handedly murder the overlord of this territory. Still, she could surprise him. Like now.

She was squatting on her heels, wedged in the far corner, between the commode and the sink. Hunched over, she had her arms wrapped around herself, her back to the door.

He didn't believe anyone could come upon her unawares, and he didn't believe he did so now. Which might explain one of the reasons his heart lurched when he squatted behind her, and she merely lowered her head further. As he wrapped his arms over hers, blanketing her, tremors rippling across her back became hard convulsions, terrible, strangled things that made him realize she was crying. Crying the way a hysterical woman would cry, only in complete silence.

I hate this, Dev. Hate it so much.

Relieved to hear it, love.

She made a noise, something like a snort and a sob. When he tightened his arms around her, the twisted sense of wrongness in him loosened. He'd no doubt she was comfortable with her dominant sexuality, her predator's bloodlust, but until Ian, he'd seen her as a beautiful wild animal, like a cougar. It all clicked together, even before she opened her mind to let him see it, because it hadn't made sense until this minute. And a different twist wrenched his vitals.

"It wasn't just what he did to your mother. Bloody hell."

Her response came in a painful flood of thoughts and images, jumbled like her emotions. *I never cared much for him, but he seemed to love her so much. When she was away . . . I was over a hundred, but he was older, and he took me by surprise. Took by force what I wouldn't give. Only the two of us here, and the staff, who couldn't interfere. Only old Jim is left of those to remember, thank God. But he was the only one who came up afterward to see if there was anything he could do. He's a good sort. But it's something you don't forget, having someone hurting you, with so many close by, but none able to help.*

He remembered the way she'd let Ian touch her, tease the strawberry over her breast, how soft and willing her gaze had been. *Ah, love . . .*

But she wouldn't take his comfort. Abruptly, she turned, putting her back to the wall. He kept his hands on her as she slid to a sitting position on the floor, planted her bare feet between his boots. She'd changed into jodhpurs and a snug shirt for her fencing. "Like I said, Dev, I'm not her. You do get that, don't you?"

"I do." He reached out, cupped her face. "You're nothing like Tina, love."

She searched his countenance, nodded. "This is the way it is for vampires. What they can take from one another through violence and force, some of that's allowed. Like me killing Ian tonight. That's okay, as long as I pay my due to Ruskin. As long as we stay within the boundaries of the Council's rules. We're monsters, playing at being civilized, that's all."

He tipped her chin. "Sounds a lot like humans."

She shifted her glance back to the tile, nodded. "I'm sorry, Dev. I used you for the distraction. Doesn't mean I wasn't glad to have you at my back. You came to tell me you're going, didn't you?"

"You're a selfish bitch. That's a fact." Pushing a lock of her hair over her ear, he lingered there, passed his thumb over her cheek. No tears. She'd allowed herself only the sobbing, and that had been stingy, hard-won. She tilted her head away, and he made himself lower his touch. He wondered at the dark swirl of his own feelings, which seemed to be intertwined with hers. "I knew that, the first time you took me to your bed. But there's more to you than that. I don't think we're done with one another yet."

Fanning out her fingers on her knees, she closed her eyes. "If it helps to know . . . I did what I had to do tonight, but I knew the highest price I might pay for my vengeance was losing you."

"Tweaking my ego, love?" He couldn't quite manage a smile.

"Well, you're so full of yourself, always putting on airs and bragging. Thought I should play to that."

"You don't have to play me at all, love. You might figure that out one day." He reached over her bent knee, squeezed her cold fingers. Feeling an unexpected brush of hair, he looked down to see she held a lock of it beneath that palm. She shook her head.

"I didn't come in here to fall to pieces. When he did it, all those years ago, I cut off a piece of my hair, put it behind this loose tile. So that when I took his worthless life, I could take this part of that younger, naive version of myself, and tell that woman it was done. I'm no victim, Dev." The truth of it was in the sharp edge of her voice, the brief glimpse of banked anger in her gaze. "The day it happened, I'd have torn him to pieces once I got free, but I wanted my mother to know the truth, to send him away, because that would be a worse punishment. She didn't. She believed him when he said I was angry because I'd tried to lure him to my bed and failed." She gave a brittle laugh. "So bloody clichéd, but women in love with monsters fall for it, all the time. And I was no better, acting like one of those ridiculous heroines. Hurt, betrayed, I left, turned my back on her. Knowing the Ennui was starting to get a grip on her, I should have stayed, figured out a way to do this then, and then forced her to see the truth. She was . . . she was never right after my father's death. Far more gullible. She needed me. I failed my father in that regard."

Turning her hand, she tucked the silken curl in his. It had been lighter then, he noted, and wondered if the older she got, the darker gold her hair would become, until she would be like a sun unto herself, moving through darkness.

"You can let the wind carry that over the desert now," she said. "That younger Danny can rest in peace, such that she is."

He nodded. "And what about you?"

Her lips twisted, and she tangled the fingers of her other hand with his empty one. Bringing it to her face, she rested her face in his palm, holding there for a long moment, leaning into his touch. "I've got one more monster to handle."

"You're not going to—"

"Not tonight." She lifted her chin, and he saw that streak of cold purpose glimmer in her gaze. "No stomach for it, and it's the wrong time. But I expect it's going to come to that. Ian was what I'd expect from most of my kind. Ruskin . . ." She paused. "Ruskin is a true monster."

As she began to rise, they helped each other up. In the small confines of the bathroom, she was nearly pressed against him. He had a sudden urge to slide his arms around her, hold her close, but she slipped by him, turned at the door, the lady of the manor returned.

"Let's go get this fucking evening over with, shall we?"

~

The courtyard was an area enclosed with a low stone wall, a frame built over it with screen curtains draped on the sides to keep the flies from interfering with refreshments. Aapti was there already, her face drawn but composed. She wore a dark, less formal garment now, a skirt low on her hips and the stretched bodice from dinner that still showed the treasures she had to offer. She sat on one of the walls, a decanter of brandy next to her, ready to serve her Master if called.

The British vampire had simply removed his jacket, already being suitably attired. Danny's tight breeches and snug long-sleeved shirt would have been an indecent outfit, but she'd obviously dressed in anticipation of the exercise, how she would need to move or bend. Interestingly, she left her feet bare. The courtyard was carpeted in flat stone tile.

When Dev took a position in the opposite corner from Aapti, he sat down on his haunches, his bootheels flat on the ground, his back curved and body balanced without the support of the wall behind him, the way he'd often gathered with the aborigines. It was a tranquil pose, and he definitely needed tranquillity.

As she warmed up, a knot of tension was forming. He couldn't help but have a man's prejudice, worried for her, thinking of a female as more fragile and vulnerable when going toe-to-toe against a man's strength and skill at arms.

"Sabers?" Lord Charles nodded to the two weapons she'd brought out. Danny nodded, tossed one to him, which he caught by the hilt and examined the blade. "Your mother's weapons?"

"One set of them. She had others, but these were the ones I most preferred. Three strikes?"

"Versus collegiate rules?"

Danny's lips twisted. "Lord Charles, we were doing this when *dueling* was rampant. I like the simpler rules."

He acknowledged it with a bow and humorless smile. "We'll speak of Ian's death and the debt you owe me after our bout. When I defeat you, I will have the upper hand. It is more advantageous to me."

"Lord Charles, whether you win or lose this match, you will never have the upper hand on me."

"We shall see." He flashed teeth. *"En garde."*

Dev tried to keep himself relaxed, at least outwardly. And he had to admit his sheila had well-developed skills. As the two circled, feinted, parried, riposted, clashed, ducked and spun, running the gamut from competitive form to straight-out fighting, the stockmen who'd completed their tasks or were idle had circled to the outside of the courtyard to watch. While they stayed at a respectful distance, the vampires didn't seem to mind as the men became more involved in the match, commenting and calling out. Dev was sure part of it was they were absorbed by their new Mistress, who was a hell of a lot better to look at than Ian or Ruskin. She was bloody mesmerizing. He had to force himself to focus past that to note the way she compensated for Lord Charles's greater reach and height with quickness and superior flexibility. The first blood was hers, a slice that went over his guard and nicked his shoulder, leaving a bloom of blood on the white fabric.

They backed off, circled again. Charles was no longer looking relaxed and urbane, the polished aristocrat. He'd shifted to that aura of unnatural stillness, and Dev knew before the second strike came that he had her on this one. She parried in, and on the riposte, he lunged forward unexpectedly and jabbed her thigh, the blade scraping off, but tearing the fabric as she spun away. She'd put up her blond hair to keep it out of her way, holding it in place with sticks. Dev narrowed his eyes, wondering if they'd come from Chiyoko's belongings. For some reason, he was almost sure they had.

When Charles gave him a disdainful glance, he also realized he'd come to his feet on that nick, his hand on his knife hilt. "Your servant doesn't know the difference between play and threat among vampires, my lady."

Danny gave a short laugh, humorless, as she backed, regrouped, and began to circle again, performing a couple graceful sweeps with the blade to loosen her arm up further. "Neither do vampires. And he's not my servant."

Charles snorted. "More semantics, my lady." He engaged again. Clash of steel, turn, the torchlight catching the blades and making them flash. Sparks when the blades hit, edge to edge, slid off, both vampires retreating and then Danny starting with the lunge again. Dev noted that Charles's men and even Danny's had fallen silent. One more strike to go. After seeing her dispatch one of his overlords . . .

bloody hell, win or lose this bout, if Charles was still standing, he'd almost have to exact something dear to her, to punish her, put her in her place. And Danny knew that.

Charles's men had shifted from observation to watchfulness. Quite a few of them had wooden knives in their belts. Charles likely wasn't planning to kill her, but he didn't trust her, either. He wasn't taking any chances that she might be working her way down her "to do" list, and he was number two tonight.

My lady, in case you've rethought your plans, now is not *the time. His men are prepared.*

He tried to make the thought quiet, unobtrusive, and realized how absurd that was, since he had no idea what difference the volume of thoughts made in the recipient's head. Her glance shifted to him, briefly, and Charles had her. Using a surge of hard-to-follow speed, he thrust inside her guard, knocked it out wide and shoved her back, stumbling.

Dev started forward, and three of Charles's men came over the wall, holding him in place with a battery of pistols and drawn knives, skirting the circling vampires deftly. "Let it play out, mate," one of them said, keeping the pistol leveled at Dev's midsection.

While she was still stumbling back, Charles plowed his boot in her chest, knocking her to the ground and pinning her there on her back. When he pressed forward, a blade shot out of the sole, the tip jamming against the base of her throat. He held the saber at ready.

"You son of a bitch," Dev swore. He plunged forward, the hell with the weapons trained on him. Three who had circled to the rear jumped him, bearing him to the ground with liberal fists. At least one gun butt rapped him so smartly he saw stars. He ended up with his back against the stone wall, held by the rough hands of the three stockmen, the other three with their weapons trained on him. It was a gratifying number, if he was in the mood to be flattered.

Stop, Dev. Wait. Her voice was sharp and urgent enough to get through. She and Charles were still in the same position, staring at each other as Charles apparently waited for his men to get the situation under control.

"Yield, my lady?" he asked. His breath came up short, telling Dev that vampires could exert themselves, and his lady had done a damn good job of that. However, Ruskin's deadly gaze was still fastened on hers, his grip on the sword sure and steady. He could take her head with little effort. The stillness of his eyes suggested he wanted her to defy him, give him the chance. "You may voice your objections to the Council about my mastery of this territory, but you cannot find fault in my fencing skills."

She stared up at him, ignoring the blood trickling down her throat. "You were lucky tonight, but I will say your skills have improved since last we crossed swords."

"So you will swear loyalty to me?" He let the tip drift down, follow the curve of one breast. "Give me your blood?"

She tilted her head, an indifferent look. "Not likely, Lord Charles. As a full-blood vampire, I'm not required to do that."

"Even"—he pressed the tip of the blade against her —"if I insist? There is no Council here right now, Lady Daniela. Protesting after the fact is just whinging, as we both well know."

"With my lineage, I'm far more useful to you alive, if you can win my affections." She glanced down at the blade. "Stop being a bore, Charles. You won the fencing match. Take your bragging rights and help me up."

Dev watched, his heart in his throat. Though he suspected she didn't know, any more than anyone else, if he'd choose to kill her, she showed no fear.

Charles sighed. "You're being stubborn. It's a small thing. I could exact a far higher price for your infraction, and you know it."

"It's not a small thing at all. Which is why you want it so badly."

"Your breeding is a matter of circumstance," he sneered, his lip curling back. "Something your back alley thief of a mother stole from Fate and gave to you as if it came from the Queen's blood herself."

"Well, my mother would have been capable of stealing the Queen's jewels right from her head. Why not her blood as well?"

The cool frustration in Charles's eyes died away, replaced by a tight smile that Dev found more chilling. Swinging his boot off her and twitching the saber aside in a harrowing move, he nevertheless offered her a hand up.

When she rose, he retained his hold, his fingers pressing down as his expression darkened dangerously again. "I doubt your affections are even winnable, Lady D. So enough of your coquettishness. I know it for a sham, and won't tolerate it."

A muscle in her jaw flexed as his grip increased, but she shrugged. "A woman uses her assets to survive in this world, Lord Charles. If it offers no advantage with you, I'm happy to discard it. I find it rather tedious myself." Nodding to the table and chairs set up nearby with another bottle of brandy, she said, "If you'll let go of my hand, we can have that drink now and discuss your terms."

Come stand behind me, Dev.

Giving Charles's men a hard look, Dev shouldered past them and moved to the side porch. When he mounted the step and came up beside her, he went ahead and poured the brandy for her. At her nod, he did so for Lord Charles while Aapti quietly watched. The male vamp's eyes narrowed, apparently displeased by his unwillingness to offer the courtesy until Danny had bid him do so.

"I miss England," the vampire commented. "Where the servants are servants. Not ill-mannered stockmen or Irish whores, trained like monkeys to make beds and curtsy."

"England was too damp for me. Too closed in." Danny sat back with her brandy. As Dev realized she'd grown paler, he noticed the swelling in two fingers on the hand she rested gingerly on her thigh. The bastard had broken them.

Don't worry, bushman. Her calm voice smoothly cut through his rage. *They'll heal within an hour, good as new. Let him flaunt his testosterone. He was probably scared to death I'd offer a rematch.*

Dev took the wall behind her, though his gut was churning. He'd never longed for a sunrise more.

"I've no objection to you reclaiming your station," Charles commented, reaching back to take Aapti's hand. As he drew her forward, she set her hands to his shoulders and began to massage them. "But since the taking of a vampire's life must be justified to the Vampire Council by the Region Master, I will set the price to vouch for your actions."

"Neither my blood nor my body is on the table. I've no concerns about making my case before the Council if you try to force either of those upon me."

"Lady D, I'm beginning to suspect you *want* me to kill you, merely to cause me trouble with the Council."

"It would be a nice memory to take to my grave." She saluted him with her brandy. "You know how protective the Council is of born vampires."

"Regardless of how undeserving you are, or your lack of true bloodline." He took a swallow of his own drink, his gaze lingering on her fingers, as if enjoying the look of his work and wishing he could lean across and do more. "As far as your body, I couldn't care less about that. I can command a common whore anytime. Unlike Ian, I won't cater to the pretension that you or your mother are anything but that."

When Danny merely smiled, he let out a nasty chuckle. "You're a hard one to rattle, I give you that." He leaned forward, the glass dangling in his hand. Aapti paused. "I can make you pay the price with flogging or branding. You cannot know how much I'd enjoy binding you to stocks in your own yard, having your shirt torn from your body and whipping that pale flesh until it bled."

"Foreplay," she commented. "I thought you just said sex with me held no interest for you."

He bared his fangs. "The other thing I can demand is the sacrifice of a servant."

Putting down the brandy glass, Danny locked gazes with him. "I've already told you, he is not my servant. I'll take the branding or flogging."

The hell you will.

Hush, Dev.

"You misunderstand, *Lady* D." Ruskin cut across Dev's next mental retort. "Outside of blood price or sex, the choice is mine. I wasn't offering you an option."

"To take his life, you *will* have to take mine."

Danny didn't move from her chair, but what emanated from her then made Dev feel as if she'd risen to her feet. He wasn't alone in detecting it, as the handful of Charles's men still loitering nearby came to attention at the tone of her voice.

"Rather fond of him, aren't you?" Ruskin's voice had a serrated edge.

"This man saved my life. I owe him a debt of honor. As an aristocrat, I expect you to understand that." With him digesting the backhanded compliment, Danny's gaze flicked over Aapti's kneading hands. "She performs many services for you that make her indispensable. And she *is* your full servant. He's the closest thing approaching one I've had to date. I don't wish to carelessly throw away his life." She glanced over her shoulder, sweeping Dev from head to toe, and lingering on choice spots in between that almost made him blush. "Not when I'm still evaluating his worth."

Lord Charles studied her for a long moment. "Lady Danny, I think you should have been born male."

"Women can enjoy their carnality as much as men. Particularly if they have no care for the expectations of others."

"Which was why you left your mother when she needed you most."

She leaned back again, that half smile still playing on her lips. "A compliment. You see me as a worthy opponent again. You've gone from crude accusations back to subtle barbs. If you're going to take up where my mother left off, blaming me for the things that were her fault alone, I will *not* make a regular habit of inviting you to dinner."

"Enough of this," Ruskin said softly at last. "You submit to my station brand, planted on your right cheek, burned into the flesh with my blood, so it will be a permanent scar you carry." He shifted. "Or you give me a game of fox and hounds, with your man as the fox. Three days in the Outback. If he makes it back to the fence line by dusk on the third day, or dies, the score is even."

"Done," Dev said.

A muscle twitched in Danny's jaw, but she didn't acknowledge him. "My employee obviously does not speak for me. I do not agree to the terms."

Moving around the arm of the chair, Dev dropped to one knee, met her eye to eye. Maybe a true servant to a vampire would bow his head, but they all knew he wasn't that, no matter Ruskin's barbed comments. "Let me have the honor of paying this debt for you, my lady. I will not fail you. Obviously." An ironic smile twisted his lips. "Because dead or alive, I serve the purpose."

"Done, then," Ruskin said.

"No," Danny said sharply. She kept her gaze on Dev's face. "It's not done until I agree to it. You do not owe me this." *I just murdered Chiyoko to settle a vengeance debt. I don't deserve your sacrifice.*

My will is my own, my lady, remember? I don't know why I continue to live when there is so little for me to live for, but remarkably, every day, with the rising and setting of the sun, something presents itself. This is today's task.

Native spiritualist bullshit. Don't throw your aboriginal blood at me.

You have no problem drinking it.

He heard an alarming sound, almost as if she'd ground her teeth. "Speak out of turn again, and I'll rip your throat out to get at it," she said.

But she turned back to Ruskin, who had a smug look on his face. "Done, then," she spat. "But I will not thank you for depriving me of the man I've brought here to run my station, Lord Charles."

"You should have thought about that before you killed my overlord, pretentious fop that he was."

Giving Ruskin a reserved look, she rose, shifted her gaze to Devlin. "If tonight is the last night I will have the joy of you, bushman, then you will come to me in my rooms. After you ensure that the stock and household are properly settled for the evening. The household staff will determine Lord Charles has what he needs."

"You are calling it an early night, my lady," Ruskin drawled. "I thought you might want to see my hounds. I've got them penned in the barn. I'm sure your man wishes to see what he's up against. The finest noses in Australia. Tireless in their tracking, utterly focused."

A muscle flexed in her jaw. "I've no wish to see your pets."

"I'd like to see them. Always good to meet the competition." Dev glanced at his lady, noting the tight lips. Yeah, she was roiling mad at him. Might be best all the way around to let her cool down. "I can get everything settled, Lady D. It won't take much time. This mob seems competent."

Danny's expression was unreadable again, but she dwelled on his face a long time, in a way he found unsettling, as if she was weighing a lot more than this moment, or even Lord Charles's request. Finally, she inclined her head.

Don't give him the satisfaction of reacting when you see them, Dev. His hounds *are not dogs. They're children.*

13

WHEN Dev reached the top of the stairs of the quiet household, he paused. Leaned against the wall to take the first steadying breath he'd taken in a while. The hallway seemed a lot longer than it had earlier, when he'd been here to wash up. Below, he could hear the house staff finishing up in the kitchen.

While there was work done during the day by the stockmen, the household staff often slept during daylight hours, knowing that they worked hardest in the night hours. Up until her death, Danny's mother and Ian had been here about half the time, but Ian had been here full-time since, probably to ensure the property wasn't claimed by Danny in his absence. Well, that was no longer a problem. Dev had a hunch if she'd had the upper hand, there'd be two bodies burning out there at dawn's light.

Christ, he wasn't used to a woman acting so much like a man. That said, no way in hell would he ever call Lady Daniela unfeminine. It just was all a little bit outside his milieu, he wasn't ashamed to admit. Tina had been spirited, but when it came down to it, he was the man of the house, and if he said it was going to be this way, she respected him. Though she might goad him with a teasing little smile later when it didn't work out how he expected.

He'd seen enough of Lord Charles to pick up on why Danny

considered him a monster, though. The clincher had been what he'd kept in the barn. Thank God she'd warned him.

He'd brought them in cages loaded into the Rovers. There were fifteen of them in all, a sizable mob, and they ranged in age from six to twelve years old, squatting up against one another in the limited space of the cages. He supposed the ages were irrelevant, because they could easily be much older, every one of them being a vampire.

But not like the vampires he'd seen so far. Well dressed, cultured, with an acceptable veneer of civility, no matter how bloody thin. The mixture of white, Asian and aboriginal children had permanent scars on their lips from the elongated fangs that apparently couldn't retract like the adults'. They were filthy, naked, and started shrieking and calling out in unintelligible noises when Dev entered with Lord Charles and several of his men.

"I don't want you to think I'm inhumane," Ruskin commented. "At home, they each have their own cage, as well as a large enclosure."

He put out a hand. One of the men reached into a meat safe and came out with a fistful of raw meat, dripping with blood. The children went into a frenzy, crashing against the bars.

"Only a little bit, my pets. Tomorrow you get real blood, but you must hunt fiercely for it." As the man handed the meat to Charles, a startling change came over the children. They shrank back, eyes rounding in fright. When he put a hand into each of the cages, without exception, they were tentative in how they reached out to take it, though once they did, they set about snarling and tearing it apart between them. Dev glanced toward one of the men as he brandished a wicked metal spear at one of a more enthusiastically savage group.

"What's that for?" he asked while Charles was crooning to the children.

"If they get too hungry and turn on each other. He doesn't feed 'em for a while before they hunt, so they'll stay on track. Most the time they do pretty good in the cages, but they're a bit crowded in. Still, they know if they damage each other, he'll punish the lot of them. He'll—"

Dev shook his head, a short, sharp shake. He didn't need to

know. He felt sick. When Lord Charles finished and turned, a cruel, satisfied look on his face, Dev didn't bother to mask it.

"You're a right bastard, you are," Dev said. "No wonder she thinks you shouldn't be running this region."

Lord Charles's lips thinned, but when two of his men moved forward, he raised a hand. "No. Lady Daniela would feel I'd been unsporting if I paid you for that remark as you deserve. You must start out in the condition you're in now." His voice dropped, his eyes as dead as a reptile's. "But tomorrow night, when they catch you, and they will, I'll have the pleasure of hearing your screams. They're children after all, and have to squabble. They usually tear apart the body in their eagerness."

~

He didn't want to be here anymore. It was a bloody shame he'd been telling Danny the truth. For whatever reason, he felt he had to stay, see this through. Not only because he'd given his word, either.

He knocked.

Inside, Danny closed her eyes. She'd been sitting on the bed, brushing out her hair, staring into space. She could touch his mind, his thoughts. Feel him move around the house, do a quick check of the outside. She'd told him to come to her, but knew after what he'd seen in the barn, what he'd seen in the dining room, he might not. And how could she blame him?

She could have reinforced the call, brought him to her. But she didn't. One, she wanted him to come to her of his own volition, didn't want to have to coax him. She had that much pride. Second, because she knew she was going to have to take another choice away from him. If he came to her room of his own free will, well, that would help her rationalize it was all for the best. Not for the first time in the past few hours, she was glad she didn't have to face herself in a mirror.

But when she bade him enter and rose, all that went away for a moment. Because his gaze alighted on her, and for a moment he had the expression he'd had at dinner, when he first saw her in the dress, before everything happened. Yes, vampires were beautiful, there was no way around it. But when he looked at her, she felt like he saw *her* in the dress, and found her beautiful, with or without the vampire allure. And that mattered to her. God, she really was young and stupid, she was sure. But maybe she'd outlive her folly. She hoped he'd outlive it.

She'd worn a peach satin nightgown and robe. As he entered, she released the diamond hook closure at the gathered waist of the robe, let the sheer cloth float to the floor. The gown had a V neckline, and an inverted V seam beneath the bust that made the nip of her waist even more delicate, the area of her cleavage more riveting. It was the type of gown he might have seen Greta Garbo or Mae West wear in the pictures in England or Europe, but here she was in full color, very real, and ready to let him touch.

She knew the color combined with her pale, cream skin to make her look both ethereally beautiful and deceptively fragile to a man, an irresistible combination. His gaze coursed over her, then dropped to her bare feet. Since he'd discovered the pleasure of worshipping her feet, she thought it was a new obsession for him. However, in his mind, she found it was more than a fetish. Seeing her bare feet helped him keep things in perspective. Her feet somehow said she was real, approachable. A woman he'd seen vulnerable, something that helped him relate to her, to what had happened tonight.

It was a rationalization to help him cope, not the true reality. For she wasn't human, and while she might have emotional moments, she was not even slightly vulnerable when it came to dealing with a human male. But she wouldn't disabuse him of the notion. Not until she had to do so. So she told herself as she moved back to the bed and turned, looking at him.

Come here. I want you.

What was the matter with her? She'd meant to be smooth, casual, seductive. And yet she had a craving for the clean, mortal smell of him. The feel of his arms sliding around her readily. As if there were nothing repulsive about her, as if she hadn't had Ian's blood sprayed all over her dress, her hair.

"You make it hard to take the reins, love."

"Yes, I do. Because the reins belong to me." Changing tacks, she turned, moved toward the night table and poured them both a strong whiskey. Brought the glass to him, peach and perfume within his grasp, his senses. "It's not beer, but you look a little pale at the edges, Dev. Drink with me."

Dev took it, and followed her example, downing it in a fiery draught that burned to his belly. When she pressed her lips together, moist with the liquor, he leaned forward, put his mouth over hers, his tongue flicking on the bottom, then the upper lip to collect the taste, giving her a not-so-friendly nip. "Maybe they change hands occasionally, those reins. Sometimes they lie loose, and the horse chooses the direction."

She tilted her head, considering him, her mouth now moist from his. "I saw you looking at her collar tonight. Ian's servant. Some vampires do that. Collar their servant, to remind them of their bond to their Master or Mistress." Her fingers lifted, traced the strong column of his throat. He swallowed under her touch. "I could imagine one on you. A thick strap with a triangular buckle. Simple thing, but very tough, what you'd put on a hunting or fighting dog. Because while I might own you, you're a bit unpredictable. That's what makes you so lovely to have."

Curling his fingers around her wrist, he held her. "You can't own someone, love."

"Maybe," she agreed softly. "But you can possess them. I think that's why you're still here."

Dropping his hand, he poured himself another whiskey. "Those sticks you wore in your hair. They were Chiyoko's, weren't they?"

"Yes."

He nodded, stared into the drink. "You typically riffle through a dead person's belongings for things that strike your fancy?"

Her gaze frosted. "I don't explain myself to others. A vampire can't afford weakness."

Dev gave a bark of laughter. "Love, we all have weaknesses. Yours are sunlight and a man's tight arse. Glad to oblige you with the latter," he added. "But don't blow smoke up it. Why'd you take them?"

Danny looked away. "I wanted something of hers on me, when I fought him. I don't know why."

Dev pushed down his irritation, though it took effort. The temptress or the bitch. She seemed adept at swinging between the extremes of each. "Staff gossip says when you do choose a full servant, it'll likely be a woman. Because you prefer them."

"And what do you think, Dev?" She turned with a waft of perfume, a shimmer of gauzy material that gave him the hint of hip and breast.

"You like girls. They're easier to dominate, because they're used to men being in charge. I suspect they're a vacation for you, the difference between taking a bubble bath and fencing an opponent you're not sure you can beat." Putting down his drink, he stepped toward her. "But most of the time you like the challenge more than the bath. Tonight was about neither. It was about distraction."

He let his attention pass with deliberate leisure over her throat, her breasts, down the slope of her abdomen to the flare of her hips, all tempting satin and silk softness. She was watching him, intrigued by his words, but beneath the softness was something as lethal and unyielding as mortar fire, as ruthless. The way he knew there was venom to certain snakes, a sting to stonefish, fatal bites from spiders. They could all be killed by man if he had the right weapons to hand, but they were going to bugger him good before they were taken out.

That had been her expression tonight when she'd faced down Ruskin, an easier look for him to accept than the one she'd had right after taking Ian's head. But the night he killed his family's murderers, it was on his own face. At times, a man snatched the cloak off the Grim Reaper, donned it himself and said hang the consequences, seizing the chance to be the bringer of Death.

"You loved her. And your father."

She nodded, a short, barely there movement, then turned toward the mirror, which confirmed she had no reflection. That, and the effect of the sun, the need for blood, those things were all true about her. But there were things that weren't true. So following that odd instinct that had guided him since he met her, he moved across the wood floor and Persian carpet as she stared at the empty image. Sliding his hands on her shoulders, the roundness of them, then down, he framed her breasts, just an easy grip. A sigh slipped out of her and she leaned her head back against his chest.

"Your distraction strategy worked, you know. I was so worked up I was going to come, right then and there, all over the nice china."

She smiled. He felt the pull of it against his chest when she turned her cheek to him. "Think that was all for you, do you?"

"No," he said. "It was done for them. But you made yourself hot with it by pointing it toward me, to make it more believable. And truth, that's what made me hard as a rock, even more than seeing so many beautiful women play with one another."

She was silent a moment or two. "We're good for one another, Dev."

"Two destructive forces usually attract," he observed. "So when they detonate, they can cause greater damage."

Angling her head to look at him with her golden-lashed blue eyes, she shook her head. "I've no desire to self-destruct. I want this station. I don't care about being more than that. I have no aspirations of being a Region Master, or going abroad to acquire a more prestigious territory, like Charles. But I'll claim this territory for my own to protect the handful of vampires who've chosen to live in it. Make it a home."

"So why *haven't* you ever taken a servant? Seems one would help you with all that. It's the person who protects you during daylight hours, your primary food source. You can communicate with him without speaking—"

"Sounds like you've been auditioning for the part, doesn't it?"

When he gave her an annoyed look, she held up a placating hand. Turning so her gaze rested on his face, Danny studied the lines of it, the shape of his mouth. "I can hear your blood, Dev. The beat of your heart, the rush of blood through it. Now that you bear my second mark, I can plumb as deeply into your mind as I wish. I have heightened senses and strength beyond any human's comprehension. Every bruise you bear is proof of my restraint, because I can crush your bones without a thought. But having a third mark is all that and more. In the vampire world the only comparison is a spiritual commitment, like a priest taking his vows."

He rested his hands on her hips, his fingers pressing into silken fabric. "Somehow I don't think most priests expect their vows to include the things you demand, my lady."

"What a lovely surprise for them, then," she rejoined, but he didn't smile.

"When I get close to you like this, your lips part before you even think about it, and your body sways toward me." His hands tightened on her in midmotion, making her aware of it. "You're conveying need. Desire. Wanting. We all have that."

"Yes, we do. But my desires and wants can kill you. Quite easily."

He shook his head. "Might as well give over, love. You're an interesting woman, a dangerous one. Can't decide yet if I like you or not, but I reckon you can stomp me like a bug. Maybe you even have the power to hold my mind, make me strut about like an emu, or think I'm a spider and try to spin a web out of my arse hairs. But it doesn't change the fact we're made out of the same dirt and air, fire and water, and whatever was in charge of that doesn't likely view us much different than one little ant and a slightly bigger one from His perspective. I understand how your world is, or at least, I'm learning. I don't have to be convinced it's sensible to get along with it. So let's just leave it there for now."

"Why are you still here, Dev?" She flattened her palms on his chest, and he was taken aback by the tension in her voice. "I've put no hold on you, offered you the choice. Given what you've seen tonight, you should be gone. Take off in the daylight. I know you know how to get out of here undetected by Charles's men. They'll never find you."

"His 'hounds' might." Dev shook his head. "Danny, that's a crook deal. How could he . . ."

"It was one of the things I went to talk to the Council about," she responded bitterly. "They agreed it was a serious transgression, *if* it was true. But none of them were willing to come here and address it. Our Council likes having Ruskin here, because they know he's a problem, though they're not acknowledging the full extent of it. Out of sight, out of mind, remember? Lord Ruskin wrote the Council, exaggerated my youth, suggested a tendency to overreact, and courteously extended them the invitation to visit anytime, knowing they won't." She gripped his collar. "You still haven't answered my question. Why are you still here?"

He cupped her face. "You can read my mind, love."

"You're doing that stillness thing. I can't really tell."

"Beats the hell out of me." He gave her a half smile, grazed his fingers over her brow. "I've lived on my gut awhile now, Danny. My gut says I'm not done yet. Though no lie, after what I saw tonight, I wish I could tell the bloody thing to rack off. Tell me more about what I'll be facing. Where did he get them? And why are they so wild? Is that from that bastard starving them?"

"You are a frustrating man," she informed him. Gripping the two sides of his shirt, she laid her forehead down on his sternum, took a deep, steadying breath that surprised him. When he laid his hands on her upper arms, intending a tentative stroke of reassurance, she lifted her face back to him again.

"Some of the children were orphans, brought here from Europe to be placed in new homes. Others are aborigines taken from their parents under the guise of the government's program to relocate them with white families to give them education, a supposedly better life." She shook her head at his look, continued. "When a human is turned, there's a very rigorous process followed to teach them to control bloodlust. In this case, Ruskin uses hunger as bait, to train them into a pack that will track a blood source at his bidding. He's also made damn sure the only thing they fear is him."

Then, before he could digest that, her blue gaze grew cold. "Dev, I know you've been a father."

When he would have pulled back, she dug into his biceps, earning a flash of temper from him. "Do *not* think of them as children. I was born a vampire, which means I grew until I reached the age of twenty-five. I will look twenty-five all my life. A made vampire child will never age. Living year after year without sexual or physical maturity, they are the most vulnerable of us. Think of the hormones and aggression that comes with youth on the cusp of adolescence, and imagine being trapped in that forever. He has exploited that, pushed their minds to the breaking point and turned them into mindless beasts. It's a terrible, horrible thing, but they need to be put down, the whole mob of them. Not out of cruelty, but out of mercy. So promise me you won't hesitate to kill them if you have to do so."

Dev thought of the hissing, naked bodies in the cage, fighting over bloody raw meat. The brown eyes of one girl as she tried to watch him, Ruskin and the others, while she licked blood residue off the filthy bottom of her pen. Releasing Danny, he turned away, went to the side of her bed and slid down to a seated position on the floor, dangling his hands loosely between his knees. "Did you know that some aboriginal tribe members adopt temporary names to explain who or what they are?" he asked. She stood across the room from him now, remote, beautiful. He could tell her anything. It didn't really matter, anyway. "What they're becoming, what they've been. Whatever has the strongest hold on them at certain times in their life?"

"No, I didn't."

His throat flexed as he swallowed. "I didn't pick mine. They gave it to me. Gravedigger."

She surprised him when she said nothing. Simply came and slid down next to him, shoulder to shoulder, drawing her legs up into a triangle, loosely linking her hands over it. The peach gown floated down, pooling around her feet, over the toe of his boot.

Dev turned his head against the mattress to consider her. One moment determined to imprison his soul, a sorceress who could seduce him to it willingly. No contest there. But it was the duality that made her impossible to resist. If she was all darkness and fangs, he could pull himself loose of what was entirely a fantasy, knowing a fantasy would wear thin after a while, become too dangerous and destructive to indulge. But she was quite real as well, particularly in moments like this, when she wore an expression of shrewd concern. Plus, he could tell she was tired.

This hadn't been her tonight, but she'd made herself play the part, do what she felt had to be done. It would bother her, weigh on her conscience, but she wouldn't go on about it. She'd made her decision, done it, and it was hers to carry. That was the way it was out here. You might bear a lot of burdens on your back, but hardship toughened you, made you what you were supposed to be, and that was that.

He adjusted so he could finger a strand of blond hair where it fell forward over her breast. She leaned back, giving him access to stroke the curve beneath, indulging his need to touch.

"You said you were born a vampire. Does that mean you were a child?"

"It usually does. My mother wouldn't have been very happy if I came out this size."

"No, I suspect not." He smiled. "What were you like?"

She blinked. Reaching up, she took his hand from her hair, held it palm to palm with hers, her large eyes staring steadily into his, so he was acutely aware of the extraordinary beauty of them, the long lashes, the preternatural focus. "You don't want to go to this place, Dev."

"That much of a brat, were you? I suspected as much." But neither of them smiled now. "Did you play games, love? Get in trouble? Have a strap taken to you?"

Danny didn't think she could keep this up, not on his last night on earth. But while she thought she'd concealed her worry and fear, knowing it served no purpose, now he scooped an arm around her, brought her onto his lap so they were heartbeat to heartbeat. Wrapping his arms hard around her, he held her close to him, reminding them both, their minds twined together, of that night they'd been together in the cave, only the two of them.

Sliding her arms around his neck didn't feel wrong, so Danny did it, and let herself be held. "I had a wonderful childhood, Dev. I was surrounded by loving humans faithful to my parents. I learned literature, art and music." She hesitated. "My mother loved to fence. All types of blades. My father taught me to shoot and fight hand to hand. I learned how to compel a human so I could drink from them unknowing, if I had need."

She brought her arms back to her lap, not wanting to feel him stiffen and withdraw from her, as he inevitably would. He needed to understand. Maybe if he did, he would abandon his foolishness. "A born vampire, from the time she attains puberty, must take an annual kill to replenish her blood, as I told you before. Throughout the remainder of the year we may feed without taking a life, but that one kill is essential. It's a vaccination of sorts, where we get vital nutrients. Depriving ourselves of it is a slow starvation of the body, a weakening of it and the mind, a dangerous state for a vampire. Plus, the life taken must be a good one. It cannot be a cruel or wasted life, because the energy in the human's blood does affect the vampire. My parents felt it was critical that I handle my first kill. That I take down the person, look them in the eye. They chose my nanny, the one who'd been with me from a babe."

"A message. That your childhood ended with that kill."

Startled, she looked toward him. "Exactly. That . . . they said that was the intent. If I look back on it," she continued, clearing her throat, "I think that was a lie. It didn't have to be her. I believe my mother did it because she knew it would hurt me, would transfer the agony of her own guilt."

Dev's brow furrowed. "What did she have to feel guilty about?"

"My twin brother." Danny's fingers twitched. Irritated with herself, she rose from his lap, moved away toward the landscapes, the substitute for windows in this room, though she missed the warm touch of his hands. "It was the first time, as far as we've heard, that a vampire ever bore twins. We're much like human children when we're infants, so helpless. It never occurred to anyone we could be dangerous to one another, that letting two vampire babies sleep in the same crib would be harmful . . . that one would wake hungry in the night and go for the closest source of blood that tasted like her mother . . ."

"Ah, Christ," Dev murmured.

"Mother vampires feed their babies on blood, not milk," Danny said tonelessly. "But it serves much the same purpose . . ." She grazed her fingers over the plump top of one breast. "Usually here. The veins in the breasts expand, become engorged with blood for the baby. It's how you can tell a vampire has been a mother, because the scar the baby leaves from the nursing is permanent. A mark of honor among our kind, since our children are so scarce.

"I killed him. Ten months old and the bloodlust was getting

stronger; my body was stronger. Strong enough. The ironic thing is when they found us, he had his fangs in me as well. I just got the idea first, and drank faster."

She turned, met his green eyes, full of horror and sorrow both. "I said I left because of Ian. I blamed him for adding to the Ennui that ultimately drove my mother to meet the dawn." At his curious look, she added, "It's a deep depression of sorts. A lack of interest in life. But somewhere deep inside me, I know I left because I couldn't change her sorrow, not about my father's loss or my brother's, and in her mind they merged so I became responsible for both."

Lifting her chin now, she took a step forward. "So don't human-ize me, Dev. I don't want you to be comfortable with me, or my kind. My mother's motive aside, another reason many vampire parents make their children's first annual kill the human closest to them is to ensure they understand the difference between us."

"That's a belief system to prop up a social order, love." He rose, shook his head. "There're plenty of blokes in the world who are stron-ger, faster and more knowledgeable than me. Doesn't mean they have the right to consider themselves superior."

"It's not a matter of that. It's knowing there are essential differ-ences between us that will never be bridged, and we forget that to our peril." She glanced toward the sticks she'd left on her vanity. "Chiyoko . . . Ian did give her the choice, Dev. Forced full servants are rare, though I'm not denying there are those servants who choose the third mark and then discover that their new Master or Mistress can be a sadistic monster. It happens. But it's the exception, not the rule. The vampire-servant bond is a treasured one. The vampire will value them more than any other relationship in their life, though a servant's place is not to stand as the vampire's equal. He or she is the vampire's shadow, to serve them with total loyalty. Some believe the reason the servant dies with the vampire is that he or she follows their Master or Mistress into their afterlife destiny."

"Why would anyone agree to that willingly?"

She gave an unexpected chuckle. "In your own words—beats the hell out of me, Dev. Remember, I've never had a full servant."

Saying the words, Danny felt a hard lurch in her chest at the idea of never seeing him again. Never having the chance to find out if he was the one who should take that role for her.

"It's not unprecedented." He was moving toward her once again, not allowing her to keep a distance. Not realizing what was building inside her. "Monarchs have demanded it; some have deserved it. The whole concept of medieval chivalry romanticized it." When he reached her, he didn't stop until her hands were against the hard muscle of his chest.

"You won't go, will you?" She tried to keep the desperation out of her tone, the building sense of inevitability.

"No, unless you knock me out, hog-tie me and cart me away. And I wouldn't advise that, because if Ruskin catches on to your attempt, it'll be much harder for me to participate in his little game with a concussion." He gave her a little shake. "Leave it, love. Let's make the most of the evening."

Tossing her hair back to look up at him, she had to suppress a smile when she caught the shift of his gaze, followed it and saw the flash of his thought. Her bushman who liked long fine hair, soft round arses. She curled her fingers in, ran them in a short strip across his pectoral, hearing his heartbeat.

"What kind of child were *you*, Dev? Did you get into trouble much?"

"All the time." He lifted a shoulder. "But my dad was pretty tolerant. Said adventurous boys grew up to be brave men."

"He was right. You are a brave, decent man." She let her hand slide up to his neck, to the artery there, seeing the flicker in his gaze as she did it. "You don't deserve this."

Curling her hand around his, she slid up to her toes and sank her fangs into his throat.

～

At first, Dev thought she'd decided to take a late supper. Then he began to feel light-headed. With the clasp of his hands on her upper arms, then the use of his mind, he tried to tell her, because his voice had deserted him.

Danny . . . not feeling right . . .

It's all right, Dev. It will be done in a moment or two. Just go with it. Don't fight.

Fire erupted through him as if it had originated from the place where her fangs pierced him. He fell back into the wall, and she went with him, directing him so they rolled onto the bed, she straddling his body as she continued to feed, the folds of the gown trapped between them, her hand alongside his face, cradling and holding him at once.

Danny . . .

Shh . . . easy. It's all right . . .

It was pain and not pain at once, the way a stretch upon waking could get to a point it was almost as good as sexual pleasure, and yet uncomfortable as well, when joints popped and sore muscles went past what they could endure. Only to find they could endure and were the better for it, stronger. The colors of the room became blinding, the smell of her perfume overwhelming, along with the soap that had been used to wash the linens, even the wax they used on the hardwood and the smell below that, of the hardwood itself. It was all bouncing against his senses, as if he were being pelted by hard, cleansing rain.

On top of that, her hands were on him, other hungers making themselves known. Abruptly, he was ravenous for her that way, too. With an unexpected surge of strength, he rolled them, reversing their position, putting himself on top. As he struggled to find the hem of the gown, she wrapped her arms around his shoulders and held on, pressing her breasts against him, the hardened nipples. He needed her, now. She had her fangs still in him, the burning pain of it something that made his skin feel hot all over. She was tearing the shirt off his shoulders as he worked off the trousers, and found her beneath the gown, cool and satiny, female flesh. Slick heat, to fan the flame of his fire.

When he slammed into her, her sharp gasp told him he could have showed more courtesy, but there was no time. There was only hunger. Driving, raging need, like bloodlust, like screaming, mindless violence, only this was more than that. Everything was so vivid and clear, and he felt so strong, strong enough to band his arm around her waist and pump into her like a young buck on his first conquest.

His chest was raw, heat coursing across it as if it were eating away his flesh. Wings. In his mind, he saw dark wings spreading, taking off, sending him soaring through an abyss of lightning, fire and darkness, but he wasn't afraid, because it was also filled with her breath, her erotic cries, the feel of her limbs clutching hard over his arse, urging him on, wanting more of him, more, more, more . . .

Her head fell back on the pillow, so he saw an ethereal blue substance glittering on her lips, glossing her canines. Holding her head still in both hands, he licked all of it off her elongated fangs, from end to tip, delicate as if he were licking her clit, while she breathed hot need into his face, panting with her reaction. Her pussy closed on him like a fist, her body undulating up and back with his, two waves hitting each other as if forced by a jetty, an immovable force causing a collision, over and over.

When she put her arms between them, he realized she had his knife in her hand. Before he could react in alarm, she'd drawn it across her forearm, the blood welling from the cut.

Drink, Dev.

He'd smelled enough blood in his life to be revolted by it, but for some reason, the smell of her blood was like the offer of sweetmeats. He put his mouth over the cut and drew her in, tasting her essence, feeling the flow increase as if in response to his need to quench his thirst on her. The taste was similar to the whiskey she'd given him. At first he thought that was because the alcohol had flavored her blood, but recalling the odd taste to the whiskey, he realized just the opposite was true.

Then that thought was swept away as she climaxed, taking him with her, so that he came in the middle of her spasms and cries, muffled in the pillow as she turned her head into it, though her arms and legs remained firmly locked around him, rocking with him, undulating, moving in tandem until he'd pumped out the last drop he could manage.

When his head dropped to the pillow next to her head, his fists were curled around her head, touching her loose hair. He felt her soft breath on his shoulder. And while she was there, pressed against his temple, she spoke to him.

I'm sorry, Dev. She looked up at him, her hair a fan around her porcelain princess features. *I gave you the third mark.*

~

It wasn't hard to discern why. He'd felt her worry, knew she'd been violently opposed to him sticking his neck out on her behalf. She didn't think he had a chance tomorrow, and she'd decided in her typically unilateral way that this would give him a sporting opportunity.

Do you know why so many seventeenth-century sailors never learned to swim, my lady? Because if they fell off the ship and were inadvertently left behind, they would drown more quickly, not prolong the agony.

It took him considerable effort, but he lifted his upper body to discover why there was a raw, burning sensation on his chest. He'd been marked in truth, by something that looked like a cross between a tattoo and a scar. The design was a raven, his skin permanently branded the charcoal color. The wings stretched over either pectoral, the lifted head and sharp beak engraved over his sternum.

As he pulled away from her and stood, examining the mark, he recalled the quote from Babylonian texts. *A raven, the bird that helpeth the gods . . .*

The Tibetans considered the bird special, a messenger. The Irish thought it was all-seeing, all-knowing. And in Norse mythology, Odin had two ravens, Thought and Memory, who brought the day's news to him. Christ, it was like everything else. A different story, depending on which shore your feet were planted. But he could see how all of it figured in to vampires.

He knew she was likely waiting for him to light into her, but he needed a few minutes. Everything felt . . . remarkable. Every detail in the room and every sound magnified, but not in a disturbing or irritating way. It was just so much clearer. And while he was a fit man, he felt better than fit. Strong enough to lift an opera singer off her pins, or run for miles without tiring.

"It's more feeling than actuality right now." She was watching him closely. "But in a few hours, your capabilities and senses will have actually improved dramatically."

"A few hours' wait to become a superhero. Well, that's pretty intolerable, love, when all's said and done." Pacing across the room with some caution, he used the mirror to examine the raven.

"When a servant is given a third mark," she explained, before the silence between them drew out further, "it always manifests itself in some way upon him or her. Vampires have no control over it or really any understanding of why it happens, though most believe it's totem-related magic. Dev . . ."

He turned, looked at her. "I understand why you did it, love. Maybe one day you'll trust me enough to ask before you leap, but I know you're trying to protect me. You think I don't have a chance in hell, and that I'm a daft bugger for not cutting and running."

She turned away, slid out of the bed. Her back to him, she straightened her gown and picked up her robe, sliding it over her shoulders. "It will be dawn soon," she said shortly. "Charles is giving you the day to get ahead of them. He'll release the children on you right at dusk."

"He's pretty confident."

"Vampires can move at swift speeds. Not as fast as we move in short distances, but still much more swiftly than a human. And they take far longer to tire. If you can cover twenty miles a day, they can cover forty-five, maybe even up to sixty."

"So I go with my strengths, instead of trying to match theirs."

"It's . . . Oh, damn it all." She turned to face him, impatience in the lines of her lovely body. "Dev, it's nothing that binds you to me. Well, bloody hell, of course it does. But I mean, you don't have to stay with me forever or anything. I wanted to give you a chance, damn it."

The look on her face was one he hadn't seen before. Sad, almost desolate. Alone.

"You've taken the choice from me, three times. Three marks. An apology's getting rather thin." But he said it mildly.

She shook her head, and that sadness touched her lips in a

poignant smile. "I'm done apologizing, bushman. You're determined to go through with this madness I've forced upon you, even though I've given you an escape route."

"You knew that I would."

"Because you think your life is worth my face, my pride. You don't want me to give anything up to Charles unwillingly."

"No, I don't," he agreed, and took another step, so now he was before her, but she turned away from him. When she didn't move away, he realized it wasn't to scorn him, but because she didn't want him to see her face.

If he'd been out on the porch, he knew the moon would have been a half crescent, silhouetting the distant mountains, the odd shape of scrub and eucalyptus in darkness. Dingoes would be howling somewhere, and since the daytime heat made many of the bush's creatures nocturnal, there would be many listening ears and eyes out there.

He hadn't touched her since he'd left the bed, hadn't been ready to do so. She'd picked up on it, was standing rigid. Not reaching out, either.

With a mental sigh, he bent enough to slide his arm across her shoulders in front, pulling her back against him. After a moment, her hands came up and closed on his forearm, her temple brushing his bare biceps, the raw skin of the mark as she turned her head. Her blond hair teased his lower abdomen, above the waistline of the pants he'd hitched back on when he'd crossed the room.

"Do you care so little about your own life that it doesn't matter anymore?" She murmured it, anger in her tone, but that desolation was there, too. "I will be *really* angry if you die in my service because it gave you a good excuse to do so."

He couldn't help it. He chuckled. When her eyes narrowed upon him, he suspected she was considering whether to gouge him with her considerable nails. He averted puncture by slipping a hand alongside her face, tunneling his fingers into her hair, letting his thumb touch her resolute jaw, the corner of her delicious mouth. "If I die out there, I'll make sure to write you a note in the sand, letting you know I didn't let it happen."

"That's not—"

"I know what you meant." His voice got quiet, and he put a trace of hardness into it that made her gaze flicker in surprise. "I don't look too deeply into my mind, love, and I wouldn't suggest you do it, either. I've been on walkabout, letting whatever will happen to me happen, for a long time." He gave a rueful smile. "So I can hardly take you to task for making choices for me, when I've done everything possible in the past decade to make sure I don't have to make any of real significance. Maybe there's a reason my feet have brought me to your side."

Tilting her chin, he looked down into her face. "I don't entirely understand your world, and I know you're no lamb. But I also know when a woman needs help, no matter how powerful she is, and I'm not walking away until I'm sure you're all right here."

"Even if you die for it."

"Worse things to die for. Like nothing." He changed topic. "Now, I saw what happens when Ian died. But what will happen to you if I'm . . . if they catch me? I can't imagine it's as simple as 'the vampire lives,' like you said."

"You think I didn't tell you everything?"

He gave her an arch look. Danny wanted to tell him it wasn't going to happen, but instead she swallowed, turned her face into his touch, closed her eyes. He had wonderfully strong, masculine hands, and she loved the way they felt. She wished she was the type of person who could easily tell him that, or even let him into her mind to see the way she felt, but there were too many things there at this moment. If she did that, it would be too easy to let him past the doors to the parlor and into the rest of the house, with its more personal effects.

"It will hurt me, physically and emotionally. But it would be much, much worse if we'd been together for years. I'll be all right."

"So you'll be able to get over it soon enough." He gave her that ghost of a smile, and she had a sudden desire to slap him, but instead she pulled back, leveled a fierce gaze on him.

"You say I don't own you, Devlin. That's your opinion, and I'll let you have it, but you'll hear mine. In my world, once a human is marked three times, he is the property of the vampire who marked him. So keep all your notions of independence you want. I am ordering you to do your very best to survive and come back to me. Whatever happens then, we'll figure out, but you *will* obey me in this. You return to me."

Picking up one of his hands then, she brought it to her face, and surprised Dev by pressing fervent lips to the palm. Sliding his other arm around her, he brought her close, cautiously laying his head over hers.

He remembered one time, when his vehicle was rolled by a flash flood. He'd nearly drowned except for the luck of working his way to a tree and holding on. Several weeks later, he was headed out for the same trip. Tina had become angry at him about some nonsense right before he took off, something about not wiping his boots on the porch and mucking up her floor. He'd tried to tease her about it, baffled by her irrational anger, but then she'd slapped him, started hammering at him until he caught hold of her, gathered her in and made her quit, let her sob it out on his chest. He realized then how afraid she'd been for him during the flood, the days of inexplicable absence with no news of him on the radio exchange. But she'd never shown it until the row over the shoes.

Now, as he held Danny, felt the grip of fingers he suspected she didn't realize were clutching him hard enough to bruise, he had an odd thought. Would a vampire know if she was falling in love with a human? Would she recognize it that way, even call it that? And was that somewhere he even wanted to go in his mind? Of course, he was the daft bugger going out to play fox to a pack of vampire younglings so she didn't have to bow to the likes of Lord Charles Ruskin. Maybe he should be asking himself a similar question.

Too late, he remembered she could drift through his mind like window shopping in Perth, but apparently, she wasn't at the moment, for he was sure the thought would have brought a mortified reaction. In her world, falling in love with a human was likely the equivalent of him proposing marriage to a cow. A smile tugged at his lips. Actually, in this case, she'd probably get the better deal with a bovine than him.

Though you're equipped about the same.

He winced, but also couldn't help the grin. "You love it, darling, and you know it. And I'll be back to bother you, so don't think you're already rid of me. The cook makes marvelous pastries, I've heard. A yeast bread so light it floats. Hotcakes, too."

"Just like a man. You'll survive for the sake of your stomach."

"Well, you never know what the afterlife might have to offer. Might be sandy mutton stew and moldy damper. Don't expect the devil's got his skillet out, flipping hotcakes in anticipation of my arrival."

Lifting her head, she looked up at him. He wondered if those clear blue eyes had ever filled with tears. If she'd ever let them.

"Once dawn comes," he said, "I'll be off. You'll watch after my swag?"

At her puzzled look, he explained, "Lord Charles set out the rules of the game while showing me his mob. I go out without any supplies, except a knife and one skin of water. Apparently, he doesn't expect me to survive long enough to need more than that."

"You shouldn't have negotiated rules in my absence. Neither should he. I can get that changed. That's stacking things unfairly on his side."

"I wouldn't have taken the pack anyway." He shook his head. "In this case it would slow me down. Don't worry, love." He let her hair slide down over one hand, watching the waterfall of it. "I can handle myself out there. Why don't you and I make a little side bet on this?"

"That's not really a bet." She managed a skeptical look. "If one of us bets you make it and the other one bets you don't, then the one who bets against wins nothing."

"Except the smug satisfaction of being right." Before she could cuff him for that, he pursed his lips, made sure the image in his mind was clear and vibrant. "How about this as an incentive? Something even better than hotcakes."

Exasperation crossed her features, taking away the sadness and worry, pleasing him. "You have a lot of gall, bushman."

"I'm doing you a pretty big favor. After saving you in the desert, besides. Not that I'd bring any of that up to have my way."

Her blue eyes softened on him in a way he liked, and her chuckle, though genuine, was strained. "Fine, then. But sure as I agree to it, you'll survive just to see if I'll live up to my side of the bargain."

"You bet your arse." He grinned wickedly. "Literally." Leaning down then, he feathered his lips over her cheek even as his hands eased down from her waist, curved over buttocks, squeezed enough to make her sidle closer in to him. Oh, yeah, she was responsive there. It was enough to make him hard again, their recent coupling notwithstanding. "I have some fantasies stored up. Not only about taking you there. I like to put a sheila over my knee and spank her good, get her all pretty and red before I do it. Use my hand. Sometimes I think about a belt."

Tina had never been into it that rough. The occasional smack for playfulness, but he was careful enough about restraining his baser urges so she hadn't been subjected to the needier, rougher side of it. Dealing with his unnaturally sized organ was more than enough to ask of any woman. But he saw the light flush in Danny's cheeks, the parted lips and considering light in her eye. It made him swear under his breath. God, he wished it was three days from now already. And that he was sure he'd survive. But it would be a hell of a fantasy to die with, all said and done.

"You come back to me, my arse is yours for the taking. Once." She gave him another exasperated look. "Food and sex. That's the value you place on your life."

"Not sex, love." Nipping her nose, he fought the surge of emotions the return of her teasing brought to him. "Sex with you. You being willing to give over to me, even the one time." As her eyes became more serious, he shook his head. "No, don't. I do understand things. About vampires, humans. But for one time at least, it will be just you and me. Give me that, and you've given me more than heaven can offer. I won't be lying down and giving up."

"Okay," she said at last, quietly. "Come back to me, Dev. I would miss you."

"If I don't"—he curled a mental hand around the pleasure of those words, and held them to consider later—"you take care how you handle Ruskin. You've got intelligence, love, but your lust for his blood almost took you into foolishness last night during that fencing match. Don't bother to deny it. Plan it out as carefully as you did with Ian. More, because now Ruskin knows how devious you can be. And get yourself some backup if you can."

She gave him a simple nod, not a mildly indignant comment about her ability to do her own strategizing. That alone told him she was still too worried. "When I get back, I will have that spanking," he added, wanting the spark back in her eye. "You gave me the third mark without my say-so. Everyone will agree there needs to be *some* penalty for that."

A flash of fire in the blue, another toss of that lovely hair, and her hands went to her hips, raising her breasts. God, she was a gorgeous thing. "You can spank me if you can hold me down, bushman. For that, *you* better bring backup."

14

DANNY was in the blackness of her room, missing the first rays of the sun stabbing over the horizon. She knew Charles would have his men out, ensuring Dev left with nothing but that meager amount of water.

She'd had people in her employ devoted enough to be third-marked servants. Some had even asked for it, in some subtle or not-so-subtle ways. Dev hadn't asked, and even before she'd marked him, he'd been acting as one.

She'd always been curious about other vampires and their third-marked servants, but she hadn't investigated it too closely. She didn't have family or friends in the vampire world she trusted enough to say some of the things she'd said so easily to Dev in the past few days. Up until now, she'd picked up snippets about that aspect of a third-marked servant, but never anything like this, which would have made her interested in having it for herself far sooner.

Now she wondered, because of the way she'd left it with Dev this morning, right before dawn. She'd heard his thoughts, been shocked by his intuitive understanding of her, even better than she seemed consciously to know herself. She considered herself happy, well adjusted, but she was also consummately shielded. Not unexpected for a vampire, but maybe even more than most her age. Perhaps that had been her mother's doing. She stifled a snort at the attempt to apply academic psychology to her family dynamics. Those three or four times during her life she'd chosen to attend a university had been educational. Far better times than this moment, for certain.

She couldn't stand it anymore. Throwing on her purple velvet dressing gown and tying the sash, she moved swiftly out of the back bedroom, into the front rooms, to the study. It had a heavily cur-tained window that provided a view of the west side of the station, with the additional protection of the porch overhang. Fortunately the house was quiet. Ruskin appeared to be in bed, all his stockmen out of the house.

Daring a slit in the curtain, standing well clear of the possibility of sunlight, she saw through the crack that there were some stockmen milling about the yard, but no sign of Dev. No, there he was. She could see him, already striding about a quarter mile from the fence line. He wasn't even glancing back, no more concerned than if he'd finished his beer at Elle's and was heading back into the Outback. She saw the men scowling about it. One of them had taken up a rifle, ap-parently with the thought of scudding a few bullets at his heels to give Dev something to be anxious about, but one of his mates wisely put his hand on the barrel, made him lower it. Charles didn't like his sport tampered with, and if Dev was wounded, there'd be hell to pay. Even knowing that, she found her fist clenched on the fabric, murderous thoughts churning through her head until the muzzle was lowered.

There was nothing she could do to help him. Except touch him with her mind, which, if done at the incorrect time, could distract him fatally. But she could be inside his mind without his knowledge, stay with his thoughts. Returning to her bedroom, locking the door se-curely, she lay down, closed her eyes. Nothing would happen until nightfall, and she could find him then. A third mark was good for hundreds of miles, though not thousands. Unless his new mark had given him black wings to fly, in truth, he should still be in range then.

≈

Dev was rather surprised the stockmen didn't take a potshot at him. They were certainly armed to the teeth, as if they expected him to put up a mighty resistance. No wonder they were a bit out of sorts when he thanked them for the water and headed out the front gate.

He circled around and headed up into the hills, but first he pushed his luck, staying within range of their guns and their attention as he squatted over a mudflat, studying the patterns left by the feet of lizards and rabbits, even a few emu. He checked out the landscape, seeing where there might be dry water channels that could help conceal a man as he headed back in toward the homestead. If he survived the next two days, Lord Charles had made sure the final challenge would be the most difficult. If they couldn't catch him out in the bush, all they had to do was line up at that fence and wait to shoot him, since he had to walk across the open ground to the gate.

He perused the sky, figuring what the weather was likely to bring him. Then, using a stick to dig into the ground, he rolled up balls of light gray mud and stripped off his shirt to carry them. When he at last rose and resumed his hike, it didn't take him long to reach the first series of rocks and gorges. The red mountain range was laid out almost like a toy stone castle, kicked over by a giant petulant child. The hills into which the station had been built were an elevated, rolling plain, followed by another series of rocky red hillocks, some grouped together, some separated by shrub and sand. There were jagged pillars and rounded marble formations scattered throughout the terrain. Once he moved into the shaded side of one such grouping, which concealed him from the station, now a small block in the distance, he took a deep breath, cleared his mind and considered what was facing him.

Laying down the shirt, he spread it out to reveal the balls of mud. One rolled out and trundled into a crevice between another cluster of rocks. He noted cracked pieces, sheared off by wind and weather, perhaps even by the odd ricochet of a bullet when the men went hunting.

Picking up one of the clay balls, Dev closed his hand on the coolness, felt the pastelike consistency. Fifteen years he'd spent with the tribe who had shared his raising with his mum and dad. A tribe that walked this land still, in even more remote regions than this. He knew how to find water and food, so that wasn't a concern. His challenge was going to be that pack of vampire children, with their superhuman ability to track, scent and find him. If he cut across the thick wire grass he saw stretching between him and the eastern series of rock hills, the tracking part at least would be more difficult, because it would spring back up as if he'd never been through.

Charles liked his sport, so Dev suspected he was being given the light of this day to get enough of a head start to provide a minor challenge. But after that, if Dev eluded him, Charles's sense of fair play, weak at best, would dissipate. He'd use those heavily armed blokes to track him during the day, the children to keep him on the run at night, leave him exhausted.

It was time to work on not leaving a trail. Or rather, leaving a deceptive one. Squatting, he began to work the ball of mud into his flesh. His face, his chest and shoulders, a sun covering and also a way to blend. As he performed the task, he studied those broken rocks, their shape. Lifting his gaze to the ranges, he considered the types of trees he'd find there.

After the war, he'd walked with the clan again, for a time. The Elders had told him he had to let the world back into his soul . . . he had to feel the earth beneath him, the weight of the sky and fire of sun above. The movement of winds, however slight. To know the world provided. The world understood. There were some things that could not be explained, but the world was an ancient being that understood all pain, was fertilized with tears. He had to know that, accept it. He had to heal, or he would become a tool of demons.

He couldn't explain to that tribesman, perhaps was ashamed to, that he'd polluted his own soul. He'd taken all the blood and pain, jammed it in there over the top of that young, fun-loving bloke he'd once been. He'd buried him alive, screaming, beneath the weight of everything that used to be his life. That Devlin, his soul, was buried in a sealed casket he couldn't open.

A simple idiot who'd loved a girl with long sable hair, courted her in the simple, sweet ways, and been blessed with a fine son with his green eyes and Tina's sweet mouth. He'd taken them to the picnic races that the remote stations occasionally arranged to give them all a chance to be a community. Working the sheep, he'd stopped as often as he could manage during the day for a drink of lemonade from Tina's hand, to see what young Rob had created out of rocks and sticks, small fortresses with soldiers and a pennant of a dry leaf.

What you will not do, the world will force upon you. That is its way, as well. He recalled the Elder's words, right before Dev chose to leave their company.

It's already done its worst to me. It knows where to find me when it wants to have another round.

It figured it would take its next shot through the cruel but irresistible touch of a blond vampire with blue eyes. Shaking his head, he rose, picking up several of the rock shards he'd studied. They'd make good spear points, and he'd find branches or sturdy stalks up ahead for the shafts. Charles had insisted he keep his large hunting knife in a spirit of fair play, but of course his stockmen had known that for the joke it was. When he'd made it clear he expected his weapons and pack in the same order when he returned, they'd had a good laugh, though it was the mocking kind. Mockery usually covered the fear, however slight, that he might be back to reclaim it.

Count on it, mates.

A tool for demons might be exactly what was needed here. While the Elder had given him the switch for that murderous rage within him, the meditative stillness to keep it from bursting free, Dev knew how to let the rage forth when he needed it. Since he was likely going to die in the next couple days, the ability to rein it in, reclaim a civilized sense of himself, wasn't all that important, right?

Shouldering the bundle of clothes, he proceeded toward the mountains, a darkly tanned man with red hair, now naked but for the smear of gray-white mud on him. At a distance he looked remarkably like one of the aboriginal dwellers of the area. The ones that had sent him away, sensing there was something broken in him that wasn't safe to be near, not if the right trigger was pressed.

～

At dusk, he was well into the steep gorges, craggy peaks and varied forest terrain of the low mountains, which were good for wild horses, sheep and cattle. By the time the red gorges and peaks started turning purple, evidence of the impending sundown, he'd made himself several spears, using torn strips from his shirt and grasses to position the tips. Planting the weapons at key points he scoped out for his first night's strategy, he moved swiftly, mindful of Danny's words about the speed of vampires. He'd disseminated his scent here and there, down into a gorge, up through a thicket of trees.

A sharp crack. Gunfire. He dropped low and froze, close to a low patch of scrub. An exuberant starting gun, perhaps? Danny would do wise to dismiss most of this lot, send them off to other places once all this was resolved. Men needed things to do to keep them out of mischief, and these had had the scent of blood in their noses too long. 'Course, she'd indicated Ian was an overlord. What did an overlord do? Probably like a feudal landowner, she'd resolve squabbles, take tithes . . .

He smiled inside, but remained motionless. At least until the rabbit wandered into his reach, missing his presence due to his stillness and wind direction. He caught the creature by ears and midbody, avoiding teeth and sharp claws. Running his hand over the soft fur, he gave thanks and an apology at once. "You don't deserve this, mate." In a quick motion, he snapped the creature's neck, making it painless and quick, but he couldn't look as the life died out of the brown gaze.

The aborigines believed that everything was meant to be, that if an animal spirit arrived in time to fulfill a need, it was a gift offered willingly. While Dev had great respect for his clansmen, a part of him wondered if it was a story made up by a parent to make a child feel better about his dinner. The reality was that the hapless victim was in the right place during the wrong bloody time.

Love? You out there?

He didn't know why he did it, but something about the warm, soft body in his hands, the cloudiness closing in on that gaze . . .

Her response was surprisingly clear for the miles between them. *Dev. He's going to send his stockmen after you during daylight. He figured out the third mark, and said I gave you an unfair advantage.*

Don't fret, love. He likely already planned to send his hands out after me. The point is to win, right?

Taking up the lifeless body and his knife, he rose, prepared to move again.

You're right. I should have thought of that. He's trying to see how upset he can make me about you. It bothers him.

Well, it's not like you had me pleasure you in front of him and poor old Ian last night so you could thumb your nose at them. Tell them that anything they could do for you, your mongrel could do better.

Don't *call yourself that.*

He winced at the sharpness of her tone. *Jesus, love. You didn't tell me you could come through like a fishwife. Don't do that without warning. You might get me shot.*

Where are you? What's happening now?

I'm just getting ready for them. Reaching a lower position, he cut the rabbit's stomach open, and removed some of the insides, leaving them in a crevice of rock, draining the still-warm blood down the other side of it. Moving through the trees, he disseminated organs, blood and bone, sinew, on a circular path. Finally, he laid the creature to rest beneath a bush, to feed the other animals who would come and find it, before he headed back toward higher ground.

He's made his point, love. I'm not saying I agree to it, for myself, but in your world you probably should think of me that way. Or he's going to keep using me against you, no matter what happens.

She went silent again. He didn't know if he'd offended her or not, but he had other matters to address now. The sound of the men was closer, so he found another tree, took one of his spears and worked his way up into the branches. He noted clouds were moving so at times darkness was total, then the shapes of the landscape would briefly illuminate, as the moon made an appearance.

Dev, is there nothing you want for yourself? Even pride?

Pride is a vengeful thing, love. Will stab you in the back every time you think you're entitled to something you most likely don't deserve. Hush, now. I've got a bet to win. They're coming.

Plus, a man who'd closed down his soul was like a closed pub. There wasn't anything to want from it, or to give to it, anymore. He got a sense she'd received that thought, but didn't have time to regret it.

The mob didn't run like a pack of hounds, full of crashing movement, baying and yipping. He counted himself fortunate that his first evidence of them was at a distance. From his perch in the large tree, he detected five of them tracking together, fanned out over the ground, slipping through the trees and rocks like noiseless shadows. Moving as fast as snakes on the hunt.

Holy Christ.

Clearing his mind, he held his position. He made his body a part of the tree, part of the low-hanging branches, the roots at its base, the leaves, even the wind that moved through it. It had picked up, become chilly. As he'd explained to Danny back in the caves, it was a technique that had worked very well for the aborigines, making it damn hard to find them when they didn't want to be found. He didn't know how it would fare against supernatural beings, but he was going to give it a go and see how things panned out. Another spear was on the ground next to the neighboring tree, half covered in dirt and leaves so it appeared just another fallen branch.

They'd found the rabbit. He heard the chilling growls and snarls, a yelp and howls. Sharp shouts, the cracking of whips as whoever Ruskin was using as his handlers tried to get them off the scent. He froze as the ground rustled beneath him, and he realized two of the children had split off and were wandering around the vicinity of the tree next to him. One scratched at the base, peering up through the leaves. It was a girl, hissing with a sinister yet oddly musing type of noise, considering. Apparently the other was encouraging her to go check out the hunch. Bloody hell. He saw a mop of snarled black hair, a flashing eye with traces of red, which he noted showed up well in darkness.

When the child started scrambling up the adjacent tree, as agile as a monkey, even faster, Dev made his decision. Grasping the spear, he saw the flick of the child's eyes as she registered his movement. He'd expected her to take several seconds to assess. He'd forgotten he was dealing with animals made rabid by hunger. Instead, she launched herself out into the air, twenty feet across, straight for him.

He threw hard, sheer reaction, and discovered the privilege of his new strength at the same moment. His skill and that strength made up for his delay in reaction. Just. While he knew the spear tip wouldn't kill her, the wooden haft did. The spear went through her chest when she was less than several yards from him. It launched her backward with an unearthly, echoing shriek.

Dev was already dropping out of the tree, landing on top of the other one, his knife clutched in his hand.

Because it was his hunting knife, it was sharp enough to cut through most living things, though he'd never tried human bone and sinew. He blocked out everything but what needed to be done. The impromptu wrestling match made it easier, for the creature that looked like an unkempt nine-year-old had the strength of a bloody bear. Dev knew if he rounded on him, he was good as gone. The child's head whipped right, the fangs sinking into his arm, one hand grabbing his wrist and elbow and shoving outward, wrenching his shoulder out of its socket as easily as he might have pulled an onion bulb from the ground.

Dev plunged the knife into the wild-eyed vampire's nape, twisting. There was a gurgling howl, but he pulled free and then slashed across, deep, severing neck tendons. As the boy tried to get away, Dev held him, pinned him with his knees, skewered his heart next. A geyser of blood struck his face, but he went back to the neck hacking, until he'd taken the boy's head half off. He finished the job with his bare hands. A bloody mess. Literally. As he'd intended.

A tool for demons . . . Damn it, keep the mind blank. He snarled it at himself as he plunged his hands into the warm liquid. He painted another symbol on his chest, a protection against his enemies, then sopped up more blood in his shirt. Retrieving the hidden spear, he padded at a silent run through the woods, slapping the rag here and there, leaving the blood trail everywhere before dropping it and cutting across a creek, moving swiftly upstream.

Slipping away, he heard the pack closing in. A few minutes later, their voices were raised in hair-raising screams of fury. No silence now. They wanted him to hear. Wanted him to know that, if they found him, it wouldn't be quick. Unlike hounds, these were conscious of the concept of vengeance. Odd, since the handler had indicated they were willing enough to turn on one another. But Dev understood it. In a way, the children were there still, somewhere beneath the savagery. And they were a pack.

Dev ignored the nauseating pain of his dislocated shoulder as he kept working his way upward, thanking God again they'd been blessed with recent rain. He cut out of the creek through an area scattered with wildflowers, most furled for the night. A dingo howled, reminding him that less than twelve hours ago he'd held Danny in his arms, the dingoes crying outside. He'd smiled at her, wondered at her.

He went in circles, double-backed over himself, moving so fast that even with his fascinating new speed, his lungs were laboring. Bloody hell, the shoulder hurt, but he didn't dare take the time. Plus, he didn't know if it was pure adrenaline or this third mark, but it wasn't inhibiting him the way he'd have expected. Slowing down only when he knew he was near the gorge he'd scoped during daylight, he located the markers he'd left for himself at the edge. He'd worked out a shallow gully here, which he hoped wouldn't become his grave. Now he lay down in it, rearranging the clumps of matted leaves, debris and dirt over himself, positioning a grass straw for air. He'd finished the arrangement, had no more than a half hour or so to settle and listen, before he heard the approach of the handlers and the vampires. Bloody oath, they were fast.

Someone stopped to the right of him. He could make out the muffled conversation, since they were almost on top of him. "Fan out over this area. Barnes, come over here."

By the shift in pressure near his calf, Dev determined one man had squatted. He'd rolled himself one, because he also detected the faint odor of smoke, heard the strike of the wax match. "This bloke's canny. Jesus, he's left trail markings in twenty different directions, and he's splashing blood everywhere. The little monsters are going half mad."

"Well, we better have some line on him, because Lord Charles is on his way. Night's half over and he expects his kill before the end of it."

A disgusted noise and then a thump. "Damn it. This would be a sight easier if we had an aboriginal tracker."

"Watch that knife, Smith. Don't want one of the kiddies getting hold of it. And ain't no aborigine that'll come within a hundred miles of this place, and you know it. I'm beginning to think they have the right of it. Come on. I'll leave you a couple of the mob to scout this area, and the rest of us will keep going up this ridge."

Dev let out the breath he'd sucked in, listening to the others move off a few minutes later. The Smith bloke who'd thrown his knife into the ground during their discussion was as fond of sharpening it as Dev was. And now, unless the shallow amount of earth had cleaned it off, his blade would smell like Dev's fresh blood.

"This way, I say. Come on, you bloody buggers." The snap of the whip, the sound of men muttering oaths and the animal-like noise of the children slowly receded. In the sudden quiet, Dev's ears were tuned to Smith and the two vampire children.

"What is it you want? Get away with you now. Stay the hell away . . . What the hell . . . ?"

He could imagine Smith holding the knife up to the light, seeing the telltale smear of blood on the blade attracting the two vamps. His eyes already closed, Dev listened to the man's approach, the vibration of his boots on the earth as he tried to determine where he'd been, see what clue he might have missed. Then the ground compressed to the right of Dev's feet as Smith squatted.

Dev exploded out of the ground, spear in one hand, knife in the other. Smith shouted in surprise, helping Dev target him, since he couldn't open his eyes, the sand tumbling from his face a distraction he couldn't afford. He thrust the knife hard into the man's gut beneath the heart. He swung him around by the knife handle, and got lucky, knocking him into one of the two vampire children, if the vicious squeal was accurate. He got his eyes open in time to see his momentum send them both over the gorge edge. It might not kill the vampire, but it would certainly take him out of range for the moment, for the gorge was deep. He'd managed to hang on to the knife haft, but it went spinning out of his hand as he was slammed to the ground by the other one, hard enough that the creature knocked his shoulder back into place with a sickening crunch.

However, a dislocated shoulder couldn't make up for a torn

throat, and the child was gouging, ripping at it with fangs and claws. Dev got the spear between them, heaved and managed to throw the vampire off. He couldn't see her move, but he whipped up the spear a scant second before she was back on him. She shrieked and spit blood in his face, wriggling on the shaft like a maddened shark.

This one was about twelve years old. Starting to develop a young woman's face, a hint of breast. Dev held his position, knocked back onto one knee by her second attack, but grimly bracing himself with the open gorge directly behind him. As she looked down at him, drool flecked her chin from her hunger and the animal growls she made. She was jerking, fighting the death, and when the moon came out from behind the clouds, he saw the brown irises in the bloodred eyes. She had the delicate, thick lashes of a child. The small mouth. Her hair, if cleaned and brushed, would have been brown, too.

The boy, the one he'd mutilated facedown, had been about the size of Rob. This girl might have been his daughter, if Tina had lived and they'd had the three children they'd planned.

Don't. Block it out.

She was batting at the spear, weakening, and her hisses and growls had become whimpers. Swallowing, Dev shifted it so she was on her side, the spear all the way through her. He stayed at the far end of it, though he had to fight everything in him that told him to pull it out, lay a hand on her small skull. Her head thrashed, her eyes darting back and forth, sometimes briefly meeting his in bewilderment.

Was she still twelve? When had Ruskin turned her? Five years ago? Ten? Two? How much of her life had she been tortured like this, when she should have been somewhere like Perth, going to school in her pressed uniform, white socks and shined shoes? Making shy eyes at a boy she liked?

She was dead, the body at last still and lifeless. A different stillness settled over him then, one far from what the Elder had taught him. The click of a pistol behind him was loud in that silence. "Glad I lagged behind the others. Could hear that bludger Smith's scream a mile off. You stay right like that. The other blokes'll be here in a—"

With a howl of feral rage, Dev spun low, sweeping out his feet, taking the man off his. He rolled, but Dev was already on him, the pistol knocked away. He jerked the frightened man up by his hair and slit his throat before he could cry out.

He'd almost let himself get taken by sentiment. Punishing himself, as well as his newest kill, he gutted the man there, a quick movement, leaving another blood trail. They couldn't keep the kids off this much blood, they were too hungry. He was wagering they were like hounds in truth. Give them too much scent, too much to eat, and they'd be useless for tracking for the rest of the night. He'd bought himself the first day, he was certain of it. He'd say the coast was clear, but he'd learned a long time ago not to measure it that way, because the gods sure as hell didn't. It was simply about surviving.

Rising, he looked down. Though he didn't want to, he left the spear in the vampire girl, just in case. He had a lot of ground to cover by dawn, a lot of traps to set for the men that would come after him in daylight. They thought they'd exhaust him. Two could play that game.

Danny?

Dev. You're hurt. Her concern reached him, almost made him want to laugh, but he was afraid any sound that came out of his throat right now would be unrecognizable. He used his mind instead, wondering if she would hear the raw savagery of the beast boiling inside him.

When it's time to take out Ruskin . . . you and me, we'll both take him. That bastard and I aren't going to draw breath in the same world, not if I have any say about it.

Then he turned, disappeared in the forest, emptying his mind again.

15

Any guilt Danny felt about giving Dev the third mark vanished after that first night, when he'd been stabbed and his shoulder dislocated. If he survived this, he'd discover near invincibility and an even greater ability to heal, once the mark had a chance to settle in. But as she'd hoped, his wounds already clotted and injuries knitted faster than an unmarked human's, and his new strength compensated. The problem was, as the number of hits mounted, it would get harder for his body to manage the process without her blood to assist him.

And the number had grown. He'd managed to go to ground during the daylight hours. Charles's men had no luck finding him at all, but they'd also become more cautious. Dev took out three of them with carefully laid traps. Two legs were broken. One man plummeted to his death into a gorge, while another was bitten by a nest of poisonous infant snakes. When night fell, the children, who found their hunger and focus restored after Ruskin had them all savagely flogged, were after him again. Danny paced the verandas throughout the night, dwelling in the background of her new servant's mind. Dawn found another child and two more of Ruskin's men dead. Dev was proving that bush craft made a vampire's powers irrelevant. If she hadn't been so worried about him, she'd have been overcome with fierce satisfaction on his behalf.

The Region Master was livid. She made sure she was sitting in the library, a book open in her lap, looking relaxed and bored, when he returned to the station right before dawn. She gave him a pleasant smile that bared her fangs before he stomped off to his room.

When she'd retired to her own room, though, she put her head to her knees, pressed her fingers over her eyes. Tonight, Dev had taken a gunshot wound in the shoulder, a deep tear across his abdomen from one of the children, another boy. They'd gone over the side of a steep hill together, rolled down rock, scrub and tree. When the child's head had hit a trunk hard enough to crack it open, Dev had finished the job before the boy's wits and vampire healing could revive him; otherwise that would have been the end of her bushman.

He'd had no sleep, spending all his spare time setting traps to slow them, planting weapons close to hand he could use. A mixture of tactics learned from the aborigines and as a soldier. He *was* tired, beyond exhausted. But the third mark gave him endurance. Army training kept him moving, thinking. And the rage that was all his own provided combustible fuel. Hovering in the back of his mind, she wasn't sure if he was even coherent anymore, or if something else had risen, as feral and mindless in its focus as the vampire children's bloodlust. *One target, one mission.* By dawn, except for his strategies, that was the only thought in his mind.

And the tone she heard was dangerous, almost unnatural. But she stayed silent, merely tracking his movements and condition, because whatever had altered inside him was keeping him alive. She'd deal with what it was when three days were over.

She made herself sleep through daylight of the third day, but she was restive. Ruskin had his men fanned out all along the plain around the front of the station, watching any approach. How in the hell was that fair? How could Dev get past the fence? She wanted to check his whereabouts when she rose, near dusk, but he'd done that still thing with his mind, shutting her out. She could push harder, because he couldn't keep her out if she was determined to get in, but she wouldn't be a distraction. If he needed her, he would let her know. She didn't even check for his geographical location, not wanting to give anything away with her expression, surrounded by enemies as she was.

Though Ruskin had gone on the hunt at night, he'd assigned one of the younger maids to shadow her every movement, because she'd rarely left Danny's side. Though she was quiet and solicitous, Danny suspected she was one of Ian's doxies loyal to Ruskin. Another one she'd probably have to load on a train out of here. The question was, would she be dealing with that by herself, as well as another burial detail?

The thought had her pausing in the hallway, pressing her hand to the wall to steady herself. No. He was going to make it back to her. She couldn't contemplate what she'd do if she had to watch Charles and his men cut him down within feet of the fence line. She wasn't sure if she might not race out there, throw herself over him and beg for mercy, willing to do anything to spare him. Which would seal both their fates.

"Marm?" The young maid's soft voice was at her elbow, and she opened her eyes, focused on her. Pretty enough, with exceptionally intelligent, jewel blue eyes and dark hair.

"I'm fine." *You little skulking rat.*

She met Ruskin in the dining area. He'd ordered the staff—her staff—to lay out their breakfast an hour early so he could be in position for the kill he was sure would be his. Of course, she could tell he wasn't as certain of that as he'd been two days ago. He'd offered three days as a joke, thinking the hunt would be over in one night. It had never occurred to him a mere human could persevere against his pack that long. She couldn't contemplate what he'd do to the children if Dev survived. Worrying about Dev was enough for right now.

Schooling her face into a neutral mask as she entered the dining room, she found the lingering smell of the staff's breakfast, bacon and eggs, drifting from the kitchen. Ruskin glanced at her over his tea, his expression brooding. Aapti wasn't present, but Danny had observed he often used the woman only for formality or for sex, apparently not having much desire for her companionship, at least here. He said nothing as she took a seat at the far end of the table from him. When the maid poured her tea, Danny resisted the urge to bare her teeth at her, send her scampering. The whole situation was intolerable.

"You order my staff about as if they were your own, Lord Charles," Danny said at last. "You've had me watched as if I were your prisoner. I've indulged these things, because of the circumstances with Ian." Picking up the cup, she examined the tea, then lifted her head to meet his dark, piercing stare. "But my patience is growing thin. I am part of your territory, but as you are well aware, you can only command me so far."

"Really?"

For all her warnings to Dev, she'd counted overmuch on Charles's devotion to the affectations of British courtesy, their mild savagery at best when offended. She hadn't taken into account his level of frustration and how easily the vampire side of him could push it into violence.

He was up and around the table before she anticipated him. Seizing her by her throat and the front of her blouse, he swung her toward the wall, sending her crashing against it, her feet off the ground, so she stumbled when gravity brought her back to it. But he was already there, plowing a fist into her face. It snapped her head back, would have broken her neck if she'd been human. She heard the cry of the maid, was startled to see the young woman lunge forward, bring the teapot down on his head, the glass shattering and hot tea scalding down his back.

Charles turned on the girl and Danny shoved herself off the wall, throwing herself onto his back with a snarl. Her nerves, stretched over three days, had had enough. But the impact with the wall had disoriented her. She couldn't get her balance back before he had her forced to the floor on her knees, arm wrenched back painfully and head driven to the rug, her hips high in the air as he straddled her, his thighs pressing either side of her body, holding her fast.

"You couldn't get me removed as Region Master, you pretentious whore. It's time you learned your place. You may be a born vampire, but you have no true leadership skills, nothing to offer the Council as a replacement but the fact of your existence and your pretty face. And believe me, while I might not be able to resolve the first without incurring unpleasant attention, I can fix the second. There are ways to inflict scars on a vampire. So horrible you could never venture from home again, for nothing mortal could have such mutations and be alive. And then there is the way that males have been uniquely equipped to remind females of their place, though I'd hate to dirty my wick in such a foul cesspool."

He knocked her knees apart and pushed the straining evidence of his cock against her, hard enough it felt like an invasion, though separated by both of their clothes. "I will leave when I am damn good and ready. Your mother was a whore and a thief, your father a dupe to her wiles. If you bait me further, I will prove the daughter is the same as the mother."

He spat on her, and withdrew. In the time it took him to step back, Danny spun and launched herself onto him, taking them both over the table in an explosion of crockery and table arrangements. They fell together, rolled, and Danny ducked under his grip, came up with one of the chairs, swinging it to strike against his raised arm. They were Queen Anne chairs, beautiful carved pieces, but she wouldn't mind driving a leg through his heart. She'd even have it repaired and sit on it for the rest of her life, a commemoration to its noble sacrifice.

But she didn't duck fast enough under his next attack, and found herself sailing through the air again, hitting the back wall ten feet away and thudding against the side bar. The candle sconce tore her shirt, gouged a furrow down her back, but she rolled as he came at her, hit the wall, and had made it back to a defensive crouch when they heard the yelling.

"My lord. *My lord.*"

It was the note of it, fearful, full of apprehension, that had Ruskin's head whipping toward the door and Danny blinking, seeking in her mind. Scrambling to her feet, she almost beat Ruskin out the door onto the covered porch, into the evening that had settled in, the sun disappearing for the day.

Dev stood, swaying, just inside the fence line. He almost blended in to the sand and scrub of the background, for he was caked with mud, sticks, spiny leaves and grasses plastered into it. Beneath all that, he appeared to be naked, devoid of even the one knife they'd let him keep. When he saw her, that void in his mind dissipated, like a dam of clay dissolving beneath a flash flood. He fell to one knee, but before he could fall face forward, she had him. On her knees, holding him up, his face pressed against her shoulder.

"He just rose up, there, right outside the fence, out of the ground, and walked in before we could do anything, my lord." Ruskin's lead man was babbling, terror in his eyes at the fury on Ruskin's face.

When Dev mumbled, she turned her head to his. "What, Dev?" she asked. God, he felt good in her arms, even filthy and reeking of three days of sweat and blood, his own and others.

"Munaintya . . . no, maybe Yertabulti. Don't want . . . to start over. Too tired."

Charles turned on them. She shot her glance up to him, her eyes narrowing, body tensing. But he shook his head after a long moment, his eyes cold. Swiping at his bloody lips with the back of his hand, he gave her a look of disdain. "As I said before this started, you are not easily cowed, Lady Danny. I give you that."

"You'll give me more than that," she said evenly. "My servant has paid your tithe. Declare our debt paid, as you promised."

He barked a short laugh. "You will say 'please,' or you will get nothing. I will hear you beg, Lady Daniela, once, or I will have him killed here, and say he never made it."

She stared at him. Dev muttered again, and this time Ruskin was close enough to hear it.

"Tell that . . . arrogant bastard . . . to bugger off."

Ruskin's eyes flamed, but Danny held up a hand, her jaw flexing. "Please, Lord Charles. You are a sporting man. Honor a worthy opponent. I am . . . begging you."

Though savor it, you bastard, because I'll never do it again.

"Very well. For a worthy opponent. I suspect he's not one who easily allows a woman to hold the reins. You may regret marking him yet." Ruskin held her gaze a long moment. "Your debt for Ian is paid, according to Council law. But you remember what I said, Lady Danny. If you cannot accept my authority, I suggest you skulk back to Brisbane and the Queensland Territory and cede this property to my holdings. Otherwise, I expect to see you with the other vampires at my territory meeting in Darwin in two months, offering your allegiance to me." His attention snapped to his men, lingered on his lead man, whom Danny knew wouldn't live to see another dawn. Ruskin would have someone's blood for this. Perhaps if it was the lead man, he would spare the children his wrath. It was a slim hope, she knew.

"I've had enough of this rustic place. We leave within the hour. Pack us up."

As they moved off, Ruskin turning on his heel to return to the house, she felt a light hand on her shoulder. The dark-haired, blue-eyed maid who'd foolishly tried to come to her defense. "What did he say, marm?" she asked in a soft voice that reminded Danny of fresh daisies. "That first thing. About . . . Yerbulti?"

She put a hand to Dev's hair, knowing he'd slipped into unconsciousness, for she was bearing his full weight against her. "Munaintya is Dreamtime. The beginning, creation of the world, according to the blacks. Yertabulti is the place of slumber. It's what they used to call Port Adelaide, because it was where the birds went to sleep. I think in his muddled way, he was trying to say he wanted to go to sleep." *Or to die.*

Pushing that thought away, she turned it to the practical. "Bring buckets of water," she commanded. "We'll wash the worst of it off him out here, and then I want a bath drawn for him inside. A full bath. He's earned it."

Danny eased Dev down so his shoulders and head were in her lap. Until he was conscious or clean, she wouldn't know the extent of his injuries, but for now, she laid her hand on his chest, where under the caked mud she knew the raven mark would be, felt her heart rate settle.

"Hotcakes. Cook promised hotcakes."

"Soon."

When he cracked open an eye, the pull at one corner of his

mouth speared her heart, because she felt how the mere effort of it tore something inside him. He was wounded, but his worst wounds had nothing to do with his flesh.

"First, you need this." Steeling herself for his resistance or revulsion, the idea of which bothered her far more than it should, she started to bring her wrist to her mouth to puncture it. "A couple tablespoons will be enough. A Mistress's blood is highly restorative to her servant, when he has need."

Reaching up with an unusually clumsy hand, he closed it over her right breast. Gently, his fingers traced a random path over it before his arm gave out and he let it fall back to his abdomen, his eyes closing. "There. Like you said. Liked the way you did . . . the water. Need . . . something . . . need . . . death."

"No. I forbid that, Dev. You're my servant. You serve me."

She wouldn't let him push her away, but he tried. She didn't want to hurt him, fight him here in the yard in front of the leers of Ruskin's men. But those words cut into her, the confusing swirl of his thoughts a mixture of pain and exhaustion, so deep she almost felt the lassitude in her own limbs.

"It will be all right," she said, letting it go for now and giving him something different. Sliding her other arm around him, she held him close, burying his face into her breast, the promise of it, letting him hide from himself. "Let me take care of you, Dev. Don't think. Just sleep."

∼

It took two rinses in the yard to get most of the surface debris off him, enough so that he wouldn't turn the water in the inside tub into a mudhole. He was only semiconscious through the porch washing, so thankfully he didn't have to see Ruskin's departure. Danny had to leave her staff to do the washing of the outer crust while she performed the necessary cool good-byes to the Region Master. Trying to block the whimpers and cries of his remaining children, she overheard one stockman relaying instructions that, once back in Darwin, they would be put back into their individual small cages and starved for the next week as punishment for their failure. She couldn't bear to look at their faces, and actually hated the Vampire Council for their apathy.

Lord Ruskin's farewell was curt, though his eyes were hard on her face. "I will restock my pack before the meeting, so they will perform far more ably. So I advise you to improve your manners, as well as those of your servant. Otherwise, you will be part of the excellent entertainments I'll have planned."

She cheerfully and viciously hoped he would drive straight into Hades as the entourage passed out of her gates and headed down the dusty track to start the long journey back to Darwin. However, she couldn't take her eyes away as the last Rover passed and the three caged children in it watched her, fear and pain in their gazes.

Damn it, damn it, *damn it*.

Turning back toward the porch, she saw her small handful of stockmen standing there, including old Jim. At her glance, he stepped forward. "Any orders, my lady?"

"You're in charge until Dev's on his feet. For tonight, have the men retire to quarters and handle their stock duties as normal."

"Yes, ma'am. Aye. Right-o." There was a general pulling of forelocks, an exchange of glances, none of which she perceived as being duplicitous, and then they were off to the sleeping quarters. From old Jim's long look, she knew she could rest easy, at least for tonight. However, she couldn't delay long in determining whom she was going to send off. The rest, including the house staff, would all need two marks for her to monitor them. Right now, though, she had only one thing to do that really mattered to her.

Her men had brought the semiconscious Dev to the kitchen and into the tub. That young maid was busy washing his hair, and the cook was pouring in some more clean water. At her entrance, they both looked up, but she waved a hand so that they could continue, though her gaze narrowed thoughtfully on the young woman.

"Ruskin didn't assign you to watch me. Who are you?"

"No, marm. I'm Elisa. Your mum, she took me on right before she died. She said . . . you'd probably like me." Her cheeks tinged and she rushed on. "I mean, that I'd be useful to you. I'm a very good lady's

maid, as well as . . . I can do household duties, also. Mrs. Rupert"—
she nodded to the cook—"she can tell you I'm a hard worker."

"A little too pretty," the cook said gruffly. "But, yes, my lady. The
blokes fall over themselves when they see her, but she keeps her
mind on her work." Her gaze shifted. "Your mum . . . she arranged it
so Elisa would never be bothered by the old master. His oath to her.
Possibly the only one he ever honored, and that was because she
hasn't been gone very long. Plus, he was still occupied with Mary.
This one was a little too strong willed for his tastes."

Danny arched her brows and the woman flushed. "My
apologies—"

"None needed," Danny said. "Thank you for that honesty. Elisa
has already proven her worth to me today. As you have."

There was a rumble, a sound suspiciously like a snort, and Danny
adjusted her glance to see Dev considering the young woman
through half-slit eyes. Elisa's position put her wobbling bosom,
though covered by the maid's uniform, right over his face. "I like her
fine already," he observed.

"Don't tempt me to drown you." Though she was glad to hear
him exercising his normal wit rather than mumbling about death,
see clarity in his eyes rather than the shadows of hell called up
from deep in his soul. Laying a hand on his shoulder, Danny bent
over him as Elisa discreetly withdrew. As she surveyed his body,
she had to admit she liked that fine as well. Had from the beginning. Now, though, she felt a rush of anger when she saw the healing scars of a half dozen wounds that would have been serious and
possibly even fatal on an unmarked human. Yes, he needed her
blood. Now.

"I'll take over his bath." She didn't care what her staff thought,
but neither one showed a reaction.

"There's extra towels right there, my lady," Elisa said. "Ring that
bell if you need anything, or any help getting him upstairs when
you're done." An unspoken message that they would have privacy.
Both women affected a curtsy, then were gone on quiet feet.

You're right, Mother. I do like her. Danny shook her head. Typical.

A small gift from a mother who'd left her so many other problems of nearly unmanageable proportions.

For now, though, she turned her attention to Dev, who had his chin on his shoulder, as if he'd slipped off again. Kneeling by his side, she put her hand on his temple, stroking through the wet hair. He had a strong neck, like a bull. In fact, he was built like that. Such broad shoulders, a burliness that hinted at the pugnacious nature beneath his good-natured exterior. Not overly tall, though a bit taller than herself.

Come on, then, bushman. Before I can let you dream, you have to eat.

But she hesitated at the wrist, thinking about what he'd asked. She should just feed him from the arm, a functional act, but he'd asked so little for all that he'd given her. Unbuttoning the first several buttons of the blouse she'd been wearing, she unhooked the bra in back, pulled it down so that he'd have clear access to the inviting curve of breast. When she turned her attention back to him, she found his eyes had opened again, though he appeared to be fighting sleep as fiercely as he'd fought Ruskin's men.

"Should have known the sound of a woman's clothes coming off would be enough to wake you."

"In a couple ways." His gaze drifted down his body, and she saw, remarkably, he was getting aroused in the warm water.

"Maybe you don't need my blood. Not if you can fill that huge thing."

"Taking blood . . . from my brain. Don't need a lot there." His eyes glinted. "Weak . . . as a baby. Do what you want . . . with it."

"Oh, Dev." She passed a thumb over his lips, but felt a warm shiver at the responsive flex of them under her pad, the attention of his eyes on her bare flesh. The mindless hunger there. "It's a survival response. You can't possibly finish. You'll probably pass out before you're all the way hard."

"Not about finishing. About . . . being inside. Please, my lady." She saw it then, in his mind, a desperate need to find something real and immediate to ground him back in the present and not the blood of the past few days.

That took away any resistance she had. Rising, she removed her clothes. His eyes followed her, and even as worn-out as he was, she saw his powers of observation had not been dulled enough. He lighted on the tear in her shirt, moved from there to the bruises she knew would be fading.

"You and the Pom have a disagreement?"

"A mild one. Your arrival broke it up, or I might have got the best of him, then and there."

Dev's gaze rose, held hers. "No," he said at last. "Not this time."

Despite her protest, he lifted himself with a grunt, so he was sitting up straighter in the tub, reached out to her with a wet hand. Biting back a sigh of impatience with his stubbornness, she let him touch her face, but the penetrating knowledge in his eyes was unexpected and unsettling. She would have drawn back, but his fingers tangled in her hair.

"He did more than knock you around a bit. He . . ." His eyes narrowed, his hand tightening.

"No." She closed her hand on his wrist, held his gaze. "Only if I were dead, Dev. That's the only way he'd get that. It was a way of threatening me," she added, when his green eyes didn't waver, a hint of savagery suggesting what his opponents had been facing these past several days. "He was trying to unbalance me. He succeeded a little bit, but he won't be alive long enough to savor it, believe me."

"Yeah, I do. But together, remember?"

She bit back another sigh. There was no way Dev could help her take out a vampire more than five hundred years old. But he was too much of a man to hear such logic, even on a good day. Instead, she let her hand slide to his shoulder, gently began to push him back. "What do I have to do to get you to shut up and eat?"

"The airplane, coming in for a landing?" At her startled look, he made the motion of a held spoon turning in the air, zooming for an infant's hopeful mouth. "Of course, I *was* thinking of something a little different."

"I *should* drown you," she decided.

"Your hair," he said softly. "Take down your hair, love. Thought about your hair. Dreamed about it."

For today, she'd overlook the fact it came out of his mouth almost like an order. There was no way he could make her do it, after all. As she stepped into the tub, she removed Chiyoko's sticks, let it spread out on her shoulders. She straddled his body, working her feet in on either side of his thighs. When he ran his wet hands up the sides of them, closing on her flesh, she let herself be drawn down, feeling the tremor in his arms.

His body was such a mess, but beneath the cuts, bruises and half-healed wounds, she saw his muscles, straining. From his mind, she knew he was right. Wounded he was, but what he most needed now was this. Truth, she was already somewhat slick for him, merely from the intensity of his gaze, his need for her. As she lowered herself, his hands moved up to her buttocks, cupped them. A wry smile crossed his face, though. "I'm afraid I'm not going to be able to do much for your pleasure, love. I'm so tired, but want you so badly, I'm sure to be the typical bastard. Go off like a geyser the minute your sweet cunt closes on me, and then fall right to sleep."

"We'll see," she murmured, and began to sink down on him. As his attention went to that joining place, his breath drawing in, she picked up the razor Elisa had left on the stack of towels and flipped it open, drawing his startled attention. When his cock had pressed several inches into her slick, welcoming channel, she drew the blade across her breast, making a bright vermilion streak of blood well up.

"Drink first," she ordered, cupping his head. "It will help restore your strength, heal your body completely."

She leaned forward, half impaled on him, her body already quivering, but it was a delicious sensation, holding still there while that broad head waited, insisted.

Beats the hell out of the airplane method, doesn't it?

His fingers dug into her hips, but she refused to budge until he complied. *Drink, Dev. Let me help heal you.*

His tongue touched her skin, took the first tentative lick of her flesh, her nourishing blood. A drop fell into the water with a soft *plop*, spreading out, a crimson flower with spidery petals. With a mental sigh, he closed his mouth over the wound, began to pull at her. The reaction from her own body was electric, spasms rippling up through her womb such that she felt the reactive flex of his hands on her, the surge of lust in his own mind, as he realized the effect it had on her.

She could hold both their bodies still with effort, but it also required pressing down, and she found herself drawing out that torment, one millimeter at a time, feeling him stretch her, demand more of her body, as she demanded more of it as well. She maintained the creeping pace, because every millimeter brought a convulsion of pleasure almost as strong as a climax. Also, she knew it was a gentler way to handle his battered torso, though he likely wouldn't care for her tenderness.

Down, down, as his mouth suckled the blood from her breast, her hand now cupped on the back of his neck, the other sliding slowly down his chest, over the raven mark, until she was seated to the hilt on him. The position straightened her arm, and he let go of one of her hips to stroke his fingers along it.

She didn't want to draw back, but she knew she needed to do so, for too much of her blood would make him sick, like a far too rich dessert. To ease the transition for them both, she arched up, lithe, and slowly drew his mouth down to her nipple, letting him latch on there instead. When she tightened her grip on him, she began to move, like the ripple of sand, the stroke of the wind, changing the face of things, the way their bodies looked together, so there was a compilation of images that began to build in her mind. Going down, seeing his lashes flicker up, his beautiful green eyes roving over her breasts, her throat, up to her face. It created an intimacy so intense she tilted her own head back, closing her eyes.

He was shaking so hard now it was making the water vibrate. Too weak for this, she knew, but this was what he'd wanted, and she wouldn't let him be cheated by his mortal strength. Searching, past the curve of her buttock, she found his muscular thigh beneath the water's surface, stroked up it to find the sensitive strip between scrotum and anus, and began to tease him there. The way it arched her body gave him a display of white flesh from her throat to the hint of the split lips of her sex, him thrust between them. Her quivering breasts, slope of abdomen and other sights all in between.

You, first . . . love. Please, let me see you go.

Not this time. You've ordered me about enough. This is all about you. Give me your seed, Dev. Come for me now.

His cock pulsed inside her, and his involuntary oath made her muscles contract on him in satisfaction. The water sloshed over the side as he bucked up into her, driving harder, once, twice, his breath rasping even from that bare effort. The hot flood of him seared the sides of her womb, bathed her inside with a feeling so strong it unleashed the band she'd held around other emotions for the past three days. On pure impulse, she leaned forward, grasped his jaw with both hands to wrench his head up and ruthlessly seize his mouth, kissing him with all the need, worry, anger and desire she had to give. His arms banded around her waist and hips. Despite his lack of strength, he let her know she wasn't alone in it. Or perhaps it was the only thing he could seize in his mind that he could bear to embrace.

She heard that thought, even as she kissed him harder, more cruelly, demanding that he surrender it all to her, let her take care of it. So he could rest. So he could be hers.

Ah, love . . .

It was then she realized she'd actually given him that thought, and that his mind was whirling around it, caught between resistance and desire for her, caught in this moment, knowing the euphoria could lead to great foolishness . . . but he didn't care.

I am all yours, love. Whatever's left to have is yours for the taking.

For now, at least. Ironically, what drove him to give so much to her now would, after he slept off the exhaustion, come back to push her away. But she took now, knowing she had a foot in the door. And to think, only a few days ago, when she'd walked into Elle's place, she'd had no desire to take a full human servant at all.

As he finished, she stilled on him, despite the demand of her own body to finish. She would deny it for now, hold the control, because she knew that would drive him crazy in itself, knowing she hadn't allowed him to bring her pleasure yet. Give him something else to think about other than the horror of the past few days.

Of course, that would occur to him later, for his prophetic words were amusingly apparent. He was unconscious again. Quietly, she lifted off him, suppressing a needy moan at the way even the semierect state of him could stimulate her pussy, but then she knelt by the tub, picked up soap and washcloth.

As she started the pleasure of giving his fine, muscular body a thorough washing, she stopped, tracing the upper curve of the raven's wings. They had overlaid the scars of grief he'd cut into his chest, so that the scars looked like ornamental lines, marking the raven's feathers.

Another reminder, a disquieting one, that often there were powers above vampires as well as humans, directing things. And those powers might decide he couldn't be hers, that she could have him for only a little time. She'd had enough temporal experiences in her life, no matter her own desires, to know it was possible. Since her mother's death, her priority had been the punishment of Ian. Returning here had reminded her that she couldn't stop there, that Ruskin must be expulsed as well.

Now she had a third goal. Would she be able to have them all, or would one have to be sacrificed for another? Or would both escape her grasp, held out of reach by the capricious hands of Fate?

Her chin firmed. Well, she wasn't one to defy Fate, but she wanted Dev to be her third-marked servant, not only physically, but in all the ways she'd ever imagined—or avoided imagining—a third-mark servant could be.

And she wanted him to want that, too. Vampires could control more things than most about their environments, and were often ruthless about doing so. She'd told Dev a partial truth when she'd implied that most vampires avoided the folly of forced human servitude. Some vampires reveled in the power of it. Others simply considered the notion of human free will a sentiment that could be indulged at the vampire's discretion, the way a parent indulged a child who really didn't know what he wanted.

It's acceptable to feel strongly about human servants, as long as you don't lose proper perspective, Danny. Your reluctance to establish total control over one is merely a sign of youth. You'll grow out of it, the way you stopped believing your dolls are alive and have feelings.

Danny winced at the memory of her mother's words. It didn't matter what others believed. Either he'd come to it, or he wouldn't.

Plus, she wasn't about to beg a human to serve her. If he did leave, at least she'd have the satisfaction of being able to bedevil his dreams and thoughts whenever she wished . . . until he got out of range. Third-marked servants didn't typically go far from their Mistresses, perhaps a day or two's drive at most, for the obvious reasons. But if he did go that far—and Australia was a large country—he wouldn't be able to hear her in his head anymore. She wouldn't even be able to hear him in hers.

Well, nothing to be done about that. She was depriving herself of the joy of the moment. Focusing on the task at hand, she rubbed the cloth over the rounded part of Dev's shoulder, lifted one of his arms to thoroughly scrub it. Then she worked between the fingers, ran the cake of soap under his dirty fingernails. When she eased his hand back into the water to rinse, she set aside the cloth, lathered up both hands and slicked them down the broad chest, up his neck, behind and inside his ears, over his face, touching his temples and the soft hair sweeping back from there. She noted every old scar and new wound, traced them all gently, put her lips on a few.

He slept through it all, exhaustion having claimed him even beyond her reach. However, when her finger touched his mouth, the slope of his jaw, he made a face and turned his head so it was against her palm, as if using it for a pillow. It made her throat ache. What if he did walk away?

Total control. She knew what it meant to the likes of Ruskin and her mother. But what did it mean to her? She was a vampire. It was a natural instinct within her, as well as a sexual drive, to dominate any creature who couldn't dominate her. But looking beneath the surface of that, she considered that she acquired total control when she had total trust from the one being controlled. Which required a willing surrender. That was the true gem she wanted. She stilled, thinking about the small handful of vampire-servant relationships that had drawn her reluctant fascination. Unlike Ian's and Charles's much more one-sided relationships with their servants, the ones she remembered had demonstrated that unspoken appeal, and *appeal* was likely far too light a word for such an incredible bond. If she wanted something like that with Dev, she had to have his willing surrender. And for that to happen, she had to win his soul, down to the darkest level.

Sliding her hand out from under his face carefully, she retrieved the cloth and began to wash him again. She was going to make sure he stayed in bed for at least a day. Once they worked out the staff issues and station operation, she'd take an accounting of the supplies she needed to make this station her home again. New furniture, carpets, artwork. She couldn't wait to get rid of the stifling English-manor feeling Ian had so loved. She wanted pictures of beach landscapes from the Queensland coast, the lightning storms over Darwin, quiet, tranquil bush settings. Comfortable, airy furniture, like what was in her mother's room.

It went without saying that she'd want to pick much of that out herself. So after she got things settled and moving in the right direction here, she'd head back to Brisbane for a few days to buy her furniture, and take stock of things. She would take Dev with her on the trip. If he was reluctant, she'd say she wanted to offer him a nice venture into the city to compensate him for all his trouble on her behalf.

After that, she would plan her strategy regarding Ruskin, which, as Dev had advised and she knew, would take far more careful planning than even Ian's demise.

But for now, it was time to get Dev to bed. When she thought about how she wanted his room prepared, she remembered no one here was second-marked, where she could speak in their minds and make sure that was done. Another task to handle. For now, she rang the bell.

Elisa arrived in less than a minute. Before she could speak, Danny asked the question uppermost in her mind. "Did my mother mark you?"

"No, ma'am," the young maid replied. "She said I was all yours, when you came. She knew you'd come."

Danny ran her knuckles down Dev's arm thoughtfully, watching the way water beaded between her skin and his. "Why did you attack Lord Ruskin, Elisa?"

"He was trying to hurt you, marm."

"You do realize that if he hadn't been distracted by Dev's arrival and my attack, he would have killed you, right? As it is, you're very lucky the incident slipped his mind, or he would have come back into the dining room to attend to it."

"I guess I wasn't thinking much about that, my lady. He was hurting you," the girl repeated.

Her mother had taken pains to make sure this one had not had the spirit beaten or frightened out of her, to the point she was almost dangerously naive. Either that, or she'd found someone as courageous as the bushman she was still caressing with her fingertips. Now over the hard plane of his abdomen, teasing his navel, the arrow of hair that would eventually take her into the thicket over his groin. She noted Elisa was having a bit of a hard time keeping her eyes off Dev, and the wandering of Danny's hand.

"Elisa," she prompted gently. "Why do you want to serve me?"

"Well, your mum, she was . . . She was kind to me, my lady. She sent me off to school in Adelaide, so I'd know how to read and write. Said that way I'd be sure to be running a household of my own someday, unless I found a nice man who wanted to marry me and let me run his house. I think it was also to keep me away from here as much as possible. I wasn't sorry about that," she said, and Danny saw a sudden flash of fierceness in her gaze. "He was a bad 'un, Mr. Ian. I assume you don't mind me saying he was a bad 'un, seeing as you cut his head off and all . . ." She brought herself up short, her cheeks reddening.

"It's all right, Elisa. Keep going. I want to know your thoughts. You can be a great help to me."

"Yes, marm. Sorry, marm. Most of them were afraid to leave. He wasn't like you, saying it was okay if we wanted to go. And please don't take offense if some do go, marm. Some of them he took unwilling, people who came traveling across the land."

Danny shook her head. "Please assure them they are free to go. And tell old Jim to assist them in whatever way they need with transportation or funds to return to their homes. In fact, I'll be heading to the coast for some new things for this house in several days. Anyone who needs a ride is welcome to join me. Just ensure we have drivers who will return the vehicles to the station. Now, as far as those who are *not* glad I am here"—her gaze sharpened—"I need to know about them. I will not cause them harm unless provoked, but I will make sure they leave this station. And I need to mark you, to make it easier for me to communicate with you. Do you object to that?"

Elisa flushed again. "Uh . . . n-no, marm. I just . . . Well, I'm Catholic."

"Really?" Danny suppressed a smile. "Elisa, you've fallen in with a strange household to be devout in your faith."

"Yes, my lady." The girl shifted, twisting her hands in the white apron. "I didn't know if it mattered to you. About me being Catholic."

"The one thing about being a vampire, Elisa, is you live long enough to see as many faiths rise and fall as governments, and very often their motives overlap. I don't care if you worship beetles, as long as you serve me well."

"Yes, marm." Danny could have sworn she saw a twinkle in the girl's eyes, and it was an unexpected blessing, a pinpoint of light in the darkness of the past few days. Then the maid turned a brighter shade of red, her hands twisting in the apron again. "I just don't know if I can . . . Those things . . . like Mary . . . I've never been part of that."

Even more intriguing. Most vampires considered sexual experience in humans a plus, yet her mother had obviously gone to great pains to protect this girl. "Elisa, what you saw tonight with Mary was not usual. Most often, that activity is confined to third-marked servants or willing human participants. I find females stimulating as an occasional diversion, but when I mark you, it will be to make it easier for me to communicate my needs quickly."

"Oh. Very well then, my lady." Screwing up her eyelids, Elisa jutted out her chin, averted her face and revealed her neck.

Danny hadn't meant this second, but then she reconsidered. Elisa was going to be a valuable resource to her, and there was no reason to put it off. Until she had access to the minds of the staff, she didn't know whom she could trust. Still, she seemed so young to Danny. Since she was two hundred, that wasn't unusual, but Dev inexplicably felt so much closer to her own age.

Rising, she moved to face the girl, touched her chin, leaned in to brush her cheek with her nose. When Elisa stiffened, Danny made a soothing noise. "Easy. It will only hurt for a second. I promise you that."

Though for that to be true, she might have to compromise her Catholic virtues somewhat. The hard injection of pheromones at the bite site left a lasting impression that tended to make her second-marked staff bond with her more quickly, even if they tucked away the experience behind their sense of propriety.

"It's all right, my lady." But the young woman closed her hands into fists, fingers tangled.

Danny laid one hand over both, steadying her, and then bit into the artery. The girl cried out, but Danny gave her the pheromone at the same moment, easing in the serum of the first mark, letting it rush through the bloodstream. Elisa's fists unknotted, then one hand found its way onto Danny's hip, digging into her waist, the bare skin beneath her loose shirt as the girl gasped in the throes of the rush of irresistible arousal. Danny slid an arm around her, bringing her closer, breathing on the bite mark even as she released the second mark injection. As the girl swayed, her mind unfolding to Danny, she saw a simple life, filled with hard work but a driving desire to be more, to travel, to love . . . all of a young girl's dreams laid out before her like a child's picture book. It was poignant and lovely, especially given how difficult a life she'd actually had before Danny's mother had found her.

But Danny's pleasure turned to something deeper when, seeing her mother through Elisa's memories, she realized her mother had seen her daughter in Elisa, the daughter she'd alienated and driven away. Was Elisa her gift of regret?

Easing the girl away from her then, Danny soothed the bite marks with her tongue, making the blood clot over the vital artery before she lifted her head. Elisa was still unsteady, so she held her for a moment, stroking her hair back, letting her lean into her like she would hold a younger sister.

"Oh. My." Elisa at last lifted her head. "I'm dizzy, m'lady. And I feel . . ."

"Like I can read your mind. I can. But I'll mainly use that second mark to communicate what I need to you. You don't need to worry, you'll be able to tell it's me speaking to you." And as proof, she showed her how she wanted Dev's room laid out. Danny chuckled at the startled look on Elisa's face.

"You put that in my mind, just like that. And here I was thinking, 'What if I can't tell my lady's voice from all the other bees Mrs. Pritchett says are always buzzing in my head?' Mrs. Pritchett's the head housekeeper, marm."

"Once we get Devlin settled, you'll take me to Mrs. Pritchett, and I'll make bees buzz in her head also."

"You're nicer than the others," Elisa said suddenly, then reddened once more.

At her averted eyes, Danny touched her face and brought her eyes back up to her. She saw the girl focus on her lips, saw Elisa's desire to kiss her. Indulging herself a little, she brushed the sweet mouth with her own. The girl's discomfiture grew with her desire and Danny reluctantly pulled back. *Tempting, Mother. Far too tempting.*

"Elisa," she said gently. "Your reaction is normal, caused by what I used to dull your pain. It might give you a little crush on me for a while, but it doesn't mean anything. You'll be mooning after Willis again in no time."

At the mention of the lean, silent stockman she'd seen featured prominently in Elisa's thoughts, the maid went crimson to the roots of her hair, but she gave a little laugh as well. "Sure enough, my lady. Of course, it doesn't matter. Willis don't . . . doesn't have time for me. And he's far older, nearly thirty. He's very experienced in the world and probably has far grander ladies interested in him."

Because there are such a plethora of them out here, Danny reflected dryly, knowing that the ratio of marriageable young women to men was such that it made it hard to keep white stockmen for any length of time. And while aborigines were brilliant stockmen, they had an unfortunate tendency to go walkabout and apparently a justified aversion to Thieves' Station. She kept those thoughts to herself, though. Problems for another day when she announced her intentions to make the station a fully operational sheep concern again, no longer Ian's play hobby. "All right, then. Let's call some of the men to get Dev to his room. I can carry him myself, but it will bruise his pride if he comes to on the way."

Elisa bit back a smile, but as she turned to go, Danny halted her with a hand on the arm and a fixed look. "One more thing, Elisa. I may be 'nicer' than the others. I am fair, at least by vampire standards. I am definitely not Ian. But don't *ever* make the mistake of thinking a vampire, whether it's me, or my mother, or Lord Charles, *is* nice. Humans are useful to us, valued by us because they are useful. You understand?"

When Elisa would have looked away, Danny held her gaze, made her see what was there. "It's important you understand that. You are very open with me, and I want you to remain that way. But if I tell you to do something, I also expect it to be instantly obeyed. I will punish disobedience."

"Yes, my lady." Elisa bobbed a curtsy again, her gaze somber. "I'll do my best to follow your wishes."

"Hopefully you'll do better than this one." More relaxed now, Danny turned her gaze to Dev. "He's stubborn as a bloody rock."

"But thank the Lord he's a rock, my lady," Elisa pointed out. "Because they did their best to smash the poor bloke to bits."

~

Children with sharp teeth, tearing flesh. Tearing his son's flesh. Rob screaming. Tina staring at him with accusing, lifeless eyes. A man's arms pinwheeling as Dev's bullet found him, ended all that he was. Bombs blowing someone into chunks, so that in some places you couldn't walk without having to nudge the body parts out of the way. Hiding in the water where he had to remain completely still, the enemy too close. A disembodied head floating past him, brushing his brow, up against his eyes. A handful of fish had been worrying on it, hanging on to the dead flesh as it rolled past him, their bodies wriggling against his own neck, a couple taking a nip or two to see if his was still attached, if he was still living . . .

Rob, backing toward a well hole with no wall or cover, calling, "Dad, throw it, throw it." And the ball left Dev's hand, even though he knew his son was going to fall down that dark, endless hole, into the depths of Hell where he couldn't follow, where he couldn't help him . . . But it wasn't Rob, it was him, and hands were grabbing at him, tearing him apart, endless horror and pain . . . A bomb shattered and the noise sent him into screaming, scrambling panic. He was falling, rolling, trapped . . .

Dev. Dev. Wake up. I'm here. Wake up, bushman. I'm right here.

He woke fighting for his life, fighting for air, tangled in the sheet that had gone with him as he fell off an unexpectedly elevated bed. When he kept flailing, the hand helped, removing the sheet, shifting him bodily. As soon as he was free, he was scrambling forward toward the closest source of light, the window, though the curtains were drawn. He went for it, tearing at the cloth, and throwing open the sash to draw in a breath. But he couldn't stop there, clambering out the window and sitting on the sill on the steep slope of the porch roof, drawing in deep gasps of air.

As his heart stopped racing, the wide landscape he knew steadying him, the open spaces where you could see enemies coming, he started to recall his whereabouts, the happenings of the past few days. A dark-haired stockman, whittling while sitting in a chair propped up against the barn, considered him curiously, and Dev realized he was buck naked.

It occurred to him then whose hands had freed him from the stranglehold of the sheet. And even as he figured out who that was, he registered it was bright daylight. Probably early afternoon.

Spinning, he leaned back in. She was backed up against a far corner, trapped by the bar of sunlight he'd sent spilling across the guest room. While she looked a bit disconcerted by that, she also had that faint amused look he found so damned appealing.

If you close the curtains for a moment, I'll leave the room, Dev, and

*you can keep them wide open. I thought you'd prefer to wake in a
room where there were windows.*

She'd been sleeping with him, he realized, keeping him company,
rather than being in her own room, nested in the rock to ensure the
sun couldn't find her. She didn't wear the beautiful peach creation
she'd had on that night she'd given him the third mark. Today she
wore a short pale blue lace thing that brought out her eyes, a sheer
confection that showed him the shadow of her delectable body. He
must really have been out of it, if he'd been wasting his time by *sleeping* next to that.

A smile touched her lips, but her gaze shifted to the window.
Dev.

"Sorry, love." Grunting, he pulled himself back in and shut the
curtains. His body was amazingly flexible, considering everything it
had been through.

"It's the third mark. It gives you exceptional healing capabilities.
Once it settles in, even very serious wounds can heal quickly, though
right now you needed the help of my blood. And you've been out of
it almost a day."

"Hmm." Moving back to the bed, he bent to pick up the sheet and
toss it on the mattress, before he considered her. Now that the light
had been blocked, she moved out of the corner, the sheer fabric molding her breasts and abdomen, whispering between her thighs. It was
such a contrast to the horror of his dreams, he continued to stare at
her, trying to use that powerful image, both arousing and soothing,
to dispel the others.

"I'm sorry, Dev," she murmured. "For all of it. You did exceptionally well. Lord Charles was beside himself."

"Well, pissing that bastard off is something." Searching for something to say, to loosen the squeezing grip of the dreams that had his
heart still pounding unnaturally hard, he found just the thing. "Don't
you owe me a reward?"

"Hotcakes?" She blinked innocently. "I believe the cook is just
waiting for you to drag your lazy arse out of bed."

He managed a chuckle, harsh and grating though it sounded to
his own ears. Her eyes softened. Lord, a woman's compassion could

kill him at the moment. He turned away, glad for the one sliver of sun that had escaped from the curtains' crack, keeping her on the other side of it.

Now wasn't the moment for him to collect the prize she'd so generously offered, anyhow. The shadows were too close, and he didn't want them to taint it.

"Dev." Her voice coaxed at him. "Look at me."

When at last he turned, she looked toward the line pointedly. He stepped to it at last, blocking the stream of light with his body, and extended a hand. Taking it, her fingers slim and smooth, she stepped across, so that when he moved out of that line, they were on the same side of the room, her body beneath his hands.

Lifting on her toes, she rubbed her lips against his stubbled cheek. As he closed his eyes, his hands gripped her hard enough to hurt a mortal woman. She made a soft noise of reassurance, moved closer, let him bury his face in her hair.

"I'm so glad you made it back, Dev."

She didn't say the wrong thing. Didn't try to get him to talk about it, but then she didn't need to, did she? And she didn't tell him she was proud of him, proud of his ability to kill men who'd made bad choices, and children.

"After we get things settled here, I'm going to go to the coast to get some new things for the house," she continued softly. "I'd like you to go with me. Will you? It will be a few weeks among the civilized."

When he lifted his head, he saw that smile again, only there was a shadow to it he found odd, like she almost expected him to say no. Or maybe, after his behavior just now, she was reconsidering.

"Don't be daft." Her blue eyes met his. "Dev, I couldn't have asked more of any man or vampire than you've given me in these past few days. Let me take you into the city, give you the pleasures of good food and drink, and what you've earned from this body." With the hint of a mischievous smile, she shifted into a turn, and he suppressed a groan because it was sheer in back as well. She was wearing some kind of pretty trifle on her waist that had a tiny tail of diamonds to it that teased over one buttock. She was so close, that sweet curve brushed his thigh. "Then we'll come back here."

"You shouldn't have slept up here," he said, wanting time to think. "It's dangerous."

"Outback vampires tend to take more chances. Live on the edge." She bared her teeth, making him snort. "After all, you have to be short of a full quid to live out here, right? Will you go with me?"

"I want to say yes, but I don't know if I should." Rubbing his chest as if he still felt the pain there, the tearing of flesh, he was startled to feel a different texture, and then remembered the raven. Evidence of the hold she had on him. He turned away before he could see if she registered that damning thought. "I'm not sure of my mind right now. Don't know what or who I'd be if I went with you into the city. Things feel raw, out of sorts. Maybe it's best if I just go. Or stay here and get your station in order."

"Then how will I give you your prize?" She moved around him, the silk of the gown fluttering against his bare legs as she tilted her head, studied him. "I've got a little place in Surfer's Paradise, right on the shore. We can take the train from Alice Springs to Adelaide, fly from there to the coast. Save our shopping for Brisbane, after we take a breather for a few days. It will work out well, because I also need to pay a call on the Queensland Region Master when we're in Brisbane. You'd be a great help. You can coordinate the shipping of our purchases back to Adelaide for trucking out here."

She shifted closer, tilted her head, her lips so close, and of course they had to be moist. Dev would have chuckled if he thought it wouldn't be more like a sound of despair. "You'll like the cottage in Surfer's Paradise. It has a nice high bed. I want to be in it with you, hear the waves hit the shore as I feel the heat of your skin, your thighs against the back of mine . . . Feel you readying yourself to enter me. You're right, I've never taken a man there, Dev. You'll be the first."

Holy hell. He really needed to put on some bloody clothes. His dog was going to be straining at the end of its leash, lunging for her in a minute. "You told me that just to get me to go."

"Yes. I want you to go. If you'd consented to being my third-marked servant, it would be a command." Unrepentant, she ran her fingers down his chest, her nails scoring the raven a little. "Go with me. Let me take advantage of every inch of your marvelous cock for several days. Until you're even more exhausted than you were when you collapsed in my arms."

"Well"—he shifted—"I wouldn't say I collapsed in your arms. Perhaps thudded to the ground in a manly fashion, and you happened to be there to break my fall."

She smiled, but kept serious eyes on his face. Her voice lowered. "I won't let the shadows have you, Dev. Come with me. I'm strong enough to keep them from taking you."

They took me a long time ago, my lady. "My cock you have. It's my mind I worry about."

"Let me worry about both," she said softly. "Because I believe they both belong to me."

16

AFTER weeding out Ian's lot and sending them on their way, Dev wasn't surprised that only a handful of her remaining staff and stockmen chose to leave the station. It was mostly those whom Ian had taken against their will that left, and even a couple of those told her, with some feet shuffling, that if she'd be willing to take them back on, they'd return after a visit with their families.

He understood it. Once they were exposed to something so far outside the understanding of what the world was, it was difficult to return to what they'd known before. The world of vampires was brutal, violent, fascinating, glittering and sexual. It might be difficult to return to something like mining, running a shop or working a regular station after that. The other part of it was her. When she locked gazes with you and said something in that right tone of voice, you knew she wouldn't go back on her word. She didn't deceive, but she sure as hell could overwhelm. Jobs were too scarce out here, and they'd wait to see how things changed. He suspected old Jim, who had the men's respect, had also vouched for the fact she was a worthwhile boss.

So, with only a couple vehicles following, he'd driven her back across the terrain, picked up the Stuart Highway and headed toward Alice Springs. Given her plans for them over the next few weeks, traveling didn't bother her; that was for certain. And this time, he made sure every vehicle carried those special canvases.

Of course, he was comfortable with travel himself. While he wasn't as used to dealing with planes and fancy vehicles, he definitely preferred that to the strangeness of vampire dinner parties and their aftermath. He'd deal with the whole idea of visiting the Queensland Region Master later. Maybe he'd make sure he was way too busy handling the details involved with getting her purchases back to Thieves' Station to participate in socializing. *Yeah, she'd accept that. Snort.*

Though it was in the back of his mind, always, that he could just pick up and leave, his feet wouldn't go. So here he was, for now, and unwilling to delve too deeply into why he wasn't running away as fast as he could.

The Wanderer's Inn hotel and pub was the first stop they saw after they gained the tarmac of the highway. Bob, the proprietor, knew Dev, since Bob's son had been a digger in the 39th as well. Because his place did have a store and facilities to wash up, they made the decision to stop there for the daylight hours. And of course they had beer.

When the sun hit the horizon, Danny was safely ensconced in a room. Dev adjusted the curtains to make sure no stray sunlight could get in, using some extra blankets he'd borrowed from Bob, who'd looked surprised that anyone would need extra linens for the hot daytime hours. Dev had wondered whether she wanted her own room, since she'd had to be lady of the station the past couple days. But she'd told him to get one for the two of them, and make separate sleeping arrangements for the others.

After he came back from doing that, she'd washed up some, and taken it upon herself to rummage in his pack, for she'd found one of his cotton T-shirts, put it over her otherwise naked body and curled up in the center of the bed. While she'd tangled one of the sheets up in her legs, in her repose she'd already kicked one leg free, and he could see the lovely length of it from the ankle to the hint of bare backside beneath, the shadow that led from the crease of thigh to sex. The sight of her there, the one bed, where he could be next to her, his body spooned behind her . . .

A few days ago, he wouldn't have hesitated to enjoy the scenery to the fullest, or become part of it. But though he'd worked hard on her station, getting up to speed on things, he'd been running from demons. The nightmares were back in force. He woke twice in her arms, screaming and bathed in sweat. After that, though she didn't like it, he'd gone off and slept in the barn when she didn't need him. No one could hear him there.

It shamed him. The bush could absorb his pain, a silent witness that passed no judgment on weakness. When a man was around blokes, his boss or especially a pretty woman, he didn't act a wobbly wuss. He should be back in the Outback, had known it, but she'd made him give his word he'd accompany her on this trip, knowing he wouldn't go back on it. They had that in common, damn it all.

She tried to get him to talk about it, but he always turned it to the things they needed to do on the station, or halfhearted flirtations. So far, she hadn't pushed it, but he could feel her watching him closely. She was too downright in her opinions to let him get away with this for long, and it increased the sense of trapped desperation.

He thought about getting a beer, but put that off for later. He sure as hell didn't feel up to talking to Bob alone. Instead, he unrolled his swag, stripped off his shirt and lay down on the floor, staring up at the ceiling. When she shifted, he lifted his head to see her hand passing over the bed, fore and aft, her eyes still closed.

Dev? You can come up here.

I know.

A quiet moment. Then, a different tone. *Dev. Come up here.*

His body felt weighted with a dark exhaustion, but when her hand slid across the mattress, drifted over the edge, the fingers with the hint of curved nails fluttering at him, he found himself rising and coming to her side. Only then did she open her eyes and look at him, but she turned over on her back, those lovely legs uncrossing, shifting apart and then coming back together as she turned away. As she did all that, the cotton shirt drifted higher up her hip, giving him more of a view of her arse, as well as the dark smudge of her nipples beneath the thin cloth as it stretched over them.

Hold me. I want to feel you behind me when I sleep. Leave your trousers on, except the belt. Give that to me.

It was indescribably seductive, the sultry cadence of her words filling his mind, the provocation of the images. He couldn't explain how his mind shut down when she spoke to him like that, but he suspected she knew it. Was she compassionate enough to know it helped? That sometimes he responded to her the way the aborigines had taught him to respect the power of stillness? Just giving himself over to it.

He slid behind her. Of course, she already had him hot and hard, so he didn't intend to apologize for that. When he pressed his hips up against her bum, cradling her with his knees, she wiggled, settling herself firmly on him, making him stifle a groan.

The belt, Dev.

He'd forgotten about it. Reaching between them, he unbuckled it, slid it free, and doubled it up. Curious, he handed it over her arm. She twisted her body enough to take it from him, then slid the tongue through the buckle until it was a cuff, looping it around his wrist. She wrapped the tail around her own forearm, threading it through her fingers, and then turned again, his arm over her so she was snugly curved into his body, her hips putting tantalizing heat on his erection again.

So you'll stay tethered to me in my sleep, bushman. You rest with me today. You've rechecked the vehicles. We'll worry about anything that needs worrying about when we rise. Sleep with me now. Just sleep.

You've made that very hard, my lady. Difficult.

She chuckled as he corrected the entendre, and did a slow, seductive circle over his groin that had his hand clenching in its cuff then, finding her wrist and circling it with his fingers, as if he were manacling her in his own way.

Sleep, Dev. Just sleep.

He couldn't. He wouldn't let himself wake her with his fears. But then she started humming, a soft, quiet tune he couldn't place. It had the rocking cadence of a lullaby. She reached back, found his face, and then began to stroke his hair at his temple, over and over, a soothing rhythm as the song continued, lulling him and his cock into drowsiness. He had the sweet soap smell of her hair, fragrant and light as feathers, against his lips and nose, where he had them pressed into the back of her head, alongside her ear. Her body pressed into his, giving him coolness and heat at once. And that soft singing, a little off-key, but soothing as well . . .

You'd make a good mother, love. . . . Gentle as a doe, fierce as a lioness.

Her hand paused briefly, then continued, but she made no reply. Just bade him with her touch and lullaby to sleep, to give himself over to her and dreams, willingly bound to her by the strap that held him to her. He knew she'd be following him into dreams, for he'd observed there was a certain lassitude to her when the sun climbed into the sky. In fact, her hand was already slowing, her voice drifting into a vaguer hum that eventually moved into his mind and then dwindled away, leaving him with the muted sounds of the desert beyond the window and Bob's pub below, all in all a comfort that promised a brief respite from nightmares.

~

After sundown, Dev got his beer and information from Bob on the road conditions, including what effect a recent dust storm out this way had had. Danny browsed through the adjoining store while the men got a quick supper.

"Elle down at the Marsten's Creek has been radioing about you," Bob said. "You want I should let her know where you ended up?"

Dev considered that as he watched Danny make a few additional clothing selections. "Yeah, Bob. But if you don't mind, don't mention anything about my lovely boss on the open airways if you can. She doesn't like folks to know about her comings and goings."

"No worries, Dev. Trouble always follows a sheila like that one." Bob gave Dev a wink, slid him another beer, seeing Dev had drained that one.

Dev picked it up, gave him a salute. "I'm going to go out and check our fluids and lines." He'd checked them earlier, as Danny had said, but a second check wasn't amiss. Plus, he also wanted to check the ammo in his rifle and pistol. Traveling with a vampire required some extra precautions.

"Right-o." Bob cleared his throat, making Dev stop in midturn. "Not sure if you'd heard, but Terry put a bullet in his brain a couple weeks back."

Dev put the beer down. "Crikey. His wife there?"

"Naw. She left him, taking their girl, about two or three months ago. Went back to town." Bob shrugged, but his eyes were somber. "Word was she could take the Outback being so empty and desolate, but she couldn't take the same from Terry."

Danny had chosen that moment to come into the bar from the mercantile, ignoring the speculative looks of the men not part of their group. He hadn't been able to contain his internal reaction, and of course he knew she was monitoring him pretty close these days. He'd accuse her of being overly clucky, but in truth, sometimes that sense she was there offered him the balance he was trying to reclaim in himself.

"Friend of yours?" she asked quietly.

"Yeah. At one time. We fought together in the war, early on." Dev lifted the bottle, took a draught from it, wiped his lips with the back of his knuckles. Danny could pick it out of his brain, but their men were sitting close, looking curious, and he had to work with those driving back. "After the militia, I signed up as a digger to the 39th battalion, part of the Maroubra force that worked the Kokoda Track. But Terry got caught by the Nips. He was part of that mob held up in Thailand, forced to build the railway for them. Messed him up a bit."

The murmurs of the stockmen behind him were part sympathy, part banked ashes of old angers. No one had forgotten the six thousand who'd died in the Japs' POW camps, or the things done to them. Dev drained that beer, slid it down to Bob with an abrupt movement. "Probably just couldn't take it anymore."

Terry hadn't been able to find silence again. A man had to find it, or the noise would drive him mad, so mad his only escape was a bullet in the brain.

From the startled look on Danny's face, he knew she'd heard his thoughts. To hell with it. Turning on the ball of his foot, he went back out the pub door, muttering about checking the vehicles. Bob let him go without another word. Dev knew he understood, being a WWI digger himself. Plus, Bob's son had died in the war, twenty feet away from Dev.

Kokoda Track had been rough. Hot, nerves-on-edge work. So many dead, casualties of battle and disease, the mosquitoes bringing a death all their own. Being in Europe had been one thing; he'd talked to the battalion mates who'd done that. But this was different. They were protecting the border of Australia, not as Imperial soldiers for the Crown, but as Oz's sons. A real threat of invasion brought something forth in many of them, a protective, warrior fierceness different from how they'd used it in Europe. This was their ruddy home. And no one was taking their home.

So they fought, day by day, for every single yard. The Japs came within a stone's throw of Port Moresby, but by God, they pushed them back to the coast. The losses had been incredible. But for all that, all the horror he'd seen, Dev had been a free man. Terry had faced captivity, starvation, disease, and the irreparable cost of buckling under the enemy's will.

Men came home from war, lived out their lives. But Terry had died in that POW camp, his spirit gone. What had come home to his wife was a shell. Dev knew it, because he'd been that shell even before he stepped foot on his first battlefield. He'd gone to the front line seeking death, but he wanted to take the whole goddamn world with him when he went. He'd wanted the taste of blood. Well, he'd found it, hadn't he? And just when he'd learned to still the screaming in his head, find that silence, he'd put himself up to the elbows in blood again.

A tool for demons . . . Gravedigger.

He had the hood up, his elbows on the top of the Rover's grill, his fists clenched and held behind his head, his eyes squeezed shut. *Go to the place of nothingness . . .* The Elder's words spun in his head. He couldn't. He just couldn't. He needed to do something else, cut the wound, purge it before the weight of it strangled him.

The tire iron was there. He'd scized it up and turned before he'd had a conscious thought of what he was about to do. He just needed an object, something to focus on. There. Bob had a rusted-out junk cistern at the side of his place, one he hadn't yet hauled away.

Dev struck the metal, using all his strength. The red flooded in, filling his vision as he struck again. And again. Images broke loose, each one jolted by the impact of metal on metal, a hammering that vibrated like electric shocks through his hands, up his arms.

Men gunned down, rows of them. When his gun had locked up, he'd simply plunged in. One bullet took him in the shoulder, but he'd pulled his knife and hacked and stabbed, screamed in a way Tina never would have recognized, never would have wanted, some kind of feral, rabid animal that should be put down, put out of its misery . . . Bodies everywhere.

Valor. Bull dust. Not valor. Savagery. Monstrous. He'd have drunk their blood if he could, bathed in it, reveled in their deaths. *Why did you take them from me? Why? Why? Why? What the bloody hell did I do to you, you bastard, son-of-a-bitch excuse for a fucking God?* Every syllable resulted in a violent clang against the metal, the reverberation singing up through his arms, welcome pain. *What did they do to you? What did my little boy, my Tina, do to deserve that? Those vampire kids. They died alone, without me, screaming . . . Why didn't you take me?*

In some far place, he realized he was screaming the words, the accusation, at a wide, unresponsive sky, echoing back at him. He was going to fucking explode into pieces. The last swing was so hard, a piece of the cistern flew loose, the jagged edge whipping up toward his face.

That's it, cut my throat, you Bastard. I've dared You to do it a hundred fucking times. Too chickenshit, aren't You? You know I'm coming for You . . .

When the haze cleared, he realized that he hadn't had his throat cut by the spinning piece of rusted metal after all. He was on one knee, the tire iron gripped in two trembling hands.

Shhh . . . Easy, Dev. I'm here.

Danny had caught the spinning piece of metal, and was tossing it aside, a nasty cut on her hand. With her other, she'd pressed him down beneath the arc of the projectile, all so swiftly that in his haze of fury he hadn't noticed any of it until after the fact.

When she touched him, he flinched, lowering his head, not wanting to look at her or anyone. Instead of withdrawing, she stroked the sweat-dampened strands from his jawline, moved to caress his nape, an almost maternal gesture that made things worse and better at once.

"I'd have been better off as an ignorant jackaroo," he said hoarsely. "The blokes used to tease me about it, say I was a bit of a snorter, being so educated and all. But poetry and literature can destroy a man, as much as it can save him. All those words . . . they all come back to haunt you."

"The day we stop striving to be more than we are, Dev, we might as well tell the world to stop turning and the sun to stop rising." Her arms came around his chest from behind then. Startled, he felt wetness against his shoulder and knew she was shedding tears for him, but her arms held him fast, wouldn't let him look.

Danny knew Dev probably didn't realize it, but she knew about the Kokoda Track, knew about the 39th battalion, the men who were sent back into the thick of it again and again. Who'd endured battles where eight hundred men went in and as few as thirty would come out. It seemed no matter how hard Dev endeavored to die, to end his own misery, Fate wanted him to live. She'd heard his words, the futile hopelessness in him, the deepest, darkest well of his soul screaming out at the heavens, and it had torn her own heart to pieces. She squeezed her eyes shut.

I won't let you go, either, bushman. The world wants and needs you, more than you know. But she didn't let him hear that. "You smell bad," she informed him after a time. "How about you go wash up, pick yourself out a new shirt? My treat."

He stayed in the same position, but his head dropped against her forearm. "You can deduct it from my salary, when you deign to start paying me. I'm not going to become your kept man."

She squeezed his chest, made him straighten and turned him toward her, helping them both to their feet. Somehow his hat had stayed on, and she pushed back the band to get a better look at the dark, dangerous eyes and brooding mouth. Taking one of his hands, she raised it to her mouth, curved his palm around her cheek. "Go wash it off, Dev. Let it go for today. You're going to get a handle on it again. Give yourself time."

Then she pressed into him, slid her arms around his back. She let out a sigh of relief as his arms closed around her at last, the hard length of his body from thigh to chest against hers as he lowered his face into her neck, into the curtain of blond hair she had loose and waving on her shoulders specifically because she knew he liked it that way. She knew she smelled of soap now, damp, clean skin, for she heard his thoughts register it. *Woman. A man's sanctuary.* The sanctuary Terry hadn't been able to keep, and so that had been the end of it for him.

Am I your sanctuary, then?

Dev lifted his head, studied her face. *You're the vampire I serve.* She felt the effort it took him to let her go, step back. He couldn't afford to treat her like this, view her this way. She wasn't Tina. She wasn't a human he could fall in love with and depend upon.

While she couldn't argue with any of those thoughts—in fact, she'd made it quite clear he needed to think of her like that—it still felt wrong at this moment. Actually hurt a little, such that it almost put her back up.

You need me. Want me. That helps.

He sighed, turned away. "No offense, but I've enough voices in my head at the moment, love. If you don't mind . . . don't add to it."

∼

God, that was a bad one. In the washroom, Dev sat down, told himself to pull it together. She might be listening, but after his uncharitable comment, he wouldn't blame her for ignoring him. That had been real comfort offered by her arms, real tears on her cheeks. Ah, hell, he couldn't go down this road. Just couldn't.

He really shouldn't be here. This was an example of why. Even without the detonator that Ruskin's actions had set off, the longer he spent with people, the more things like this boiled up. And yet, he couldn't shake the notion she needed him.

You're a daft bugger. She's not Tina. You don't have anything to prove; she's even said so herself. A vampire with ten times his strength and speed, with enhanced senses, and as rich as Methuselah to boot.

Tina had been like wildflowers. So perfect and marvelous, a joy in every way. He couldn't be with a flower again. Too delicate, too easily crushed. Here today, gone tomorrow, before he even understood the miracle of it. It wasn't that she hadn't done well as a station wife, because she had. Most women couldn't handle the life, and she'd loved it.

But she wasn't spinifex. Something that looked attractive, almost soft, but had barbs, a clever, deceptive mind. Someone who might get overwhelmed by other men's evil, but who had a core of fury to her that would take them with her, deliver them to hell herself. A lot of *men* didn't have that in them. Danny had it in spades.

There were different types of fragility, though. Different needs. He'd felt them in Danny, couldn't shake that feeling, no matter how he wanted to do it. So, cursing at himself and the whole situation, he went the back way out of the washroom, looking for her. Bob was there, taking out some trash. He gave Dev a glance.

"You all right?"

"Yeah, I'm good, Bob. I'm sorry, mate. I turned the corner there, big-time."

"You never need to say that, Dev. Ain't no sorries ever. Just is what it is. You come take it out on my cistern anytime. But leave the working one be, if you don't mind." Bob gave him a grin and a steady look, which Dev managed to return. "Left you another beer on the nose of your Rover. Your lady and her men are waiting, I think."

He was right. As Dev went out front, he found Danny sitting on the tailgate of their vehicle, gazing up at the night sky, the other stockmen leaning on theirs, waiting them out. Because of Bob's outdoor lights and the moon, he saw the sheen of her hair, the paleness of her skin, the slim jaw and high cheekbone. Her clean ivory shirt billowed against her. It was open at the throat, so that when she twisted and looked toward him, the movement revealed the cleft between her breasts. Since she loved her opals, she was wearing one now, shaped like a flame, the light blue swirling color like the fire in her eyes. She looked beautiful, delicate, and yet invincible and calm, all at once.

She'd been that way from the beginning, he realized. Even when she knew she was out of her element. Somewhere along the line she'd learned you couldn't show weakness to your enemies, and often even to your allies, or they wouldn't be allies any longer.

While he could only make out an idea of her expression, he knew she'd been listening in. It was odd, how that had bothered him so much when it happened, for all of about two minutes. Then it didn't bother him much at all. Maybe because he really didn't give much of a dead dingo's donger about anything. If anyone found anything in his head worth knowing, good on them.

But that wasn't it, and he knew it. *She* didn't bother him, hadn't bothered him from the first, in a way that was uncanny. He kept his own counsel, preferred his solitude and privacy. Hadn't told anyone about his life who didn't already know about it from having been around him when it happened, or like Bob, connected to it indirectly. But she knew all of it now. Hell, he'd told her the worst of it the first night, before she'd ever drilled into his head. Maybe he'd been lonely long enough and she'd been there at the right time. Maybe he felt comfortable with her because there didn't have to be any promises between them. Nothing but lust, for that matter.

Are you going to stand over there and beat a dead horse all night?

He narrowed a glance at her shadowed silhouette, heard her chuckle at his retaliatory thought. *Now that wasn't nice at all, Dev. I might be of a mind to make you pay for that one.* Then she straightened from the tailgate. Even in the darkness, her movements suggested the deadly purpose to her, that stillness that reminded him forcefully, when he was of a mind to forget, that she wasn't human.

Grab your beer, bushman, and let's go.

~

When they at last reached Alice Springs, they had a private berth on the train to Adelaide, two narrow stacked beds and a sitting area by the window. They boarded at night, but when daylight came, he pulled the curtains. Not for the first time, he thought of what she'd said, about how few vampires risked living out here, where it would be easy to get marooned during the daylight hours. Even now, all he had to do was reach over her and pull back the drapes to puncture her body with an unrelenting square of bright sunlight. Why did she trust him so? Why did the idea of someone doing such a thing to her send his hand automatically to the knife at his side?

The trip by vehicle had been long, so almost as soon as she washed up, she'd lain down on the long seat by the window, blinked sleepily at him.

Come take off my boots, Dev.

He'd arched a brow at her. "Expect you've known how to do that since you were a little one, love."

I have. Come take them off.

Meeting her eyes, the blue that could pull him in so deep he was reminded again of swimming in the beauty of the Great Barrier Reef, he'd put his swag and weapons in the corner and moved toward her.

"You playing games with me, love?"

"Would it be easier for you if you thought I was?"

He shook his head. Not a denial, but a resignation to the peculiarity of her ways that compelled him to go to one knee by the long seat, shifting her sole to his knee so he could unlace the boot and slide it from her dainty foot. He unrolled the sock as well, letting his palm slide over the ankle and smooth flesh of her sole, tease the tips of her toes. She stayed on her side as he shifted farther down the cushion, worked the boot off the next one. On impulse, he bent and put his lips on her insole, teasing it with the tip of his tongue, feeling a tremor run up her calf beneath his hand. Then he laid his head there, feeling a temporary easiness to it.

"What will you do while I sleep?" Her hand passed over his hair, grazed his shoulder before he straightened.

"You brought along some books. I'll probably read. Get some sleep myself." He gave her a half smile. "You know, they say mothers need to sleep while their babies are sleeping, to keep up with the little tykes when they're awake."

She gave him a soft smile. "I'll bet they tell them a story before they go to sleep. Tell me a story. Come up here. Let me put my head on your leg."

When he obliged, sliding under her, she coiled her arms around his hips, her fingers stroking his buttocks in a very distracting way. With her cheek pillowed on his thigh, he told her one of the Dreamtime stories, the story of creation, when the Father of All Spirits woke the Sun Mother and had her create all living things . . .

When he was done, she was quiet for a bit, her breath even, and he laid his head against the wall, his hand absently tracing her temple, that baby-fine hair that everyone seemed to have there, human and vampires. As well as every man he'd killed . . .

Shh . . . Not asleep, obviously. She began to sing to him, this time in his mind, a peculiar but soothing sensation as she chose another lullaby, all about a cradle rocking in the clouds, carried along by the wings of angels, never to tip, always to have sweet dreams, of unicorns and birds, bright sunlight and sparkling water . . .

He was starting to rely on it, another coping mechanism, the way she had of drawing a curtain over his memories. "You can wander the train a bit if you get restless," she murmured at last.

"I'm fine." He wasn't leaving her alone while she was sleeping in a strange place.

Another moment of silence. "Dev, you did what you had to do. And you did it for me. To protect me from having to swear loyalty to Charles. As well as to save your own life."

"One of me for six or seven of them."

"Who all tried to kill you. That was the point. To run you down and make sure you didn't survive. Worse, they did it as a game."

No. Men don't play games like that. If they call them games, that's just a ruse for what they're really about. Dev turned his gaze down to her, found her half-open eyes watching him. "Like having me take off your boots, right?"

"Mmm." A light smile touched her lips. "There are places I could take you, where I could chain you up, and tease you to hardness, over and over, until you'd beg for the barest friction of a wet pussy against you. Make you mindless except to my commands. Work you so hard I'd break down your mind, let all the shadows escape. After that, all you'd have is my commands to obey, nothing else, until you could get enough rest from the chatter in your head that you'd become the man you were meant to be again."

The berth had grown much smaller, warmer, as his body warred with his mind over the unlikely words. He noted the faint sheen of moisture on her lips, and wanted to taste it. Instead, he curled his hand into a knot and stared down at her. "Promise me you won't do that. Chain me up."

She held his gaze. "I promise I won't, until I know you trust me enough to let me do it."

"I wouldn't hold your breath for me to say those words, love. Nothing personal."

"I didn't say I'd be waiting for your permission. I said I wouldn't do it until I know you trust me enough. That day will come, Dev. And when it does, you'll be scared, and furious, and gloriously violent, but you'll also be yearning toward me, daring me to take everything, your heart, mind and soul, and make it part of myself. Then, when I unchain you, it won't matter." Her hand reached up, traced his throat. "The collar will still be there. Forever. It doesn't take anything away from those you've loved before. Every experience you've had before this moment has made you who you are, what I want. What any woman alive would want." Her fingers settled on his shoulder, the dangerous light weight of a spider, drawing his attention to the coolness in her eyes. "But which I alone will claim."

Turning his head, he brushed his lips over her fingers. "I told you, I'm no one's possession."

"That's only because you hear the word and you think of a loss of freedom. With surrender comes release, Dev. Remember that."

∽

When she slept at last, he was loath to move from his position. Feeling around in her travel bag, he came up with Walt Whitman's

Leaves of Grass. He wondered if she cared for it, or if she'd brought it from her library, suspecting he would find it enjoyable. Taking him back to a time when his life was all about study, debating points of philosophy with fellow students, or playing English rugby. Of course, he'd also introduced his classmates to aerial pingpong, the chaotic Australian footy rules. In wry hindsight, he realized his knowledge of that sport had been good preparation for the battlefield. He'd just begun to teach Rob before . . .

As the train rumbled, he opened the cover and moved into Whitman's world, before he could get pulled into his own dark one.

I have perceiv'd that to be with those I like is enough . . . His hand drifted over her hair, down her back. How often he'd had thoughts about that, when he took his trips in to Elle's place, or walked with the clan for a day. Or when crossing their tracks, he'd stopped to examine the different patterns of their feet, identifying who was heavier or lighter, who bore a burden and who did not. Who was in good health and who might be feeling poorly. A way to connect, without being with them.

> *This the nucleus—after the child is born of woman, man is*
> *born of woman,*
> *This the bath of birth, this the merge of small and large, and*
> *the outlet again.*

Then, regarding women . . . *You are the gates of the body, and you are the gates of the soul.*

"The gates of hell and heaven both," he murmured, his hand resting upon her. "And when you possess our soul, we will follow you to either one." *I know what being possessed is, Danny. I do.* He just didn't know if he was that strong.

> *By my side or back of me Eve following,*
> *Or in front, and I following her just the same.*

She shifted then. Moving with her, synchronized with her body as if he were the wind and her limbs the branches of a tree, flowing together, he brought her up into his lap. Leaning against the back of the sleeper, he let her dream on that way, her body laid out between his spread legs, her upper torso propped against his. One arm was hooked loosely at his waist, the other resting in her lap, her cheek pillowed on his abdomen. At this angle, through the curtain's crack, he could see Uluru in the far distance—or Ayer's Rock, as most of the whites called it—the vast formation of sacred rock. The sun was starting to spill out over it, an awe-inspiring sight, even at this range. He'd stood in its shadow, knew what had once rested there, so many sacred items and stories of the aborigines, many of those spirited away before others could remove them for museums, souvenirs. You had to protect what you treasured. Otherwise it would be taken away when you least expected it.

No, he couldn't afford to be possessed again. But he was well aware the choice might no longer be his to make.

17

IN some part of her subconscious, Danny was aware of the many hours he spent, letting her pillow upon him while he read. The rails clacked beneath them and the train halted and started again for the few stops along the way, a comfortable rhythm.

After watching him deal with the aftermath of Ruskin in his own stubborn way for the week, then seeing the darkness pour off him at Bob's, she'd realized it was past time for her to lance the boil. The verses he'd found in the poetry to stir the things festering in his soul were the final sign. She let it percolate in her mind now, gave herself the luxury of a slow rousing while the brooding man remained oblivious to her state of wakefulness.

At last, with an easy movement, she pushed herself up on his thighs, nudging the book out of the way. Before he could greet her awakening, she'd curled her arms around his neck and teased his mouth open with hers, feeling a surge of need when he clasped her in his arms, his hand cupping the back of her head, taking over control of the kiss, making it deeper, more insistent, like the pressure she was feeling against her hipbone, the hard bar of iron at his groin.

"Good dreams, then?" he asked at last when she drew her head back. She noted his voice was thick, his arms not easing from her a bit, so she felt the tension of his biceps, the broad shoulders.

"Almost as good as the real thing." She touched his mouth. "It's time to give you that reward, Dev. I don't want to wait until we get there."

It took a moment to register, then she was surprised to hear the thought in his mind, see the charmingly embarrassed flush. She laid a hand on his cheek. "I will heal, you know."

He cleared his throat. "I . . . One of the prostitutes I was with, she said it's so awful for so many women because they don't use things . . . of different sizes . . . to stretch themselves out first."

"I will heal," she repeated gently.

He shook his head. "It's not that. I know that. I want you . . . to enjoy it. I don't want to hurt you that way."

"Don't you?" She raised an eyebrow. "That first night, with the whip. You knew exactly how to do it without causing me pain, but you chose to give me that sting. You like it, giving out some pain, Dev. Making it part of the pleasure. You might have a drop or two of vampire blood in you somewhere." Leaning forward to his mouth again, she stopped to breathe on his parted lips, her blue eyes lifting to embrace his green ones. "The key to making it pleasurable for me, bushman, is to make sure I'm so wildly aroused that I'll tear the flesh off your bones if you don't take me down."

Dev swallowed. The power of his lust was rising, and the feeling of it washing over her was enough to heat her own skin, make her hungry for it. Make her hungry, period.

Sliding his belt free, she unbuttoned the front of his trousers. As he watched her, she reached in and teased his thigh above the hiked-up edge of his boxers. "Ease these down," she whispered. "Just to the tops of your thighs. I'm going to prove my point."

"Danny—"

"You think it's lust that makes what's between us bearable, addictive." Her gaze glinted. "Take your trousers down."

A muscle flexed in his jaw, but he complied, shifting her weight as he did so. It kept him hobbled, she knew, because he still wore his boots, but she was going to use that right now.

"Now, spread your legs for me. A few inches." She was still lying halfway over one thigh. When he obeyed her, she let her gaze drop to the delectable outline of his testicles, straining against the seam of the boxer shorts, and from this angle, she could see the flesh color of one of them, the full ripeness of it, revealed by the open leg.

"Pain and pleasure. They go together," she breathed, and bent her head.

As she pierced the femoral artery in his thigh, he arched up against her mouth, his breath drawing in sharply. She caught the rich blood in the back of her throat, savored its rapid pump, even as she placed pressure above to slow it down. She wanted time to linger, enjoy, let her lips nuzzle his flesh. Her hair and the shell of her ear were so close to that erect organ that her other hand found, clasped and began to tease it with slow strokes, up and down.

"Jesus, love." His hoarse groan, the sudden grasp of her hair in hard fingers, told her that pleasure had kicked in, dragged the pain with it. She would make sure they'd intertwine the same way their bodies would, very shortly. By the time she finished her meal, his upper body was jerking, movements he was fighting to rein in, but emulating the rhythm his body most wanted.

Taking his hand, she brought it down and placed it on the pressure point she'd been holding, even as she took the time to make sure his blood was clotting. His heart was beating fast, his throat working, a reaction to the dangerous precipice. But as a third-mark, she could almost drain him and he would live, as long as he received her blood in a prescribed time.

Then she rose, surprised when he caught her wrist. "Where are you going?" His green eyes devoured every part of her, his voice a low growl.

"Wherever I want to go, bushman." She gave him a teasing smile and, with a quick, easy movement, freed herself. Her gaze lowered to the hard length of him, now trying, with success, to point up along his belly, stretch beyond the waistband of his shorts.

Going to her small carry-on, she withdrew the warm oil and sat it on the built-in shelf, the bottle vibrating with the clicking of the train. "You can use me gentle, bushman, or throw me down on the bed, use me like a whore who likes it hard and rough, pour all that fury and pain you're carrying into me." She gave him a steady look as she slid her shirt off her shoulders, then took off her trousers. Then the scraps of knickers, leaving her naked to him. "Time to draw off the poison, Dev. Give you a rest from it."

"And you think one good arse fuck will do that? Christ, you have a high opinion of yourself."

Dev was startled by the sudden flood of his anger, but she'd pointed so easily to that darkest part of himself, the desires any other man would have suppressed. And she'd done it without reading minds, he was almost sure of it.

"I don't know, Dev. Will it?" She took a step back, away from him, toward the berth, a glittering light in her blue eyes. In the dim light, with the curtains drawn, they were almost black.

"Unbraid your hair. I want to wrap my hands in it when I fuck you."

She cocked her head. "You're my servant. You do it."

Yet when he leaned forward to yank off his boots, get the bloody trousers off so he could go after her, she beat him to it. Putting one lithe pale leg over his knee, so she was practically sitting in his lap in the confined space, she straightened his leg, took hold of the toe and heel and pulled. The rounded cheeks were like two curved flower petals in his face, inviting touch. He ground his teeth together, everything in him drawing together like a coiled spring. A snake in the sand, waiting to strike.

As soon as she removed the trousers, he whipped up off the long seat, seized her by the waist and turned her, bringing her facedown on the lower berth, his body insinuating behind her, close enough that the jut of his cock pressed against her arse, though separated by the straining thin cotton of his boxers.

"You don't move," he said, his voice not his own. A way he'd never talked to any woman, but needed to now. But even as he got the boxers halfway off, she'd slipped away from him, her laughter torturing raw emotions in him.

When he was completely naked, she was in the corner behind him, a taunting, intimate display, her fingers drifting down the front of her body. She made a fair dodge around him on his next lunge, but he caught her waist, turned her and slammed her against a wall, going to one knee himself before she could anticipate him. Taking hold of her arse with both hands, he parted her and began to lick her rim, that oh-so-sensitive area for women. She was already wet. He could see the silver tracks of it on her inner thigh, and when he started doing this, he forced his hand up between her legs, widening her, and teased her opening with his fingertips. He was rewarded with another flood of moisture that bathed the digits as she worked herself against his mouth. She hit the side of the train wall with her mound, a fierce impact that reverberated into her clit, if her breathless moan was any indication.

"Oh, God, Dev. That feels . . . marvelous."

She sounded amazed, as most sheilas were who'd never contemplated it, who were too embarrassed about it. He'd had the pleasure of far more virgins than his mates who preferred only the one orifice. But he'd never been able to unleash himself, take it beyond her pleasure into the darkest realms of his own. He was holding on to sanity by a thread, the taunts of bloody faces, the sound of bullets and men's screams, the dying eyes of a twelve-year-old, closing in on him.

I can't . . . Danny, are you sure? I'm dying here.

I won't let you hurt me more than I can bear, Dev. Know that I can stop you at any time. Do your worst.

He turned, bit her buttock, deep enough to break skin, and she shuddered. Then he pushed her facedown on the bed again, pulling her knees up on the mattress, keeping her hind end up in the air as he used the moisture between her legs to lubricate his cock, as well as the oil she'd provided, until he was dripping onto the covers and the skin over his organ was painfully tight. God, the way she looked, sitting there, haunches in the air, that tiny pucker waiting for him, damp from his mouth as her lips glistened with arousal.

Between her splayed legs, he saw her breasts mashed against the mattress, the press of the nipples against the cover. When she began to rise, he caught her neck and shoved her back down, holding her there as he began to guide himself in with the other hand.

He didn't take his time, wasn't gentle. Drawing a deep breath, she pushed against him, exactly what either an experienced whore or a woman who had no fear of it would do. Swallowing, he let go of her neck, took hold of her hips, and rammed into her with a savage snarl.

Her cry of pain was music to a damned soul, freeing it. Her hands went to the covers, grasped it in fists, tearing it with her strength, but she didn't stop him. He pumped hard and sure into her, feeling the convulsive flutters of her inner muscles, even as he worked her hard enough his testicles began to slap against her clit, a sensual spanking that had her hips tentatively lifting. But she was biting her lip, tears on her cheeks from the pain, and it maddened him like an aroused bull. Falling over her, he reached beneath with one hand and found a breast, squeezed it hard, took his pleasure in the wobbling feel of it, of his leg pressing hard against the back of hers. Insisting, he knocked her out wider, stretching her farther for the other hand he now used to press two fingers into her, engorging her clit with his thumb even as he knew her rectum had to be on fire.

She hissed, but he held her down, made her take it, scissoring with his fingers as she began to make raw, bleating cries, her hair spilling forward as she thrashed. Crowding his knees against her fulcrum as he kept pumping into her, he yanked her head up by the hair so he arched her like a filly under a cruel bearing rein. Each pounding of his cock, the tightening of his fist, exacerbated that straining angle. His testicles were still slapping against her clit, which was spasming beneath his working fingers. Even that wasn't enough. He wanted to hammer into the center of her, make her feel his agony and need all the way to her heart, to her soul, if she had one. Dropping his head onto her shoulder, he bit savagely, holding on to her, tasting the unusual exotic flavor of her blood, that rejuvenating stuff that could heal physical wounds, that he was using to heal his emotional ones.

More, deeper. His belt was on the bed. Seizing it, he ran it beneath her body, just above the sensitive nipple tips, and pulled her up off her arms so that he could slam into her at a different angle. She'd caught the curtain, ripped it in their struggle. The now fortunately dark landscape flew by, lights of the infrequent stops strobing across his face, leaving his ghostlike reflection when darkness fell again. He saw a man whose face was contorted in battle rage, not pleasure, but his body didn't care, for his release was coming, making his thighs tremble.

Don't worry about me . . . all for you . . .

But he didn't want it like that. He demanded that she release with him. Forcing himself to slow, he made his penetration of her rear opening a smaller motion. Reaching under the belt, holding it one-handed, he found her nipples, circled them with now excruciatingly tender fingers. It made her spine curve impossibly, so her hair brushed his chest, his jaw, and he turned his face into it, smelled the soap she used. Her hands found his thighs, gripped him, long, slim female fingers. Soft female arse and cunt.

Releasing the belt entirely, he began to stroke her clit with sure, clever fingers, even as he kept up his teasing of her nipple, the weight of her breast, kept his hips moving, working inside her.

"You've got the tightest, sweetest arse I've ever buggered, love," he muttered against her ear, and saw her lips pull back in a soft smile that revealed fang, even as he also saw the strain on her face, the tracks of tears. "Come for me. Let me hear you cry out."

And judging her ready, he eased up the clit hood, claimed the sensitive bundle of nerves beneath between two knuckles, and returned to being ruthless. Her scream reverberated throughout their car, lost to the other cars in the rushing wind outside, the vast, empty spaces of the Outback. His cries joined her, for he could hold back his release no longer, taking her body back to the bed as he crouched over her, using her hard, pistoning his hips with all the finesse of a stake and mallet.

When he was done, his body rested on top of hers and his arm was banded around her front, the other bracing them on the bed. She was gasping, breathless little sobs. As he turned his head, he felt the wetness on her face.

"Love?" He lifted up, but her hand gripped his, keeping him where he was.

"No, just turn, Dev. Stay inside me, but turn."

He did as she bade, spooning with her with some difficulty in the narrow bunk made for one. "Did I . . ." Rationality was returning, and with it, incredulity. What in the hell had he been thinking, listening to her? Yeah, she was invincible and all, but pain still hurt.

Shhh . . . you're fine. She was shaking, and he wanted to pull out, see her face, but she simply held his arms banded around her, so she could shelter inside the weight and size of his body, while he still impaled her. He knew he would soften and gradually slide out of her, but the sphincter was such a tight ring of muscles, sometimes a man had to work his way out. And she didn't seem to want to let him go yet.

"I'm a bloody bastard," he muttered against her ear. "A fucking monster."

"No," she said softly, and now she turned her face enough that his lips brushed her cheek. He saw one blue eye, too close up to distinguish the look in it. "I owed you that one, Dev. You wouldn't have had to do everything you had to do in the last three days if it hadn't been for me seeing you in Elle's. If anyone's the bloody bastard here, it's me. I've used your darkness, needed it."

He did pull out then, slow and easy, though she still bit her lip as he completely got out. Turning her over to face him, he pulled her up close. She allowed it, letting him wind his arms around her body, rub soothing hands down her back, over the tense buttocks. "Over on your stomach, love. Let me help."

"No, it's fine."

He tipped up her chin, gave her a look. "Don't make me pull out the Superman strength I've been holding in reserve."

"Really?" She arched a brow. "And here I was, already impressed by you." But still she balked. "Dev, I can take care of things like that . . ."

"Yeah, you can. But wouldn't a servant take care of all sorts of things for you, including intimate things like that?"

"Some do, but—"

"Well, then." He rose up on an arm. "Don't make me resort to tickling." At her look he sobered. "Please, Danny. Let me check."

"I'll heal."

"Yeah. But I can make it easier."

When he tugged on her, she capitulated, but he could tell she wasn't very excited about it. As he'd figured, he'd torn her, and there was blood. He hitched his pants and shirt back on, went and found some hot water, coming back with that and some cloths to do a hot compress.

Danny put her cheek on her hands, watching him, the concentration on his face as he gently parted her buttocks and cleaned her, then pressed the hot compress to the abused area. It did make it much better, and she let out a hum of relief. "You might have some blood on you, too," she noted, glancing at the heavy weight of him, held in his strides again.

"I'll take care of that in a minute, after I take care of you." He blew out a breath through his nostrils. "Danny, it wasn't supposed to be like that. I know . . . it was our bet. But if ever you're willing to trust me again, I promise I'll show you how much pleasure I can give you from doing it that way. If not, you don't have to worry. I won't ask again."

"You asked for it to be the reward for your survival and I obliged. And you can ask again, for less dire reasons, I hope." She smiled at him as his gaze turned her way. "Dev, it's far easier to trust you than for you to trust me. I can read your mind, after all. And I see what kind of man you are." Lifting up, she feathered her fingers over his cheek. "This is how I wanted you. Raw, uncontrolled. I like everything about you, bushman. Except your sadness. That I can't bear."

Dropping her hand after that surprising statement, she changed direction. "After we get cleaned up, let's go eat in the dining car."

～

They sat at a corner table. The other passengers gave them a close scrutiny, because he supposed they did make an odd couple, a rough stockman and a woman of obvious aristocratic lineage.

Danny was amused by his thoughts, for he didn't recognize that the female attention was almost exclusively on him. They checked out her appearance in that catty way women did, but he captured their interest and didn't let go. *You should have seen him an hour ago, ladies.* Sitting on the edge of the bed, his hands so gentle, face so concerned, easing her pain. Or a half hour before that, raging like an oversexed stallion let loose on the first filly he'd seen in ages. It had hurt like holy hell, but she'd taken every inch of him, knowing she'd given him a way to eradicate some of the darkness in him, take it to a manageable level again.

Completely bound to him in mindless need and pain, she'd found a tranquil center, an almost Nirvana where the pain didn't matter anymore, only the connection between the two of them. It was quite peculiar, because she'd seen it demonstrated before, by third-marked servants completely enraptured by service to their Masters. It had happened to her, because she'd been immersed in the need to take away his pain and see what lay at the darkest depths of his psyche.

A curious thought. Mulling on it, she chose several items off the menu, handed it back to the waiter without giving Dev any options, waving off the man imperiously when he tried to ask. Her bushman studied her. "What's going on now, my lady?"

As he asked, he picked up the glass of water they'd brought out, downed it in about two seconds, so that she pushed hers over to him, let him finish that one.

"Dinner," she said simply.

When the food arrived, she gestured to have it put before her. After they had arranged it suitably, she took up the knife and fork and cut the meat. "Slide your chair over here."

Giving her another curious look, Dev slid his chair over. He almost jumped when her hand ran along his thigh beneath the tablecloth, high enough that her smallest finger grazed his groin. She didn't worry with the fork, simply picked up the piece of cut meat, the juice staining her fingers, and brought it to his lips.

"I'm going to feed you every bit of this, because I like the way you take it from my hand."

"You really needed a dog as a child," he observed. But he took the meat from her fingers.

Christ. From that first bite, he had a desire to taste more than the food, pull her fingers in as well, but they were causing enough of a scandal as it was. She'd moved to his testicles and was stroking over him, easy, calm, as if they weren't surrounded by thirty other people taking their meals. While they couldn't see beneath the tablecloth,

Dev realized it was the way she was toward him that had glances coming their way. Blatantly sexual and possessive, attracting attention because of the subconscious recognition of temptation, even if the brain wasn't sophisticated enough to name it that. There were some castigating glances, but he saw a few surreptitious, fascinated ones.

Here they were, sitting at a table in the first-class dining car, his arm comfortably stretched behind her chair, certainly a more intimate pose than most chose for a public meal, but it was evening, after all, and they weren't having sex. Though, Jesus, Mary and Joseph, her knuckle was continuing to glide up and down the curve of his testicles beneath the inseam of his trousers to the base of his cock, a teasing swirl, then back down again. And the fingers of her other hand, now stained with the juice of the meat to the knuckle, were still extending the bits of it toward his mouth. He wondered if that waiting look, that stillness to her, explained the erroneous lore that vampires were dead. She didn't move her eyes, no quiver to her hands, not even a flutter from her bosom from breathing. Anyone who studied her long enough would get the uncomfortable impression he was viewing something not human. But her beauty would continue to hold him as she approached, closer and closer, until a man realized he didn't really care if he was prey.

"Do you feed on other men, the way you've fed on me?" He asked it before he thought it through, realized he had a burning need to know, and not know.

"I've fed on no one in the same way, ever," she said in that erotic hum, collecting juice at the corners of his mouth, teasing his lips and tongue with it. "But what you're asking me is whether I always take them to my bed. Sometimes I do. Often I don't. Most of the time, they're merely a meal. Taking blood alone almost matches the ecstasy of sex, so it's only when a face or body particularly stirs my baser hungers that I indulge."

"And does a full servant eliminate the need for that?"

She gave him a feline smile. "I expect that depends on the servant, doesn't it?"

He closed his hand over her wrist this time when he took the food, licking the crevices between her fingers before he withdrew, chewed. But he kept his hold on her wrist, his thumb tracing her pulse, eyes locked with hers.

"While you were recuperating at the station, I gave every stockman two marks." She straightened her fingers to tease them along his jaw. "Each one took a knee by my chair. Then I placed my hand along the side of his head, his throat, and sank my fangs here." She extended one finger, made a bare line along that main artery, the blood escalating at her touch. He dipped his head, licked the center of her palm where juice had trickled, kept exploring her palm with his mouth. Her blue eyes fired, particularly when he gave her an ungentle nip.

"Do you want me to say I'm jealous, my lady?"

"No," she murmured. "Your thoughts already told me. You don't want me to touch another, and I've told you, as long as I wish you to be at my station, I won't take another to my bed." Extricating herself, she leaned back, perused him with heavy-lidded eyes. "But the very nature of a vampire is to touch, to experience. I might enjoy watching you take another . . . lie in the bed with you, hold her body to mine while you plunder her from behind. Kiss away those sweet tears you'd make on her face, as you made on mine. Clasp my legs around your hips and hold her tight between us as she comes to climax, cries out in my ear, digs her nails into my back as she'd like to dig into yours."

Dev stopped in midmotion. She'd not only spoken it, but injected it into his mind, complete with the girl's sharp gasps, the feel of her nails, of Danny's legs holding them both. In a moment, they were both going to be arrested.

Her voice had lowered further as she leaned forward. For dinner, she'd changed into a tightly laced corset and a snug riding skirt. The thin cotton shirt she wore under the corset did little more than create a gauze whisk over the expanse of her elevated breasts. She wore her opal again, teasing his gaze down the deep valley of cleavage, making him imagine vividly what he'd do if one of those pieces of steak had dropped into it. He'd eat it out as thoroughly as he would her cunt, the sweet taste of the two fleshes on his tongue.

"Nice," she murmured, her voice husky. "But I have another image, Dev. I'm imagining that same situation as before, only it's not a girl between us. You're in my arms, my cunt impaled by that large cock of yours. But behind you is another man, and he is rutting upon you, his cock in your arse, and he will send you into unwilling screaming ecstasy as you bring me to mine. His touch on you will be ruthless, relentless. But you will be there because it serves my pleasure, because it's my fantasy to see you ridden so rough, that hard male way men fuck one another, to be a part of it."

Now he was dearly glad there were no tables close enough to be privy to their conversation. Otherwise, he was sure some comfortable matron behind him would have thudded to the floor. He was feeling a little dodgy himself at the vision. "And you think I'd submit to that, ever? Being buggered by a man?"

"It's not about being buggered by a man," she said, studying him with those large eyes that looked like they should be in a Walt Disney movie, the long lashes and pouty red mouth. He could imagine birds twittering around her. A moment before her forked tongue shot out and captured one, like a dragon zapping flies.

Humor twinkled through her eyes. "That's a power I don't have. But it's not about being buggered by a man," she repeated. "It's about wanting to serve someone enough you get beyond questions. You simply serve."

"I'm not the right man, if you're seeking someone for that. I won't give up my brain, my right to make my own decisions."

"This is the opposite of that. This is the most conscious, relevant decision you can make." She pushed the plate to him then, laid the fork alongside it, but he stifled a groan as her touch returned to his cock beneath the table. "Eat the rest now. I want to watch you."

What if I wanted to watch you, my lady? See you take pleasure in my blood, the way you take pleasure in watching me eat this steak? The moistness of your lips, the way you swallow?

Her gaze flickered, her lips parting at the image he gave her. *You are very adept at this, Dev. I'm not sure if I shouldn't block you from my mind altogether.*

In answer, he picked up a piece of the meat, just a small one, but one with plenty of red juice glistening in the folds, and extended it to her mouth. As she held his gaze, he shifted his foot, prodded her calf so she slid her foot out of her shoe, laid her stockinged toes on top of his boot, against his ankle.

I think you would miss having me there, my lady.

Her mouth opened, her delicate lips closing over his fingers, the scrape of a fang arousing him further.

I think I might at that.

~

When they took the plane trip from Adelaide to the airstrip nearest Surfer's Paradise, Danny was delighted to find out her bushman had been to Surfer's Paradise before and found it a bonza place. It was one of her favorite vacation spots as well. The small, quiet town consisted of a few cottages by the sea, a couple of hotels and restaurants. Her structure was not a large place, a bungalow on pilings that had a lovely ocean view and comfortable furnishings. While she endeavored not to be intrusive, she enjoyed staying in his mind during that first day, registering his surprise that a woman with her obvious relaxed urbanity preferred a place like this for her leisure time.

You're surprised, even though I want to live out on a solitary station with only my staff and the great wide plains for company?

Well, I reckoned that had to do with Ian taking what you thought was rightfully yours. At first, I didn't expect you'd be staying. Maybe you'll explain your contradictions one day, my lady.

He'd been out on the beach in the sunlight when they had that conversation, him taking in the sunrise within view of the cottage while she prepared for sleep. Since he was stripped down to his shorts, obviously ready to go for a swim, she left him with the question unanswered and the advice to beware of sharks and jellyfish. To all appearances, she let him be, though she stayed in his mind almost as a form of bedtime story, following his thoughts and reaction to the water, the surf, other early bathers . . . his laughter.

When she woke in the early evening, she found fresh flowers, pink and white everlasting daisies, in a vase on the side table. She was still alone in the room, but located him just outside the door.

Wrapping a sheet around herself, she cracked it and peered out, finding she had to suppress a smile. Her swagman. He had a chair leaned up against the wall beside the door, whittling on a piece of wood, watching the people go back and forth along the boardwalk down closer to the shore. The soft rush of the ocean, the familiar music of it, was a pleasant background. Stars were already starting to come out, promising a beautiful and romantic night that stirred her in ways she knew it shouldn't.

But what woman could look at him and not feel that way? Despite it being past sundown, he was still wearing his hat. As always, she liked the way the brim shaded his face, emphasizing the strong jawline, the day's worth of stubble as he tilted his attention toward her. The carving process drew attention to the capable, strong fingers, the length of his forearms, the column of his thigh he had braced against the chair leg to hold it back and steady himself.

"G'day, love." He slanted her a half smile. "Slept the whole day away, didn't you?" His gaze traveled over her loose hair, down to the looser hold of the sheet, her bare shoulders and glimpse of bosom. "You might want to go get dressed before you scandalize these nice family people."

"I don't seem to be scandalizing you."

"Oh, I'm a worldly sort of bloke." He shrugged. "Manage to keep my tongue rolled up in my head most days without the help of clothespins." He flicked away another shaving. "Do you like to dance?"

She cocked her head. "I can manage. I learned some belly dancing in the Holy Lands that would scandalize these fine wowsers."

He grinned then, making a turn on what he was whittling. "Well, Jezebel, if you can manage to do a proper waltz instead, they're having a dance, main hotel in town tonight. We can go do some moonlight swimming or walking along the sand when you get tired of it, whatever suits your fancy."

"You suit my fancy, quite well." She smiled at him, trailing a hand along his shoulder. He was relaxed, making her very glad she'd brought him here. "What are you doing there?"

Blowing the shavings off, he offered it up for her inspection, sheathing the whittling knife in the smaller scabbard next to his hunting knife. He waved toward someone on the beach, one of their passing neighbors, she supposed. As she took it from his fingers, she was charmed into another smile when she recognized a kangaroo. "This is quite deft, Dev. I don't think I've ever had something so fine."

"Well." He cleared his throat, looked away. "Your apologies, my lady, but I didn't make it for you."

She shifted her attention back to him. "Oh, really?"

"Nope. Another sheila whose affections I've managed to win. I'm quite the popular man about town already." He crossed his arms over his chest while she considered giving the back leg of the chair enough of a shove to send him toppling.

"Well, maybe you should take *her* to the dance, then," she suggested, showing a hint of fang.

"Might want to sheathe your blades, my lady," he responded with a twinkle to his eye. "We have an impressionable visitor."

She really needed to get in the habit of stripping his mind bare so he couldn't tease her. A young girl of about eight approached them now, with a shy glance at Danny. Danny could see now that she'd come from a picnic area up on the beach, where she'd been sitting with her family. His wave toward them had obviously been the signal that he was done. Danny relinquished the toy to him, watching as he placed it in the child's flat palm. He made it bound up her arm so she giggled. Taking a piece of twine, he tied it around the roo's body and then made a necklace of it, putting it over her head. "There, love. You won't lose it while you're playing in the sand. Have fun with that." He waved genially to the watching parents, as she thanked him politely and scampered back to show them.

"You have made quite an impression."

He snorted. "They like to romanticize us bushfolk, you know that."

"Like American cowboys."

"Aren't all Yanks cowboys? Saw enough of them in the war to think so."

"Not all." She gave him a smile. "It's more a national spirit. The same way most Aussies identify with folk like you when they think of themselves as being Australian, but you couldn't get them out of the cities with a crowbar. Can't imagine why. Winds that raise up enough dust to block the sun, heat to fry your liver, rains that bring floods to drown you but rush away to drought, leaving your skeleton lying on the desert sands."

He gave her a considering look. "Not fooling me, love. You're drawn to it. Quite the bushie yourself, even when you don't know enough to stay out of trouble."

"Well, lucky I have you, isn't it?" She swiped his hat and put it on her own head, cocking a hip against the door.

He laughed. "Don't pout about the roo, love. I'll make you one, too. Do you want children?"

The question caught her off guard, but she shrugged. "Most vampire females can't have children. That's why born ones are so rare and so treasured."

"Well, genetically speaking, you might be predisposed, though, right?"

She shook her head. "No proof so far that it works that way. And I really haven't thought about it. Too young yet."

"Too young," he murmured. "A young woman at two hundred?"

"Exactly." But she looked back toward the family. "You're barely forty. It's been over ten years since you lost your family. Why—"

"I had that. Man only deserves that once, if he lets it get away."

She stopped, not because it was a good explanation, but because of what she saw in his mind. He couldn't do it. He'd be paralyzed, unable to leave them alone. He wasn't like the smiling young father examining what his little girl had secured from one of those famous bushmen. Dev wouldn't ever be able to get past the choking fear that when he left his family, he'd come back to the smell of blood and waste. That he would have to use his rifle to drive off the dingoes and buzzards circling the house, seeking a way in because they could smell the flesh, calling to them . . .

Abruptly, he rose. "I'll be back."

"No." Before he could get away, she curled her fingers in the open neck of his shirt, pulled him to her. With his body half shielding hers, she let the sheet drop, the breeze from the ocean blowing her hair back in a ripple, drawing his attention to the expanse of breast revealed.

"Christ, you have no sense of decency." Easing her into the room, he closed the door with a snap behind him. But she was already back onto him, sliding her arms up to his neck to bring his mouth down to hers, knocking the hat off her head. He surprised her this time, though, putting his hands over her wrists to still her. Lifting his head, he touched her cheek and jawline with his fingertips, studying her so hard in the dimness she knew even without looking into his mind that he was contemplating the day she'd no longer be part of his life.

Don't do that, Dev. Don't say good-bye, bushman, when you haven't even said a proper hello, by my accounting of time. Two hundred years is young for a vampire, remember?

That twist of his lips again, and it punched her low in her stomach, that sensual curve of mouth. His hands went to her waist, finding the small of her back, the rise of her buttocks. She brought all her soft curves and willing flesh against the cotton, denim and leather covering his. No wonder the little girl was enchanted. He *was* a romantic figure with the stock whip coiled at his hip, the handle fitted into a slim pocket along the thigh, the knives on the other side. Reaching up, she took off his hat, raking her hand through his copper red hair. "Did you used to keep it short for her?"

"No. I kept it short because that was the way I was raised. She liked it longer, like this, though. She understood I needed it the other way, for the heat and dirt, all that. But she liked it like this," he repeated.

Danny nodded. "So do I." *Touch me, Dev. Kiss me. Hold me.*

But she didn't beg any man, so she held those thoughts in her own mind only, began to draw away, giving him a coy smile when his hands tightened, drew her back, close enough that muscled leg found the seam of her thighs and pressed, so he rode her on it as he leaned back against the door and brought his head down to nibble on her lips.

"Hold still, love," he murmured. "Let me enjoy you. Give you pleasure."

Was it to make up for his roughness before? Whatever his reasons, this was pure devastation of thought, everything given to her senses as he teased her mouth over and over with his. Lips, tongue, working intimately to explore her mouth, her lips, the wetness just inside them, the tender, moist flesh so like another part of her body. He eased up her sides, tracing her rib cage, sliding around to her back again to play in her hair, following it to where the tips teased the tops of her buttocks. When his hands formed a butterfly shape, the thumbs pressed together in her cleft, up against the sensitive opening, his other fingers spread out over her cheeks to grip with the right firmness.

He moved against her then, his leg insinuating farther so she held on to his shoulder and he took her off her feet, working her against his thigh, a delicious pressure to her clit that had her tossing her head back and giving him access to her throat for more of the magic of his mouth, moving down her sternum, his stubble scratching her breasts, his hair brushing her skin. She gripped his arms, the loose stuff of his shirt, undulating against the hard column of his thigh, rubbing his cock with her hipbone. When he turned his head to her shoulder, nuzzling the point of it with his lips, his pulsing artery was there, before her eyes, her mouth. He'd registered her hunger.

She brushed the offered area with tender lips, a thank-you before delicately piercing him, using only one fang so she could sip from the bite area. Feeling his cock grow harder against her, she knew how much it aroused him, she feeding on him, he serving her needs, even if he didn't think of it that way. Giving something simple, life sustaining. No gray areas to consider. Just pure, red blood.

Hitching her up on his body as she drank, he moved them to the bed. As he took her down, she watched him fan out her hair with his fingers. This intense attention was an irresistible seduction, the way he looked at her, his only focus her. Whether he was doing it deliberately to force out other memories or not, the only thing she felt in his mind now was his absorption in her. She liked it, and pushed away her own discomfiting thoughts, not wanting to remember her reaction when she thought he'd been flirting and making friends with a town girl.

A stroke of sadness came with the thought. No matter how he denied it, he needed to have a family again. He needed that to heal. Which meant, third mark or not, he wasn't going to be hers forever, no matter how much she wanted him to be. When it came time to leave, she wouldn't hold him. It was what was best for him.

But for now, she focused on this. Divesting himself of his clothing, he came down upon her on the bed, sliding his arm under her waist to move her up, adjusting her where her head could rest on a pillow. He entered her, slow, sweet, pulling everything in her yearning body toward that joining point, taking his body all the way down on hers so they were simply intertwined, their gazes holding, so much going on that wasn't being said, even in their thoughts.

Dev might be right. A woman's heart was a woman's heart, no matter whether it rested in a human form or a vampire's. It could break in either vessel. It just couldn't kill the vampire, much as she might wish to avoid the pain. And it made her wonder if the desolation of having loved her father and never found a replacement for him was what had sent her mother walking out into the sun, that last dawn of her life.

This was a thought she didn't want, couldn't be having, not at this moment. But she couldn't prevent the wave of feeling, as vast as the ocean so close to their door, when he leaned down, kissed her lips again and spoke to her in that tender whisper. "Gate to my soul, love. That's what you are."

She drew him down to her then, clasping her arms over his broad shoulders, pressing her face into his neck as his strokes began to quicken and her body began to lift to his, to demand, to come closer to that pinnacle where both of their unsettling thoughts would be swept away by the incoming tide. She would take it, even knowing that things washed away by tides had a way of returning, again and again. Marking the beach with their impression so they could never be forgotten as well as never kept, temporary and yet eternal marks in the sand.

18

ANOTHER plus, he was a man quite comfortable with dancing. At the hotel, he handled himself handsomely in a waltz, his hand sure on her back, fingers supporting hers.

"So, did the aborigines teach you to dance?"

"Aborigines don't dance." He gave her a smile as he turned her. Most had turned out for the hotel's entertainment, so the waxed and swept wooden floor was semicrowded. "They imitate animals or hunting scenes. They use music as part of the ceremonies, so people think it's dancing."

"You've participated in them?" She raised a brow.

He shrugged. "Because of my ancestor, I'm accepted as a member of a particular clan, the family descended from the aboriginal woman he married. But yeah, I've done my share with the men of the tribe. Done a passable bird, horse, camel . . ." He winked at her. "They said when I did the bird, I looked a bit frightening, this naked white thing flapping his arms and cackling at the sky. They weren't sure I hadn't been possessed by some kind of evil spirit instead."

"You didn't stay with them, though."

"I'm welcome to walk with them on occasion, but they won't let me stay with them. They said the white world has more need of a Gravedigger than theirs."

Then that brief shadow passed, good humor returning to the hazel eyes. "I could imitate a bird for you, but I'd be afraid of offending my totem." He flicked his eyes toward his chest, the raven they knew was concealed beneath his shirt. "His power might desert me."

"Somehow, I doubt that." Sliding her hand up to his nape, she played under his hair as they turned together. His hand was low on her back, and she supposed it was clear to anyone watching they were intimate with each other. She'd seen more than one woman's eyes seeking wedding rings and tutting when they didn't find any.

Bugger them. They're just in a blue because their husbands can't take their eyes off your bum.

"Behave," she reproved, though her eyes twinkled. "You still haven't told me how you learned to dance."

He grinned. "Maybe it's from sheep shearing. The key is keeping the sheep relaxed, so she'll turn in your arms like a lady dancing." He took her smoothly under his arm and then back to him again. "When the shears run along her fleece, you keep one hand ahead of the blades to pull the skin smooth so you don't cut her, and so you'll cut the fleece even. I expect that feels like a soothing stroke up a woman's back." His fingers drifted along her spine. " 'Course, you're spinning her this way and that on her arse. May explain why my first few dance partners didn't take well to me."

She chuckled. "Care to walk on the beach with me after this dance?"

Dev nodded, gave her another stylish spin to maneuver her off the dance floor and made her laugh again. He liked the sound of it, relaxed and almost girlish. She stopped at the boardwalk to hold his shoulder and remove her sandals, leaving them tucked in the shadows as they continued down to the shore. She'd worn a proper sundress tonight, and he liked the way it bared her arms, the flare of the modest skirt that fell to her calves. She'd clipped her hair back with a barrette on her shoulders. She looked pretty this way, a young woman walking along the beach with a beau.

However, despite her attractive but relatively demure appearance, he noted her direct gaze was disconcerting to most. Whether consciously or not, parents had a tendency to move their children to the outside when Danny passed, hurry them along and steal a nervous glance over their shoulders as if they'd encountered a dangerous lioness who happened to look like the Cinderella of the fairy tales.

In contrast, when they went down the stairs to the beach, he automatically took her hand, making sure she maneuvered the rickety wooden steps safely, though she was lithe as a cat in truth and probably could have vaulted down them.

They encountered another swagman a few feet away, up against the dune. He'd collected bits of trash off the beach and created a giant lizard made of wire, paper, string and other bits of debris, delighting the children and Danny. She circled it several times and made the old fella's night, with her interest as well as the few dollars she gave him.

When another group of children came to see, they moved on toward the shore. Danny held up her skirt to avoid getting the hem wet, while the tide bathed her toes. He offered her his hand and she took it, wrapping her fingers in his as they ambled along in companionable silence.

"I've seen the world's largest ball of string. And the world's tiniest dollhouse. Why do you think people do that? Make things larger, or smaller?"

"Well, the miniature stuff seems easy to understand. Your own tiny world."

"It always boils down to control." She sent a smile toward him.

"Care for a swim?" he asked, nodding toward the ocean.

"No." When he raised an eyebrow at her emphatic response, she grimaced. "Vampires can't swim, Dev. Our bodies . . . there's no buoyancy. We don't float. We can walk along the bottom, but most of us don't like getting our heads wet."

Which explained how cranky she'd been when he'd tossed her into the billabong. She snorted. "I heard that. I was not cranky."

"If you don't like what you hear in my mind, my lady, you can always change the radio station."

He drew her close enough to brush his jaw across her fair brow. Shaking her head at him, she bent to examine a shell. Her hair fell forward, baring the side of her throat, making him want to kiss it, blow on her nape. She tilted her head slightly toward him, telling him she was listening, still preferring to tune in to his channel.

"Why did Ruskin want to take your blood that night? Does it give him the same access to your mind as you have to mine?"

Putting the shell back down, she moved on, her footprints leaving a trail in the wet sand. "Yes and no. If he took just a small amount, he could locate me in his territory, have some sense of my thoughts or intentions. But more than that, and he can get deeper into my mind. It's not as easy. I could block him in a way a human can't, but it would take fairly constant effort. For instance, vampires have used a forced blood exchange, combined with torture, to find out secrets from other vampires. Council plans, family fortunes, et cetera. Most vampires in a territory don't have a choice, and it was set up that way to help Region Masters and overlords enforce our tenuous order. But if you have a choice, you don't willingly give a vampire access to your mind."

"Have you ever?" At her wary look, he squeezed her hand. "I want to get at that family fortune. You know I prefer the finer things in life."

"Idiot," Danny muttered, though she didn't know which of them it was directed at. She could trust him, she knew that. "Two. One was a first crush. He . . . I was a total bogan, about thirty-five, which is like a teenager to vampires. I did it in a flush of feeling, sure that he was everything, my whole life. My father killed him when he tried to make me do things for him by manipulating my thoughts."

"How long did it take you to forgive your father for that?" He lifted a shoulder at her surprised expression. "Most kids, it would take them a while. They wouldn't see anything but their feelings."

"It was long ago, and there was nothing to forgive. My father saved me from disaster. It taught me an invaluable lesson."

"Hmm." He wondered at the flat tone of her voice, but let it go. "And who was the second one?"

Danny picked up another shell, held it up to the light, showing him the delicate lavender interior. It reminded him of the delicate shell of her ear, and he bent, nuzzled into it, seeking it with his mouth as she leaned into him. While she was still looking at the shell, he could sense her body humming with the contact, the way she pressed her hip against his thigh. "Her name is Lady Lyssa," she said at last. "She's the only direct line royal we have left. Used to be, vampires were in clans, headed up by royalty. Dukes, kings, queens. She was Queen of the Far East Clan. She's very old. Over a thousand, some say, but no one knows for sure. You'll get to meet her in Brisbane. Though I'm fond of Alistair, the Queensland Region Master, I admit she's the real reason I'm stopping there. She's come to Australia to stay with Alistair for a couple months, and wanted me to visit if I came to the area."

He glanced at her, amused. "So you and she are mates. Like for girly stuff. Shopping and whatnot."

Danny laughed. "I'm not sure how she'd react to that. Oh, her servant is a monk."

Dev's brow lifted. "As in celibate, a church monk?"

"Are there other kinds?" she responded dryly. "But yes. She's married, so some of us figure that's why she chose Thomas, but then, she was with him before she decided to marry Rex. He won't be with her this visit, though. Rex," she added.

"Sounds like you're not unhappy about that." Dev was watching her face closely.

She shrugged. "He's not a very easy person."

"Considering the majority of you are big mobs of fun, that's saying something."

She elbowed him. "He used to be better. He's been . . . changing. Remember, I mentioned the Ennui? Vampires, as they get older, can get a bit sick of life. If we have a predator of any significance, it's that. Many vampires succumb to it when they reach five or six centuries. The vampire gets tired of everything and either self-destructs by running him- or herself into trouble, or chooses to walk into the sunlight with dignity."

"That's what your mother had."

She nodded. "She was a bit younger than Rex, but I don't think she ever got over my father, not really."

"How did he die?"

A shadow crossed her gaze. "Vampire hunter."

He stopped and looked at her. "There are vampire hunters? Here? In Australia?"

"They're everywhere." As she laid her shell back down again, she squatted in the sand looking for more. Gathering her skirt up beneath her, she kept it from trailing in the wet sand.

"But I thought you said the Ennui was your greatest predator, after other vampires."

"It is. Vampire hunters are mainly fringe groups who don't always know what they're doing, easily killed if they stray where they shouldn't go." Her tone was flat, emotionless. "But because there *are* so few, it's hard to stay vigilant against them."

He thought of the way she had watched everyone who passed her on the boardwalk, how she insisted that he be armed, even when they were traveling on Stuart Highway or in the desert.

"My vigilance is mostly for attacks by other vampires," she answered, "but dissolute vampires also tend to breed vampire hunters. Which is another reason vampires like Ruskin are a problem. A vampire who takes his maximum kill, or engages in atrocities with children like he does, tends to create family members who find us out in their search for vengeance. But my father wasn't like Ruskin. He was set up by his enemies."

"Your family seems to attract an awful lot of trouble." Dev squatted beside her, ran his hand down her back.

"We're the only major landholders in Australia," she said vaguely. "The rest have property, but nothing like ours. And my family is well established, old. You know how it is, Dev. There are always some who feel they can take what they haven't earned just because they haven't been as fortunate, or made decisions as wisely. Or fate hasn't blessed them with the same luck. That sort of thing."

When she finally lifted her face, he was struck by her classic beauty and reserve. As well as why her explanation seemed lacking to him. He rose with her, closing his hand on her arm before she could start walking again.

"It's you," he said. "You're the draw of it. It's this crazy mating courtship you were talking about. That's why you left forty years ago, as well. To take you out of the equation, let your mother live in peace for the remainder of her life, because it was the only thing you could think of to help her. But you've suspected, ever since you killed him, that Ian may have driven her to her death specifically because it would bring you back."

"Dev, don't." But he saw the truth of it flash through her eyes, the guilt and useless anger. He shook his head, took her other arm.

"You're the prize. You're young, and the property and title pass to you. Not to mention, I don't give a damn what Ruskin says, he and every one of them know you're extraordinary, independent. You have integrity and power both. You should be the Region Master. He knows that. So he wants you gone, or under his thumb. You're Oz's princess, love. That's what it is."

"I don't want that. I've *never* wanted it." She pulled away from him. "My father told me the same thing after he killed Sean. There are five thousand of us in the bloody world, Dev. You'd think we could spread out far enough not to bother one another, but no, we have to act like a bunch of rats packed inside a damn barrel, squirming and biting to get to the top of that stupid heap. It's suffocating, and I *won't* bear it."

"Some things aren't a choice." He caught up with her as she muttered an oath and started striding off in the sand. It would have been amusing, for she swore pretty crook, and her frustrated stomp in bare feet through sand was as waddling as a human. Except, with the truth of it staring in his face, he wasn't feeling amused at all. When he pulled her around by her arm, he met her killer look and hiss.

"Knowing all this, you set out across the desert with two guides and three men? And now you're planning to run a station with a handful of stockmen and a bunch of maids? You need an army, love."

As well as a servant, linked to her mind, who would protect her during daylight, could telegraph information to her through her mind. Now he understood the look that passed between Ian and Ruskin that night when she'd brushed off the idea of having a third-mark servant. She was denying herself one of the most potent weapons a vampire could have. And she would still be without one, if she hadn't decided it was the only way she could try to save his life.

Because he sure as hell wouldn't have tolerated her being branded or flogged, unless he was a corpse.

"I don't have a full servant," she retorted. "I've neither asked for that commitment from you, nor have you offered it, for that matter. And I'm not in as much danger as you think." Jerking free, she leveled a glare on him. "The Council particularly protects the born vampires."

"You forget I was there, love. Ruskin is right. Seems to me, they might get worked up about your death, but only after it happens. They're not near protective enough, not if I was the only thing that kept you from being barbecued out in the desert."

"Why, Dev, I didn't realize you had a clucky side. Are you mothering me?"

"No," he snapped. "If I were your father, I'd put you over my knee and blister you for being so careless of your own life."

She stopped and turned. Blinked at him with those luminous blue eyes. "Well, that makes me think some rather incestuous thoughts . . . Dad."

When he lunged at her, she was ready for him, slipping past with an infuriating peal of laughter, dancing away and around him as he did his best to catch hold of her. Then he grasped the stockwhip coiled on his hip and snapped it out. It not only caught her in midspin, but the end popped high on her arse. He might not move fast as a vampire, but he was learning a lot about using the element of surprise.

"Ouch!" she yelped, but then he'd brought her in to him, loosing the whip with another deft twist of his wrist so it fell down along the outside of her leg. When he clamped a hand on the abused area, she sucked in a hissing breath, but her reaction wasn't anger. Seeing it, he muttered an oath, but she was done playing or fighting. Curling her hands in his shirt, she yanked him down for the kiss, roughly enough she ripped the fabric as she pressed herself against his chest.

You're avoiding the issue.

It's not your place. Shut up and kiss me back.

With a frustrated snarl, he did, though he squeezed her buttock hard, conveying his annoyance with her. When at last she drew back, he gave her a stern look. "You've made it my place, my lady, if you remember. Without giving me any say in it."

He'd managed to get his own thoughts turned in a different direction as well, unfortunately. With the whip wound around his knuckles, holding her cinched to him, it was under her buttocks, taut enough to lift them and send a shiver through her. She could throw him off with barely any effort, but she wasn't, was she?

"Let go of me," she said softly. "Right now. Or I will make you very sorry."

He cocked his head, lifting a brow. "What will you do? Beat the shit out of me, shoot me? Tear my heart out of my chest and play with it, take every drop of blood? You've made all that happen or done it yourself, my lady. I'm still here."

"Yes, you are." Abruptly she sighed. "Okay. Let go. I'll tell you some things."

"I'm happy to hear them like this."

A slight smile pulled at her mouth. "I'm sure, but it's rather hard . . ." Rolling her eyes at his look, she struck his shoulder, none too gently. "Don't be obvious. *Difficult* to think. You know vampire appetites well enough by now. As long as you shove that great thing against me, all I'll be able to think about is taking you down on the sand and raping you. Wouldn't the matrons strolling about with their kiddies just love that?"

He loosened the whip, recoiled it. "I'm sorry, my lady. But you do act like a spoiled brat sometimes. No offense."

"Why would that offend me, coming from a man less than a quarter of my age?" She bared her teeth in a smile. Then at his expectant look, she gave an exaggerated petulant sigh that made his lips twist, even as she moved up onto the dry sand and sat down. She bent her legs before her, smoothing the skirt as he dropped down next to her, resting on an elbow and hip.

"You're naive, to boot," he continued.

"And how did you come to that conclusion?"

"Well, you offered me the job of station manager based on one night with my cock."

She gave him a severe look. "That's offensive enough I might withdraw the offer. And have the blood squeezed out of your heart *again*. I had my men ask about you thoroughly, bushman, before I left that note. I was informed by anyone who knew you at Elle's that you were no sundowner, the type who drifts about, doing as little work as possible and scrounging up free handouts. Instead, they were told you knew the bush better than most, could live off of it for months at a time. When you needed a bit of quid, you were a better than fair ringer. In fact, one man even informed me you're a bonza shearer. A gun shearer, he called you. Which, if I remember correctly amid all my spoiled self-absorption, means you'd be good to have around on a sheep station." ·

She lifted a brow as his jaw flexed. "Not as dumb as I look, am I? And from our one night together, I did manage to accumulate a few sound impressions. Like that you're the sort a woman can trust at her back. Plus, you say very little, but you see a great deal. That's tremendously useful to me. So stop being cranky, *Dad*, and I'll tell you a few things about vampires you don't know."

He gave her a gimlet look, but inclined his head. "I'm all ears."

"Actually, from my perspective, there's a different organ that holds that distinction."

"Now who's being obvious?" He tugged a lock of her hair. "I'm listening, love. The more I know about you, the better chance I actually have to guard your back."

She inclined her head, giving him that, then directed her gaze out to the water, the sliver of moonlight creating a jagged silver track on it toward shore that reflected in her eyes. "Vampires are attracted to weakness and fear, like all predators are to wounded animals. Being overly cautious is a similar type of beacon to them. I won't live my life like that. I don't want to be part of all these politics, but if I have to be, it's going to be on my terms, damn it." When he would have responded, she shook her head. "Dev, I know you haven't been thinking it, but I want to make sure you know I didn't make you my third-mark servant to save myself the inconvenience and vulnerability of being marked by Ruskin. He was boxing me in a corner that day, testing me. I just about failed that test, when he threatened outright to kill you. But if I had let him mark me to spare you, a human, I would be admitting I valued my freedom over your life, which . . ."

"Meant he would have killed me, then and there." At her surprised look, he nodded. "I picked up some things at that dinner. Male vampires don't seem to like it when you sheilas get too fond of your male servants."

She nodded. "There are rules, and laws, but the Council is all too aware we have fairly base instincts. I am sorry, Dev. Please believe that no matter what you've seen, what choices I take away, that was one I never intended to take from you."

She could tell he was surprised by her candor, and in truth, she was surprised by how fervently she needed him to believe her.

"No worries, love. You were right. I wouldn't have made it otherwise." He feathered his knuckles over her cheek, surprising her further. "I realized it during my very first bout, with that boy beneath the tree. The way I could move, the strength I had. It wasn't like anything I'd experienced before, and he still would have beaten me if I hadn't lucked out and been a little smarter on my feet than he was, poor bastard."

She nodded. "I'm sorry for that, too, Dev. I know it was awful."

He had his attention on her hand, braced against the beach, and so now he scooped up some dry sand in his palm and let it pour over her knuckles. He kept doing it, a rhythmic, circular exercise, engaging both of their silent attentions for a few moments as he buried her hand to the wrist.

"You know the silver lining they always talk about?" He watched the grains fall. "Well, it's damned odd, but after finding your wife and child murdered, you *know* there will never be anything as bad as that. Doesn't matter what atrocities or horrors exist in the world—I mean, the whole damn planet could go up in flames. That's the simple truth. So though I've seen some terrible, terrible things since then, for certain, and those kids rank right up there, it wasn't something I couldn't handle. Though I admit, Bob's cistern did push me over the edge that day, the foul thing. I'm an even-tempered bloke, when all is said and done."

She cocked her head, looking down at him. "You are. That's the truth. After the thirty-ninth, that was when it all hit you, didn't it? The war just delayed it awhile. That was when the Elder taught you about the stillness."

When he gave a slight nod, she hesitated, drawing his attention up to her face again. "What did he do to call you back from that edge?"

He met her eyes. "I know where you're going with this, love. You're not me."

Danny looked toward the ocean. "I . . . I've killed, of course. My annual kill. But I make that as pleasurable and quick as possible. Try not to let the person even know it's happening until it's all over. And I've had some near misses with other vampires, but other vampires, more experienced ones, have handled the situation. Ian was the first I'd killed . . . that way."

"Premeditated and with malice."

She kept her eyes trained on the water. "I didn't care for it, Dev. Made me feel tarnished. Wrong. Other vampires . . . we don't talk about things like that. Killing, taking full servants, it's all part of who we are. I wondered . . . No, my experience isn't yours, but I wanted to know what the Elder said."

When Dev's hand touched her face, she resisted a moment, then looked down at him. He passed his thumb over her cheek, her lips. "You're not a killer, love," he said quietly. "And for who you are, that's a bad thing."

She nodded. "I know."

"All I wanted was to lie down and stop existing, like an old member of the tribe," he said at last. "The Elder, he was a karadji of sorts, a medicine man, if you will. He told me I would make the spirits very angry if I wasted the life they'd given me. He told me I was moving further and further from my path, and whether I liked it or not, the spirits would send something to put me back on it." He shrugged. "Don't know if I believe all that or not, but there was something about you that night I couldn't resist. And though you are irresistible," he said with a light smile, "it was more than that."

Danny laid her hand over his on her face, then lifted her other one from the sand to tip up the hat to see his face. "So you think it was destined, you becoming my servant?"

"I think it was destined that you mark me three times, and I be with you for a while. Don't know about the future, short or long term. I haven't planned that way for a long time now, love. I just know things seem to happen sometimes."

Drawing up her knees, she pulled away to lock her hands around them. Wanting to eradicate the ridiculous sense of disappointment, she turned her mind to a few minutes before, when his arms had been around her, his whip holding her. In that position, she could have swayed against him as he rocked her side to side, a pleasant friction of motion as she let her belly slide across his groin, the head of his cock, which would become engorged by the motion of her body across it.

"God, you're insatiable," he said. "And you're trying to distract me."

"It's your fault for distracting me. You brought the whip into it." But she let the shadows go. "Too bad you didn't bring your swag. We could find a secluded spot, and I could ride you until dawn."

She liked the flash of heat that went through his gaze. "Well," he drawled, "that's just going back to the room and getting it. But there's a float somebody's left tied up over there." He nodded toward a clump of vegetation flanking the dunes. "We could borrow it for some land-based uses. Or I could push you out into the water, so you can enjoy without sinking."

"If I fall off, I will be extremely irritated."

"Well, they haven't had a good shark story to report around here for a day or so. Those poor noahs, if they tangle with the likes of you."

Dodging her swat, he took her hand again, caressing her fingers, twining with them on the swirl of cool sand. She raised her gaze to him. "Dev, I don't want to ruin a lovely moment, but I can't act this way with you all the time. We can't be this informal when we're with other vampires. Like Lady Lyssa and Alistair."

"You've made that clear from the first, my lady. And if there was any confusion, it was taken care of during that dinner with Ruskin and Ian. The whole standing behind your chair and ordering me onto my knees to lick your cunt etiquette."

A tinge of color stained her cheek at his crudeness, but she nodded. "Even for those I trust, like Alistair and Lyssa, there are things that vampires view as inappropriate, almost as an illness. Too much affection for a human is one of them."

"Hmm. And *do* you feel inappropriately about me, my lady?"

Danny looked sharply at him. His mind was open to her, and she saw curiosity only. Concern as well, because he didn't know how he'd react if she did admit to such a thing. That concern was a relief to her, though it came with another twinge of disappointment she chose to ignore. Instead, she gave him a smile. "No, Dev. I don't. But I tend to be more informal with my staff, and you are my first third-marked servant. I just don't want there to be any confusion between you and me."

Particularly since he made her feel confused enough inside without her projecting it to those who might understand it even less.

"There isn't, my lady. Never fear." But when he raised his gaze to her, she got a little lost in the hazel green of his eyes, the fan of brown lashes. "And I thank you for this, these few days . . . to just be."

"The pleasure has been all mine," she responded. He shook his head, increased his grip on her fingers.

"No, my lady. The pleasure has been ours."

~

They spent some more time wandering the shore, because shell study was a favorite pursuit of hers. She told him their names, stories and legends about the shells, as they both kept an interested eye on the dwindling number of other vacationers sharing their beach.

Well past the midnight hour, when the few families at Surfer's Paradise had gone to sleep, and the moon was turning the surf the color of foaming milk, they returned to that float. Danny straddled the muscled body of her bushman, his hands helping her slide the skirt in soft folds up to her hips so she could take him inside her. Pressing her hands down over his thundering heart, she watched him look at her face, her breasts, the cream color of her skin in their shared passion. After he tangled his hands in her hair, drawing her down to kiss her throughout a screaming, shuddering climax, she let herself be coiled on his chest, clasped tight in his arms, their bodies still joined, his cock a welcome, insistent pressure against the walls of her channel. Sand crusted on her feet as she dug her toes into the cool stuff outside his long calves.

"I'll build you a sand castle," he said at last, after they'd been quiet for quite a while.

She smiled against his chest, hearing the slow heartbeat, the sleepy note to his voice. "How many rooms will it have?"

"At least three or four hundred. You can have a different world in every room. There will be a library, a room with a huge fountain. With a giant lizard sculpture," he added. "Another room will be completely empty except for a tree growing up through the floor. The pattern on the floor will be thousands of the most beautiful shells in the ocean. Starfish will decorate the tree's branches. They'll be alive, because everything will be possible inside the castle."

"Everything, hmm?"

But she'd heard the slurring to his words and let him drift off, have his doze. She'd wake him again, another couple times before dawn, to feed on him, to bring him to release again as he serviced her needs as well.

I'd have a room in there for you, too, Dev. A room with your green Queensland station and your son and wife. You'd live there as long as you like, laughing with them. Telling your son stories, teaching him how to be a man like you . . .

She tried to be good, tried to imagine him with his wife, but she found she didn't want to do that. She settled for having the well-meaning thought and then shut it down, preferring to listen to his heartbeat, and his breath stir her hair. The tide rushed in and rushed out, like the tide of her feelings. They'd get higher and higher, until she couldn't hold off any longer and would rouse him to her once more.

19

HE'D really enjoyed Surfer's Paradise. He wasn't going to examine whether it was because he'd liked the people he and his lady became there, no matter how insulated a bubble it took to accomplish it, or because he was nursing a gut-level uneasiness about Brisbane.

Though Brisbane wasn't Melbourne or Perth, it was sizable to him after having spent so many years in the Outback, with only occasional forays into places like Elle's.

Danny's place just outside the city was a large home, dating from the eighteen hundreds with traditional architecture. The house was raised on stilts to promote airflow, and possessed wide, shady verandas. Tropical vegetation was cozied up to it like a beautiful nature sprite's lush green hair, dotted with splashes of color from blooming bushes and clusters of artlessly scattered flowers.

Despite its size, the house captured the same quiet peace he'd felt at her place in Surfer's. He was given a guest room with floor-to-ceiling windows that overlooked a garden. While he was used to the sweep of wildflowers after rains in the desert, the vibrant color of everything was absorbing and overwhelming at once, from the royal blue and gold of the carpets that didn't have a constant layer of dust to sweep off, to the ruby red of flowers the size of his hand on the bushes below his window and the bright green of the lush ferns. Even at Surfer's, there'd been enough of a monochrome theme between sand and ocean to help him ease into a different environment.

Bemusedly, he also found several changes of clothes, slacks, shirts and collars, appropriate to diverse occasions and his size, waiting in the wardrobe for him. The room even had a private bath.

It underscored again that he was traveling with a woman of tremendous wealth, which gave him some discomfort, particularly when she seemed to be picking up the tab for everything. He'd had to argue to pay for his own meal and beer when they went to a restaurant, and she laughed at him for it, reminding him he was her employee. Which, of course, he was.

In the desert, you saved my life. You think I don't know you're the type of man who'd work ten jobs to care for his family? I don't need that. I need other things from you.

And do I provide them, my lady?

She'd given him a leisurely glance, that distant smile. "In spades."

Still, he felt damned uncomfortable with it, though he wasn't quite sure why. And he paid for the bloody beer.

Lady D, as she was known to the staff, had her own private wing, and it was clear no one ventured there unless invited. She underscored that herself when, arriving just before dawn, she left him with a lingering kiss and smile, and told him the maid would show him to his room. Then she disappeared.

As he prowled the room, he found himself tempted to reach out, try to speak to her. The bed looked solitary, lonely. He'd stay on the floor in his swag.

Bugger it. If she liked her alone time, he couldn't cast stones, could he? When she wanted him, she'd let him know. That suited him fine. It wasn't like he'd had the time to get so used to her company he couldn't do without it.

Dev, find the pen and pad in the desk. There are people I need you to contact today, arrange for their stores to be open after dark. Use my name and they'll agree.

Startled by her intrusion into his thoughts, he assumed, with some relief, that she hadn't heard them. He jotted down the names and stores she noted; then, before he could speak further, she added, *If you have any difficulties, see the staff and they'll help. Also, please check over the house accounts and review maintenance with the property manager, Mr. Forbes. As my third-marked servant, you would oversee the maintenance and operation of all my properties.* He sensed a smile in her voice then. *That should keep you busy, but be sure to get some sleep. I'll be up by sunset. Be ready to go with me.*

Keep him busy. Bollocks, she *had* heard his thoughts. However, it hadn't escaped his notice that part of this trip *was* about exposing him to the wide variety of things a third-marked servant was supposed to know and do, to see if he could handle it.

Right. Because, whereas being the bait for some psychopathic vampire's three-day game wouldn't faze him, knowing he had to inventory a pantry might send him screaming.

The echo of her laughter in his head had his gut easing, if not his loneliness.

For the next two nights, he revised his opinion of shopping as a leisure pursuit. A human woman could be singleminded in the pursuit of her goal, he knew, but a vampire female was dedicated to the hunt, and tireless. At the end of the evening, when they got in, he was exhausted by all the choices, decisions and—he shuddered—color swatches, such that he practically staggered, falling facedown on his swag. Almost exhausted enough to ignore the fact she was shutting him out of her room and sometimes even her mind, far more than she'd done before.

Hell, he missed her. And of course she knew it, so there was nothing to talk about. She was doing it for some mysterious purpose of her own, and he had too much pride to act shirty about it. But not too much pride to stay around and endure it.

Sometimes when he woke during daylight, he had to put his hand in his shorts, wrap his fingers around himself and imagine it as her. One thought of her sweet mouth closing over him, her hands digging into his thighs, and he exploded in a matter of seconds. It didn't fix the gnawing in his gut, though.

He got cranky about it, truth be told, though he didn't know if his irritation was primarily with himself. So he did his job. He handled the transportation details, coordinating with a freight company to have the items they would truck out to the station coincide with their return. Thinking ahead, he noted that they might also have items returning for consignment, and after he described some of the antiques and rich appointments Ian had preferred, the proprietor was more than happy to coordinate the details of that with him as well.

～

"Well, that's done," Danny said, as they stepped out of the drapery shop into the darkness of the near midnight time. "And thank God. You were starting to be grumpy. Next time I'll carry a few lollipops in my purse for when you get fussy. Of course"—she arched a brow at him—"the assistant to the proprietress in there seemed to perk up your spirits considerably."

"We were just chatting while you two discussed taffeta silk versus cotton. Floral versus animal prints."

"We did not discuss animal prints. And you won't distract me. You were flirting."

"She was just a nice girl, love. I was being nice back." It had been . . . nice to talk to someone simple and down to earth, who was going to university and liked going to the pictures with her friends on Saturday mornings.

Dev looked up to see Danny studying him with that doll's mask of hers, but at his puzzled regard, she turned away. "You'll be relieved to know our shopping trip is over. Tomorrow night will be for fun. Alistair is expecting us to join him and Lyssa for cocktails."

"Not dinner?" Dev tried to keep his tone bland, but she cocked a brow at him.

"Not dinner."

"No decapitations planned."

She stopped, looked back over her shoulder with narrowed eyes. "Not yet. But that could change."

He smiled, but when he moved to her, intending to offer his arm, she'd sidled off a few more steps, and was peering down the street. Dev followed her glance.

There was a man leaning up against the wall, smoking a rolled cigarette. A stockman on holiday probably, since he was wearing the clothes of one and looked as if he'd wandered out of one of the pubs at this late hour. He gave Danny a thorough, appraising look as she stopped there in the flood of the streetlight. In return, she cocked her head, the lamp catching the considering look in a predator's eye.

"I'm feeling hungry," she mused. "But for something a bit different. Wait right here in the shadows, Dev. Where he can't see you."

Before he could respond to that, she was moving down the street. As she came toward him, her walk changed to a provocative saunter that couldn't be mistaken for anything but an invitation. No decent woman would be out this time of night unescorted, anyhow. The man straightened from the wall. If he'd been a smarter bloke, he would have been wary, for she didn't look like any kind of whore. Of course, he hadn't been any smarter that first night, had he?

Dev set his jaw, tried to cross his arms and lean back against the wall, almost a mirror of how the man had been standing. It wasn't his business if she wanted some variety in her meals.

Except, for her, the taking of blood brought the same pleasure as sex. She'd said so, hadn't she?

That wasn't why he took after her. He wasn't sure why his feet were moving, but they were. When he got into the alley, she'd turned toward the stranger, her face lifted as if she might take a kiss. Dev gripped her upper arm and pulled her away from the muddled bugger.

"Rack off," he snarled at the man. The stockman needed no further invitation, apparently registering the blood in Dev's eye, the feral amusement in Danny's. But when he'd disappeared, that amusement disappeared. Reversing their grips, she slammed Dev against the brick so hard, his breath left him in a grunt. He tried to shove at her, but then he was gripping her waist, for she'd seized his jaw, jerked his head to the side and pierced him, her body pressing against him from neck to groin.

"You want to be mine," she whispered. "You are mine."

"No." He denied it, even as his body betrayed him, hardening against her, his hands under the shirt now, curling into her flesh.

He didn't want her feeding on others. Didn't want her to seek another man's flesh, his heat, to nourish her. Jesus, he was torn between being a moony, lovesick calf and wanting to cut and run.

Maybe she had the same problem, for with an oath, she pushed away from him, wiping at her lips with the back of her hand, her irises tinged with red.

Withdrawing his handkerchief from the jacket he wore, he reached out, slow, careful-like, for her expression was that of a spitting cat. She let him touch her, though, wipe the blood off the back of her knuckles. Keeping his gaze on that, he spoke, low.

"I was just being nice to her, love. She was young enough to be my daughter. Truth was, that's what it felt like, like I was talking to a kid. Though a pretty kid, I won't deny that." He pocketed the handkerchief with a bitter smile. "I told you when you took another man to your bed, that's when I'd leave. I don't expect you to have a lower standard. I'm all yours, until I've had enough or you send me away."

He glanced up then, and she was staring at the contact between their hands. "This isn't the way it's supposed to be, Dev. Between vampire and servant."

"What? They have a manual? Like Emily Post?"

She lifted her attention to his face then, and he shrugged. "You've made me learn all sorts of things these past couple days. I could have been reading that, brushing up for this get-together tomorrow night."

"Larrikin," she said at last, and he squeezed her hand.

"Daft girl. How could I want any other woman? I'm aching for you, love." He took advantage of the softening of her eyes to bring her closer, where her breasts brushed his chest. "Take me to your bed tonight," he demanded.

As she touched his lips, he caught a finger, drew it in, teased it with his tongue. He felt her pulse elevate, for he closed his hand on her wrist. When she drew back at last, he damn well knew she was aroused.

"Not tonight," she said softly. "And as stimulating as it was to be in your mind early yesterday morning, feeling you bring yourself to climax alone, I want you to keep your hands off what's mine. Then, tomorrow night, we'll see."

"More games, my lady?" He tried to push down his frustration. "It's never a game, Dev. Remember?"

∼

For some reason, Dev had pictured Lyssa as matronly. More than a thousand years old, after all. Danny was probably laughing at him, though he wouldn't know, since the bloody woman hadn't had a bloody word to say to him beyond perfunctory instructions since she'd left him in the foyer at dawn.

Lady Lyssa, Queen of the Far East Clan, had eyes with irises like jade, but large, dark pupils that could almost obliterate the color when her moods changed in intensity. The long black hair she had twisted over one shoulder went to her hips. He suspected whatever she chose to wear would be stunning on her, but tonight she wore a Japanese-style jade green and blue dress with mandarin collar and a single frog that reminded him somewhat of Chiyoko. However, this one of course covered most of her small bosom, though it was blessedly short, only to midthigh. She wore earrings that were emerald pendants set in a frame of dark blue sapphires to match the two colors of the embroidered silk.

Appearances aside, Dev had no doubt the woman was more than a thousand years old. When she took a seat on the beach chair Alistair had provided, her elegant hands rested comfortably on the chair arms, her posture erect. If he had been in the presence of Queen Elizabeth herself, Dev couldn't have been more aware that he was before royalty. Lady Lyssa's royalty wasn't merely the entitlement of blood or birth. She projected it in strength of purpose, character and sheer *power*.

When Danny looked at him certain ways, he *sensed* he was dealing with an otherworldly creature. In contrast, what emanated from Lyssa was like the punishing strength of dangerous surf, wave after wave of it, impossible to get your feet beneath you once you'd waded in past the ankles. Any man in his right mind would be scared shitless of her, vampire or not.

It was okay, Dev reminded himself. They weren't having dinner.

Just visiting, cocktails and such. Surely they only indulged in their depraved Roman-style orgies in conjunction with seven-course meals.

Alistair had a beautiful Victorian on a private stretch of beach outside of Brisbane, versus the more removed Surfer's Paradise. He'd had his staff set out chairs, a table with chessboard and refreshments for his guests, even a side table with a selection of beverages for the human servants, under a colorful pavilion he had permanently erected on the sand. The decorative wrought iron frame was wound with streamers and fresh tropical flowers. When the three vampires lost no time settling down to catch up with one another, Danny waved Dev away like a mother shooing her boy in short pants off to play.

He was distracted from that irritation when Alistair's servant joined them. Nina was well along pregnant. She took a quiet seat on a towel folded on the sandy surface between her Master's spread feet. While Alistair continued conversing with the two vampires, he stroked her hair, her temple resting against his knee. Like a devoted pet, Dev told himself. But he couldn't help remembering Danny's hand upon his hair, her soft eyes studying him with a gentleness he saw in Alistair's gaze when he occasionally glanced down at her. Or how sometimes Tina had leaned against him at night when she was carrying Rob, seeking that reassurance and bond at once.

If Danny had reminded Dev of Grace Kelly, Alistair was Rudolph Valentino, the sculpted planes of his face immortalized in black and white. Tall and virile, he had dark straight hair that followed the shape of his skull closely, and direct, piercing blue eyes beneath etched brows. A disturbingly sensual mouth, because it was distracting to either gender. Dev wondered if God had ever created a homely vampire.

"You must be Devlin."

Devlin turned to find himself face-to-face with Lyssa's servant. Thomas was about his height, an inch or so taller, with closely trimmed brown hair and wire spectacles over remarkably vivid gray eyes. His brows had a golden color that suggested, if his hair grew out, it would have blond streaks from the sun. For a monk, he had an athletic, lean build and a firm grip as he shook Dev's hand. "It's a pleasure." He gestured with two towels. "Why don't you and I wade out while our host and the ladies enjoy their game of chess? As long as your Mistress doesn't object?"

Dev slanted a glance toward Danny. "She doesn't seem to give a rat's arse, mate."

Thomas looked startled by the caustic observation, then an unexpected slow smile crossed his face. "You haven't been with her long, have you?"

~

"I figure it's temporary for the two of us. I mean, it happened out of circumstances, and you, Aapti, even Nina over there, you're all polished and groomed for this. So when she turns her sights on another bed warmer, or I get the notion it's time to go walkabout again, it will end. But on the other hand, I want to know more about being a servant. You know, until then. I don't want to botch the job, no matter the rest."

Jesus, Mary and Joseph, you could bury a man's Scotch-Irish Catholic blood, but it would boil up like tea in the billy in the face of a priest. 'Course, Thomas was a monk, not a priest, but it was all the same. The monk's first insightful observation, followed by some other pointed questions during their swim, had made it too bloody easy. Dev had nursed questions about being a servant since the beginning, and for the first time, he'd found someone more than obliging to answer them. The couple beers he'd had, plus the two rather potent drinks brought to them by Alistair's staff, hadn't hurt with the loosening of his tongue. Being third-marked apparently didn't inhibit the ability to hit the turps, though he'd hardly call a handful of stubbies that.

Now they sat side by side on the tide edge, letting the ocean waves lap at their toes. It had taken him aback, the lack of swim trunks, but Thomas had patiently explained that the vampires preferred to see their servants swim naked. So, after their clothes had been taken away by the far too helpful staff, they had enjoyed a swim, though Dev made use of the towel, wrapping it around his waist when they took a seat in the sand. Thomas simply folded and sat on his, obviously comfortable with nudity, or perhaps obeying his lady's wishes. Despite the fact he was a monk, he did have a body that would more than please a woman. Of course God had that kind of sense of humor.

Only one thing marred that perfection. Having been in war, Dev knew there were things one didn't ask another bloke unless he volunteered to talk about it. But it was hard not to let his eyes stray to Thomas's back as the monk leaned over to take up another, smaller towel and mop his face, reclaim the wire-rimmed glasses he'd left on them. Old scars, but they'd been deep ones. Lash marks, so many that they striped his back, made it hard to figure what the count had been.

"My fealty oath to my lady. The Ritual of Binding to a vampire queen."

When Thomas turned, he lifted a shoulder at Dev's expression. "The lash marks. That's what you wanted to know. You might as well ask the question if you're staring."

"Sorry, mate," Dev offered. "Bloody hell, though. She did this to you? Lady Lyssa?"

"Yes," Thomas said, unperturbed. "Well over a century ago, when I chose to become her full servant. In order for a full servant to scar, his vampire Mistress, or Master, must mark the weapon with their own blood before they use it on the servant. She had me draw the blade across her arm, and anoint the flogger myself. Then she did the honors."

Dev looked up the beach. He'd caught Danny indulging in a few nice, long looks at him as he swam in the waves. But otherwise she seemed unconcerned with him, playing chess with Lyssa and laughing at the dry comments Alistair was throwing in. The vampire queen even had a faint smile on her face.

"Ah, hell, I'm in the wrong bloody place." Dev scrubbed frustrated hands through his wet hair, slicking it back. "I should—"

"Keep doing exactly what your heart tells you to do."

Dev started as Thomas reached out and rubbed a quick hand over his head. A tousle, the reassuring gesture an older man would offer to a young boy, and strewth if it didn't actually make him feel a bit better. The bloke had a way about him, for certain. That could be a problem. Looking down, Dev spoke to the ground between his feet. "Are you fucking with me, Thomas?"

"Excuse me?" The monk sounded startled.

"I think the lady Lyssa had the staff bring us those drinks. I think you're getting me to talk because she wants to know more about Danny. I don't know all the politics, as I said. But I've learned enough to know that it's entirely possible every vampire she meets either wants her dead or between her legs, so if you're up to either of those—"

"Good God, no." Thomas's eyes crinkled in a smile. It was reassuring, but Dev held Thomas's gaze, saying nothing. "It's not Danny she wants to know about," the monk relented at last. "She already knows a great deal about her. She wants to know about you. Though I'm glad to see you're already paying attention to what's going on around you," he added. "And even more importantly, what's going on around her."

"So why does she want to know about me?"

"Lyssa is very fond of Danny. She's worried about her for quite some time. Danny is different from other vampires."

"A gentler sort," Dev remembered. Thomas nodded, and his gray eyes sobered.

"Yes. Which shouldn't be a flaw, but you can't change the reality in which you live. She has no political aspirations, but she's not willing to have anyone tell her what to do, either. Lyssa has hoped, these past few decades, that she would find a servant to help her. On the other hand, she believes Danny held off so long in choosing a servant because she was afraid of shortening a servant's life, if she was killed."

Dev's back straightened, and he set aside the beer. "What the hell does that mean?" His gaze flickered back up the sand to her, verifying she was still there, safe. As well as noting the ripple of her hair, the light smile and delicate movement of her hands as she moved a chess piece.

"It means," Thomas said patiently, "she either has to be willing to be in charge, or bow down. If she does neither, she's in no-man's-land,

and she will die there. Danny has traveled extensively, refusing to swear loyalty to anyone. Cut herself loose from the protection of her family with her falling-out with her mother. I suspect you don't understand what a miracle that is, or how that makes her such a desirable feather in the cap to others. If you carry a death wish, Devlin, you couldn't have picked a prettier one."

Dev stared at him. "Nobody's getting to her while I live. Or making her do anything she doesn't want to do."

"Your lady has spoken very warmly of you. I understand why." Thomas tapped his temple at Dev's surprised look. "When she chooses, my lady Lyssa can allow me to hear their conversations."

"While mine won't speak to me at all," Dev said, despite himself. "I feel like she's put a fucking wall between us these past couple days."

"She's chosen to avoid having a full servant for nearly two hundred years. I'd say what's remarkable is that she's let you in at all, not that she has a few days here or there where she keeps her own counsel. She's likely dealing with the way she feels for you. It's difficult for vampires to figure out the relationship, the first time they have it. It's much like a crush, very passionate and romantic. That's normal, but she's worrying it's more than that. The process of establishing some distance to prove to herself she's still in control is as natural as any of it."

It all sounded rational. And annoying. Dev picked up his beer, took another hard swig.

"Pay attention to my words now, because you won't hear them from a vampire." Thomas reached out, took the beer from his hand and set it aside. Anyone else, Dev would have thumped in the teeth for that, but Thomas's expression conveyed the gentle rebuke and obedience only a priest could. Even sitting there without a stitch on his knackers.

"She's your Mistress. Your employer," Thomas amended, with a note of irony to his voice as he registered Dev's discomfort. "How many things in this world are labeled one thing, when we all know they are another? The human servant is the cornerstone, Dev, when a vampire allows the relationship to be what it should be. If you are the person meant to serve that role, you already feel it. That's why you get uneasy when she shuts you out. If you both decide the bond is permanent, as it grows, she'll do that less and less. But vampires are not humans. They'll never feel the same responsibility to ease our worries as we do for them."

"I guess I should count myself lucky that her silent treatment is the worst thing I'll face today," Dev said after a bit. "I was worried this would be another thing like that dinner with Ruskin. But you're a monk, and now that I know Alistair's servant . . ." He stopped. "He doesn't make her do things *now*, does he?"

"Vampire children are rare, Dev," Thomas reassured him. "Alistair is very devoted to Nina. If he thought something as simple as walking would cause stress, he'd pick her up and carry her everywhere himself." He hesitated. "However, as much as I hate to do this, you *did* ask me to help you understand more about vampires. And I'm afraid you're suffering a false sense of security."

Dev closed his eyes. "I've changed my mind. I don't want to know more."

Thomas chuckled. "Dev, I'm unusual in that my celibacy is permitted within the boundaries of my service to Lady Lyssa. Not that she doesn't enjoy tormenting me with it. I help bathe her, do her hair, massage oils into her skin . . ." He blew out a breath at Dev's look. "It amuses her, to torment me that way. That's part of what vampires are. While I try very hard to remain humble, sometimes I feel there should be a special room in heaven for me. Or that I should have myself castrated," he added dryly.

"You love her."

Thomas looked toward him, some of the humor dying out of his eyes. "Yes. But I do not love God less. And so I hold to my vows." He sighed. "My lady asked me to break my vows of celibacy once, to prove my loyalty to her. And yet, she has honored my vow ever since, no matter how others, even her own husband, have challenged it." A shadow crossed his gaze. When Thomas turned his head, looking out toward the ocean, Dev understood that was a dark area he was not invited to enter. They sat in silence for a while, Thomas a silhouette.

"Because of her status, her indulgence of my vow is excused. Vampires do not tolerate or comprehend a vampire who doesn't offer her servant for sexual entertainments, unless there is an accepted excuse, like Nina's. And whenever vampires get together, there are *always* sexual entertainments. It's like . . ." He considered it, thinking. "Like when humans get together for dinner. They eat. That's what a dinner is. When vampires get together, they expect to satiate a different appetite.

"As a student of history," Thomas mused, "I believe the tradition developed a long time ago, when some intelligent vampire realized that vampires would be less likely to kill one another if they could indulge a different form of lust when they gathered socially or on business of mutual benefit. Very politic."

"Ah, Christ." Dev lay back in the sand, stared up at the stars. "Guess I couldn't throw a sickie and get out of it, could I?"

"Think you signed up for the wrong job," Thomas said, with a half smile. "You're not working on a factory line. And your head will clear within the hour. We can get drunk, but the duration is much shorter."

"So that's what they get with this third-mark gig. A permanent sex slave." It sounded ridiculous, coming off his tongue, but as Dev thought of the different things Danny had done with him, the way she'd deprived him the past couple days, denying him the ability to relieve his simmering lust so it had built ever higher, it made an alarming kind of sense.

"Vampires are extremely carnal creatures, Dev. They need sexual interaction almost as much as they need blood. But a third-mark . . ." Thomas's words stopped, his gaze drifting to Lyssa. "This isn't just about sex, or even blood. And it's definitely not a half-measure thing. I think you know that. Think you both know that.

"I don't claim to understand or know why a person becomes a vampire's servant. You just know it's meant to be. The moment is coming, very soon, when you have to accept it, or walk away. Third-mark is being *everything* to your Master or Mistress. We help them dress, make sure they look appropriate before other vampires, since they can't see mirrors. We run their houses, handle daytime business transactions. We serve their sexual needs and, though you'll never hear a one of them admit it, their emotional needs."

He nodded. "That group up there, they're a little more informal than most, because Danny and Lyssa get along so well, and Alistair is very devoted to Lyssa. He's almost like a son to her, because she sired him three hundred years ago and mentored him through most of his life. But vampires never truly relax their guard around one another. They can't. They need companions, someone they can trust. They can trust us, because they can be in our heads whenever they wish. We are here for their needs."

"Pets," Dev said, bitterness creeping into his tone.

Thomas gave him a shrewd look. "What bothers you more? Thinking she believes that, or knowing that when she looks your way, you don't give a damn if she does? And you shouldn't give a damn about it. It's bullshit, as well. We're not pets. We're human servants to vampires, and it's a relationship like nothing you've ever had in your life. Tell yourself you love her or don't love her, it doesn't matter. If you are meant to be her full servant, you are bound together in a way that would tear out your heart and half the things in your gut if you decided to walk away from it."

"Jesus, I met her a week or so ago."

"And when she feeds, do you turn your head, offer your throat, before she even asks?"

Dev shrugged, but Thomas was watching his face. "If I were a Baptist, I'd bet good money you won't leave her," the monk concluded with a somber twinkle. "You'll likely reach some point where you tear loose, needing to prove something to yourself. But within a couple days, your gut will cramp with how lonely you are for her. Something calls a person to be a vampire's true servant, something more than fascination or a fear of death. It's a desire to surrender, only to that vampire."

"I suspect I'd feel a lot more comfortable with the idea if it wasn't put in those terms."

"No doubt," Thomas said dryly with a smile. "But I suspect you're as brutally honest with yourself as a man can be. If I dressed it up for you, you'd tell me to bugger off or speak plain." Sobering again, he looked toward Lyssa. "Vampires such as my Mistress frown on vampires who abuse or even kill their servants, though it happens, far more frequently than it should. Because it's a betrayal, for the reasons I just noted. Whether conscious or not, when you do accept the idea, you're offering them everything you are. To devalue that, to throw that gift away or, worse, brutalize it, a vampire might as well brutalize their own soul. Because we become that much a part of them. The question of inferiority or superiority, the right or wrong of it, becomes irrelevant. We are interwoven."

He gave Dev another straightforward look. "As to the issue of boundaries and limitations, you'll find eventually that doesn't concern you as much as wanting to please her does. Even as you occasionally—or not so occasionally—have the desire to choke the life out of her for acting so superior sometimes."

There was a glint in the monk's eyes at this, and Dev swore he saw Lyssa flick an amused glance toward him before she returned her attention to the game. It made him swallow, because something did, in fact, cramp in his gut. He missed having Danny in his mind like that, as short a time as he'd had it. But how could he ask her to reassure him, when he hadn't even made his own decision?

Thomas touched his arm then. "Time to go in and get ready for cocktails and appetizers. Thank you for the swim. And good luck this evening."

"Don't be smug." Dev shot him a narrow look. "It doesn't suit a man of God."

"Are you so sure it's smugness? It might be envy." Thomas laughed. "I've seen a great deal of these vampire *social* events, Dev. While they can be harrowing to the servants involved, one thing they never lack is pleasure. The stripping away of all shields is the most frightening part. Once you surrender to your Mistress, there's no worry in any of that, anymore."

"Like surrendering to God?" Dev offered the resentful barb, but the monk didn't seem offended by his defensiveness.

"Very similar. I'm not so sure that the hand of God isn't in this relationship," Thomas added. "Who is to say a full servant isn't the one who helps a vampire remember there is something in this world to embrace other than bloodlust? And if you think that is a small thing, think how powerful and intelligent these beings are, and what they could do to this world, if they put no constraints on their behavior."

On that enigmatic note, with another affectionate squeeze of Dev's shoulder, Thomas excused himself to change for the more formal indoor gathering.

~

Dev had been given a room to wash up and reattire himself as well. He was tempted to barricade himself in there. 'Course, he couldn't argue with the household uniform for the all-female staff. Black short skirts fluffed out with a layered slip so that it was clear they were wearing no underwear. The only thing on their upper bodies was a string of pearls, run between their pierced nipples. Chiyoko had worn nipple jewelry, but he'd never seen pierced ones before. They drew his eyes, no matter how hard he tried not to stare. All the women wore their hair swept up and pinned, showing slim, artery-rich throats.

"Alistair, you *really* need some male staff." He heard Lady Lyssa make the comment as he approached the spacious solarium. As he stepped in, Dev saw it provided a dramatic nighttime view of the ocean and white sands. After seating Lyssa, Alistair returned to the couch, where Nina was curled up on a pillow, dozing. When he sat, she scooted closer, and he gathered her in, putting her head on his thigh, his hand lying on her hip.

"Now, my lady, you know I have some excellent male flesh working in the stables. You've already sampled it. Don't deprive a man the simple pleasures of his home."

Thomas brought Lyssa her wine. When he proffered his wrist, she shook her head but held the glass as he produced a slim, elegant blade and made a deft cut, letting the blood from his body trickle into the crystal. She swirled it with her finger, but then spread the damp, wine-stained tip over his cut, brought it to her lips for a single, easy caress that clotted the flow.

It was so painfully obvious Lyssa communicated with the monk often. Though they spoke very little aloud to one another, the compatibility between their movements and actions was uncanny. More than a hundred years they'd been together, Thomas had told him. What would it be like to share that time with Danny? Cultivate that closeness?

No, he couldn't think like that. Hell, only a few days ago, he was living basically hour to hour, and now he was thinking a hundred years? Jesus.

When Thomas bowed, and stepped back to take his place along the wall, Dev hoped to see Danny entering. He'd wanted to come in after his lady, though he suspected that was a breach of etiquette of some kind. Instead, she was exercising a woman's prerogative to be late. Probably on purpose.

"So you're Danny's servant-in-training, so to speak. Come over here and let me have a closer look."

Definitely on purpose.

He'd stood quietly by the door, thinking that was the most unobtrusive location. He wasn't a coward, by any means, but he had a healthy sense of self-preservation. Nevertheless, there was no mistaking Lady Lyssa had issued it as a command, one she expected to be obeyed. Trying to quell his uneasiness, Dev moved around the chair and came to stand before her. She was petite, and it seemed logical and not too much of a compromise to take a knee before her. As she watched him in that peculiar, still way, again he couldn't imagine any human spending more than a breath in her company without realizing she wasn't mortal.

"Nice. You have manners, and can think on your feet, perhaps a little too much. You're very rough around the edges as of yet. But I'm not surprised at Danny's taste."

"I agree," Alistair observed. "He's got a style to him. Very . . . appealing."

"Hmm." Lyssa touched Dev's face, the sweep of hair he'd had the rare occasion to brush, settling her hand on his shoulder. It was peculiar to sit still like this, her tracing the bones of his face as intimately as a lover while she studied him like a bug under a microscope.

He'd donned the broadcloth jacket over shirt and slacks again, the clothing Danny had provided him at her Brisbane home. Her gaze coursed over him now, slow, taking an accounting of every length of limb, the broadness of his chest, lingering at his groin in a most unsettling way. "I'll be interested to see how she lets us play with you tonight. She told me you were fearless. I think she told us that to give us a challenge. Do you agree? Are you fearless, Dev?"

"Depends, love. I—" He about bit through his tongue as her brow lifted and Alistair choked on his wine. "My lady," he corrected himself hastily, feeling a flush stain across his cheeks. Hell, he didn't know how to deal with this class of people. "I'm sorry. I meant, it depends, my lady."

Dev glanced toward Thomas. The monk's face was mostly impassive, though his gaze flickered, a warning. Bloody hell. Dev jerked his attention back to Lyssa.

"Keep your attention on the vampire who is addressing you," she rebuked him, confirming his error. "But it's good for servants to have mentors among our ranks, to help you understand us better. You chose wisely with Thomas."

Shifting her attention, she nodded toward Nina. "Alistair, let Thomas rub Nina's feet. She's been overdoing it in the kitchen again, to make sure the appetizers and sweets your chef has prepared please us."

"I'd be grateful." Alistair nodded, then gave Nina a light pat on the bum. "I'll punish you for that later." He gave her a warm look that made Nina smile a shy but entirely unconcerned smile, lowering her eyes so her lashes fanned her cheeks.

Thomas moved to comply, kneeling at the woman's feet to begin a massage of swollen ankles. Lyssa turned her attention back to Dev, and something shifted in those unnatural eyes, something that had tension drawing up from his testicles to his throat like a rubber band that would snap and sting the hell out of him. However, she merely waved him off.

"You may rise and return to the door. She's coming down the stairs now, and no vampire likes to see her servant at the feet of another female when she enters a room."

He returned to his position, relieved, as Danny did in fact make her entrance. The one thing about these gatherings he could honestly admit liking was the way she dressed for them. Tonight she wore a black dress with spaghetti straps. The deep-cut neckline was draped, the skirt of the dress so snug it was obvious she wore nothing beneath it. She also wore stilettos that put her eye to eye with Dev as she stopped before him, gave him an assessing glance. The only jewelry she wore was a tiny gold cross on a long chain, giving him another myth about vampires to discard. Simple gold dangles adorned her ear lobes. She didn't have pierced ears, so they were affixed with a gold cuff high on the curve of her ear, and attached with another cuff a little lower, decorating the entire shell. Her hair was up, and scattered with gold dust, further adorned with a comb that had a porcelain blue bird in it. He thought she looked somewhat like a dark elfin creature from the Underworld.

"You must have an excellent lady's maid, Danny," Lyssa observed.

"Thank you, my lady. Actually, this was thanks to the help of one of Alistair's people."

You look beautiful.

You look positively edible. After several days of nothing more provocative than instructions on shipping furniture, she staggered him with a flash of images, goading his cock to instant attention.

Christ, love. You might want to tone it down.

She smiled, moved into the room to take a seat in a wing-backed chair, leaning back and crossing her legs with a show of thigh that Dev sourly noted Alistair openly appreciated. The downside to her distracting fashions—he had to share his enjoyment with other leering buggers.

As the staff brought in wine, tea and appetizers, the three spoke comfortably of things that were occurring in Alistair's territory, improvements in commerce, Australia's continued allegiance to Britain versus control of its own governance, the possible visit by Queen Elizabeth and its impact. In some ways, it was little different from the conversations he'd hear at any other gathering of Aussie urbanites, except he was listening to three intelligent vampires who had

centuries of experience between them in the cycles of change in governance. At another time, without apprehension of what else the
evening might bring, he would have found it interesting.

"Well, I will say the new immigration policy is bringing them
into Oz in droves, so we're finally getting some decent food in this
part of the world. My latest cook is from Italy. These appetizers will
taunt you to come back for dinner soon, Danny." Alistair sent an
amused look toward her. "Since you insist on staying out in the bush,
I'm sure you're more than ready to see something on a plate other
than lizards and kangaroo."

"Well, we have other offerings, but when you visit, I'll make sure
a bowl of Bogong moths is prepared specially for you," Danny returned sweetly. "Seriously, I'd love to have you and Nina out once
the baby is born. I still can't believe you're going to be a father."

"A frightening thought, for certain." Alistair cast a fond look
down at his reposed servant. "No one was more surprised than I
when she conceived."

"I was," Lyssa remarked. "I didn't think you'd leave off your strap-
ping footy boys long enough to dip your wick into a female. Are you
sure it's yours? Your ego has been known to inflate enough to crowd
out truth."

As they bantered, Dev decided there was another conversation
going on between Master and servant. For Nina had twined her
hand with his on her hip, and was tracing the creases between his
fingers in a decidedly stimulated way. He thought of Aapti and Chiyoko again, their obvious enthusiasm to flaunt their sensuality. Was
it just a matter of time, experience, as Thomas said? And was it a
matter of "the mind doth protest too much," given that his cock
wasn't protesting at all, but rising to the occasion like a damn cheer-
leader, merely contemplating what might happen tonight?

"Nina's been mine from the beginning." Alistair defended his
honor without rancor. "And even if I couldn't plumb her mind to the
depths of her soul, I would not doubt her."

Lyssa nodded, studying their linked hands as well. "Then we will
guard her carefully, Alistair."

Alistair's grip tightened on Nina. "No one will touch her," he said, a dangerous look crossing his face. "Or our child."

"They better not," Lyssa responded. "Or I'll feel I've failed in everything I've taught you."

The dessert was brought out then, a confection of chocolate, cream and strawberries shaped into a star on each plate, and the tense moment passed as Alistair smoothly became the affable host again.

Who would harm the baby, love?

He wasn't sure Danny would answer him, but he couldn't not ask, not after that frisson of danger had rippled through the room and he saw worry cross Nina's delicate features. When Danny's answer came, he felt an easing of his shoulders from the connection, though her answer itself was far from reassuring.

No one would harm the baby. But there are vampires who would try to pass it off as their own if they could take the mother before she gives birth. They would kill Nina the moment the child was born, because she would be only a liability to them then and they would want the baby to blood-bond with them.

Alistair had moved their intertwined hands down to cup over Nina's belly, a reassurance to the mother-to-be. Dev felt a surge of protective anger himself. *Lady Lyssa might have waited until Nina wasn't in the room.*

No. It may irritate him, but Nina needs to be as alert as he is. He knows that. He's just being a typically overprotective male. He heard the smile in her voice, and again, it gave him a shot of warmth. *Nina may seem fragile, but she is quite capable. However, it's another reason Lyssa is here. She'll provide additional protection until the baby is born next month.*

Alistair spoke then. "Lady Lyssa, as our guest of honor, would you choose the evening's entertainment, while we enjoy our dessert?"

And just like that, Dev's warm feeling disappeared, swept away by anxiety.

20

"Though of course," Alistair continued, "I beg the indulgence of a protective father-to-be and prohibit Nina from anything too exerting. With your monk enjoying a similar status, though no one in the vampire world but you understands why"—he apparently had the privilege of teasing his sire—"we can involve the house staff, though regrettably they're not as well versed in such matters."

"I like being a woman of mystery." Lyssa took a small bite, her eyes closed as she sampled the dessert. "Marvelous, Alistair. My compliments to the chef." Then she opened her eyes, turned them to Devlin. "I don't think we'll need any of the household staff. I'd like to see how Devlin handles pain at the hands of his Mistress. See if he will submit to it."

Danny had lifted her fork with a bite of the chocolate star and was inhaling it, her delicate nostrils flared. As far as Dev could tell, the suggestion didn't cause even a hitch to her movement. "Chocolate liqueur . . . A very nice touch." She placed the morsel in her mouth, savoring before performing a comfortable single swallow, all her vampire constitution would accept of human food, that one tantalizing taste.

"Dev," she said at last. "Please go to the room Alistair provided and bring me your whip and your hunting knife. When you retrieve them, strip off all your clothes and leave them in the room."

A pair of household staff entered as if summoned by Alistair, to shift a decorative silk screen panel, revealing a spoked wheel hung parallel to the floor from a large hook embedded in the ceiling beam. From the sections of the wheel hung a series of chains.

Can you submit to me, bushman?

As she turned her head farther, he locked gazes with her. The soft wetness of her lips, her long golden lashes, even the porcelain trifle in her hair, all spoke of a beautiful, desirable woman. Most men would say they'd do anything for the touch of such a creature, the privilege of her bed. But taking that step with this one was more than an empty declaration.

At the dinner with Ruskin and Ian, she'd had him do something he'd like to do anyway. Even pulling the other two women into it had fallen in line with male fantasy. Uncomfortable and over the top, it had still been doable.

What are you willing to do for me, Dev? Be for me? You come back, you'll be forced to face that question. Maybe it's best if neither of us ever know the answer. If you leave, before or after, I will not suffer consequences from this company as I would have with Ruskin or Ian.

He gave her a bow, lifting his head to meet her eyes. "I will return, my lady."

Maybe he was the only one who saw the faint tremor that went through her hand, resting on her thigh. If he hadn't seen it, perhaps he would have chosen differently, but he didn't think so. Thomas was right. There was a moment when you accepted things, or walked away.

Not only did he suspect whatever would happen in the next few hours was going to answer that question, he believed she'd planned for it to be brought to a head tonight. He understood Danny's quiet for the past few days better now. His lady had been thinking. She was tired of waiting. She wanted it settled. Whatever happened, while he was sure that was probably for the best, he couldn't deny the panicked feeling roiling in his gut, his surprise that she hadn't given him any warning, any time to prepare for this. He perhaps could handle what was about to happen in this room, but could he handle walking away, if that *was* the answer?

◦

When he returned, stripped as she'd requested and carrying the whip and knife, her expression was unreadable, her mind closed. That was unsettling, particularly since he was still recovering from the trauma of stepping out of his room in the altogether and running right into a maid coming down the hall with a stack of towels. That stack was the only thing that averted a pleasant collision between her generous bare breasts and his chest. She'd given a startled yelp and blushed, but when he snagged the top towel, which turned out to be a hand towel, he'd heard her whisper to another maid, "I don't think that's going to be big enough," as they went giggling on down the hall.

He didn't dare look back to see if they were ogling his arse, because he was fairly certain they were. Well, hell. He'd swum this way with Thomas, had stripped down in the army and in the Outback for years in front of the eyes of God and everyone else. And of course, Danny had told him things about vampires who refused to let their servants wear clothes at all when they were in the privacy of their properties. If it was expected behavior, like the attire of Alistair's house staff, why should he be embarrassed?

So he'd pushed down his discomfort and made it back to the solarium, though he did use the towel, tossing it away before he turned the corner and stepped into the room.

Stand there, Dev.

He came to a halt while everyone in the room, with the exception of Thomas, studied the breadth of his shoulders, the slope of his chest, the tapering of waist and hip. He should have shot through like a Bondi tram and kept on going.

"Holy God," Alistair said reverently. "You have a good eye, Danny."

Okay, that was it. He was mad as a hatter for not bolting.

Then Danny rose from her chair, studying him as she balanced herself and took off one shoe, then the other, a curiously domestic gesture, losing several inches of height as she went to stockinged feet. She extended her hand. "Bring me the whip and the knife."

Having been in combat, he had the same hesitancy as most about giving a weapon to another, particularly a person who'd made it quite clear she intended to use it on him. He knew what the hunting blade could do to flesh, after all. Though of course he had no one but himself to blame. He was the daft bugger so accustomed to having the bloody things close to hand he couldn't leave them at her house. Hell, he'd been uncomfortable leaving them in the guest room.

Nevertheless, he crossed the floor to her, came close enough that he could have reached out, drawn her to him . . .

Setting the knife aside, she threaded the whip through her fingers, reminding him of their first night. *I have some skill in using a whip as well, bushman.* Using his closeness against him, she looped it once around his head, letting it settle around his throat. Watching him all the while, she slowly drew in the slack with both hands until it cinched against his windpipe, until his breath registered the restriction and his heart rate began to speed up.

"Are you prepared to accept pain from me?" Her voice was a murmur, but his gaze was on the quickened pulse in her own throat. Somewhere in the haze of oxygen deprivation, he wondered if it was excitement.

"I can handle anything you've got, love."

Alistair's lips curved. Nina's doe brown eyes got wider. Lyssa and Thomas remained expressionless, though Dev could imagine Thomas inwardly rolling his eyes and thinking he was a complete fool. He didn't disagree.

"New servants are such a delight," Alistair observed, and asked for more wine to be brought in.

"Go stand over there," Danny ordered, yanking none-too-gently to bring the whip slithering off him and back to the floor.

The chains had been unraveled, and four manacles hung from the iron wheel. With the spokes, the manacles could be hooked at a narrow or wide span. Two longer manacles went all the way to the floor, their chains swaying slightly in the sea breeze that was filtering through the screens, for Alistair had ordered the windows opened.

He made his feet move. When he got there and turned, she was standing in the same place. "Raise your arms over your head."

When he complied, Thomas moved from behind Lyssa and came to him. The monk's gaze met his briefly before he reached up, guided Dev's hands into the manacles and locked them into place. There was a switch panel in this corner, and when Thomas flipped one, a mechanical whir ensued. The chain retreated, drawing up the slack, so that Dev felt his heels leave the floor. Quelling the sudden clutch of panic, he watched Thomas then kneel to clamp a soldered pair of cuffs around his ankles. He also wrapped a strap around his thighs, cinching in tight so his legs were held together, ankles to crotch, making his testicles a swollen nest for his rising cock. Since Thomas appeared to be doing this without any verbal instruction, he determined the "guest of honor" was providing the guidance. When he looked toward Lyssa, she was appreciating the stretch and strain of his body.

Danny had moved closer, was examining his bonds. She tilted her head toward Thomas. "That's good. Take him up."

Before he could get his mind wrapped around that, Thomas had flipped two more switches, made several adjustments, and Dev's feet left the floor altogether, which put his weight against the wrist manacles. Thomas had adjusted the chains at opposing points on the diameter of the wheel, balancing it so his arms were stretched out, almost four feet between them. God, this hurt the shoulders. He suspected the vampire queen had done some time with the Spanish Inquisitors.

Then Danny moved in, close enough to touch, only he couldn't touch her. Instead, she ran her palm up his chest, over the raven mark, then back down, slow. He noticed then she'd set aside the whip and held the knife, the blade catching the candlelight. While Alistair had electricity, like most vampires he seemed to prefer candlelight, which made Dev wonder if their eyes preferred darkness entirely. Which also explained why there'd been no torchlight around the covered tent where they'd played chess.

"I'd be worried about a servant who used knives like that." Alistair chuckled. "He might cut off something you could use later."

"He's very careful about his knives. Takes good care of them. The way he takes good care of me."

Dev turned his attention to her still face at those words. He wished so damned much she would talk to him.

What would you have me say, bushman?

He closed his eyes. *Anything, my lady.*

She caressed his chest again, only this time she did it with the tip of the sharpened blade, drawing it down his sternum. When he opened his eyes, she still hadn't taken her eyes off his face. But she drew the knife down, down, sliding left to follow the pectoral to the nipple, bore down as she cut him there. His breath clogged in his throat as she bent and teased the nub with her tongue, taking the blood away.

"He didn't even flinch," Lyssa murmured. "Are you warning him, Danny?"

"No. No warnings."

"He *is* fearless," Alistair said.

No matter what I do, do not go to that still place in your head. I forbid it. Stay with me.

You only have to ask, my lady. He couldn't seem to summon her familiar name right now, though he knew that might have helped keep some sense of an equal connection between them, even if it was only an illusion. The title seemed more intuitive, more from his gut, despite a confusing swirl of emotions.

Her blue eyes were very close when the blade sliced across the other nipple. He shuddered at it, but again, didn't flinch. Wherever she went with that knife, he was ready for it. He just wasn't sure he could withstand the emotions, the power of them growing stronger with every pain, with the contrasting gentle touch of her hands. He wanted to disobey, needed to go to that still place before they all spilled out and he couldn't control them.

"More . . ." he muttered. *Please, God, let her hurt me more, give me the pain, because I can't handle the rest.*

You don't need to control or handle anything, Dev. Don't you yet understand that I can handle your rage? Don't shut down. Let yourself understand why you're doing exactly what I want you to do, even as you're daring me to make it hurt more than your flesh can bear. Is it your soul that needs scourging? Do I need to cut or lash you that deeply?

He yanked against the chains, forcing his body against her, which, as he twisted, made the knife arc over his abdomen, slicing through his epidermis. *Damn it, use the thing instead of talking me to death.*

He never saw her move back, but now she was truly out of reach, though her eyes were on the wound he'd made her inflict on him. The blood streamed down his stomach, fast enough he felt it tease his cock, run down the base to his testicles. *Thinking of dinner, love? Here it is. You just have to get on your knees for it.*

Her gaze flicked up to him, her mouth tightening. She brought the knife up quite deliberately, ran her delicate tongue along the edge of the blade. *I don't need a servant whose only reason for serving me is to exercise some twisted punishment upon himself.*

"Blindfold him," she said, before he could think of a response, though he felt the rage of it sing through his muscles, his clenched jaw, even the hardened state of his cock. "And bring me a gag."

~

Apparently, while most people had extra cloth napkins and spare silverware sets handy to the solarium, Alistair kept other things. Thomas removed a cut blindfold from the drawer of an antique wooden cabinet and came to Dev.

"Do not put that fucking thing on my face," he warned.

"Step back, Thomas." Danny took it from the monk's hand and came right to Dev. When he tried to avoid her, he found Alistair behind him, the vampire seizing his hair in hard hands, holding him still as she fitted the blindfold and then thrust something like a rubber ball past his teeth, using straps to hold it in place that Alistair buckled in back.

He struggled, snarled, made the wheel turn and his shoulder joints scream. As darkness descended, he was even more aware of their attention on him, the heat of the candlelight warming his skin.

"He's bloody marvelous, Lady D," Alistair said. "Holy God, that cock alone is worth salivating over."

Tell that son of a bitch to stay away from me.

The lash came down hard on his flank, telling him that Alistair had moved back, but only to give Danny room with the whip. It cut deep, arching him forward with an exhalation. *You do not command me, Dev. Not ever.*

Another strike, this one high on his shoulder, and Jesus, but she didn't believe in preliminaries. She was going for blood. Another, across the center, and he could imagine the artistically placed three stripes as her body brushed against his. Her mouth touched his skin, feeding on the blood coming from those welts. *Is this what you craved, Dev? I can make it hurt so badly you will beg me to stop.*

God help him, but his cock responded again, leaping at her as her hand caressed him, clasped the base and tugged.

All mine. My possession, my slave. My servant . . .

Had she intended he hear those fervent words, the desire behind them? He didn't belong to anyone. He didn't.

Unless he chose to.

Holy . . . Apparently she'd pulled something else from those drawers, for he felt her hand, now slick with some type of oil, teasing the crease of his buttocks. *Danny, no . . . Women don't do this . . .* And yet, even as he tried with futile effort to tense against her, her much stronger fingers simply found him, eased into that tight, un-initiated opening.

"So you've never had anyone there . . . Interesting, considering how much you like to take women there."

"Really? Nina loves it." From Alistair's voice, it sounded like he was back on his couch, which Dev knew could be false reassurance, but he'd take anything he could get right now.

"That's a fortunate thing, considering your usual preferences," Lyssa noted dryly.

Dev tried to draw a steadying breath during the banter, but Danny didn't give him the opportunity. She'd withdrawn, moved back again, and the whip popped across his shoulders. She went for the sting this time, not the cut, and she worked it with a will, proving she was as capable as any cattle drover he'd ever met. His body jumped and flinched so that she had him dancing in the chains, twisting, making them clank in a primal rhythm. Because of his suspended state, he had no anchor, no ground to hold on to. While his shoulder joints were screaming, apparently he was putting on quite an erotic display, if the appreciative comments from the other two vampires were any indication.

The spoked wheel holding the manacles spun him this way and that as she struck. With the blindfold on, he had no orientation, nothing but the sensations closing in. Pain, blood trickling down his body, her perfume, coming close, moving back again. The tease of her hand, stroking his cock. Her lips brushing his chest.

Reaction was spiraling up from inside him. An overwhelming sense of panic that caused him to snarl, but his aching jaw was bound up by the hard rubber of the gag. Then he tried to go to that state of stillness, his promise be damned, and found, with true panic, he was too far gone for that. That whip and the rousing touch of her mouth and hands gave him no escape from what he'd allowed her to do. Would allow her to do.

Abruptly, the spinning stopped, her hands steadying his body in front. It took a few moments, but some of the dull roaring in his mind eased off, enough for him to realize that Alistair had put on music, so that he was hearing the drifting and sorrowful "Für Elise." Soothing. Setting a different tone.

Now when her arm curled around his neck, she brought his head down to hers to play over his stretched mouth with her lips. She'd taken down her bodice, for her bare breasts pressed against him, the soft, willing flesh against the mark she'd given him. The raven, the all-knowing, all-wise. The bird who knew without knowing. The messenger.

"Shall I let you go, Dev? Or shall I continue?" *I'm so aroused, I want to take you right now. You are beautiful, Dev. Absolutely magnificent.*

Like she'd praise a stallion, and bloody oath if he didn't respond to it. The whip had lashed close to his cock several times, but it had never flagged. If anything, even stained with his blood and his body running with sweat, it was hard and heavy, standing up proud near his belly.

A pair of male hands had steadied him from behind when she stopped the bucking of the chains. Now he stiffened a different way as he realized they were not Thomas's hands. Alistair's capable, strong palms moved over the welts, digging in a little as his melodious voice offered a sensuous, low chuckle. "It hurts, but he likes it, too, Lady D. It's almost fate, the way those that like the pain sometimes drop in our laps. I'm just sorry I didn't find him first."

Don't let him touch me. I don't . . . I don't have any interest in men.

I know you don't. But I want to see him touch you. It gives me pleasure. One handsome man caressing another. Will you surrender to my pleasure, let it become your own? Feel it, take it for yourself?

He sank his teeth into the ball as Alistair's touch dropped, stroked his buttocks. He growled in vicious protest, a promise of retaliation as male fingers found his rectum, eased into the area Danny had already greased. The male vampire's lips pressed against Dev's nape and he bucked helplessly, his naked, straining body held between the two vampires. Danny's hands were on his cock, working him, an irresistible pump that leaked his response onto her fingers. A scraping sound told him she'd pulled a stool around and stepped onto it. When her thighs enclosed his cock, her breasts rubbing high on his chest, he felt the fabric of her skirt, pulled up but brushing against his groin.

"There's the spot," Alistair crooned, and Dev strangled on a cry as his body convulsed at the male's stimulation in his virgin rear passage. "You're quite ready for us both. Don't you think, Lady D? With your permission?"

Danny's breath was soft, shaky, as she worked her clit slowly over the length of Dev's cock, a wicked caress. "You have it, Alistair. Take your pleasure with my servant. And he likes it rough."

I can't do this, my lady. Please don't—

If you called me Danny, I would stop. You know that, don't you? But you're torn. Put your mind out of it. Feel how it pleases me to share you with another vampire, knowing you are all mine.

What is it you want? God damn it, what . . .

Your soul, Dev. A third-marked servant must give a vampire his soul. I need to know you can surrender to me enough to take my pleasure, wrap it around you, make it your own. To come for me, and have no concerns about the fact a man is fucking you. To have serving me be what drives all your other desires, no matter what I ask. You know that's what this is about. Game over. Tonight's the night you face it, and decide whether to run or stay.

He struggled, he cursed, and yet he could not loose either one of them. They were much stronger, and he was bound. Again he struggled with how she'd given him no warning, little time to prepare for this. It was as if she'd wanted to force the issue so abruptly. Why?

Then the thoughts were pushed away, for Danny reached high, closed her hands around his biceps, adding to the weight against the chains so he groaned. With a flexible athleticism he almost wished he could see, she lowered herself onto his cock. From a shift, another scent, he realized Lady Lyssa was behind her. Was likely holding Danny as she released his arms, leaned back and changed the angle to take him in completely, her legs sliding around his hips and then Alistair's as the male vampire pressed against Dev from nape to arse, and began to guide his thankfully well-lubricated cock in between his buttocks. With his ankles chained together, it made the opening that much tighter, and Alistair's explosion of breath, a sound of pleasure, couldn't help but remind Dev of when he'd penetrated Danny in a similar way. God, it hurt, it stretched him, but as if his arse knew, the muscles released, let Alistair in, and the sensation rocketed all the way to his testicles.

The hard male grunt, the flex of strong fingers on his hips, the muttered, "There you are, let me in, you gorgeous, tight-assed bugger," made him want to escape, tune it all out, but Danny was slid down to the root, drawing him up, even as Alistair's skill in the back was doing the same. He was going to come explosively, harder than he'd ever come in his life, and everyone was getting off on it. He could smell the heavy musk of arousal as if it had blanketed the room.

He was the center of it. Danny gave that to him, opened her mind and let him slide over that waterfall, rush down into the arms of the tumbling waters below. Seeing what she was seeing, the clench of his jaw on the ball gag, the furrowing of his brow, every sweat-glistened muscle from shoulders, to chest, to abs, buttocks, thighs, shuddering from the dual stimulus, his resistance to the typhoon of pleasure that was going to roar over and take him soon.

He moaned against the gag as she looked down, let him see how her cunt was sliding up and down his cock. Lyssa holding her body, letting Danny's head lie on her shoulder as the vampire queen watched Dev's struggle, as she might study a particularly amazing sculpture. How he was undulating rhythmically in the chains, caught between the two pistoning bodies like a well-oiled machine. The way Alistair's hard male body, so like his own, was pressed close, his arm across Dev's chest.

"After this, you should let Nina clean his cock with her little mouth," Alistair rasped against his ear. "She can make him spew again in no time. Ah, Christ, he's priceless. He's still fighting me as hard as any footy player I ever bent over my bed."

Let go, Dev. Let it go. Feel it.

She drew him into the seductive web of her mind again but not to see more images, which were devastating enough. No, this time she let him feel what she was feeling. How fucking aroused she was by all of it, harder and more intensely than she'd ever been aroused before, so that she finally understood the deep fulfillment that came with having a third-marked servant. Something that belonged to her, that she could share, but in the end was hers to take home and fuck however and whenever she wished . . . A servant who got off on her pleasure, by whatever route it came.

Oh, God, she was worked up, spinning, her cunt contracting, milking him valiantly, the thick girth of him as Alistair kept ramming him, burning, mindless pleasure.

Serve me, Dev. Come for me now, upon my command.

He cried out against the gag, an animal scream as the climax detonated. The chains clanked hard and the stool that had been beneath her, which she no longer needed, clattered away as his swinging toes hit it. Both vampires held tight to him, Alistair gripping his forearms below his wrists, his fingers bruising. Another form of manacle that would remind Dev of this moment before the third-mark healing took it away. And Danny, her lovely slick lips working up and down his length as she found her release right after him, her voice lifted in a cry that was musical, like the sigh of the wind across the barren desert, a gift to the ferocious heat. He wished he could see her, for he knew she wouldn't see herself as he saw her, but he could imagine it. Her body's angle making the movement of her breasts an erotic wobble back toward her throat, drawing his gaze onward to the smoothness of Lyssa's hands holding her, the two women's hair mixing, black and blond . . .

Alistair released right after, his strokes becoming more punishing, burning like fire, but it was all right, for his working against that pulsing gland had Dev's cock spasming with one more strong release, a final expulsion of fluid into his lady's cunt that had her crying out again, one of her hands digging into his abdomen, a passing, grasping touch.

Slowly, things settled. Gasping breaths eased, and he felt Alistair's hands, the bastard's touch actually fairly gentle as he removed himself from Dev and gave him a passing caress on his buttock, the small of his back. His lady slid from him as well, and he heard the rustle and adjustment of clothing.

"Outstanding, Lady D." Alistair took another moment to catch his breath. Dev felt his arm slide around his side, the point of his elbow resting briefly on Dev's waist, the angle of his body suggesting he'd gathered Danny to him in the other arm, and even Lyssa. He brought them all close together, an oddly sentimental cuddling, Dev sandwiched between all three, so he felt the erotic press of flesh on all sides. "You've made a beautiful choice. At least in terms of bedding. The question is, will he be suitable for the rest?"

Lyssa's hand touched his face, stroked briefly over his stretched lips, her nails scoring a welt on his neck made by God knew who. "Time will tell that, Alistair. Let the poor girl get her breath. It is their business, not ours."

There was an intriguing note to her voice. He wondered if he would have been attuned to it if he hadn't been blindfolded and all his other senses enhanced by that deprivation. But it made him wonder if Danny had reacted more strongly than even she'd anticipated to the situation she'd created, or allowed Lyssa to orchestrate.

Love? Danny?

He heard her breath catch, a small sound almost like a sob, and then Lyssa's voice cut over it smoothly. "If Lady D has no objections, I'd like him left like this while we enjoy the rest of our cocktails. Watching a muscular naked man swaying in chains, with his seed running down his thighs and glistening on his cock, mixing with his blood, is something we should savor before we let him down. After he catches his breath, we will let Nina service him with her mouth and watch him come again, as spectators this time."

"Thomas." Danny spoke then, and her voice was back to that neutral, smooth tone which told him nothing, but he caught a slight quaver on the syllables. That could be from the aftermath of her climax, of course. "Put his feet back on the floor to rest his shoulders, but otherwise Dev will pleasure us according to Lady Lyssa's wishes."

21

So it went. Nina did put her mouth on him, something he was powerless to refuse. Because her pregnant belly was pressing into his shins, he was afraid to move too violently for fear of hurting her, resulting in a slow build to a climax almost as intense as the first. When he spurted into her mouth, care washed away as he groaned out his release.

Before and after, they went back to their conversation of politics and past experiences. His presence there was one more adornment to enhance their evening, and he was expected to submit to display.

In fact, I gagged and blindfolded you in deference to your inexperience, Dev. A seasoned servant would *have stood quietly, without those things, waiting to be released.*

He could hear the rustle and shift of bodies moving. Clothing. The clink of teacups and silverware. The occasional hiss of a dying candle, mixed with the smell of the women's perfumes, Alistair's aftershave. Even the quiet, clean scent of Thomas, nearer than the rest. Dev wondered if he'd shifted closer to give him some steadying reassurance.

While he hung there, exhausted, he became aware that his muscles were trembling, and it wasn't from fatigue, but something far deeper. As clear and sharp as all those separate impressions were, her movements, her scent, her voice, were the most precise, like etchings on the fragile glass he felt he'd become. Transparent, exposed, breakable. When he'd worked as a stockman on a cattle station, or did shearing, he'd had days he'd felt beaten half to death by the time he laid his body on his swag. But this . . . he'd resisted all of it with muscles drawn so tight he knew he must have knots, and now, in this lull, he felt as if he'd been beaten, dragged and then done all over again. And they still weren't done with him. He knew it.

She'd offered him the way out, not once, but twice.

If you'd called me Danny . . .

I don't need a servant whose only reason for serving me is to exercise some twisted punishment upon himself.

He did relish the pain when she offered it, God help him. But there was no voice in his head telling him he should crave pain because he deserved it. It was something about the way she dished it out. The wave of desire he felt with her, the connection that was established, it didn't matter if it was from the cut of a knife, the lash of a whip, the touch of her lips or the gentle stroke of her fingertips. Or another man's cock plunging into him.

It was too much to handle. But throughout the two hours they made him hang there, his shoulders screaming despite the fact his weight now rested on the floor, his legs bound so close together with the ankle and thigh manacles, there were moments when his thoughts and the physical state of his body overwhelmed him. A wave of violent panic deluged him, an overwhelming need to fight his bonds, gnaw his damn arms off at the wrist if need be.

Each time that happened, before he could start struggling, do more than twitch in the chains as if he were preparing for seizure, she was there in his mind. Crooning to him, a soft lullaby, like she'd done before. That instant presence told him that, despite her casual conversation with the others, she was watching him closely, watching over him. Christ, he was so bloody twisted up.

"Lady Lyssa?" Alistair spoke. "It's getting time to draw the evening to a close. You've taken precious little from Lady D's servant. Would you like to sample him before we retire? I feel certain he has one more in him. Too much energy seems to be pouring off him still."

"Try not to sound so envious, Alistair. Be warned, Danny. Keep Dev around him too long and he might decide to trade his baby for him." Lyssa's cutting amusement was met with mock outrage by Alistair and a short chuckle from his lady. Then the vampire queen rose, evidenced by a soft whisper of her legs, which, not stockinged, had a different sound from Danny's.

"Unlike you children, I prefer anticipation to saturation. The taste of it has a sharper edge. So perhaps I'll get him warmed up for the lady Daniela to take him once more before she sleeps. If she'd like that."

"Of course," Danny said courteously, though Dev thought he heard something in her voice, some level of reluctance.

She was right. You can share me with another male, or his servant, but a female vamp's a different story, isn't it?

She didn't deign respond to that, an answer in itself. He wasn't goading her, not exactly. His body and spirit were exhausted, numb, leaving him hanging on an odd precipice between yearning and despair. Then, from the exotic scent and that emanation of heated power, he knew Lady Lyssa stood before him. He made a hoarse sound behind the gag as the chains were drawn taut. Not to the extent as before, but enough his heels left the ground and he cried out as even the slight pull on his shoulders was enough to spark pain through the tendons. Her long nails trailed down his chest, slow, slow, and his breath stilled, his heartbeat conversely speeding up.

He'd been touched by his lady, and her skill was enough to make any man cross-eyed, but something about Lady Lyssa's touch... Jesus, this woman had been alive more than a thousand years and had all the mysterious magic of a sorceress behind her touch, paralyzing a man.

She'd reached his abdomen, and now her fingers caressed the silken mat of hair above his cock, teased one finger down the length of it. It had been drained by Nina just a little while ago, but now, at that touch, it stirred weakly.

"There you are." Her voice was a purr. "You need to be ready to service your lady again. Lady Danny is so aroused, even now. Watching Nina put her mouth on your splendid cock, then seeing me touch you. All the while, everything that has happened tonight replays in her head. When she takes you to her bed at dawn, she will be so hungry to have you all to herself, to mark you with her scent as only hers again. She'll shove you down on the bed and take you hard, too needy for your cock to pretend any formalities, any thought that she is giving you foolish choices."

The bite to her words now was obviously directed at Danny. But then Lyssa's slim, small fingers curled around his cock and pulled with a skill that had him sucking in a breath.

"If I were Lady D, I *really* wouldn't let you out too much. Someone might be tempted to steal you away." As she drew closer, the brocade and silk of her dress pressed against him. "Thomas is removing your gag, but you will not speak unless spoken to."

The buckle eased, and then Thomas's fingers were there, guiding the ball from his mouth, his body pressed briefly against the back of Dev's, another reassurance. "He bit into it quite fiercely, Lady D," Lyssa observed softly. Then her hand was on his shoulder. When she gripped it, and leaned into him, her body elongating as if she was rising onto her toes, he realized she was bringing her mouth up toward his.

He jerked back and away, avoiding her lips.

He hadn't thought about courtesy. He'd just reacted. Now a tense silence fell over the room, just long enough for him to think, *Oh, bugger.* Then Lyssa's hand was on the side of his face. But not to turn him back and force him into the kiss. Instead, she went for his throat, grazed him with her fangs.

He had a band around his chest so tight he could barely breathe. He didn't realize how tight until Danny's hand touched him. Traced his mouth. Then she was next to Lyssa, so close the women had to have an arm around each other to balance. They pressed against him to add to that anchor, but Danny's other hand moved to his nape, and when her mouth covered his, he gave himself up to that kiss. The softness of her mouth, the reassuring touch of her hand tunneling through his hair as Lyssa teased his carotid with the threat of her fangs, her hand still working his cock. Then there was Alistair again, God help him, his strong palm running down Dev's back, down to his arse to give it a kneading squeeze, his fingers playing in the cleft.

Nina's mouth and hands came back as well, along his right thigh. Her flexible tongue worked around Lyssa's fingers and underneath as Nina started to do as Aapti had done that night, sucking one testicle gently into her mouth, then the other, then licking both. Alistair's fingers slid back into his still well-greased backside.

He couldn't take it again. He couldn't.

Stay with me, Dev. I'm here. Still Danny kissed his mouth, pricking him with her fangs, sweeping her tongue inside, tangling with his. Despite the excruciating discomfort, his arms grew taut in the chains as he strained toward her, his body surging to life with need. While the stimulus of the other three helped his cock reach its turgid state, it was that mouth, the smell of her in his nostrils, the brush of her blond hair against his cheek and temple, that had him needing. Wanting Danny to do exactly as Lyssa described, when Danny took him to her bed before dawn.

He knew a lot about patience, having lived in the bush. Where so much had to wait on the elements. The sun, the rain, the wind. Where one might have to be still for hours to catch food, or walk for miles to find it. How you had to pay close attention to find water.

But patience had a different quality in creatures who lived forever. Danny was content to keep kissing him as long as she liked, knowing she could have more whenever she wished, even as his body jerked and arousal built, and built, until he was groaning into her mouth, telling her his need. His cock was an iron bar in Lyssa's grasp, his arse clenching rhythmically around Alistair's fingers, electric sensation jolting up from his testicles under Nina's clever mouth. He didn't know where Thomas was, might be glad he didn't know. He was probably saying rosaries or whatever a monk did in his mind to overcome the temptations of the flesh displayed before him so blatantly.

He'd played some games with whores, but even when he'd blindfolded or restrained them, it had been temporary, play only, no matter how hot his need had been at that time. He hadn't realized what it would be like to be blindfolded and restrained for hours like this. It was entirely different, what it did to the body, the mind, how it broke things down. He was making unintelligible noises into her mouth, into her mind, an animal level of communication somewhere between plea and threat. He knew his cock was leaking over Lyssa's ring-bedecked fingers. Once or twice, she turned and raked him with the sharp edges of her gems, causing him to flinch at the unexpected pain, but then Nina's warm, wet mouth followed the blow, soothing and keeping his cock hard and upright despite the scraping pain.

"You should consider piercing him, Danny. There are some wonderful practitioners in Singapore." Lyssa's voice came slow and thick with pleasure toward them all. She teased his throat again, another prick. "Seems a shame to have a cock this large and not be able to adorn it. They have gold rings like manacles they can size so one locks behind the head, one around the base, and then one around the top of the scrotum. You connect them with chains, keep those chains short, and when he gets aroused . . . Ah, the pleasure and discomfort it puts them in . . . it's a delight to watch."

He rocked into her hand, expelling more fluid, and she slicked it over his head with her thumb. "I think he's ready for you, Danny," Lyssa said in that throaty purr. "Taste him from my fingers."

Alistair released the blindfold, so Dev got to see Danny suck Lyssa's fingers into her mouth. Lyssa stroked her blond hair with the other hand, turning it over so she could caress the side of Danny's face with her knuckles, an affectionate, almost loving gesture. When Danny had cleaned the last of his essence, her blue eyes lifted to Dev's face. She reached out with her fingertips, grazed them down his cheek. With the blindfold on, he hadn't noticed, but he didn't want to believe that what she was tracing were the tracks of dried tears on his face.

"I want him here. Now."

As if prompted, Thomas brought several cushions from the chairs and sofa. Nina withdrew, Alistair gallantly helping her to her feet as Thomas arranged the cushions on the floor. Danny eased down on them, Lyssa holding her arm and back to assist before she, too, withdrew. Candles were extinguished, all but those closest, so it became just the two of them there, even as Dev could sense the vampires in those shadows, following him with gleaming fangs and watchful eyes.

He'd expected to be released, but the mechanics engaged again. The chains holding his arms began to tighten, and those holding his ankles did as well, so he was pulled off his feet and pitched forward, a short but harrowing fall before he steadied. He was adjusted so he was close to parallel with the floor, facing down, though his lower torso was kept higher, so he was almost in a shallow dive position, being lowered toward Danny's waiting body. He remembered then what she'd said in the cave, about suspending a man in manacles.

God in heaven, his lady was drawing up the edge of that tight stretched skirt, to expose long pale legs, the slick, pink lips between them. Her fingers were there now, teasing herself as she arched in sensual invitation, her eyes watching him come down upon her. As he came to a halt, his chest barely brushed hers. Now he knew the reason for the angle, for his overly blessed cock was so very close to her wet heat. Just not close enough. Her blue eyes devoured what he was sure was a very needy expression on his face. He wanted to kiss her, and could, but somehow knew he had to wait. Strewth, she was killing him.

"Just for me, Dev," she said softly.

She stretched up to kiss him. He kissed her back, as hard and demanding as he could, and when she drew back, he fought the chains, wanting to follow her, but they merely clanked and bounced, pulling at his shoulders until he was sure they might dislocate. It didn't matter. They would bloody heal, right?

One slim leg lifted, the heel of the foot tracing the back of his calf, up, up to his thigh, then his buttock. His cock was at her mons, and she lifted enough to rub herself there, pleasuring herself with that tip on her clitoris, her breath coming short, skin flushing. She could come just from doing that, he could tell, and she might. While it would leave a gnawing in his gut, it would be . . . okay. He just wanted her. Needed her to look at him with her blue eyes, feel the passing touch of her hand . . . Feel her inside his mind, his body. He wanted to fuck her until he drained himself to a skeletal husk, but he also wanted to hang here, his shoulders screaming with pain, his buttocks drawn up tight, and see the way she looked at him, with so much hunger in her eyes. A hunger that went beyond lust and blood, and encompassed both.

She would make him wait, because that increased her desire, watching him go mad with pain and lust. He found that state of mind was similar to his place of no thought, only this was not a conscious choice, not an effort to stave off destructive blood rage. In this place, he was capable of doing anything and nothing, for though violent desire and need tore through his body, he was bound, not only by chains, but by her will.

An experienced servant will simply wait, unbound . . .

She made the first bite hurt, spearing her fang into his pectoral, an inch or so above the sensitive nipple. When he arched with a snarl, Danny licked his blood away, then bit his abdomen. His arm. His shoulder, his throat. A dozen different places she sampled, including high up on his thigh, sliding her body as needed, until she was aligned with him again, face-to-face. Then her legs lifted, slid over his hips, her hands clutching his overstrained shoulders, causing him to let out a short exhale of breath at the additional pressure.

"Bring his cock down to me."

Danny took him, inch by inch, clinging to his shoulders. They kept his upper body several inches off her, reversing the angle so he was stretched over her like a warrior leaping off a ledge to strike, his manacled wrists and interlaced fingers over his head, back arched. His body was still shuddering, doing that outer and inner trembling that made it difficult for him to determine if the cause was physical or emotional.

Her lips parted, those amazing eyes fathomless pools. As she took him in deep, she began to work her lower body up and down, teasing his shaft in long, slick strokes. He was going to die, for it was entirely perfect, the slow, slow build in his own groin, the knowledge that he would come, but only when she'd worked him past the point of insanity.

You're my pleasure, Dev. In every way. God . . .

Her breath started to quicken and her eyes glazed, chin tilting back so there was that tempting throat, the pulse beating hard in it.

He almost wanted to do as she did, sink his teeth in, taste her flesh and blood, but she wasn't going to let him do anything but serve her now. His mind was spinning in a cataclysmic free fall so that he didn't know what he'd be striking when he hit bottom.

"Time to come for me once more, Dev," she whispered, and her muscles drew taut, her body moving more swiftly now, that friction that could bring fire to wood.

He cried out hoarsely, his body straining, working against itself, pulling ligaments and tender muscles into blood-and-brimstone agony. It must be the third mark that gave him this ability, for nothing else explained why his cock, heedless, spurted into her welcoming heat. Her cries were hoarse, needy, tumbling over the raw field of his emotions like a wind, stirring them up further.

It goaded his climax to monstrous proportions as he writhed in the chains, his lady fucking him, not letting him get away with anything less than full, mind-altering release, leaving no part of him hidden as he cried out, cursed her, begged her, threatened her. Adored her.

~

When he was done, his head had fallen down so his temple pressed into her throat. The chains were removed, his arms remaining limply over his head, along the sides of hers, his body shuddering, his breath coming in short gasps. As the manacles were removed from his thighs and ankles, his knees settled between her spread legs, a cradle for his hips, cock still inside her. Laying her arm around his back, she murmured to him. Meaningless things, gentle things, soothing him almost as one would soothe a child. He felt like a child, something broken so deep inside him, he wanted to hold it up to her, ask her to fix it. But his arms were too tired, and it was something he knew couldn't be fixed. Not like this.

Slowly, he managed to rise up on his knees, to take the edge of her short skirt as he came out of her and draw it back down so she wasn't exposed to the other two men in the room.

My chivalrous, possessive bushman . . .

The emotion she let wash into his mind was of tender amusement, but in truth Danny was feeling something much deeper at the look in his eyes. She'd stripped him to the bone. She'd done what she was supposed to do, the highest level of what her kind demanded at an event such as this. But the deepest level of her soul said she should have left him at Thieves' Station. Maybe even left him alone at Elle's.

The truth of it wrenched her. The man trying to get to his feet, who had been used in such a callous and depraved way, who'd been whipped and whose seed glistened on his thighs, had been a laughing young man who'd married an uncomplicated, loving woman. They'd had a son and a flock of sheep, a simple, beautiful life. She'd seen the memories in his mind, and it very much matched the life she herself wanted, but could only have as part of her much more complicated world.

As he moved to the side, she lifted up on her elbows and stroked his calf, feeling the quivering muscle. When he swayed on his knees, before she could rise to hold him, Thomas was already there. Lyssa propelled her to her feet, took her arm in a companionable grip and steered her toward the archway. "Alistair, why don't you set us up for a final brandy while we ladies go freshen up?"

"It would be my pleasure." Without another glance toward Dev, he took Nina's hand and guided her out the opposite door with him.

"Don't look back," Lyssa murmured as they moved outside the archway. "Alistair is still watching."

The vampire queen took her directly to the rooms Alistair had provided the monarch. She brought Danny into her private bath facilities so she could straighten her clothes, clean the dress where Dev's semen had stained the fabric. However, as she started to wipe her skirt with the cloth, Danny found she couldn't stand. So instead she sat down on the edge of the tub. Looking down at her hiked-up skirt, she held the wet cloth balled in one hand, but couldn't yet use it to erase the lines of fluid he'd left on the insides of her bare thighs. Proof of his body being part of hers. The flushed color of her labia, her still-swollen clit that would likely want him again in no time.

So deep was her absorption that she started when Lyssa's hand appeared in her vision, took the cloth away. However, she was more than startled when the woman knelt in elegant silk and glittering gems to wipe her thighs, holding one hand on her knee to keep her open. Danny swallowed. As she'd explained to Dev, all vampires were sexual dominants due to their predatory nature, blood and lust too closely intertwined in their psyche to divide them in the bedroom. When one as powerful as Lyssa touched another vampire, Danny therefore sat still beneath her touch, unresisting as she passed the damp cloth over her mons, her still-sensitive lips. Danny caught her breath, gripping Lyssa's shoulder in one hand. The woman glanced up at her, the jade eyes assessing.

"You forced the issue, didn't you? You stupid, stupid girl." But her voice was gentle. "I thought you overdressed a bit for cocktails. The way a woman does when she's preparing herself to do something she expects will take exceptional effort."

"I don't know what you mean."

"Don't take me for a fool, Danny," Lyssa said, and Danny saw a flash in those green eyes that had her pressing her lips together. "You've given him every way out, and he hasn't taken it yet. So you've skinned him alive tonight, gutted him, because you want him to run. It's time to grow up. You marked him three times. You cannot just cut him loose."

"I marked him three times to save his life. I have no right to hold him. He has a death wish, that's all it is."

"You've got something worse. His death wish comes from having needed someone too much. You're afraid of needing anyone at all. Well, open your eyes," Lyssa snapped. "That boy has been hurt, far beyond what you've experienced, even in your extended lifespan. Everything you told me ... He lost everything a soul can bear to lose. And yet, he's primed to love you, serve you. All you have to do is let him. Let him do it."

"I'm too caught up in him. You proved it. I would have looked back, gone to help him, if you hadn't reminded me Alistair was watching. What if a male vampire of Alistair's standing, or even a territory male with powerful connections, thinks I've been compromised by a male human?"

"The more power you acquire, the more choices you can claim for your own in our world."

Danny closed her eyes. "It always comes back to that. Sometimes it feels there are less."

"Hmm. Stand up and turn."

"Lady Lyssa, I don't—"

"Stand up. And turn." Lyssa fixed a dark gaze on her. Danny, swallowing, obeyed. The female vampire folded up her skirt in the back and began the same process, this time cleaning the dampened cleft between her buttocks. It reminded her of Dev there, on the train, tearing into her body like an animal determined to get to her very heart and soul, the agony and pleasure of it. She trembled.

"It will pass," Lyssa said quietly, her fingers pausing, resting on the curve of Danny's hip. "It does for all of us. Getting a third-marked servant is a process, much like falling in love. You get perspective after a while. They are an important tool, a vital extension of ourselves, Danny. Don't deny yourself that." There was a pulling at her waist as Lyssa returned the skirt to its position, turned her and rose, studying her face. Picking up a brush, she gestured. "Sit back down on the tub. You're too tall."

Danny complied, stared at the wall. "So it will be okay."

Lyssa lifted her chin. "If you take control of yourself, him and the situation. But there are no fairy tales, Danny. Don't ever think that things just work out of their own accord."

Danny closed her eyes. She couldn't look at the other woman, but she was going to ask the question. "Do we get to be close to someone, Lyssa? So close it's like they're inside you and you're inside them, breathing together, your bodies like one? Do you have that with Thomas? Or Rex?"

When Danny opened her eyes, she saw the shuttering in Lyssa's. "Oh. My apologies, my lady. That was too personal."

Lyssa kept working on her hair. "Tell me what's in your heart, Danny, and don't concern yourself with what's in mine. You can trust me. Tell me what this rough bushman makes you feel."

Danny studied her hands. She so rarely wore rings, she realized, unlike Lyssa and many other vampires. As if she expected to work with them, do something with them. Like her life. "As if I've been encased in ice forever, because of my mother, my father's death,

Ian . . . I understand what we are, what we need to be. But I'd be content to live in a territory with no particular power. That said, there's a part of me that knows I can be a territory overlord or Region Master. I can do it. But I want something of my own, something that connects to my heart, a place I can go and be a woman, a child. A temptress. And not because I'm a vampire and have that allure."

A smile touched her lips. "When I'm with him, when I was with him in the bush, I felt that. He knew what I was and he wasn't afraid. He only wanted to help and be with me. I like his mind, his body, his heart. Is all that normal? Temporary feelings you say will pass?"

Lyssa was silent for several moments. "Yes," she said at last.

Danny pressed her lips together. "Though I know Alistair would disapprove and you will call me foolish, I'm ashamed of what I did tonight. He's a brave, decent man, and I'm not sure we have the right to take that away from him, just because we can."

"You didn't," Lyssa observed. "He capitulated to you, Danny. He surrendered. Remember that. Some part of him needs you, the way you need him. That's what being third-marked is about. You're providing one another something that neither of you can find alone. We get to delve into the soul of the servant we bind to us in a way those who fall in love and claim to understand one another never will. There are no hidden dark secrets or yearnings. They are there to see clearly. That's why he surrendered. You gave him what he needed, though you both may not yet realize it."

Danny's eyes had become distant, and Lyssa touched her shoulder. "Danny?"

Danny turned her gaze to the vampire queen. "It doesn't matter," she said softly. "He's decided to leave. He just said good-bye."

22

A FTER all the vampires and Nina left the room, Dev's strength deserted him. When he fell forward, he didn't expect the arm he put out to stop his fall, let alone hold him. Fortunately, he was caught in the monk's strong arms. Thomas's quiet, even voice soothed him.

"Easy, boy. It's done. Nobody's going to want anything from you for a while."

Dev sagged in his grip then, choosing to believe him. Thomas managed to coax him up on wobbly legs, and got his arm over his shoulders. "Let's get you to my quarters."

On the way there, they moved through the servants' hallways, so they were alone, the rest employed in the care of the master and his guests. It was blessedly dim here, for Dev didn't think he could stand the glare of light on his shamed soul right now. Thomas took him to a room outfitted with a simple cot and nightstand, the bath across the hall.

"Lie here for a bit. When your strength returns, you can go clean yourself up. I can help you with that if you have need, no shame."

"There's no shame in a monk handling the body of a naked man? Strewth, the world has turned upside down."

Thomas gave a grim smile, the dim sconces making the metal

rims of his spectacles gleam, passing a shaft of light over his closely shorn hair as he tilted his head. "I've no designs upon it."

"I've never wanted a man to . . . and yet, they . . ." Dev's throat worked. Now that it was all passing, he felt a sudden desire to get up and run, run until the aching in his chest abated.

"She knows that. It was about what you would do for her, if commanded."

"How can anyone be suited for this?" Even though the ground tilted alarmingly, he had to get up, regain that much control. As he pressed tented fingers against the wall, holding himself up, he saw Thomas tense, ready to avert a fall. "I'm fine." He gave a derisive chuckle. "Christ, my stomach's rolling enough to chunder. Oh, sorry . . ."

Thomas shook his head. "I've called on Him more than once since I became my lady's servant. In various ways. Dev, do you love her?"

Of all the questions he expected from the monk, that wasn't one he'd anticipated. He eased back down to the bed, acknowledging the fact his legs weren't ready to hold him up for the duration of a prolonged conversation. "I had that once before. This is different. I'm not sure if it's a different face of the same, or it's just . . . fascination, self-destruction, or something else."

"If we could go back five hours, and she told you everything she'd expect of you tonight, in detail, would you have done it?"

"She'd have thought I'd turned the corner if I did. Cripes . . ."

"Not what I asked." Thomas's gray gaze was cool. "Would you have done it? Without analysis or understanding why you actually did it, would you have?"

When Dev's gaze rose, helpless to answer, Thomas inclined his head. "I told you earlier, there's something in a man's makeup, or a woman's, that makes them a human servant. It may defy everything you've ever known about yourself, but for some reason, you can't refuse her. My lady . . ." He cleared his throat. "I told you she only asked me to break my vows once, to prove my loyalty to her. But if she'd asked me twice? Or maybe even every single day from then until now, I'm not certain I could say no to her."

"So why doesn't she keep asking?"

"You know why. Because they are ruthless. Violent. Insatiable. As well as honorable, intelligent, courageous. Loving and nurturing even, at times. They like pushing the edge, there's no doubt of that. They do it to break us down, help us remember our place with them. And for their own pleasure, for our pleasure. Perhaps it fascinates them, the depths of what we are willing to give them, such that they plumb that deep and deeper, longing to know what it is in us that gives them what they cannot give back themselves, in the very dangerous world in which they live."

"If I've decided I *can't* handle it," Dev said slowly, staring down at the floor, "when's the best time to leave her, so it doesn't affect her standing with other vampires?"

The utter silence in the room wasn't even punctured by the sound of Thomas's breathing for a moment. Then he let out a quiet sigh. "You could leave on this dawn. Lyssa would not betray her confidence, and while Alistair will disapprove of her decision to release you, he will not speak of it, either. You can disappear back into your world, and she can manage your disappearance in hers without too much incident."

Dev nodded, rose and began to work his way along the wall, headed toward that bathroom, all muscles aching. No worries. That third mark would make him hale and hearty as a teenager in no time, right? But he needed the water. Needed to be clean to wash away how his body had responded to all of them so shamelessly. "Guess I'll have to think about that, then."

"While you're thinking, remember what I said earlier." Thomas rose, drawing his attention. "Being a full servant may serve God's purpose for you."

Dev stopped, glanced back at Thomas. "Perhaps your sense of divine purpose is the excuse you use to stand by a woman you can't help loving in a way you shouldn't."

Thomas lifted a brow, his shrewd eyes never wavering, and damn if he didn't have that priest look still, as if he could see every corner of Dev's battered soul. "That's as good an excuse as using what happened tonight to drive you away from the woman you love, who can give you a chance to serve a true purpose again. Because no matter what form it takes, love always serves a divine purpose, Dev. *Always*."

~

It was close to dawn when he'd regained enough strength to come to the room Alistair had provided her for the daylight, so they hadn't had to rush their evening. Well, he sure as hell could vouch for the fact they'd maximized every moment.

He'd dressed, planning to take a cab by her place to pick up his swag, leave her these clothes and don his own again.

Come in, Dev.

She was on a divan, her feet tucked up under her in a lounging position. Her gaze was calm, serene. "So you're going walkabout on me," she said without preamble. "I appreciate you facing me with it."

As he shifted uncomfortably, she shrugged. "Dev, I told you I'd let you go if you decided this wasn't for you. It's best you made the decision now, when you're so new. I would like to thank you," she added. "You've made me understand why so many vampires choose a third-marked servant. And you're right, it's foolish of me not to have one. Once I return to the station, I'll start considering my staff there. Choose one who will serve my needs and yet is perhaps a little more suited to the role."

She gave him a light smile, gestured to the couch. He didn't feel like sitting, but he did, perching on the arm. "We've had quite an adventure together, haven't we?"

A muscle twitched in his jaw. "Can you bloody stop this?"

Her brow creased. "I'm trying to make things easier for you."

"Don't." He stood up abruptly. "Nothing's going to make it easier. I'm going to your house to get my things, but everything's set up to truck your purchases back to the station. I'll leave you the paperwork so you can see everything's in order. Thomas said if anything goes amiss after that, he'll be here a bit to help you sort it out. He seems a very levelheaded bloke."

Danny rose, faced him. "You didn't fail me, Dev," she said softly. "If anything, I failed you."

"No." He shook his head. Hesitating, he reached out, lifting her hand to bring it to his lips. But her fingers opened, so she ended up cradling the side of his face and he was leaning into her, drawing her body up against his, holding tightly. With an oath, he broke away. "It's what it is, love. I've enjoyed the ride. Just wasn't cut out for the whole journey. I want to thank you, too," he added awkwardly. "It's been brought to my attention that the way you left the door open isn't the usual thing."

She nodded, her countenance as smooth as a lake, as lovely and mysterious. However, he thought her fingers had almost closed on him, as if trying to hold him, before he pulled away. "After . . . well, about a few days after this is done, I'll block the mind link, Dev. I can open it when I choose, but you'll feel . . . It will feel odd, like something's missing at first. You'll get used to it after a while, but if you do run into vampires down the road, it will be harder for them to detect you were marked by one."

His lips twisted in a bit of a smile. "Not a whole lot of them in the Outback, love. You're unique."

She swallowed then, the first indication of a real emotion. "You're an exceptional man, Dev, a treasure to any woman whose heart you steal. Seek a family again. You owe it to yourself. You have love to give."

He swallowed as well, glanced to the left, made the automatic note that the curtains were properly sealed against the coming dawn. Of course, he was sure Alistair's staff was well trained in that. "Ruskin. We still need to deal with him. You call me on that mind link thing of yours when you're ready. I'll back you up."

"No." Now any softness disappeared from her gaze. "I won't. Let me deal with him, Dev. I promise I will, and there's no shame in you letting me do it. A human cannot stand against a mature vampire and live. I'll take care of him in my own time, my own way. All right?"

When his lips firmed to that thin, stubborn line, Danny had to resist the sudden, desperate urge to follow the hard jaw with lips or fingers, make the green eyes soften or fire with lust, instead of anger. But something was tearing inside her now. It was a crush, Lyssa had implied. Emotions running high and strong like a flash flood. Like a flood, it would pass, and she'd have lovely, delicate memories, like the sudden fields of wildflowers that sprang up in the red landscape after such storms.

"Your word, my lady. Or I seek him out myself, at the earliest opportunity."

"Very well," she relented. "When I get ready, when the timing is right, I'll contact you. We need to get past this vampire event of his first, because we don't want to do it when he has so many in attendance. I'll be going to that, of course, to determine if there are other weaknesses we can exploit."

His hand shot out, caught her wrist. "I don't want you anywhere near that bastard."

"That is not your decision," she said, meeting his gaze. "But know that I will be safe from him until I choose my strategy, if that brings you comfort."

He searched her face, nodded. "All right, then. But, Danny, it can't be like Ian. You have to step back, keep yourself separate from it if you're going to get where you're going." At her furrowed brow, he shifted his glance away. "I'll only say this once, and only because I think you need to hear it. That's how I hunted down the men who killed my family. I didn't let myself feel any of it, until it was over. You've got to do it like a god. As if it's all for the best, really. No regrets. That comes after."

With the nightmares, she thought. Who would be near him during his sleep to keep it tranquil? Hold him when the nightmares couldn't be outrun?

Hesitating, he withdrew his hand, but then offered the right one. "My lady."

Danny took it, but instead of a formal shake, she simply slid her hand into his palm, laced their fingers and gazed up at him. With another oath, he leaned down, took her lips in a hard, needy kiss, pulling her up against him. The sweep of his hands up her back washed all the rest away, made her long to beg him to stay, no matter what, damn the consequences to his heart and soul, or hers.

He saved them both. Tearing away, he spun on his heel, striding out of the room without a look back. Danny was glad for it, because she didn't want the shame of him seeing the tears that gathered in her eyes and spilled out onto her cheeks at the close of the door behind him.

She stood there, her hands opening and closing. When her father died, she had hidden her grief away because her mother couldn't bear her tears. She hadn't cried when her mother chose Ian over her. But now, this was something she'd wanted for herself, and she'd underestimated how much. She didn't give a damn about the vampire world and what they thought. He'd seen *her*. Liked her. Known her heart. And she'd gutted him for it. It didn't matter that she'd had to do it. If this was all that life was, holding oneself aloof, century after century, not giving oneself a moment of intimacy, a moment of meaning, then what was the point? He'd looked at her the same way he looked upon the landscape of the bush, and he hadn't seen emptiness in either one of them. But in the end, he'd chosen the Red Heart, because it hadn't betrayed his, the way she had tonight. Like a sailor returning to the sea, because he was too much a part of it to refuse its call, he was going back to his desert. Which was where he belonged, where she could think fondly of him.

She'd sat down on the divan, bent over double, the pain too much to bear, when she felt Lyssa's hands upon her. She'd given Lyssa a bloodlink, and while the queen could avail herself of it at any time, she didn't often, as a courtesy. But apparently Danny's pain was too loud to ignore.

What she'd never counted on her mother to give, she took from Lyssa now. Turning in the older vampire's arms, she sobbed, while Lyssa held and rocked her silently, her jade green eyes full of sorrow and knowledge. Thomas stood at the door, his gaze locked with his Mistress's, both of them understanding all too well the young vampire woman's grief. And while Lady Lyssa might not fully understand what a servant provided, or how it balanced a chosen vampire's world, Thomas did.

"Figure it out, Dev," the monk murmured. "And come back soon."

~

Lyssa had stayed until Danny was collected, then helped her wipe her tears. Said little, for there was nothing to say. By the time Danny went to bed, well past dawn, she was exhausted and thought she'd perhaps won the ability Dev had, to go to a place of nothingness in herself.

"It will be fine," Lyssa had murmured, her last words as she smoothed a hand over Danny's brow, dropped a kiss on her forehead and left her. "You're so young, darling. It will be all right, I promise." Danny sensed the presence of Thomas for a while, knew what an honor it was that the queen had left her own servant to watch over her. Or perhaps it had been a protection for her, from herself.

When she rose at dusk, she'd had a pleasant enough breakfast with Alistair and Lyssa, then bade them an affectionate good-bye, her usual composure locked in place, though it wavered when she was provided a cranberry concoction flavored with Dev's blood. Alistair reported that before her man had departed to attend to his duties, he'd left that with the kitchen staff, to ensure she was properly nourished by her own servant. She sat back, listening to the pleasant conversation, tasting his blood on her lips, savoring the last taste of it, aching.

When Danny took her leave, Lyssa gave her a long look, squeezed her hand before Danny turned away and let Alistair offer her a hand into the car.

She didn't linger long at her house, finishing up with her servants and packing. The flight to Adelaide she chartered for that night was uneventful. During it, she reviewed the paperwork and found all was as Dev had promised. Everything she'd bought in Brisbane would reach Adelaide and be transported by truck train to the station in the coming days. The rest of the time, even the refueling stops, she spent staring into space, trying to think about what lay ahead of her and not about where Dev was.

Once in Adelaide, she verified what had already arrived. She also informed the charter company she'd need the plane's use again the following week and set the itinerary for a trip to Darwin.

She'd been telling the truth to Dev, at least the part about taking care of Ruskin without the other vampires in attendance. Because when they arrived, she intended to be there to greet them—as the new Region Master, with Ruskin's head on a pike on the front gate. Based on the savage turmoil she carried within her now, she couldn't imagine a better time to challenge Ruskin to a duel.

~

When she returned to her station, she'd originally intended to divide her time between preparing for the duel and anticipating and then arranging her new items the way she desired. Making Thieves' Station her home. If Dev had been here, she was sure he would have needled her with dry observations about females and their need to see a chair in every possible location before deciding on the spot they'd first chosen. Or quip about how she was abusing the stock-men, making them push the furniture about when she was so bloody strong she could twirl the sofa on her index finger like a circus player.

No, her heart just wasn't in it right now. She refused to let herself think that, in such a short time, she'd decided Dev was an irreplaceable part of what she considered home. That was ludicrous. She merely had to get this matter with Ruskin out of the way first.

So she let Elisa and the house staff handle the planning for the new items, giving them a general idea of how she wanted them arranged, and turned her focus to that one thing.

But as she spent hours in the courtyard, practicing with her two sabers, she found it hard to concentrate. She imagined the crinkling around Dev's eyes when he smiled. The way he'd doff his hat and wipe his brow before he stepped into the house in early evening, after working all day with the stockmen. The gap at his throat from the cotton shirt that lay just right along his shoulders and chest, the mole-skins he'd worn at Surfer's Paradise, just snug enough at the hips and backside, the eye-engaging groin area. Those beautiful sea green eyes studying her, thinking. She remembered the way they looked when he quoted poetry, when he shouldered a rifle to deal with the dingoes, when his lips curved in that smile.

Damn it, damn it, damn it. She pushed herself, wondering what level of exhaustion it would take to drive him out of her head.

Her fencing match with Ruskin had not been idle play. She'd wanted to know his capabilities. His arrogance, his anachronistic grasp of himself as an English lord, would all work to her benefit, as would her defeat in their earlier round. He didn't believe she could beat him. She was younger, female, less experienced with the blades. She'd lost with enough of a struggle to convince everyone—including Dev, with his alarmed reaction—that she'd been trying her best to gain the upper hand, perhaps slaughter Ruskin on her own property as a follow-up coup to Ian. He'd thwarted it, soundly defeated her.

If he would accept her challenge to another duel on fair ground, she could take him. She would take him. And she was counting on that fair ground, if he thought he had superior advantage and so had no need to cheat. However, she'd be leaving sealed instructions with Elisa and Willis so if she didn't return, they would know how to handle the station. But damn it, she *was* going to return. And she was going to arrange her furniture and enjoy it, damn it. Lyssa was right. A woman's heart could break, but it could heal. Anything could heal, as long as you were still drawing breath, and the sun was rising and setting. She'd deal with her feelings of anger and loneliness after handling Lord Charles.

Cutting off the Region Master's head would take care of the anger. As far as the loneliness, well, she'd force herself to consider the idea of another third-marked servant. Maybe not a man. While most chose their sexual preference, she thought she might give Elisa the honor. The girl seemed potentially suited to the life, and less likely to cause Danny the same problems with her heart being involved. Perhaps she needed to grow up a little more before she could handle a male servant. And she thought Elisa would be lovely to cuddle with in bed before the dawn, her blood sweet and feminine, her arms wrapped around Danny's waist and hips, head pillowed on her breast. She'd be devoted, loving and undemanding, but intelligent and useful as well. Everything a third-marked servant should be.

Danny went to the courtyard wall, picked up the soft cloth she'd left there and brought it to her face. She wasn't wiping sweat, of course, because a vampire had to be sick and wounded to perspire, but she hoped her staff didn't realize that. For she needed the reassuring touch of that cloth—Dev's cotton T-shirt, the one she'd slept in and he'd inadvertently left behind.

23

I T was easy enough to catch a ride out of Brisbane. He could head from there into northwest Queensland, and move at his leisure out into Western Oz again. Instead, he found himself taking a room in the hotel at Surfer's Paradise. He watched the waves move in and out, and the other families there. As he studied the clouds floating over the blue sky, he thought of how, in the Outback, there was so much blue sky the clouds looked like a complex, shifting world of their own, suspended above the earth.

He reoutfitted himself with some new gear, drawing on his little-used bank account. Spent a couple of the nights in the hotel pubs, intending to get drunk enough to justify a harmless fistfight or two and be unconscious if she tried to speak to him during her waking hours. But then he recalled it took an extraordinary amount of alcohol to keep a third-marked servant drunk, and with his enhanced strength and speed, he might easily kill someone in a friendly brawl.

That depressing knowledge, and the fact he didn't hear a peep out of her, just made his mood more savage. It was done, he'd said so, and it would be unkind, not to mention pathetic, for him to try to keep talking to her. Like some girl asking to be "friends" with the bloke whose heart she'd just mangled. Of course, he hadn't mangled Danny's heart. They didn't love like that, the vampires. He would have been her tool, her . . . God, he knew some of the terms for what he'd done at that dinner, and didn't want to think about it anymore.

But as he lay there on the veranda of the hotel with other single men, at the end of a full week away from her—which would have been an accomplishment except he couldn't get his arse to leave this damn little town where he'd enjoyed so much with her—his mind went there anyway. Remembering the glimpse in her mind, how absolutely absorbed she'd been, taking him over that way, making him the center of all that pure sexual pleasure, washing over him like the waves here. Salty, punishing, pummeling, a challenge to those who couldn't surf well, but exhilarating and dangerous at once, something that called you back to it again.

Not a bad description of her, for that matter. He'd have to walk-about the whole of Australia before he could deal with her again, as much as she was haunting him. But he wouldn't be given the blessing of that much time. The faces of those children pricked him hard. Ruskin would replace the ones Dev had killed; he knew it.

Danny said they had to wait until after that vampire gathering thing, and that rankled. But maybe she figured Ruskin would be too busy to recruit new kids until after that. Of course, if he had entertainments planned on a larger, party-sized scale, sure enough those monsters he'd created out of innocent souls would be a part of it. And new ones would bring him even more of a charge.

As badly as it bothered him, he knew it had torn at her as well. When something genuinely pissed her off, her mouth tightened slightly, and there'd be a flash in her eyes, like the hint of a lightning storm. She'd had it a couple times on the trip to the station when she'd talked about Ian, but at that point Dev had read it only as a bit of pique. A mistake he wouldn't make twice. When she'd fought Ruskin, fencing, it had been there, and he'd known she'd been prepared to go all out then, if she'd had the opening. He was a pretty damn good poker player himself.

She was cool, cool as the desert nights, but only as a prelude to the blasting heat she could summon during other times. She *did* feel. She'd let him see some of what she felt, opened up to him in those few days they'd been all alone. And that was what had captured his heart . . . because in those few days he'd met a woman as unflinching as himself, one who didn't ask him to love her more than any other . . . just to love her as much as he could, and perversely, it made him want to stretch himself beyond what he'd thought himself capable of giving.

He sat up, letting the light sheet fall away from his body, and stared out in the darkness. She *was* a lot like him. Except she was also a vampire, which meant she wouldn't hesitate to lie to a human, to *him*, if she felt it was in his best interest. Wouldn't even flicker a guilty eyelash over it. The supercilious, blond, blue-eyed delicious pain in the arse.

She was going after Ruskin alone. He'd bet his life on it.

∾

Thank God there was phone service. He got the shipping company in Adelaide on the wire in the morning and verified his lady had indeed chartered a Dakota back to her place. He was thinking himself a bit paranoid when the clerk added, "And we've still got her down for another trip out to the Top End."

Dev froze, his fingers squeezing down on the heavy receiver. "When?"

"Oh, right, sorry. Actually I should have said we *did* have her down for that trip. Plane should have picked her up for that last night."

Dev swore, and hung up. "I need a car," he told the dispatcher. "Where can I get hold of a fast one?"

∾

It was full daylight when Dev got to Lord Alistair's home. Dev asked to see Thomas. When the monk appeared, Dev wasted no time on greetings, explaining the situation in terse sentences.

"She's gone after Lord Charles Ruskin on her own," he concluded. "I know she has. She'll have some strategy in her head, but she's . . . I think we need to be there."

Thomas rubbed a hand over his face. "I sympathize, Dev, but if you think Lord Alistair will involve himself in another Region Master's territory fight, you haven't learned enough about vampire politics."

"What about Lady Lyssa?" he persisted.

Thomas gave him a look. "Dev," he said gently, "we can't interfere—"

"Oh, bollocks," Dev snapped. "I saw how it is between the two of them. Will Lady Lyssa sit by while Danny is torn apart by Ruskin and his pack of vampire puppies? Call it vampire politics and let it go? Because that's what will happen."

"I think you underestimate her."

Dev turned to find Lady Lyssa standing in the shadows of the darkened dining room. She wore a velvet dressing gown that clung to her curves, her dark hair waving around her face like a sorceress's tresses. Jesus, apparently vampires didn't even wake up looking bad, except when they'd been burned half to a crisp. It was an interesting thought to contemplate, if he'd been willing to spend several centuries with Danny.

"No," he said. "I don't. I know she can fight like a tiger, and she's more than a fair hand with a blade. But I think Ruskin will cheat. And she doesn't cheat." The irony of Lord Charles's purported adherence to the code of the English gentleman, and Danny's actual observance of it, was not lost on him. Or Lyssa, he would guess, from the spark in her eyes.

"I'm not asking any of you to interfere," he said carefully, fighting his own impatience. He suspected if he told the high-ranking vampires to get a move on and rattle their dags, it wouldn't go over very well. "I do understand that much. But if you're there, you can guarantee it's a fair fight. If she loses"—he swallowed—"then she loses. But if she loses, you'll ensure he makes it quick."

Lyssa raised a brow. "You think she would go, knowing she'd be killed?"

"She's no coward," he asserted.

"No, not in the least," the vampire queen returned. "But there are two things to ensure that will not be the outcome if she loses. One, she is worth far more pleasure and satisfaction to Lord Charles alive, not dead. If she makes this aborted attempt on his life and fails, he will force her to offer her blood and submit to his will, in a variety of ways."

Dev's eyes grew hard, sea glass in truth. "That's not going to happen. She'd let him take her head first."

"No, she won't," Lyssa responded. "Reason two. Danny would not have risked this if she thought it would truly end in her death. Because of you."

"Because of . . ." He cut it short, remembering. *Oh, Christ.* "So she's given herself no out. She's either got to win or she becomes his plaything as long as he wants to treat her that way."

"Yes. A fate far worse than death to a beautiful, independent spirit like Danny. She is young, but she's not as inexperienced or gullible as might be thought." Her gaze fastened on Dev. "I think she gauged your character true. You will come with us?"

"You couldn't keep me away," he said grimly. He shifted his glance to see Alistair now standing behind Lyssa.

"Lyssa, I can't join in this. I won't leave Nina alone, and she can't make a trip like that."

"Yes, I can, my lord."

Dev was surprised to see Nina step out of the shadows behind Alistair. The heretofore quiet and deceptively meek servant had a look in her dark eyes that was pure determination, reminding him of what Danny had said.

Nina is very capable . . .

"Lady Danny needs our help, and I won't be the cause of her falling to the likes of Lord Charles Ruskin. I am strong. The baby is strong. We will all go together. And Thomas will watch after me." At his expression, her own softened, and she reached out a hand. "My lord, please. You are being overprotective, and I am grateful, but I think we should do this. Not that I would ever presume to overstep my place," she added.

"Of course not," he said dryly. "I *am* keeping a tally of how many beatings you deserve, once you are no longer carrying this child of mine."

She gave him a smile, dipped her head. "I am ever yours to do with as you will, my lord."

Alistair turned his gaze back to Dev. "As Queensland Region Master, I will not interfere with the fight itself. Only if Ruskin does something to weigh the odds unfairly in his favor. We will not allow you to do so, either. Those are the conditions of my participation."

Lyssa glanced at Dev. "I must abide by it as well, but for more reasons than form. She has chosen this course, and will want to do it herself. It is a matter of honor and pride. You have accustomed yourself to much that is unusual about female vampires, compared to human women. You must accept her right to defend herself."

"I met her in a hotel bar, where no human woman I know would be," Dev said wryly. "I think she pretty much set that standard from the beginning."

As Alistair began to make arrangements for their transportation, Dev did something he hadn't, in a long, long while. Stepping outside, he cast a defiant look at the sky.

Get me there in time, so she'll know I'll stand with her. So she'll know she can accept death instead of defeat, if she has to do so. I won't live, knowing she's under the thumb of that murderous bastard.

Let me be there in time, so she doesn't have to face it alone, no matter what happens.

~

Danny studied the tarmac at the Darwin Aerodrome. The town was struggling to survive, like so many in the Western gold territory, its heyday come and gone. However, she'd lived long enough to see such things turn around and wouldn't be surprised to see it become a thriving city again in the decades in the future, particularly with its beautiful curve of beach and proximity to the Asian coast.

The pilot had engaged her in some brief conversation. Since it was unusual for someone to pay the exorbitant amount it would cost for a nonstop flight, most of these small plane runs necessarily performing mail stops or pickups of stockmen between stations, he was naturally curious. However, Danny made it clear she had a great deal on her mind. So in time, he just enjoyed the unusual pleasure of flying over the bush on a moonlit night, leaving her with her own thoughts.

She'd sent a telegram ahead to Lord Charles through the radio exchange, telling him she had business to discuss with him and her approximate arrival time, and received an acknowledgment that he would be in attendance at his Darwin estate. Upon reaching the ground, she found that he'd sent a car for her, which told her he'd used his informants to keep him apprised of her movements, since the plane's arrival time couldn't be easily predicted. There were about three more hours of night left, and Darwin was of course silent and still. The driver was a silent sort himself, who simply got out at her approach, took her one bag, tipped his hat and held the door for her to get into the second seat.

Lord Charles had a stunning place built out on one of the cliffs overlooking the sea. Unlike the bungalow and Victorian architecture of the other homes, after the WWII air raids, he'd built it in the likeness of an English manor, underscoring again how closely he felt tied to the country he considered home.

While she suspected he might have enjoyed the slight of not meeting her at the door, he was too much of a British gentleman to abandon that courtesy, and so Lord Charles was in the drive when she pulled up. She noted there were four men with him, and off to the right she saw the large cluster of outbuildings, which she was sure held his various twisted entertainments, such as his "pack."

He wore riding breeches, a well-cut broadcloth coat and linen shirt beneath, along with polished boots and spurs. His ice gray eyes revealed little as his man moved forward to open her door. Not himself, underscoring his status as ruler of this domain. While it was undeniable that all male vampires reflected masculine beauty, she remembered the ugly snarl twisting his face as he forced her to the floor and tried to intimidate her with a turgid cock. She could be nothing but revolted by the sight of his face.

With that in mind, she coolly ignored the hand he extended as she approached. Not just in calculation. If he kissed her knuckles, even a brush of lips, she was fairly sure she'd vomit. "Thank you for responding to my telegram, Lord Charles."

He dropped his hand. "Did you come merely to insult my hospitality, Lady Daniela?"

"No. I have other matters, in addition to that." She raised a brow, pursed her lips and glanced at his men. "You insulted *me* deeply, at my home. You attacked my person, made free with it in a manner that I cannot overlook."

He rolled his eyes. "So what, do you again go whinging to the Council? Give them more pathetically weak reasons to remove me? Faith, you know so little of our world, for having been in it for nearly two centuries. That's why I'm Region Master, and it took you so long, and with female trickery at that, to win a simple poor overlordship. Which I warrant will be taken from you before the year is over. I will not apologize for it." When he took another step closer, Danny forced herself not to move, not even twitch, as his breath touched her face.

"You may complain to the Council"—he bared his teeth—"but only after I've had you bound in stocks in one of my barns, buggered in every orifice you have. I'll roll you in manure and cattle urine, staple a tag in your ear so you finally know your place. *Then* you may crawl off to them. If I am merciful."

Force and fear were the only way he could get a hard-on anymore, she realized. He probably viewed seduction as too close to begging. Ruskin only took now. What wasn't given to him freely got his blood up. And strewth, on his home turf, he wasn't even pretending at civility. Pushing down an uneasy reaction to that, she arched a brow, swept an unimpressed look over his face, over the grounds around her.

"You're king of a tiny, inconsequential kingdom, Lord Charles. Despite all your pretensions, you know you are Region Master here *because* the Council doesn't care what vampires do in Australia. We can be as savage as we wish, ruling with our brutality instead of our brains, because it's in the more important areas of the world they need vampires who can manage affairs with intelligence and skill. Here, you can be as ham-fisted as you wish."

She was ready for the blow, could have ducked it easily, but she took it, knowing he would be doing it as a chastisement, a humiliation, not to knock her down. Even so, it knocked her head back, shoved her into the car door, denting it, and broke open her lip. She straightened, wiping the back of her hand over it, taking in his angry eyes, the hope for fear to flare in her eyes. She laughed instead. "And obviously too thick to understand the irony of that response."

Stepping forward again, she threw down the gauntlet. "The Council may not care about the vampires in Australia, but I do. I'm here to challenge you to a duel, Lord Charles Ruskin. Fencing. I win, I become Region Master. You win . . . you get to treat me like a cow, if that's your best idea of what being a vampire leader is all about."

"And how will you treat me if you win? Relegate me to a pathetic station like yours, out in the middle of nowhere?"

She didn't blink. "If I win, Lord Charles, you will be dead."

"And why wouldn't I take your life?"

"Because you want to punish me for being what I am. That's too tempting for you to pass up." Retreating enough to manage a mocking bow, she raised a brow. "So, blades until one yields or the other is dead? As I've said before, Huntington's rules are a little too modern and civilized for two such old souls as ourselves, I think."

Charles studied her a long moment, then inclined his head. "Done, Lady D. I will look forward to driving your mockery from your eyes, replacing it with fear."

"You will never have that satisfaction, no matter the outcome of our duel."

"That's the important difference in our ages, my dear," he said. "I know all things come with time." She noticed his dangerous cordiality had returned, as if the anger he'd displayed had never existed, as if he'd produced it simply to see how she would react. The four stockmen who'd been standing off to the side were moving closer, and as they approached, Danny realized she was wrong. They weren't stockmen. Not human ones. Four adult male vampires, likely Ruskin's spawn.

"My sons, so to speak," he confirmed it. "The best wealth a man can have in this country, to help him work his land, manage his interests. It's almost dawn now. You shall have your duel at dusk tomorrow, after you've had a good day's rest and a chance to feed. I am nothing if not fair."

Fairness was becoming an elusive hope, she knew, and quelled the frisson of uneasiness again. He had to be stopped. This was just more proof of it. A vampire had to have Council permission to make a vampire, and she doubted he had that for any of these. He thought himself outside of all rules.

"I would prefer to be done with it now," she said. "I expect it to go quickly."

"So do I, more's the pity, but I do not prefer it now." When he shifted his glance to the silent, still group of vampires, four pairs of eyes fixed on Danny in a manner that made her skin crawl, though she managed an indifferent stance. "We prepared quarters for you. With the children. They are looking forward to seeing you again."

As she turned toward him, he gave her a mocking bow. "I wouldn't suggest resisting us, Lady D. You are heavily outnumbered, and you will need all your energy to keep my darling tykes entertained through the long hours. Being penned up so much, they don't sleep much during the daylight hours. And if you can keep them from feeding on you, you're welcome to try and steal a sip from them." As he jerked his head toward the barn, the males closed around her.

Lyssa had reckoned that no matter Danny's strategy, based on her flight plan, it would be tonight before she and Ruskin got into it. Dev had to appreciate Alistair and Lyssa's willingness to fly during daylight, with heavily draped windows and backseat, such that there was almost no air back there at all in the stifling heat, the plane bouncing erratically over the thermals rising up from the Outback. Thank God that Alistair also had his own private plane that could carry up to ten, so there'd been no need to wait for a charter. Dev rode in the copilot chair, and Nina and Thomas sat in the row of seats behind them. Nina was unruffled, humming to herself as she gazed out at the view, holding on to the strap to buffer the jostling. Thomas tried hard not to get airsick as he watched over her.

Dev tried to doze, knowing he might need the sleep, but he had a hard time of it, not only because of the cramped quarters and loud roar of the engine, but because of that nagging sense of urgency. He'd had the desire, every other second it seemed, to reach out to Danny, speak to her, tell her he was coming. He didn't know if it was pride, residual awkwardness or intuition that made him hold off. Or if knowledge of what was happening to her might drive him mad.

Elisa had surprised him with her candor when he'd managed to connect with her by radio. "She's gone, sir," she'd reported unhappily. "We think she's going to challenge him to a duel, for she was practicing with her swords. We couldn't get her to pay attention to anything else. Left me and Willis this sealed envelope, I'm sure with instructions of what to do if she doesn't return. Oh, Mr. Dev . . ."

"You did fine, Elisa," he said. "We're going after her. You hold tight. Light a candle for us. And it's just Dev."

Hell, light a whole bonfire, because he was sure they were going to need it. He had the same feeling Elisa did. He stifled a curse. Challenge Ruskin to a duel, as if they were at some kind of fucking court event with king and country looking on. But following Danny's savvy mind, he figured that was what she was counting on. She was playing on the old bastard's pretensions at being a bloody noble. But she was also underestimating the sick underlayer, the one that would trump all that if he thought she had a shot. To Ruskin, to vampires as a whole, it seemed honor lay in winning, not necessarily in being honorable. And from watching her fence, Dev knew she had a hell of a good shot of winning.

Sitting in the plane, he'd gone over that first duel in his head a million times, every step she'd made, down to the one that had cost her the match. The subtle shift when she lost her balance and Ruskin cut under her guard, barely. Another second left or right and she would have avoided it. It had looked purely like a mistake, caused by his interruption in her mind, something she'd never taken him to task about, oddly. Because she'd intended to lose. She'd been gauging his strengths, setting Ruskin up to be overconfident.

With Ian, until the actual decapitation, she'd been dispassionate about her feelings for him. Such that Ruskin was as astounded as anyone in the room with the vicious decisiveness of her attack.

Yeah, his vampire had a bit of the sociopath in her, she did. The planning and patience required for Ian's death would have been admired by any soldier who'd had to lay motionless for an ambush. Hour after hour, as mosquitoes settled on flesh burned by the sun and flies crawled up your nose until you thought you'd go mad with it. And maybe she had, because she certainly hadn't put that kind of planning into her confrontation with Ruskin. Maybe because of Dev. She knew he wouldn't wait forever, because he'd said so, and she didn't want him involved. To protect him. *Christ.*

They still had an hour to go before reaching Darwin. And night was closing in.

∼

Lord Charles could have sent his men to retrieve her, bring her to the practice courtyard where he would complete his exercise in domination. However, he couldn't deny himself the pleasure of seeing his guest, normally so well put together and remote, reduced to rags and blood, carrying the exhaustion that would have come from fighting for her life until dusk. It was unlikely the children had killed her, of course. Not only did none of them have access to a stake or cutting tool, they'd be more interested in draining her rich vampire blood. And the more blood she lost, the harder she fought them, the weaker she would be.

As they slid back the door to the outbuilding where the cages were kept, as well as the communal pen where they'd released them last night, his gaze went to the latter area.

He didn't see her at first. He'd brought the original pack numbers up with another handful, but he wasn't surprised to see some of the newer ones dead. They weren't properly seasoned yet. He was impressed, regardless. She'd killed about six.

No matter. The orphan service was good about sending replacements whenever he asked for more, citing the growth of his interests and more placement opportunities. Particularly when he coupled it with donations to their cause and requests for more school materials because of his desire to educate them. His lips twisted. His money and position made it easy for them to accept it, the bleeding heart

fools. He told them he'd found the children various homes with remote station families, to learn the trades of shearing and cattle.
Forged happy letters from the tykes. The white ones, because, of
course, aboriginal children were no problem at all, their parents having no rights to reclaim or locate their snatched children anyway.

Still, it was a loss. The remaining children were milling on one
side of the pen, pacing, snarling, but at his presence they cowered
back, always uncertain of his mood until he produced food or a demand. Many of them had been wounded, repeatedly it seemed. Arms
at odd angles, some limping. There was torn flesh that would mend
in a day or two, perhaps longer, because even with the conversion,
children did not heal as fast as adult vampires. One or two had been
blinded, eyes gouged out. These whined piteously, even as they hissed
at their brethren who came too close and tried to take advantage of
their weakness. She was a nastier fighter than he'd given her credit
for, and of course some of them had taken the easier route of satisfying their hunger on their fallen brethren.

That was the problem he couldn't surmount, that he'd had when
chasing her servant. They were scavengers primarily, and would take
a fresh kill over pursuing the stronger, moving trophy. But older
children had more of the craving for the hunt in them, so he'd made
sure the newer ones were older. Ten and twelve years of age. With
satisfaction, he saw those were still prowling, looking for an opening
against her. Though she was a vampire, they still knew the rich aroma
of prey.

She'd struggled to her feet at the sound of the door rolling back,
for there was straw sticking to the back of her shirt and trousers,
though that could have been from her struggles throughout the night.
Her hair was an unruly mess, no longer the soft style that had made
her face look so deceptively angelic when she'd stepped from the car.
Remembering how she'd disdained his hand on his front porch, his
lip curled. She wasn't getting the opportunity to scorn him, ever
again.

If she'd shown him one moment of favor, bowed to his authority,
he might have entertained the idea of an alliance, for her standing
was strong among the vampire world. And she did have her appeal.

When she turned her face to him, the defiance in her eyes aroused as much as angered him. The latter was mollified by her pallor. They hadn't let her feed. Good pets. He would make sure his vampires tossed them a whore from town tonight or a swagman drifting through that no one would miss. While they fed on the blood, he would feed on the screams of the confused and terrified humans. Better than sex, practically. Able to be enjoyed by oneself, fully. When he had such thoughts, he knew he was meant to be a king. Perfect isolation in one's own mind, while dominating the world around him. He didn't need Lady Daniela or anyone else.

The blood on her clothes, copious amounts of it, told him she'd likely been wounded numerous times. While she was almost two hundred and her healing was swift, vitality had to be restored with blood. Blood she wouldn't get.

What had happened with that servant of hers? Why wasn't he with her? He would have enjoyed tormenting him in ways that could stretch on for days, but he put that dissatisfaction aside when he noted some of her struggles had landed her in the waste often left in the pen by frightened human victims. They had it mucked out once a week for that reason. However, he didn't want the stench to distract him from the pleasure of bringing her to her knees. Because while he had her down there, he'd make her suck him off. Yes, he liked that idea exceedingly well. Once she was under his control, he'd even fit her with a permanent bit, stretching and tearing those pouty lips, so she would have to service him whenever he desired, with no ability to dismember him with her teeth. It made him hard, just thinking about it, and he was almost impatient with the duel, wanting it out of the way.

"Take her to a room, let her clean herself up and prepare her weapons."

~

"Coward."

Danny stepped out of the corner after Lord Ruskin issued the command, causing him to stop and turn. Sending a warning look to the two circling vampire children, she made it clear they'd regret making another move forward. Probably because they'd had enough of her blood to be halfway sensible, they hung back. Still, they were opportunists, so she proceeded carefully to the front of the big pen. "My mother told me you were not even man enough to stay in Darwin during the war, when it was bombed. You fled, like a dog with his tail tucked between his legs." Thinking of Dev, the battle wounds he'd sustained, her voice strengthened. "While Aussies and Brits alike went toe-to-toe with the Japanese."

"Why do I care who wins human wars?" He scoffed. "We're far superior to them. It affects me not at all."

"No, you wouldn't care. Any more than you care what true honor and courage are." She spat then. The tomboy skill she hadn't exercised in years kicked in enough to win her the small victory of the saliva striking the front of his perfect linen shirt. "You wouldn't know true nobility if it bit you on the backside, *Lord* Charles."

"I've changed my mind," he said after a long moment, when it was obvious that fury had robbed him of speech. "Take her out in the yard, strip and hose her down like you would stock."

When she saw the imagining of it flash through his eyes, she sickened at the visible swell in the front of his breeches. "Let her change into the appropriate clothes out there and give her the blades she's brought," he continued. "Don't leave her alone for any reason."

~

Danny knew it was a futile expenditure of energy and a telling one, for she should have been able to give considerable trouble to vampires under the age of fifty, as these "sons" of Charles's were. However, she wouldn't capitulate, strip before those leering male eyes. So they closed in on her and she struggled while they tore her clothes from her, rolling her over in the dirt of the yard, kicking at her, punching when needed, groping whenever they could get lucky, while she screamed and fought back. She landed a few blows of her own that, like the children, had them somewhat wary by the end, but only the way men around a calf were, knowing they would overpower the poor beast with only a certain amount of caution.

At least the water was not cold, but the humiliation made her wish for Dev's ability to block things out as she stood in the center and they washed her down like cattle, then made her stand, naked and shivering while they retrieved her travel bag with her blades and fencing clothes.

In those long daylight hours, she'd been bitten numerous times, had bones broken, skin ripped from her. Once or twice, they'd piled up on her so skillfully that several had been able to get nice long drinks before she could struggle free. Of course it had all healed back, but there were some places, closer to dusk, she'd not allowed to heal fully, conserving her strength. While she'd managed to catch one or two a couple times, reclaim some of that blood, there were too many. Before she could get too much sustenance, her flank and back were attacked and she'd had to fight again. They might have no true feeling for one another, but they'd learned the laws of being a pack.

She blocked out the faces she was smashing, arms she twisted, eyes she gouged. Nine-year-old boys, ten-year-old girls. One girl, perhaps six, who couldn't possibly survive long in this mob, for the other children were much stronger.

She'd understood why it haunted Dev, but she couldn't deal with that right now. It didn't matter that she was weak, that she'd lost so much blood. She was going to fight the bastard, and she was going to win, on strength of will alone if she had to. There were soldiers, or diggers as Dev'd call them, who'd fought and won battles far past the point when their bodies should have given out, when something far more elemental kicked in and said, "Bugger it, I'm not going to stand for it."

The thought of the bushman brought the yearning that had recurred through the night. Hell, she hadn't been able to push it away since he'd left. If she'd thought he was close enough, she'd have reached out to him. She'd been tempted to try to locate him, but what would it avail her to find he was still in Queensland, probably trying to erase her memory with a fat-arsed whore with a kind heart and soft hands? Or that he was deep in the bush again?

He'd made his choice, and she'd respect it. If she tried to reach out to him now, it wouldn't be fair anyway. She couldn't let him know what was going on. The noble daft bastard would feel he had some obligation to her, though nothing could be farther from the truth. But she couldn't help but long for the sound of his voice, that relaxed drawl. The dry, self-deprecating humor that made her picture his half smile, the Gallic shrug.

It had been wrong, what she'd done to him that night. Didn't change the fact that it had given her such pleasure, or that, to be her servant, he'd have been subjected to more and worse at future vampire gatherings. Particularly if she was going to subject *herself* to the politics of being a Region Master. He wasn't cut out for it, never had been.

Which brought her back to the present. Probably knowing it didn't take much to get on Ruskin's entertainment agenda for the evening, most of the staff moving about their daily business between the outbuildings didn't linger. Except for one.

Aapti stood on the back porch, the servant motionless and watching. Danny suspected Charles had her there so she could give him a play-by-play without him appearing to have vulgar curiosity. Remembering Chiyoko, she pushed the bitterness about that away, and locked gazes with the woman.

"I'm sorry," Danny said. "Not for what I intend to do to him, but for what it will do to you."

The servant's dark eyes flickered. Without a word, she turned and went back into the main house.

Her bag was tossed to her. The vampires stood, arms crossed, staring at her with hungry eyes, anticipating what Ruskin might yet allow them to do to her. Ignoring them, she imagined she was in her bedroom back in the station as best she could as she wrung out her hair. She dearly would have liked a brush. Her hands wanted to tremble as she lifted them to tie it back. Weakness in her arms, her wrists. Damn it, she could *not* lose this.

She'd brought a snug top, no loose sleeves. Cotton pants that clung indecently for a woman, as Dev might think, but stretched and moved with her as if she wore nothing. Slippers with traction on the soles, making it easy to spin and lunge, regardless of the surface. She blotted her face dry and then turned to the case that held her blades. When she closed her hands on the hilts of the two sabers, she saw the gleam of the silver on the curve, a reflection of the moonlight above. Thinking of it glimmering with the crimson of Ruskin's blood gave her some extra energy. As well as the fact his men had come to attention, watching her closely. She spun, arcing the blade out, and the four either ducked or jumped back. Her lips curved in a feral smile.

"If we're done with Ruskin's little tantrum, I'm ready to go cut your Master down to size, boys."

~

He did like ceremony. She had to suppress the desire to roll her eyes. The practice yard had been lined with unnecessary torches, and he had the four vampires each take a corner, like an honor guard. Except she noted they all kept their weapons, an assortment of pistols, rifles and knifes.

"Don't think you can beat me on your own, Ruskin?" she asked contemptuously. "Not that you've already made that patently obvious, by how you've tried to weaken me. It must twist your cowardly gullet, knowing you fear a woman's blade."

Lord Charles, on the other side of the tourney area, gave her a disdainful look. "You are a fair hand with a blade. While I'm better, stronger and faster, I'm not going to leave my victory to skill alone. No wise leader ever did that. The elements of luck and surprise have been known to favor the less deserving."

"Well, at least that explains why you were allowed to become Region Master."

Without waiting for response, Danny took position on the mark that had been etched approximately fifteen feet away. Ruskin shed his coat and took up an *en garde* stance mirroring hers, his eyes glittering. He'd chosen his own saber this time, but had opted for one blade versus her two, perhaps indicating his confidence, or just that he'd never learned to fight with two. "I will take such pleasure in bringing you to heel."

"God, you've got tickets on yourself. Nurse that fantasy when I take your head."

He leaped forward on a simple attack and she met him, changing her crossed sword stance to a dual sweep across the body that deflected his blade as she spun, bringing the one down toward his calf even as he recovered and came overhand at her upper body. She caught that but felt the shock of it reverberate through her shoulder. Danny ducked under and spun, but he pinked her, tearing a hole in the sleeve of the shirt. She rolled back as he roared, lunging forward. When she brought the hilt up, she took his blade on the guard with enough force she thought her wrist might have cracked.

He's strong, well rested. Outthink him, you idiot.

As she admonished herself, they circled, engaged. Danny countered the increasing complexity of his attacks with parry and riposte, use of her blade and quickness, but her recovery time was off. Thank God her footwork was holding, but she couldn't get herself positioned for counterattack. She found herself quickly on the defensive, which she knew would wear her out in time. He knew it, too, his lips curving in a smug smile.

Though she knew it unwise, she let anger and frustration give her renewed energy, and lunged, scoring a slash across his chest, damaging his shirt, but he twisted away, came back and sliced her side, causing her to cry out and stumble, momentarily unsure if he'd damaged her spine.

He was back on her, and she rolled backward, coming up in a half squat, one blade extended, the other pulled back to her ear, holding it in the upper line of defense, and he snarled, slashing across, which knocked the lower blade free and sent it clattering across the cobblestones. She surged up, coming inside his defenses. Punching him in the jaw with the guard, she nicked his ear with the blade before they sprung apart and circled again.

Her breathing was labored, while his eyes were alight with the victory he knew was coming, the simmering anger in his eyes promising her hell on earth. When she lunged again, he was ready.

After another hour of these tactics, she knew she wasn't going to win. It was creeping into the back of her mind, despite herself. She could force him to finish her. She'd rather die than . . .

No, she wasn't losing this match, and even if she did, she owed Devlin. She wouldn't take the coward's way out, no matter what.

He tensed his back leg, an indication of lunge, and she was ready with the riposte and parry when it came, but instead of checking himself against her blades, he plowed forward, locking their blades together, wrist to wrist, and used the brute force of his body to knock her backward, take them both to the stones. When he got her there with the unexpected move, he had his body full on hers. Danny promptly reared up, seized his ear in her fangs and snapped her head back. With a howl, he rolled away and she spat the flesh out of her mouth, managed to get to her feet as he came at her again. She got one arm up in time, but he came down on it like a crashing wave, enough to crush her. She cried out and fell. Though she scrambled to get up, he shoved her back and slammed his boot down on her throat, the sword point hovering over her eye.

"Yield, Lady Danny. You are outmatched."

"I think not yet."

24

LORD Ruskin's head snapped up toward the imperious and unmistakable voice of Lady Lyssa. Danny caught his foot, wrenched it, heaving him off her and sending him stumbling back as she brought her sword up. Their blades crossed, a holding point, and Charles turned his attention to his visitors again, registering Lord Alistair and Dev behind the vampire queen.

"My lord, Lady Lyssa," the terrified butler stammered, "she insisted on being seen into your presence at once. I could not—"

Dev noted that Lord Charles had a Herculean struggle to rein back his irritation at being interrupted. Though Alistair had made himself quite clear, Dev supposed he should be grateful for the crushing grip the vampire had on his arm, which had kept him from rushing the field and leaping on Ruskin himself when he took Danny down.

Now the Northwest Territory Region Master stepped back from Lady Danny, putting several paces between them. Dev assumed it was to give the appearance that they'd interrupted a civilized fencing match. Danny was paler than he'd ever seen her, obviously weak and injured, though they hadn't been fencing long enough to warrant that. It looked like she'd been drained of blood. The bloody bastard. Dev had seen her fight, and the few minutes they'd seen as they came in wasn't her best fighting, not by a long shot. Her speed was down, and her strength was lacking. If anything, Ruskin was likely getting off on toying with her, or she had superb footwork, enough to make him fight for his impending stolen victory.

"Lord Ruskin, it appears you have a territory matter in process," Alistair noted smoothly. "I understand Lady Daniela challenged you to a fair duel for an insult done to her. While you are allowed as Region Master to answer such a duel, I believe it is only fair play that she be allowed to fight you on the terms she has offered. Which"—his gaze went to Danny's pallor—"does not appear to be the case."

"I am not responsible for the condition in which she comes to me to offer her challenge." Lord Charles shrugged. "If she has not fed as she should, that is her own handicap."

"Well, being the sporting gentleman that you are, I'm sure you won't mind a recess to offer us a welcoming cup of wine and allow her to regain some of her strength with the assistance of her servant, will you? Then we can come back here and enjoy watching what appears to be a truly excellent match. If honor is satisfied after that, and you are the victor, we will escort the properly chastised Lady Danny back home."

"You do not have the authority to set such terms. This is my Region—"

"But I do." Lady Lyssa pinned Ruskin with her gaze, held it there with ice-cold intent until he shifted his own gaze with little grace, unable to match her power. "As liaison to the Council, I even have the right to stop this bout if I deem it disadvantageous to their interests."

"With all due respect, great lady, I do not believe the Council has invested you with that power, either. You did not allow them to grant you such influence." Ruskin's voice held satisfaction underneath the barbed words of deference. "I do pay attention to Council communiqués. Quite closely."

"You are correct," she said, unruffled. "But by the same rules you yourself have exercised to unfairly weigh this match in your favor, I can cross this courtyard and rip your head from your shoulders before you have a chance to blink. And no one here will go against me when I report to the Council the unfortunate nature of your passing. You do not have a good reputation, Lord Charles. I would not test me."

Dev felt the cold wind that moved through the courtyard, as if ice attended her words. It was obvious she had not issued an idle threat. At the four corners, the other vampires shifted, disturbed, even as Lord Charles sent them a quelling look.

He brought his sword up, an ungracious salute. "Well, then, I welcome you to my home. If you will come with me, I will see to your refreshment, while Lady Danny is attended by her servant. But she will not leave this courtyard, and I only agree to a half-hour break of the bout."

"That seems hardly—" Alistair started.

"That will be enough," Danny cut in. When she got to her feet, Dev detected a slight sway as she made it upright, but her pale face was resolute. "One half hour, my lord. Go take your last cup of wine. I'd make it one of your favorites, because as far as I know, there are no libations in hell."

Lord Charles's lip curled back. "That's the last order you'll ever give me, whore."

"You will give her the privacy of this courtyard with her servant," Lyssa said sharply. "Your cronies will come with us or wait elsewhere. She has acted with honor in coming here and requesting the duel. If she gives us her word she will not leave the courtyard, she won't."

"Yes, my lady," Danny confirmed. Lyssa glanced at her. From that look, Dev had a feeling that if Danny survived this, she might be in for an equally terrifying dressing-down from the vampire queen.

Lord Charles made a curt gesture to the four vampire males, and they moved to the nearest exit from the courtyard area, disappearing. Then he turned and swept his arm forward. While his gesture bordered on rude, Lyssa and Alistair let it pass, accompanying him from the courtyard, though Lyssa gave Dev an even look before they departed. "Give her what she needs," she said.

The second they vanished, Dev lunged into the battlefield, for

Danny fell to one knee, the blade clattering to the ground. He caught her before she could join it there, and felt somewhat relieved when her hands clutched his arms. "You are an idiot," he informed her. "No offense, my lady. Ah, Jesus." This close, holding her, he could see how truly pale she was, the glassiness of her eyes, the faint tremor in her body. "A half hour's not going to be enough."

"Yes, it will." Though he wanted to get right to giving her blood, she was staring up at him in a way that suggested she wasn't ready for that yet. Her fingers touched his jaw as he settled to the cobblestones, stretching out one leg beneath both of hers, his other knee up to support her back along his arm, cradling her. "It's nice to see you again," she said. "Why did you . . . Ah, God. You figured it out, and you're being bloody noble. I'm *not* your obligation."

"That cold wind thing Lady Lyssa does would have been nice for us to have when we were in the desert."

"It's not a vampire gift. She's got Fey blood. And don't change the bloody subject."

Spearing his fingers through her hair, he cupped the back of her head, gave her a hard look. "Can you drink before we argue? I'd like you to be around to finish our fight."

"I wouldn't . . . He wouldn't kill me. I wouldn't do that to you."

"Yeah, so I heard. You think I'd be all right with that, knowing you'd become his bitch hound, and those poor kids still suffering?"

"You weren't supposed to know, one way or another. And I'm supposed to beat him, so it's a moot point."

"You've got that one right. Drink, damn it." Realizing she might be too weak at this point to cut a vein herself, he drew his knife. "Which cup you want it out of, love? Throat or wrist?"

She was studying him in that intent, mysterious way of hers, but before he could take the decision from her, make an incision and force it to her lips, she slid her hand to the side of his throat. He took his cue, tightening his arm around her slim back to bring her close to it, lifting his chin and feeling a wave of inexplicable emotion choke him as her teeth sank in and she began to drink, take what she needed from him. Putting the other arm around her, too, he held her closer.

I have to drink a little more than usual, Dev. I'm sorry.

You take everything you need, love. It's all yours. Unless you're doing it to keep me too weak to try to kill that bastard if he does anything else to you.

You'd never get near him. You can't fight a vampire.

It isn't always about succeeding, love. Sometimes it's just the doing. And if you lose, but I'm dead, you can still take his final victory from him, can't you?

She pulled away briefly, and he felt the seep of blood as she gave him a look that was far more like herself. "I told you I won't be your death wish, Dev. Not now, not ever."

When she put her mouth back on him, he gave her the answer to that. *It's not that, love. I'm not sure I could stand to be around if you're not. I won't bear anyone harming you, you hear?*

Her grip on his shoulder slid around so the fingers were at the base of his skull, caressing his hair. For only a moment, he felt a trickle of the feeling moving through her, but it was enough to make him cinch his arms around her, his thoughts speaking forcefully into her mind.

I'm here, and I'm not going anywhere. Even if you lost, I'd stay. I won't let you be alone, no matter what they do to us both.

You don't have to stay. You're—

"I'm your servant." He said it out loud, cutting over her. He was feeling a little light-headed. Jesus, but the blood rushed out of the throat fast. He could feel her closing it up, doing that provocative little teasing thing she did with her tongue to make it clot, sealing the vein. When she leaned back, he was glad to see there was color seeping back into her face, though her body was still too heavy in his arms for his liking. But her eyes were riveted on his face.

"I'm your full, fucking human servant, and that's what I'm going to be for the next several hundred years or so. At least that's what the judge says this convict's sentence is." He gave her a wry grin, but his heart tore with the effort of it. "You did it, so you're going to have to put up with me, you hear? You can't change your mind in a few years and realize you'd like some English butler type who will 'yes, m'lady' and 'no, m'lady' you and kiss your arse. You're going to have to put up with a rough stockman who speaks his mind, but who'll manage the hell out of your place."

He stopped abruptly, realizing he was talking nonsense. She could, of course, do whatever the hell she pleased. He wasn't going to bloody beg her.

"Dev?" The scattershot of his thoughts was dispelled by her soft voice, the way her blue eyes rested on his face. "You don't understand what you're getting into." But her hands were curling into his arms, and he hoped it was because she didn't want to let him go.

"No, I don't. No bloody bloke understands what he's taking on when he tells a woman he's going to stand by her no matter what. I can handle the sheep and the books, drought and dust storms. But your moods, and Lord God, the dinner parties, are going to take me some time."

Her lips curved. "We'll see if we can't take those slow, then. We have more picnic races out in the station area than vampire get-togethers. I like the way you dance, bushman." But then the serious look came back into her eyes. "Why, Dev?"

Because, of all the things I've seen, people are what they are. You either accept them that way or move on. You have to accept what you are yourself, as well.

"So you decided not to move on."

He nodded, meeting her gaze.

What type of person does that make you, I wonder?

"I guess God will answer that one day," he said. "Until then, I'll answer to you, my lady."

"When it suits you," she said, reading the unconscious flow of his thoughts. He looked startled, but then matched her smile.

"Well, I did say you'd picked the wrong person if you were looking for someone who says 'yes, marm' all the time."

She squeezed him. "It's good to have you here, Dev. I'm as fit as a mallee bull now, but think you can help me up? We can talk more about this . . . after."

"Right-o." Clearing his throat, he got to his feet, and lifted her onto hers, inspecting the slice on her side, which had almost healed now, as well as the pink on her arm. "You need some more."

She shook her head. "I can't take any more of yours without debilitating you for a much longer time. And I'm not sure it would make much difference at this point."

"Then you'll take mine." Lyssa had returned, and she stepped into the courtyard now, studying the two of them, Danny in particular, as she turned. "Because it *will* make a difference."

"My lady." Danny seemed at a loss for words. "You've already done me a great service."

"Your man has done *you* a great service, pulling us out of bed, something I will be certain to take in trade next time he's at one of *my* dinner parties." She gave Dev a veiled look, but she was already unbuttoning her cuff and pulling back the sleeve. "There's no time, girl. Take more."

"You—"

"I trust you, Danny," Lyssa said gently, drawing her forward with a hand on her arm. "Take it now, and no argument. You've only got about a quarter hour left."

Danny nodded, and then surprised Dev when she went to one knee by the petite woman, an act of decided deference as she put her mouth to the woman's wrist. "Keep my arm steady, Dev," Lyssa said. When he moved forward, sliding his hand under her forearm to form a three-way link, Danny bit, much more carefully than with him, he noted with grim amusement. Lyssa absently lifted a hand to stroke it over Dev's hair, along his back and to his arm, giving him a pet while allowing his Mistress to drink. Another small price she was extracting, he expected, but he found the sensual touch almost reassuring, a connection between the three of them.

When Danny sealed the wound and rose, she did it without help this time, and the color was back in her cheeks. There was also a bolstering flash to her eye. "My thanks to you both."

Lyssa inclined her head. "Your mother, before she lost her mind through grief, would have been very proud of you, Danny. Live up to your family today. Take this bastard down."

"I will."

"I suppose you understand, now that we've interfered, if he wins, he'll do it by taking your head. He will not permit you to leave this property, and that's the only fair way he can accomplish it."

"No." Danny shook her head. "When he comes back, I'll make it clear I'll honor our bargain, no matter your presence or what Alistair said. If he wins, I won't leave here. I won't sacrifice Dev."

"Yeah, you will." Dev took the lead now, taking her hand and giving her a hard look. "We stand or we fall together, love. Don't piss me off by doing it half measure."

Dev had been through bombings, ambushings, even faced off with tai pans and crocs, and a near deadly run-in with a funnel web spider once. He didn't care about his life. It was what it was, and if it ended today or tomorrow, it was of no great consequence to the world. But he didn't want anything to happen to her, and that issue was oddly disconnected to what would happen to him if she was struck down.

As he saw her register it, he sent her another thought, one intended to dispel the somber cast of her eyes, to bring back the flash of fire.

It's a moot point anyway, remember? You're going to take his ruddy head.

～

Unfortunately Ruskin returned with restored spirits as well and renewed determination. He couldn't have what he wanted, but it was obvious, as Lyssa implied, that he would improvise. Dev could imagine his thought process. If he struck down a born vampire of consummate fencing skill, like Danny, that might improve his standing in the eyes of others.

The duel resumed. The four vampires were in the corners again, but they were unarmed now, and their attention was diverted between their sire and Alistair and the deceptively relaxed pose of Lady Lyssa. The latter was seated in a chair while Alistair leaned against the courtyard wall behind her, his eyes watchful, dangerous. Nina and Thomas were within sight of the vampires, but on an upper balcony overlooking the courtyard, well away from the action.

As for Dev, he'd chosen a squat on the ground just outside the match boundaries, balanced, solid on one foot, the other heel out, a pose he could hold for some time and which kept him from jumping up and surging forward each time Ruskin pressed an advantage.

She still wasn't full on, but she was doing a hell of a lot better, and the sneak suspicion he'd had about her was being reinforced. Those forward lunges, her deft counterattacks, the parry and ripostes, showed her footwork was better than Ruskin's, her compound attack strategies and secondary intents obviously superior. This time it was the older vampire whose breath started to labor, though hers did as well. They'd nicked each other a few times, and she'd managed a good cut across his side once, quid pro quo for his earlier take in that area.

Back and forth, the cobblestones ringing with the sound of crossed steel, the shuffle of slippers and boots. At first, so involved in the duel, Dev didn't pay attention to the weather, but then he noted the stars had disappeared and the wind was kicking up. A flash or two heralded the impending storm, and thunder began to be heard over the constant roll of the ocean off the cliffs where Ruskin's home was built.

A Darwin lightning storm was an extraordinary phenomenon, but Dev could have wished for better timing. The wind started blowing out the torches, so soon the vampires fought in darkness, silhouettes that spun and moved in full shadow, making it hard for him to see who had the advantage. He couldn't see Lyssa or Alistair to gauge their reactions, either.

But then the flashes began to spin into a full-course light show, shards of light cracking through the air above them, giving the display of skills an ethereal spotlight from time to time, catching the flash of an eye or baring of a fang, the glitter along a blade or curve of a guard. They had to treat wind as a factor, of course, with it whistling in through the various entry points to the courtyard.

A particularly loud crack came in darkness, a clatter, and he saw one of her sabers skitter across the ground, coming to a spinning stop close to him. When he reached for it, Alistair spoke sharply. "No. This is their fight."

He might have ignored him, but Dev's attention was caught by the two combatants. They appeared to be grappling. Then they pushed away and Ruskin lunged forward, skewering Danny through the abdomen.

Dev surged to his feet as she screamed, but her other blade was in motion. With a savage snarl, she brought it around in an erratic sweep. On a strobe of lightning and Ruskin's bellow, he saw her notch it under his ear, the force of the swing biting into his neck enough to hold the blade in the bone, but not enough to go all the way through. A brief glimpse of her savage, blood-smeared expression, then she was in darkness again. Her silhouette held there for one more blink while Ruskin's body jerked, his strangled scream of rage vibrating through the air. When his arms started flailing, trying to grasp or knock out the blade, she let go of the weapon.

Dev was unable to follow her with his eyes, but he felt the breeze of her passing, heard the scrape of the other saber on the stone. As Ruskin staggered, trying to reorient himself, lightning flashed again. So Dev *did* see her sweep back in over the other blade and take his head.

Thunder reverberated, a low growl. Dev went for his knife. Alistair and Lyssa were already moving as the four young vampires lunged forward, their movements strobed by a staccato of storm flashes. The thunder's voice was enhanced by a warning hiss from Lady Lyssa, a chilling sound that came from the darkest worlds of children's nightmares. Though Alistair had drawn a pair of wickedly sharp daggers, that one sound settled in the vitals with the weight of imminent death, bringing Ruskin's progeny to an uncertain halt.

As Thomas had joined them with a lantern, Dev quickly shifted his focus to Danny. She'd backed away from the fallen body, and was peering through the darkness. She was looking for him. Her clothes and face were splattered with blood, her midriff soaked.

With an oath, he was moving toward her, heedless of any other threat now. When the sword dropped from her hand and she fell to one knee, holding her abdomen, he was there, holding it with her. Blood oozed around their tangled fingers.

"Bloody hell, that hurts," she said.

25

RAIN at last came, as if it had only been waiting to lash the courtyard and the fallen body, the gruesome staring head. Despite the fleeting feeling of amusement Dev felt from his lady, he insisted on carrying her, and wasn't sure he was wrong about it. She was weak again, and he didn't believe it was all from the stomach wound. With a savage wave of fury that made him want to kick the head across the courtyard for extra measure, he realized whatever Ruskin had done to her in the hours before their duel was going to take some time to rejuvenate her fully. His blood and Lyssa's had carried her through this, though. Just.

He took her to a couch in the nearest room, which appeared to be a study. He heard Lyssa ordering the servants to bring them some wine while Alistair instructed the four vampires on the disposal of Ruskin, and other matters.

"Until the Council rules one way or another, that woman is your acting Region Master," he heard the vampire lord's warning. "So I'd pay particular attention to the things she wants, or it's likely to be your head rolling around that courtyard."

Danny made a noise of protest as Dev lifted the shirt. The stomach wound would have eviscerated a human. The kind of wound he'd seen men die of, in agony. Her free hand shifted, laid on his.

It's fine, Dev. We just need to bind it up to hold everything in. "I hate to ask"—she gave a weak smile—"but if I can get some more blood, it should knit up, good as new."

"You don't ask a servant for blood. You take it," Lyssa said shortly, materializing at his elbow like a malevolent dark witch, her hair brushing Dev's arm. "Here. The household staff provided us bandages. Apparently they have frequent need of them."

"Don't be angry," Danny said. "And don't take it out on him."

"You would be wise to say as little as possible to me," Lyssa said, pinning the younger vampire with a dangerous look. "Until I decide not to kill you myself."

"She's right, though," Dev said, cupping Danny's face, drawing her attention. "It's past time for asking."

Danny closed her eyes. "Bandage the wound first."

It wasn't easy, for it did hurt her terribly. He had to steel himself to her gasps, her death grip on Lyssa's hand, vampire bones the only ones resilient enough to take her grip as he and Thomas worked as quickly as possible. Nina proved a competent nurse as they wrapped the gaping wound tightly so the skin could mend without her insides dropping out, something that would disconcert him greatly, whatever Danny herself felt about it.

As they cleaned her up, though, Dev noted bruising, gashes that were half healed. Teeth marks. *What the hell . . .* "These are older." His fingers passed over them. "Why aren't they healed?"

"When I take blood, I can divert the energy from healing to physical strength, when I need it." She lifted a shoulder. "Given the situation, I thought it might be best to augment my strength for the fight."

"They will take longer to heal, as a result." Lyssa bent to take a closer look herself. "But still within a few days. How did he do this?"

Alistair came in then, and regardless of the sense it made, Dev shifted her shirt to cover the lace-covered breasts. The male vampire drew Nina close to his side to slip an arm around her, offer a tender squeeze of reassurance before he nodded her toward a chair.

"Danny," Lyssa repeated with far less patience.

Dev thought it odd to see Danny hesitate the way she did now, waiting for Nina to get seated. Then he saw the shadows gathering in her eyes and understood. She wasn't trying to avoid Lyssa's question. She just couldn't bear to say the words, because of how she'd had to deal with it.

"The children. He put you in with the children during the day, when you should have slept." He felt a renewed surge of rage, and his hand clenched into a fist on her leg. "That bloody bastard."

Danny's gaze flickered, locked on his to say the words. "I killed another handful."

"You had to do it. You know you did."

She made a half shrug, looked down at her hands, then back up. "I'm thinking . . . Well, I'm having a daft thought, Dev."

She spoke to him, as if no one else was in the room. It was a unique feeling, since he'd already noted that when there was more than one vampire about, servants were treated as children—best seen, not heard.

"How many are left?"

"About eight."

They held gazes a long moment. "You think they can be tamed down."

"I know I should kill them. It would be the most merciful thing. They'll never grow up, never have adult bodies. But they've had nothing but cruelty and abandonment. I can't do it." She turned her attention to Lyssa. "It's one of the things I brought to the Council, but Ruskin convinced them I'd been misinformed. They've been dealing with the territory war in Germany, and that was taking precedence. Ruskin changes orphans and aborigine children, uses them like a pack of hounds for his sport."

"If you don't kill them now, it will be much harder later on," Lyssa said impassively as Alistair muttered an oath.

"We all have the option of walking into the sun, when we're in sound mind to make that decision," Danny responded slowly. "I'd like to give them more of a life than what they've had, let them make that decision for themselves. Will you give me that right?"

Lyssa exchanged a long glance with Alistair. "Well," the vampire queen said at last. "As we know, I am merely a powerless figurehead. Who am I to make such a call?"

Danny smiled as Alistair snorted. "You are Region Master of the Northwest Territory now," he said to Danny. "Or will be, if Lady Lyssa and I have anything to say about it. As such, it is your call."

Dev felt some of the tension leave her body. Her fingers twined with his, drawing his attention back to her tired face. "I'm thinking Elisa and Willis might help us care for them. If we get the children's bloodlust under control, then the two of them can help take care of them, until they mature enough to need individual servants." A glimmer of something that might have been humor, if it hadn't been clouded by shadows of the past day, passed through her blue eyes. "Your job managing my sheep will include an additional herd, I'm afraid. A far more unpredictable one."

"We can negotiate better wages later. I expected the job to be a bit different than most."

"They'll never grow up. Never sexually mature," she repeated.

"Maybe that's a good thing. A man's pecker can make him do a lot of daft things. Like fall in with a sharp-toothed sheila."

She gave him a narrow look. "Here I was thinking it was your overdeveloped sense of honor that gets you in such trouble."

"Pot calling the kettle black, love. Let me give you more blood." He was worried that she seemed to be getting noticeably paler.

"Not quite yet." Drawing a deep breath, Danny moved her attention back to Lyssa's dark eyes, the rim of green iris a faint glow of emerald fire in the candlelight. "I have a feeling my lady Lyssa has other things to say to me, and that she might be kinder about them if she feels I'm not up to full strength."

"You ascribe qualities of mercy to me I may not have, Lady D," Lyssa remarked. She glanced at Alistair. "My lord, will you please go check on these children? I want another set of eyes to confirm Ruskin's actions, to help with our report to the Council, which will include what I expect was an unsanctioned making of these four vampires. You will need to accompany me and Lady Danny to Berlin, when she accounts for this matter. I will watch after Nina while you're checking the grounds," she added, glancing toward the woman.

Alistair nodded and withdrew. Then Lyssa looked toward Dev.

Anticipating, he shook his head. "Danny needs blood," he said stubbornly.

Dev.

"And your lady *Daniela* will have it. But you will obey my direction. Go stand there." Lyssa pointed to the other side of the door where Thomas had slipped in and taken up a silent post. When she looked in his direction, he spoke.

"Aapti was in the upper chamber, my lady. She died in her bed, it appears."

It jolted Dev, the reminder that the death of a vampire meant the loss of more than one life, though he was more concerned about the additional pain that crossed his lady's face. Surely she'd weighed the consequences of her actions. But it didn't make it easier, he knew.

"Go to the door, Devlin," Lyssa said, and that cold note was in her voice. "You may stay in this room, not because you've done anything to deserve it, but because I want you to hear what I say to your Mistress. Perhaps between the two of you, you will have enough sense to survive another decade or so."

Go, Dev. Do as she says. I'm all right.

Though he had his doubts about that, Dev rose. As he did, a hint of sharp fang appeared beneath Lyssa's curled lip. "Given the evening's circumstances, I will let your defiance pass. But never again refuse a vampire that outranks your Mistress, unless it is at her direction you do so. You may deprive her of a servant in as little time as it takes to rip a man's heart out of his chest." Her eyes held his so intently Dev felt pinned by the hypnotic gaze of a serpent. "And believe me, it takes *very* little time."

"Lyssa." Danny struggled up to her elbows. Dev wanted to help her, but before he could step forward, Thomas's hand was on his arm, drawing him back.

"Don't be an idiot," he muttered. "In this mood, my lady is apt to put you through a wall. And your head could cause these walls serious damage."

He saw then that Lyssa had moved in, helped Danny to rise. With some pride in his sheila, however, he saw she shook her head at further assistance, putting her feet to the floor and bracing herself in the upright position, though it looked as if a feather could knock her down.

Despite that, and the fact her torn and bloody shirt was still open, she sat straight and tall, unconcerned about her appearance. "I am at your disposal, my lady Lyssa," she said.

"You are at the end of my last nerve, is what you are. You came here, by yourself, thinking that you could outwit a five-hundred-year-old vampire into playing a game by your rules."

"Yes, my lady."

"Do I need you to confirm the obvious? Don't speak until I give you leave to do so. The problem with born vampires is they're often overly spoiled by their parents, leading them to overconfidence in their abilities."

Dev noted, with some relief, that while Danny's eyes flashed, she pressed her lips together and remained silent. Even Thomas seemed tense and alert, not a good sign. She'd held her own, though, damn it. Lyssa had to give her that.

As if she heard him, the vampiress continued. "You have great potential, Danny. I know your desires are simple ones. But my hope is that you have now learned we only have any peace and enjoyment in our lives if the remaining ninety percent of our time we remain vigilant. You have finally grown up enough to take a servant." She glanced toward Dev. "He seems to have the mettle, and perhaps a stable core that will help balance your flightier moments."

"With all due respect, my lady, I thought my actions through thoroughly."

"Did you now?" Lyssa eyed her with a cringe-worthy disdain. "So you told the Council your complaints about Ruskin. When they did not respond the way you wished, your backup plan was to come back here and launch a one-woman vigilante strike against him. Oh, and as a side matter, dispatch your mother's lover. It succeeded, only because of your servant's loyalty to you, as well as my regard and Alistair's, and that was all luck. If we had arrived an hour later, you would have been defeated, and you would have been Lord Charles's to punish for however many decades he felt it necessary to underscore his authority in this territory."

Lyssa rose then, paced across the room. Dev didn't need any help from Thomas this time to know it would be wise to try to blend with the wall as much as possible. When the ancient vampire turned back, Danny was staring at the wall, but there was a misery to her face.

"I am sorry to have disappointed you, Lady Lyssa. I . . . I never wished to take advantage of our friendship. I hold it a great honor. Dev shouldn't have—"

"Dev did exactly what he should have done. It is you who failed in this instance. You could have tried again with the Council," Lyssa said curtly. "Visited Region Masters such as Alistair. Brought them here as unexpected guests during this upcoming gathering Ruskin was planning. Let them see the children, then bring them to speak before the Council with you. I was visiting, and had I seen them, I would have lent my voice to your appeal. Patience is an important virtue for vampires, Danny."

"They didn't have that kind of time, my lady. He was taking more children to replace those he lost during his hunts."

"You are noble, but a dead noble idiot serves no one. Intolerable suffering occurs every moment, Lady D. Stopping any instance of it, effectively, permanently, often requires planning. Time. *Patience.*"

Dev had changed his mind. He didn't like Lyssa's ability to bring the temperature of a room down to arctic levels at all.

"Through our help, you are now Region Master, able to assist in a far more potent way." She sighed, made another lap around the room and stared out the window. "But if you insist on acting in this impetuous manner, it will be taken from you in no time. So I am faced with the interesting question of whether you are ready for the position you've just taken by force. Or if I should recommend to the Council that you be chastened for your rash act and relegated to a territory in Europe where we can keep a closer eye on you."

Lyssa was in profile to Dev now. His reaction to her words was likely no less violent than Danny's. His blond sheila's head whipped around, her blue eyes widening. "My lady, you couldn't—"

"I couldn't what, Lady Daniela?" She arched a brow, turning to look at Danny. "I will do whatever I feel is necessary to protect you.

From yourself, as well as others. Before today, the general opinion was that Lady Daniela, daughter of Lady Constance, was a lovely young vampire whose main political value was whose arm she would choose or be compelled to adorn. A nonentity except for the circumstances of her birth."

Danny rose from the couch then, and her eyes flashed in a way that had Dev tensing, particularly when he saw Thomas doing the same. "And after today, my lady?"

Lyssa considered her. "The tragedy is that as word of this spreads, many will think that has changed. That you are a force to be reckoned with. A force that should be tested and challenged, not admired like a harmless hothouse rose."

"I am not, nor have I ever been, anyone's political pawn," Danny spat. "I won't allow myself to be used that way. Vampires willing to be led hope for Fate to give them someone with fairness and intelligence, *and* the power to protect them. I don't know if I have the power to resist every vampire who would try to take this territory from me, but I have the other two."

"You use that intelligence to *make* them believe you have that power. That goes for your allies as much as your enemies. Because a powerful vampire has far more allies than a weak one."

"I'll learn—"

"Then do so, *damn you*. Before I am too late and standing over your body. Or I am forced to see you become some broken, dispirited thing subverted to the will of a monster like Ruskin."

Lyssa's fierce directive reverberated through the room as if a cannon had been shot off right outside the window. Dev felt the vibration through his chest, his head, the soles of his feet. And even as the power of it overwhelmed him, the tension that she actually might do something to harm his lady loosened within him.

She loved Danny. It was clear as the sky after a hard rain. While her anger was like that of a goddess, fearsome and destructive, what he was seeing was little different than two sisters in a blue, one more experienced and angered by the younger one's inexperience and folly. Unfortunately, that was a reassurance that his lady, as the recipient of the earbashing, didn't seem to be feeling.

Danny had flinched at the tone, but now her hands slowly closed into balls at her sides. She faced Lyssa square, her blue eyes holding the green ones. "No one will ever do that, my lady. I can assure you. But I will learn. I promise you, if you support me as Region Master for the Northwest Territory, I will not fail at it."

Lyssa studied her a long, long moment. "Fine, then," she said at last. "But you owe a debt to Alistair and me of a magnitude I expect you will keep in mind if he ever needs a favor." Her glance shifted thoughtfully now, to Dev. "I will collect my payment now. It has two parts. First, I will feed on your servant tonight, because I am going to second-mark him. I will have access to his mind when I wish, so I may check in on your progress."

When Danny's gaze flickered, Dev was interested to see cobalt fire there, a different kind. "My lady, you have my blood. You can have access to my mind as you wish. I would deny you nothing, but . . ."

Lyssa raised a brow. "You act as if I was offering you a choice, Lady Daniela. I will take your servant's blood. Second, for the remainder of this night, you will follow my direction as if you were a servant yourself. I have one more lesson to teach you. To teach you both."

~

Once things were settled in the household, Lyssa retired to one of the guest bedrooms, and had Dev and Thomas help Danny get there. Frustratingly, Lyssa still hadn't permitted Dev to offer his lady blood, but she allowed him to help Danny stretch out on the bed while the queen took a seat on a nearby chair, laying her hands on the arms in a regal pose.

"Remove her clothes," she instructed Dev. "And clean up the rest of her. You will lie still as he does it," she commanded Danny.

Dev obeyed, because Danny appeared to be willing to submit to Lyssa's demands, though he chafed at it on her behalf. For quite a bit after that, Lyssa was a silent presence in the room, a sensual weight like an exotic scent.

It was then he realized this was more than a lesson or payment. This was a punishment, making Danny submit to her own servant in front of the queen, forcing her to share that servant. He wanted to keep bristling at it, but as he took care of her, he sensed a quiet acceptance in Danny. As if it was a consequence to her actions she was willing to bear, much like a child realizing that the punishment could have been far, far worse. Of course, it could be his fiery lady was out of fight, worn-out by blood loss.

As for him, he had no complaints, except he wished his lady had not been so abused. When he gently divested her of all her clothes, he used a basin of warm water, salts and herbal additives provided by Thomas, gathered from the kitchen staff, to sponge over the wounds. She quivered under his touch, sometimes at the pain and sometimes at something else he sensed going on beneath the surface of her otherwise smooth face. When he turned her over, did the back, he was angered anew to see it all, to imagine what the past day must have been like for her. And he was torn between wanting to paddle her, something similar to Lyssa's reaction, and feeling a bit amazed by her.

He was a traditional man, used to protecting women, as Danny had implied more than once. But she was different. It was almost as if Danny and he were . . . well, they were like mates, on a lot of levels. He could fight beside her, drink with her. But he could also hold her, love her. He'd known he couldn't handle a soft one again. But her, he could want. Did want, with a fierceness that had nothing to do with logic. Thomas might be right about the vampire-servant connection being predestined, since nothing exactly explained it, but here he was regardless.

When he had finished cleaning his lady, Lyssa at last shifted. "Set aside the basin, Devlin. Take off your clothes, and then I will tell you what I intend you to do next."

It went without saying that she overrode his lady, but he still wasn't completely reconciled to the idea she could override him. He wasn't sure he'd even accepted that from Danny. But as he turned toward the vampire who had implied she could rip out his heart almost as soon as he had the thought, he saw something in Lyssa's face, the way her eyes rested on Danny's mauled flesh, the many bruises and bites, mottled areas where bones had broken and then re-fused. Mutely, he removed his shirt, then sat on the bed to pull off the boots. Behind him, Danny remained on her side, turned away from him. He'd found it odd she hadn't turned at Lyssa's words, but drew her legs up closer to her body, making him think she might have dozed off. He was sliding the trousers off when he heard it. The smallest of noises, a caught breath, a tensing of her shoulders.

"Ease her pain," Lyssa said quietly. "Start at her feet, and work your way up with your mouth. Leave no part untouched. Cherish her with your lips and fingers."

As punishments went, he thought there might indeed be worse. Putting a knee on the bed, he noticed Danny's tiny shudders coming closer together and more frequent. She was fighting, as hard as she fought Ruskin, to keep the sobs from becoming noticeable. Bending, he placed his lips on her arch. The foot flexed, pressing against his cheek, another tremor.

Easy, my lady. It's all right. Just feel.

I killed them, Dev. Him, and them. Ian.

Yes, you did. Let it go. It's done, and we'll make it right with the little ones. Though he knew nothing ever really made it right. The most damnable thing about the soul was that it went on, no matter what things it had done. Would keep doing.

As her body jerked with the next sob, he put his hands along her calves, sliding up toward the backs of her thighs. He didn't leave an inch untouched with his mouth. Giving her his heat and comfort, he emptied his mind of everything but the need to take away those tears, the determination that he would do so. She'd drawn up her legs farther, gone to a fetal position. In some part of his mind, he realized despite her pain, this was an incomparable gift of trust, letting him see her this way. Letting Lyssa see her this way. The three of them were enclosed in this quiet, still place in the universe, lit by candlelight as he cosseted her with his mouth.

I know this isn't what you wanted. He made the thought gentle, soothing. *But I'm here. I'll be with you.*

This isn't what you wanted, Dev.

You're exactly what I want, my lady.

He coaxed her to loosen her thighs, let him stretch out one leg, kiss all the way to the hip, slide a hand beneath to lift her, brush his mouth over her sex. He took the pleasure of a deep draught there before turning her to her stomach, licking his way over the arse and to the tender lower back area, her long, freed hair teasing his nose.

She'd clutched her hands on the pillow now, and he traced his lips up her spine, between her shoulder blades, moving the hair to the side and wrapping the silk of it around one hand as he reached her neck. Turning her on her back again, he worked back down the sternum, mouth worshipping the high curves of breast, tight nipples and tender crease beneath. Then the slope of her abdomen, the navel. His turgid cock brushed her thigh, leaving a track of moisture, he was sure.

"Now inside her, bushman. Sink deep. Danny, your hands over your head. It is all him, what I am ordering him to do to you."

Danny held Dev's gaze, tear tracks on her face, and slowly lifted her hands over her head, taking hold of the iron rails. Scratches on the bars told him someone had been chained to them before. It might have been Danny.

He pushed that away. This moment wasn't about rage or fear over what-ifs. Though this was Lyssa's punishment, he wanted Danny to feel cherished, to reduce her to mindless, trembling release, let everything bad about this night wash from her. So maybe they *both* wouldn't be haunted by what could have happened.

"No, don't hold on to the rail," Lyssa ordered. "It's far harder to simply let your hands lie above your head, surrender to what is inside you."

New tears welled up and he turned his head to Lyssa. "Is that bloody necessary?"

The queen had blown out several of the candles, so was sitting in shadow. "Yes."

Yes, it is, Dev. I need this. I need you.

Turning back to face Danny's expression, he saw it there, the anguish and exhaustion, the fear she hadn't allowed to show, the revulsion with herself. She needed him. He realized she likely had never done anything so violent in her life as what she had plotted and executed since he'd known her. The vampire that, according to Lyssa, was considered little more than an excellent arm adornment with a good pedigree.

They'll never think that again, love. Not after this gets around.

"Do not kiss her until you are inside her." Lyssa's voice arrested him in midmotion, his face halfway to hers. "Hold right there, and put your cock inside her, slowly. I want to see it happen, and I want her to stare into your face while you do it."

He swallowed and began to do just that. It was harder than burying his face in a girl's neck and sliding in, that was for sure. There were so many expressions crossing Danny's face, he couldn't track them all. She was having a difficult time keeping her hands lying loose on the bed, and he missed them, touching his back, grasping his arse sure and steady, telling him what she wanted. But God, her cunt was heaven itself, distracting him from all of that.

So empty . . . I'm so empty, until you're inside me, making me feel real again . . . Alive. Like I can feel, and love, and laugh . . .

It was all there in her eyes, her mind, offered to him, only he wasn't sure which of them was offering it or, like their hands when he reached up to clasp one in his, their fingers intertwining, it was what they became together.

He was all the way in, her body having tilted upward to take his girth and length. The tiny tip of tongue touched her lip in the way that bespoke the concentration and effort it took to accommodate his size. The way that drove him crazy with need.

"Take her up, now, Dev. Give her pleasure."

That was an easy one, and he began to move, the friction between them instant and needy, sharp like the pop of a whip over his flanks, as if to break him into a gallop. But he didn't. Despite the drive of that whip, he worked her slow, deep, absorbed in every change in her face, how her eyes got darker, more glazed, the spasmodic way her body moved, pushing out sadness for pleasure.

It was like the rocking of a boat, being inside her, how the ocean would carry them to their fate, no matter what, and for now there was just this. He wasn't overly surprised when Lyssa's hand touched his bare back, but it certainly ratcheted up his own response when he realized the vampire queen had disrobed. Now she put her knee between his spread ones and lay her petite body all along his back, giving him the extra weight to bear, but also the sensation of her bare breasts and smooth mons at his shoulder blades and top dent of his arse, respectively. Her thigh pressed along the inside of his, so on the withdrawals, his testicles brushed her skin.

"Feed, Danny," she said in a soft purr, a whisper of sound in the darkened room. "Let us share this delicious servant of yours."

The two women came from different sides. As Dev tilted his chin up, he realized Thomas was right. It had become an instinctive, automatic response to his lady's need for nourishment. Danny's fangs pierced one side, her mouth sealing over the heated gush of blood, as Lyssa latched on to the other, her hand slipping around his waist, her hand pressed against the raven mark on his chest to hold his body, trembling with the exertion of keeping still between the two women.

He was half on his knees, most of his weight resting on one arm, because he had to caress the side of Danny's face, her hair, cup the back of her skull tenderly as she drank. But in the end he had to put the other arm down, needing both for support as the two vampires drank from him and he continued to move his hips, stroking his cock into Danny again and again. Feeling the marvelous slickness of her contractions on him, as Lyssa rubbed against his buttocks, her thigh teasing his testicles in light touches. The sound of the queen's drinking became more of an animal growl, her arm constricting around him so he experienced just a hint of bone-crushing strength. Crushing, hell. He expected she could turn his into a fine powder.

And his lady, ah, her lips against his throat, her arm winding around his waist on the other side, and under Lyssa's body so her fingertips rested high on his back, below the distracting slide of Lyssa's breasts against his skin. The vampire queen shifted, making him realize she wanted him down, all the way upon his lady. He was only too happy to oblige, feeling her soft breasts against his chest, her legs now rising and locking over his hips, over Lyssa's body, too, he suspected, holding them all together.

Danny was quivering, drinking hard, her body moving restlessly enough he knew she was close. He strove to hold out, the blood loss making it difficult to stay oriented. The buzzing in his mind told him Lyssa had in fact second-marked him, and if he had any doubt, now her imperious voice was in his head.

Hold out to satisfy us both, Devlin, and you will have done your job well. Another few moments . . .

He actually lost track of time, so dizzy did he get, but he was aware of his body becoming taut, gathering for release as Danny cried out, her nails raking his skin, her mouth releasing him as her head fell back to the pillow and neck arched, her fangs glittering with the blood he'd given her. And Lyssa, stroking her clit against the upper taut curve of his buttocks, released as well, a sensual moan, reminding him of the contented but intense purr of a tiger.

He couldn't hold out in the face of such overwhelming stimulation. He climaxed then, his body too foolish to realize he risked passing out.

It's all right, dearest. Danny's voice was in his head, two women's arms tightening around him. *You've cared for me well. I'll care for you. That's the way it's supposed to work.*

~

It took some time to get things sorted out. There was the arrival of the vampires as Ruskin had planned, only they received the surprise of finding that they had a new Region Master. Lyssa and Alistair took their leave before then, for Danny and they agreed that the vampires needed to see her standing on her own as their leader, with no sense that when the other two vampires left she might be fair pickings. That gathering lasted a week. Dev supposed he should be glad for the few initiations he'd had into vampire gatherings, because while he really didn't want to think of the variety of things he'd done during the evening meetings, meals and various entertainments with other servants, he found himself curiously accepting of it, sometimes almost eager to see how those things would stoke his lady's pleasure. Perhaps it was simply a measure of how harrowing the politics were during that week as she established her authority, that he found wild sexual games where he was a pawn a light relief from the rest.

Then again, no matter what happened, what challenge they faced, there was always that precious time just before dawn. When it was the two of them in her bed, and she wanted him in ways that obliterated everything else. That made it all worth it.

Teaching the little ones to drink moderately after having been regularly starved to a killing frenzy was going to take some time. For now, they had to keep them in separate cages. They experimented with giving them some creature comforts, like mattresses or some clothes, but right now their reaction was to tear those things up in their mad rages. So Elisa, who'd come in with Willis on another flight, had picked up toys in Darwin—dolls, stuffed animals and the like—and had them positioned in front of the cages, just out of reach. Like tiny groups of motionless friends come to keep the kids company.

He knew Danny frequently questioned whether they should put a bullet through their heads to knock them insensible and then stake them or cut off their heads and burn the bodies, the most painless death a vampire could seek.

Amazingly, it was often Elisa who deflected Danny from that course. "Ah, nothing to it, my lady," she'd say, putting her hands on her hips, though her clothes might be torn or she'd be sporting a gash on her cheek from where she'd been too close. "They're babies. They're going to test us until they learn a firm hand doesn't mean a cruel one. They've got to learn to trust us, is all, and that'll take time. It takes time for all of us to trust someone else." And off she'd go again, a slip of a maid with the quiet, lanky shadow of Willis flanking her protectively, taking the next supply of blood to them. It had been provided by contributions from Ruskin's household after Danny had made clear the contributions were not optional.

"So when do you think Willis will tell her he's mad about her?" Danny had observed, a smile in her voice, some of the shadows in her eyes banked.

"Hopefully before the kiddies eat her," Dev replied wryly. "But you heard her. You've got to establish the trust first. And you sheilas, you can be pretty mean."

Danny gave him an arch look, but left it there. Another day passing with a few smiles, a lot of worries.

She'd been tempted to have the pretentious manor torn down, but for that it was Dev who'd convinced her that the stone edifice would stand up well to the storms, be a good shelter for the townsfolk. When she left—for she'd adamantly insisted her base of operations would remain her own station—she could simply donate the use of the house to them, holding the ownership on the condition that they agreed to maintain the property at their own expense. He visited the town mayor himself and won almost instant agreement and gratitude. While they knew nothing of what Ruskin was, all knew he was a bad sort. He'd kept his nose clean in the town, wisely not taking any of the town children, but people had eyes and ears. Plus, Dev had learned the aborigines in the area had standing warnings about the place.

Of course, he'd disregarded such warnings the first night he met Danny. But then, he was the Gravedigger. What better match for him than a vampire? *You will travel far until you find your place. And until then, you will dig or walk over many graves . . .*

I feel alive with you. That was what his lady had told him. Death had its own rotten place in life, but he was ready to put it down and not carry it with him anymore. It could find him all on its own.

Maybe for a time, it would let him rest in peace. If, for no other reason, than because it was leaving him in equally demanding hands. Sure enough, being with Lady Danny wasn't conducive to peace *or* rest.

The thought always brought a grin. What a daft bastard he was. Her daft bastard.

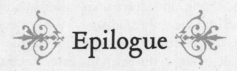

Epilogue

HE'D been rootless for so long, he was surprised by how welcome it was to see Thieves' Station again. And even more to think of it as "home." But then, in the two months it had taken them to get back here, it had also been a surprise how many avenues opened up to bring the two of them closer together. It was a lot like running a station, watching for her cues and leads, anticipating what she wanted from him and doing the job well, everything from handling how they'd transport the little bloodsucking blighters, as he not-so-fondly had dubbed them, to how he'd make her sigh with pleasure in those early predawn hours.

Sometimes he understood what Thomas was trying to say to him about his relationship to her. It still kind of slipped in and out of his mind, eluded his full grasp. During those times, he could still manage to step on her nerves, as she ignited his temper. They settled it out of sight of those who might question such things in the wrong way.

He had his own mind about that. Despite her formality, he suspected even Lady Lyssa had understood he and Danny were a bit of a different entity from the more ritualized European vampires. He wondered if the American vamps had a bit more stockman in them as well. Or as they'd call it—cowboy.

So it went for the first few weeks. He got in step with the stock-men on the handling of the sheep, coordinated bringing in more breeding stock, and worked with Elisa and Willis on making the best accommodations possible for the children in the outbuildings. Even integrated the wildly unpredictable feeding and training sessions with them into the daily routine.

It was all starting to settle in. Enough that on this late afternoon, he found himself sitting on the porch in a rare undisturbed moment, staring out at a glorious sunset as he drank his tea on the top step, listening to the wind settle, the last call of birds and the hum of the flies.

If he'd been out in the bush, he'd have wet the billy and been taking a cuppa about now, watching the spread of color from one end of the earth to the other, nothing in his view but that sky and the low-lying scrub leading up to it. He'd have been alone, purposefully mindless. Now, he was a bit tired, a lot of things still running through his head. He supposed he hadn't yet figured out how to take care of things during the day and be around when she needed him at night.

"That's because you're not going to delegate until you're sure everything's being done right, and you're so head-over-heels about me you can't stop fawning over me at night, whether I need you around or not."

He glanced back, saw her standing inside the screen door, watching that sunset from the safety of the shadows. "Think you've got me all figured out, do you?"

"There are flies swimming in your cup," she noted.

"When you come out here, they'll stop pestering me."

"I think my chief value to you is as an insect repellant."

"Well, it does make the evenings far more enjoyable than they used to be. Can even wear my shorts despite the mosquitoes."

She made a face. As the sun cracked on the horizon, spreading out and then disappearing quickly, as it was wont to do this close to the edge of the earth, she slid out the door and took a seat next to him. She was as female as they came, but out on the station he knew she had little patience for anything but her moleskins or jodhpurs, combined with some soft, flowing tucked shirt that always made his fingertips itch to follow the line of her bra beneath the pale fabric, tease the cleft of her breasts in the neckline. Her eyes smiled at him, a slow, sensual response, picking up his thoughts, but she leaned back against the opposite post and comfortably braced the sole of one boot against his hip.

"You said you'd tell me one day," Dev said, "why you wanted to come back here."

When she made a noncommittal hum, he took another sip of tea, looking out at the spread of darkness over the flat terrain, the transition of the mulga and gums to intriguing dark silhouettes. The last rains had put a touch of yellow on the mulga, and he'd thought about cutting her a sprig, giving it to her tonight to put in her hair, but one of the kids had escaped and he'd had to help Willis corral her. They were going to have to come up with a safe way to get them out, let them stretch their legs.

"I always liked living out here," she said at last, surprising him. She straightened and turned next to him, the snug stretch of her jodhpurs allowing him to feel the length of her thigh against his. "It never gets boring. I can hear everything. The whine of the mosquitoes, flies . . . the movement of lizards, a snake twisting through the sand."

She nodded into the darkness. "I used to sit here and look at the trees and saltbushes and tell my mother that they became something else at night. A tall stockman with one arm raised, an aborigine bending with his straw to find water, a two-headed roo with a wallaby's head for an arse." She pointed and it was a remarkable description for the shrub she indicated, such that he smiled.

"I like quiet, Dev," she continued, giving him a speculative glance. "I don't need a fast-paced life. I can sit on this porch for the next twenty-five years if I want, and I'm sure I'll still see something new every day. When I left all those years ago, I traveled to all the busy places. Paris, London, Berlin, Beijing and Hong Kong. New York and Hollywood."

When he raised a brow, she nodded, humor in her gaze. "Places where you don't have to put the feet of the safe in pots of water to keep the ants out of your tucker. But I don't need fancy places like that. I have some reading I want to catch up on. Do you *know* how many hundreds of books are written every year?"

Her eyes lit up with the idea of it, and he couldn't help but smile again. Seeing it, she nudged him with her shoulder. "I love to read, and haven't done much of it lately. Now that I've got a scholar in residence, maybe he can recommend some things to me. Maybe I'll even coax him to read aloud to me, listen to Yeats or Dickens in that drawling sexy voice of his."

"You might get him to do that."

She gave him an amused look. "One of my favorite things, when I was here before, was staying up long enough in the morning to tune in to the radio calls."

"Hear the messages being passed up the line about births and deaths," he remembered. "And all the local gossip."

"*Yes.*" Her mouth curved. "When life is this simple, there's a purity to it."

Looking at her then, Dev wondered how she might feel if he took her hand. Her gaze flickered to him. "I wouldn't mind it," she said. "You're a bit of an old-fashioned romantic, you know that?"

"Pot calling kettle again, love. Does it bother you?"

"No," she answered, with such sincerity he believed it. "Another thing about vampires. Innocence goes very quickly. It's not something you lament, because pleasure is, by its very nature, something worth the sacrifice if done right. But sometimes I miss the sweet joys of romance. Think that's a female thing?"

He shook his head. "I can only speak for myself. I like a woman's body as much as the next bloke, but sometimes, when a sheila looks at you with soft eyes and says she wouldn't mind if you held her hand, something inside you gets all coiled. It's almost better than having her on her back. Though you won't find me admitting that to any mate," he added. "Just to girls with big blue eyes that I want to shag."

He ducked the swat, but then she reached out, touched his face. "Sex and violence . . . sometimes they're too close. Particularly the way vampires practice them." Her eyes turned outward again, her hand resting in his, their fingers comfortably interlaced, sitting on his knee. "Maybe that's why I like the tranquillity, the sense of something perfect unfolding right before us. It gets inside you, rests there as delicate and momentary as a butterfly. It's a balance that can be pushed off by too much . . . force."

Her fingers twitched in his, a passing caress. "Romance is tenderness. Joy in just breathing together. Like this, when everything is perfect." She slanted him a smile. "When you're with a bloke who fancies you enough to hold your hand."

"That's not just romance, Danny. That's love."

When she stilled, he released her hand, stared down at his tea. "It's a problem, isn't it?"

"Is it?"

Devlin looked back up. "You can see in my head, love. We're a pair of odd birds, really. Just resisting the natural order of things."

"And what's the natural order, Dev?"

There was a tension to her now, as he knew there would be. They worked well together on so many things, seamlessly. But on this, the stitching was uneven, snarled. Most of the time they'd been too busy to do anything with it, though he'd suspected a few of the arguments they'd had were centered on this unresolved core. It was the elusive thing, the one that kept escaping his grasp when he looked too hard at it.

"I need to know what I am to you."

"My human servant."

"And what is that to you?"

At her look, he lifted a shoulder. "Church means something different to everyone, love. I want to know what it means to you."

As she remained silent, he blew out a sigh. "Thomas thinks I've survived all these bloody challenges because his God knew you'd need me. My take on it is that He's a bloody bastard. Or that He doesn't think of me at all."

Danny's brow creased as she laid a hand on his shoulder. "I think of you."

"Yeah. Like you think of them kids, the others on this place. The stray dogs you feed."

Her eyes darkened. "Don't be putting words in my mouth,

bushman. I think of you, Dev," she repeated. "There are the way things are, and the way I feel. You understand the difference."

"I do," he responded. "What I want to know is if you're brave enough to say it yourself."

When she didn't respond, his jaw hardened. "Let me have a go at it, then. I know you can read it, but maybe you could stay out of my head and let me say it."

She straightened, her blue eyes sharpening in that way that could slice at him with ruthless mockery, but she nodded. "All right. Say it, then."

"Here's what I think." He set the tea aside and locked gazes with her. "I'm in love with you. You're in love with me. And since I've been down this road, I'm pretty sure it's the kind of love that lasts until one or both of us is dead."

~

As he said the words, Danny saw his green eyes grow more intent, that sensual mouth going firm. When he looked like that, she knew his will was a match for hers, no matter what physical differences they had. Still, she hadn't been prepared for the conversation, so she said the first thing that came to mind.

"We're vampire and human. We can't be equals."

"It's not about that, damn it, and you know it. It's an understanding between you and me. That's all that matters to me. I've no plans to take up missionary work and try to convert the vampire horde." She couldn't help a small smile at that, despite the flare of temper. His eyes glinted. "For one thing, it's enough bloody work to keep this place running and deal with that menagerie of blood-sucking fiends you had to drag home like stray cats."

"But they help with the rats," she observed primly. She knew very well that he'd been wholeheartedly supportive of the idea, but now that he was working as her station manager, he had to gruffly disapprove of anything that added to the daily chores or costs about the place. It was one of the many enjoyable rituals she was developing with him. Which brought her back to the topic he was patiently waiting for her to stop avoiding.

"I'm not avoiding it," she said mildly, putting annoyance in her tone.

"Thought I asked you to stay out of my mind."

"I find your mind far more poetic. You're speaking rough and plain tonight, bushman."

Restless, she rose, moved down the several steps and stood in the yard, staring up at the sky, wondering how many stars might come out tonight. Stars that didn't give a hang about vampires and how they were supposed to feel about human servants. It was a land that was so large that many found it overwhelming, a reverse form of claustrophobia that sent them scurrying back to the noise and comforting closeness of others in the cities, so that the stillness of so much open space couldn't reach into the soul, unfold the things too large to be held inside.

A land that defied classification. According to geology, Australia had been unchanging, an island to itself, while the other land continents were still shifting for a few million more years, trying to sort themselves out. While the bulk of its people might be uncertain whether they were British or Australian, Australia herself apparently had no confusion on the matter. She was the one and only Oz. And that was what Danny liked about her. She liked a woman who knew her own mind.

Danny turned to look at Dev, sitting on the top step in his casual pose, his hat at a low-brimmed angle. The slope of his jaw, a dark shading from a day's worth of stubble. He'd saved her life, but more than that, when he'd let her inside him, she found a man she wanted to keep close to her throughout her life. By her side, at her back. He was the type of man who'd try to be in front of her when there was danger, but he would readily turn around, let her walk into his arms.

She'd fought Ruskin, a purported nobleman. For a truly noble man, she'd needed to look no further than a dusty bushman she'd picked up in a pub. A bushman who'd avenged his family, stained his soul with blood. Had gone to war and tried to cleanse it with more blood, and then sought absolution in the damning silence of the bush. And he'd ended up with her, perhaps his penance, but perhaps her salvation, too. Maybe that was another vital element a servant provided—keeping Dev at her side was the key to keeping it in perspective, knowing right and wrong, the difference between power and enlightenment.

She took a deep breath and met his eyes, already seeing in that beloved crinkle around the green irises he could tell her answer. She wanted him to see it in her face as well as hear it in her head, though.

I love you, Dev. I fell in love with you during that very first dance.

He smiled then, and that smile was like the sunset, stretching from one end of her existence to the other, lighting her way not by sight, but with a slow kindle inside she knew would never leave her bereft for the sun's warmth.

As Lyssa said, may you serve me long and well, despite my bloody foolishness.

She moved back to the stairs, toward the embrace she was sure would always be there, and chose not to question that need in herself. As she put a knee between his feet on the step, his arms closed around her, strong and sure, bringing her in against the delightful planes of his hard body, his reassuring scent. Perhaps in the end, it wasn't about vampire, human, or any other question of power or place. It was about finding the other half of the soul, in whatever vessel it rested.

Daft romantic nonsense, he'd say, if she let him hear her thoughts. *Just like a sheila.*

"Dev?" She spoke quietly.

"Hmm?"

"If it's true about vampires and their servants being bound even after death, and if I have any say in it . . . I would release you. Tina and Rob had you first. They deserve to get you back."

She felt the emotion fill him, thickening her own throat. "Ah, love," he murmured. "I wouldn't worry about it. I suspect whatever's running things on the other side will know the best thing to do. It may not be as simple as being with one or the other. Maybe it's like falling into a marvelous treasure chest, made up of green hills, cooling rain, beautiful beaches and all the people you've loved. You don't have to choose only one treasure from it."

Raising his head and drawing her chin up, he quirked a brow at her. "In fact, having both you and Tina . . . that might be heaven." And he gave her a vivid image of what he had in mind.

"Oh, you rat." She managed to give him a smart smack on his head because of his bark of laughter. "That was from me *and* Tina."

Despite her reproof, his laughter warmed her to her toes, for it was the first time she'd ever heard him invoke his family without pain. When he caught her wrists, and brought her smile to his mouth, she thought he might be right about one thing. The treasures of love were bottomless, because she thought she'd found that treasure here, even outside the gates of Heaven.

She was sure of it a moment later. In the midst of the kiss, the beauty of the Outback closing around them, she felt the sense of home envelop him, within and without, making her heart rejoice.

He was truly hers.

Turn the page for a sneak preview of
the next sensual novel by Joey W. Hill,

BELOVED VAMPIRE

Coming in August 2009 from Heat Books.

T HE Sahara had once been green. Lush, a verdant land supporting civilizations. Then the earth's orbit changed, the sun came
a little closer and the land altered, becoming a desert that swallowed
armies. It had happened three or four thousand years ago, barely a
blink in the nine-billion-year life of Earth, but in that blink, Heaven
and Hell had switched places. Had it been boredom, a need for a different perspective? Life giver, life taker.

Jessica wondered which face the Sahara preferred. Since she'd
come here to die, it was a point of interest. Barely two years ago, her
body had been vigorous and fertile as well. Now it was a barren skeleton that repelled most sensible life forms, so she felt almost at home
here.

It was the largest desert in the world. A place one could walk for
days—if one had the constitution of a camel—and see no other human life. But one could see the history of the area still mapped on
this wasteland, if one had eyes trained to see it. She'd done little else
of importance but study this region for the past several years. She
didn't really count killing Lord Raithe as significant. The vampire
who'd forced her to be his servant for more than five years, and who
was the reason she was dying now, was relatively nothing in the
scheme of things. Creatures lived, creatures died, and their bones

became sand like this. They all walked over the remains of their ancestors. At least he'd never torment anyone again. *That* mattered, though in truth, she'd been so sick for so long now, she couldn't even recall why that had been as important as it had once seemed.

But Farida had remained significant to her, from the very first moment Jess opened the ancient binding and discovered the written memories of the sheik's daughter who had lived more than three hundred years ago.

In the midst of a life so horrible Jess often thought she'd already died and somehow deserved Hell—though she couldn't recall her crime—Farida had given her a spark of light. It was amazing to find that the body's desire to live was stronger than anything, even despair. Maybe that was why she connected with a woman who had chosen love and then lost it, as well as everything else, but who still spoke passionately and vibrantly in her memoir of a love worth any torment.

Once she'd killed Raithe, Jess had spent the time between running and hoping she had the strength to keep going the next day studying those words. Hiding in dank places that only society's forgotten frequented, often there was nothing else to break her thoughts except the trickling background of an internal hourglass, the sands of her life running out. Her cells were being subsumed in that flow of sand, as if she were becoming part of a place like Farida's Sahara. She was okay with that. There were those who believed that the Sahara would return to greenness, that the cycles of climate change would evolve again, the sun getting less hot and the rains increasing. A different way of life would return.

That was when she realized where she was going to go and what she was going to do with the short remainder of her life. It was no more fantastic than what her life had been for the past five years. And no one would look for her in the Middle East.

But when she arrived in the Sahara, she realized that those who wrote of it as a desolate place devoid of life didn't know it. There *was* life here. Not just in the few people and creatures that called it home, but in the ghosts that whispered, finding voices through the movement of the sand, a haunting noise similar to blowing across the top of a soda bottle—something she'd done as a teenager as she clustered with her friends on the curb outside the Quik-Stop with soda and Cheetos, eyeing the boys who came in after school. Boys who eyed them right back.

God, that was a long time ago. She held those memories to her occasionally like a favorite doll, crooning to it, taking comfort in nurturing something that could never give back to her.

The three men she'd paid to accompany her this far thought her a madwoman, of course. But she'd paid them enough to indulge her, and there was nothing to lose, no liability. Take a crazy, dying woman out to a remote part of the desert that wasn't on any map, and she'd either eventually tire of her fantasy of finding the marker for a dead woman's grave or die. They'd be rich men, either way. She'd shown them the jewels, what would be theirs if they helped her. She thanked whatever capricious deity watched over fools that she'd had the foresight to return to Raithe's home for Farida's book and take what amounted to a full measured cup of diamonds while everyone was still out looking for her. Raithe had a hoard to rival a dragon's, so they'd never be missed.

Now, as she rolled the comfort of familiar thoughts through her head, a reminder of where she'd been, where she was going, she looked over the endless stretch of dunes. The breathtaking artistry of the wind upon them rivaled the greatest sculptors of the ages, and the sun collaborated, providing a different view with each degree it descended. But even that beauty couldn't distract her from the fact that night was drawing close. God, she hated darkness. But she fingered the compass in her pocket, reassuring herself. The stars would help her find Farida tonight.

Reading the words had made her feel as if she were in Farida's silken tent, where they cuddled on the pillows, girlfriends pressed forehead to forehead. The Arab woman had confided through every page that, while everything in life could be taken away by forces unable to be controlled, there was always a choice left. Something overlooked, if one did not let fear overwhelm desire. Farida had chosen an incomparable man. Jessica would choose where she wanted to die.

Killing Raithe had seemed impossible, of course, enough that Jess never even entertained it, not after those first six months as his slave in a world surreal compared to her twentieth-century white-bred life. Since he could read her mind as easily as she read Farida's pages, he'd delighted in punishing her every time she'd thought of murder . . . or of running. Eventually, she'd learned to make her mind blank, a dumb, self-lobotomized creature who would do anything, endure anything, her life merely a muddy haze of images and obstacles to avoid. But that hadn't been sufficient. Raithe wanted her full attention and enthusiasm. She'd learned vampires were not only brutal and ruthless, but they knew humans so well they could use kindness, cunning and desire to bait them into awareness, no matter how often their cruelty taught a woman to retreat into the apathetic pit of her mind.

At that point she'd believed he could do no worse to her, but evil was bottomless—it used every horrific torment as a shovel to dig a little deeper, giving her one less place to hide.

Oh, Jesus, was she destined to follow him to Hell? Some said vampire servants followed their Masters into the afterlife. Another good reason not to die any sooner than she had to. She'd already proven the will was far stronger than X-rays and blood tests. Though Death wouldn't wait forever, she'd faced down the Grim Reaper and made him blink, made him back the hell off until she accomplished this.

"So we wait here until dark, then?" Harry, one of her trio of opportunists, stood at her side.

While she needed the three men for passage and protection, for their knowledge of the language and the Sahara, she would have preferred to do this alone. However, there were things she couldn't do by herself anymore. Harry had put her before him on his camel a couple of times when she fainted into one of her hours-long stupors. She'd warned him of it, instructed him to keep moving no matter what. Time was too short for her. She'd given him the compass heading and some landmarks, but not all of them. They thought they were seeking only a grave marker, not the tomb that was her true goal.

When they found the obelisk, she'd have them leave her there. She wasn't sure she could make the final leg of the journey on her own, but she certainly wasn't going to dishonor Farida by exposing her secret resting place to others. She owed that not only to Farida, but to the brokenhearted spirit of the man who'd loved her enough to place her there.

"So are we in the right place?" Harry repeated patiently. They'd gotten used to her silences, her slow response time.

"I think so." She considered the lay of the dunes, checked her compass and then shuffled through her sheaf of notes, checked the GPS. They'd made camp a couple hours before and her camel's resting body was warm and solid at her back, a rhythmic vibration as the creature chewed her cud.

Harry sat down and leaned against his pack, considering her. "You know, you remind me of crazy Daisy Bates. She lived in the Outback desert for years among the blacks. Was as at home there as a baked lizard."

She glanced up at him. Harry was an expatriate Australian, one who'd lived in and around the Sahara for the past twenty years, a swagman gone walkabout far from the Outback, saying he'd come here because he'd heard tell it was even hotter than Oz. He'd stayed merely to test it out, and claimed with dry humor it was the most air-conditioned place on earth. 'Course, she knew he'd left Australia because he was wanted for the killing of a man in Queensland, a cuckolded husband who came after him with a knife. When one was a fugitive, thieves and cutthroats with some type of honor code were the best partners, when one had to have them, and she'd done well in that, for the most part. He could have been the sort to take her out in the desert and leave her during one of her unconscious spells to die, going back to try for the jewels she'd promised.

However, though she knew Harry had a code of honor, she didn't count on it carrying him too far. She'd made it clear the bank would be expecting a specific password before they'd release the jewels to the three of them. She was too weak to do anything but die under the least amount of torture, so any temptation Harry or Mel might have to beat it out of her before they got her to her destination was obviously futile.

Mel was far more unscrupulous, but Harry kept him in line. She worried little about being a woman traveling alone with them, and not just because Harry's tastes didn't run to forcing women. She was skin stretched over bone. Her hair was brittle, lackluster. If she brushed it, it came out. She was as likely to vomit up a meal as digest it, and her hacking cough kept the clothes she wore flecked with blood and sputum so that sometimes she was too tired to wipe it away. The odor coming from her body was noxious, that of a sick and dying animal. It was a wonder buzzards weren't following them.

This journey had not been so long that Mel or Harry was that desperate. Even so, Dawud, her third man and Islamic native guide, often gently reminded her to keep her head and face covered, since she was unmarried and the three of them were unmarried men. It was also better for when they met caravans, before they left the known routes.

At one time, his kindly meant reproof would have rankled. Now she didn't mind wearing the head covering. It saved questions. It also provided a protection, an unspoken barrier. She'd come from a modern world, full of the ideals of equal rights and independence for women. But in this culture a woman who demonstrated modesty, who respectfully kept herself covered, sent out a signal that she was deserving of respect. Didn't always work, of course, because the world was also full of those who did as they pleased, took what they wanted. But she'd take advantage of any protections the world offered to survive to her final goal.

She liked young Dawud very much, besides. He hoped to use the funds to bring irrigation and education to his village, and she wanted him to have that. For him, specifically, she made it clear to the other two that the bank would *not* be giving Dawud the jewels directly upon successful completion of their task, but handling the liquidation and management of funds for the village in trust. Mel and Harry could plan to rob and kill each other as they saw fit after they got their share, but she wasn't risking an innocent.

In fact, she could have done with just Dawud, except it would take two strong men to shift the obelisk. Dawud also might not be willing to touch it, because of carved ancient warnings and protections that would not concern Harry and Mel. Another way Farida's lover had protected her body, though he'd been unable to save her life.

The sun was setting now, the stars starting to appear, one by one. She watched them like beads on a rosary, a mantra of hope said over each one. She was so tired. Of course, she didn't remember what *not* being tired was, or not being sick. But it was almost over, and this would be an accomplishment she'd done just for her.

Would Jack, her murdered fiancé, have understood that about her? If so, he'd have understood it before she even understood it herself, because until all this had happened, she'd had a laughable understanding of what sacrifice and true determination meant. They'd had so little time to get to know each other, but he'd been willing to die for her. When not a split second instinct, that was too precious a gift to ever explain, a deep, soul-level treasure that foretold what would have grown between them. But why Heaven dangled a precious gem before its children and then took it away was anyone's guess—perhaps Heaven had been in that periodic transition flipflop with Hell. Like the Sahara, from green to fire. Or maybe it was the same as that ridiculous story about the one tree in Eden that couldn't be touched. Did *anyone* think an all-knowing deity had been that naive about the tragically curious nature of its offspring? More likely, He'd just found a way to kick their asses out of His garden, tired of their incessant questions.

Of course, that same fatal curiosity had drawn her to Farida's story. She'd likely sacrificed her sanity to it.

Jess picked up the binding, rubbed her hands over it. While she knew the men thought her obsession with the book was odd, she needed the comfort of those words now, to stave off the unease the deepening night always brought. Harry was moving about, working with Mel to make their dinner. When the full canopy of stars shone above, she'd be able to locate the obelisk. Persephone would show her the way.

Opening the carefully preserved but well-read pages, she began to read her favorite passages. While she knew them by heart, enough to mumble them as she'd rocked along on top of her camel during their journey, she liked to see the words, pass her fingers over the ink. Connect with Farida, as if that touch between paper and flesh could draw Jessica fully into her world and out of this one.

Three centuries ago, when Prince Haytham came to the aid of Farida's father against another warring faction, riding at his side was a man who'd fought and adventured with him, a man he referred to as Lord Mason. It suggested he'd been of British aristocracy, likely a second or third son who'd become a traveling soldier seeking his fortune, a common enough tale. Though according to Farida's words, there'd been nothing common about him at all.

If Jess could paint a picture of Heaven, that would be hers. A world where she could be Farida, their merged soul belonging to the love of Lord Mason, for all eternity.